1. Contents

For

Don Lane

Colliery Manager

28th March 1940 – 29th July 2013

2. 1987 – The Job Offer

I'd just sat down for breakfast it was the best time of the day. Television was on I was ready to watch the TV show Kilroy. My way of relaxing after the nightshift at the local coal mine. I didn't know it at the time but as the day progressed my life and that of my family was about to change. The house phone rang.

"Mick it's for you…. The Manager!" Annie Gibson my wife shouted out.

"Who?" *Why is the Manager phoning me at home? Obviously, a problem at the pit. Both faces were coaling when I'd left. I'd made sure of that.*

"The Manager." My wife repeated as she walked into the room. She was smiling she knew when I was agitated. "The Manager for little old you."

"Boss."

"It seems you've got one of the Undermanager's jobs….in North Wales." I never replied at first it was December; Christmas had come early. I was just about to get my first job as Undermanager. It was going to be in North Wales!

"You still there lad?"

"Hmm sorry boss yeah."

"You might want to get over there at the weekend and start looking for a house."

"Thanks boss." The line went dead. He'd hung up. I stood in the hallway so many questions – *when would I start? Would I be released off nightshift? Where would we live?*

"What did he want?"

"The interviews I attended back end of last month for an Undermanager's job seems I've been successful."

"Where?"

"Point of Ayr."

"Scotland?"

"No North Wales."

"How are you going to manage that travelling each day?"

"We'll have to move!"

"Tell me you're kidding. You've spent the last year on regular nights and before that eighteen months on afternoons and this is the result. What about Mum and Dad I can't leave them, Dad's not very well. We've only just had all the windows replaced. Will it be more money?"

I could hear my wife talking but I wasn't taking much in. My dream had come true. I'd always wanted to be an Undermanager, not a Deputy Manager or a Colliery Manager. That may come later the Undermanager was the responsible position I had always craved.

We all have a dream of what we'd like to be when we leave school. I was never one hundred per cent sure. I'd come into mining by accident. The first and only in the family. My parents hadn't been happy either.

It was during my time of underground training at Bold Colliery my eyes had been opened. A group of us, sixteen years old were returning from a training session from the underground gallery. Wearing our pit boots and yellow helmets. Old jeans, T shirts and jumpers. Workwear was yet to be provided. One of our trainers was the brother of the President of the National Union of Miners. He had the same distinctive eyebrows.

Training that day included using lashing chains to attach vehicles to a moving steel rope. The vehicles ran on steel rails and were the means by which materials were transported underground. Such things as steel girders, arches, pipes, and timber. We'd even learnt the benefits of the scotch not the drink but a short stubby metal rod with handle. Placed between the wheel spokes to slow the moving train of vehicles down. Nothing was left to chance even a de-railment. The requirement to use pieces of timber for packing to bring the vehicle back onto the track. It was our first introduction to pull lifts and the tirfor. There was something called a Sylvester too. We were informed its use now prohibited.

Arriving at the manriding station there was the usual assortment of lads and men. Mainly those off the haulage and transfer points. Out early to ensure a decent seat on the loco manrider for the travel to pit bottom. That's when I heard someone shout.
"It's the Undermanager. He's on his way out." Panic set in; men darting in all directions. The manrider had just arrived, the smell of diesel drifting down the tunnel to where we stood.
"Where?" someone shouted.
"The air doors he's coming through from the main return."
Then the sound of air rushing through the steel hatches reducing the pressure between the intake and return. The clang of the door closing, those men who'd

not run off hiding in the manholes fighting to get in and then…. He appeared, a huge figure of a man resplendent in his white donkey jacket, oil lamp hanging from his belt around the waist of his blue boiler suit. He was holding a wooden walking stick. On his head a white helmet cap lamp in place.

Arriving at the manrider, now in position, he looked left and right. He walked towards the end carriage followed by two smaller colleagues. There wasn't a sound to be heard from anyone, other than his stick tapping the rail sleepers and the loco engine beating.
"Wow," I said to no one in particular, "Who the hell is that?"
"That's the Undermanager lad, he don't take no prisoners." And that was it I had my eyes set on what I wanted to become.

Back at the pit the following week I reported as usual to the Training Officer. For the first time I took an interest in the organisation chart on one of his office walls. At the top of the chart was a box labelled Manager in brackets alongside in italics *1st Class Certificate of Competency* below which a further box entitled Deputy Manager followed by Undermanager. Brackets again *2nd Class Certificate of Competency.*
My thoughts interrupted as my wife shouted.
"Are you listening to me?"
"Yeah. Of course, it'll be more money." Little did I know!!!

Returning to work that night I was excited thinking about the future and my new role. I was currently on regular nights as the backshift Undermanager, but this was different. After the call from the Manager I'd spoken to the Deputy Manager. He advised me I would remain in place until Christmas. That was three weeks' away.

I arrived at the usual time, nine o'clock, although the shift didn't commence till ten. I preferred to arrive early for the shift handover. That took place with the afternoon shift Overman Bennie. Bennie was usually still on the phone with the Manager. Quietly listening to him barking orders down the phone depending on how the afternoon shift had gone. After handover I got changed and headed underground.

I had a lot of respect for Bennie particularly on his handling of the Manager. Better than most I'd observed. He knew when to speak, when to listen and not to interrupt. Above all else to have an answer for every question asked. I'd spent eighteen months with him on regular afternoons in preparation for my current role. During that time, I'd seen other potential Undermanager's provide the afternoon report to the Manager.

5

It was an experience to see how they reacted. Some unable to speak through fear of saying the wrong thing, others stuttering through the report often drying up during the ordeal. There was even one guy who'd come out with a small red blotch on his neck. Depending on how the conversation went the blotch would remain during the call. If the Manager became angry the blotch would spread up his neck to the side of his face.

I could only ever recall Bennie getting into trouble once. It was towards the end of my tenure with him. Bennie twice divorced with five kids had entered into an extramarital affair with a middle-aged lady from the local Labour Social Club. She had as he'd described "sexual needs" her husband was unable to provide. She was being ignored in the bedroom and he'd been chosen to fulfil those needs, according to him anyway.

On the night in question he suggested it was time I experienced the call with the Manager. Not to improve my education more to do with a promise he'd received from his mistress. She was going shopping and was investing in a number of new items of underwear. Including suspenders which if he'd mentioned once to me during the shift, he'd mentioned a dozen times.
I wasn't sure how exactly this was adding to the sexual encounter as any intercourse that took place was in the back of his Ford Capri outside the social club whilst her husband was at the bar.

"Right you okay if I shoot off now?"
"Yeah fine with me." It was approaching eight thirty. The preceding shift had gone well. The call to the Manager was due in half an hour. We were both stood in the colliery Control Room.
"Go on get yourself gone." Bennie gave me a pat on the back.
"Thanks mucker I owe you one." He started to make his way out.
"If he asks, which I'm sure he won't just say I've had a call from home and had to leave early."
"Yeah okay. Oh, and don't forget."
"What?"
"Don't get your dick caught in your zipper!"
"Fuck off!"

I'd received all the reports from the afternoon shift it was just a matter of filling out Bennie's pro forma he used to collate the information. Most of the afternoon shift had now gone as the nightshift began to arrive. One by one they'd enter the Control Room some already changed to go underground, most accompanied by an unlit fag hanging from the corner of their mouth. The nightshift colliery Overman greeting each as they arrived. I sat in the corner reading the afternoon report anticipating any questions the Manager may ask.

"Big night tonight Mick? Getting your first chance to speak with the Manager." I didn't answer I just smiled. "No fuck ups lad he won't forget." I ignored the last comment and continued to assess the information before me. *Where were the next supplies for the development headings? What was available immediately for the nightshift? Had all the pre-shift inspections been completed? How much conveyor was left in the loop for a conveyor extension on L31's main gate? Were there sufficient Victaulic pipes available for a water extension in L32'S maingate? Had the lads we'd left roof bolting the main gate finished their work?*

"Mick you'd better ring him now it's time. For fucks sake don't be late!"
"Fuck is that the time." I jumped up from my seat and walked across to the outside line a large black phone alongside the emergency red phone. I licked my lips. My mouth was dry. I tried producing some saliva as I took the phone from the Control Room operator. He had already dialled the number I could hear the ring tones from the Manager's phone. I placed the handset to my ear. Then silence.
"Hello Manager," he didn't answer immediately. "Hello Manager."
"Where's Bennie?" *I wasn't expecting that to be my first question neither had Bennie.*
"I'm sorry Manager he's had to nip out he's asked me to call you." Once more silence.
"How would you like me to start developments first?" I attempted to fill the silence.
"Where's Bennie?" His voice louder this time.
"Not too sure, we've had three shears off W11's."
"Where's Bennie?" I moved the handset slightly away from my head. I sensed the background noise in the Control Room had stopped.
"I........."
"Get Bennie to phone me!" The line went dead.

"Well Mick that's the quickest conversation I think I've heard anyone have with the Manager." The colliery Overman responded laughing. My head was attempting to recover. I couldn't speak my mouth was salivaless. I reached across for my cold mug of tea.
"Do we know which social club Bennie frequents?" I seemed to have everyone's attention.
"Leigh Miners?"
"No that's on Thursday."

"What about St. Helens Labour Club?"

"No, I'd try Haydock No. 2."

I realized then no one had a clue. I kicked myself for not asking him myself just in case. Twenty minutes later after a number of calls.

"Mick it's for you."

"Bennie?"

"For fucks sake Mick I was on the vinegar stroke, her husband came out looking for me." I had visions of his yellow Ford Capri in the car park. The only one with windows steamed up.

"Sorry mate, the Manager wouldn't speak to me he just wanted you."

"For fucks sake what did you say?"

"Never got the chance he just wanted you."

I smiled to myself that was nearly twelve months ago, how time flies.

"Hello Mick, hello Mick." My thoughts were interrupted as the tannoy burst into life. It was the Control Room.

"Hi Mick here."

"EWR is gassed out the Deputy wants a call."

"Thanks Steve I'm on it."

I put the call through to the Deputy in charge of the heading. He had everything under control. The place was renowned for sudden emissions of methane even after our attempts to pre bore between shifts. We'd leave two men to drill in the sides of the roadway holes up to ten feet and then couple to the methane range. The Deputy had detected the gas during his increased inspection regime. Two per cent in the general body meant he'd have to withdraw the men.

The Dosco Mk 2 Roadheader had been stopped and isolated whilst the men extended the ventilation bagging's right up to the face of the headings. I guessed the problem had been caused due to the unavailability of ventilation bagging in the first instance. We were required by law to keep the ventilation within five yards of the face. I was happy with his actions and decided to visit the heading later. The incident had confirmed my intentions for the shift. I would visit the developments, nine in total. The two coal faces I would leave until the following evening.

The coal faces in question were W11's in the Wigan Five Foot seam and C16's in the Crombouke. 11's an advance face; was to complete a shear and then carry out an extension in the maingate. The extension consisted of adding additional conveyor belting into the maingate conveyor loop. Thus, allowing the face conveyor to push over and the stage loader to follow without interruption. In addition, a number of men were to assist the electricians to extend the electrical cables. Rehanging them as the panel train, pantechnican as it was known was moved in.

Whilst this was happening the rails on which the pantechnican was sat were extended allowing the whole train to move forward. Speaking with the face Overman he confirmed they were on target to achieve the required work and leave the face in a position for the day shift to commence shearing as soon as they arrived.

The other coal face 16's was already onto its third shear nothing unusual about that. Of all the coal faces this place was guaranteed to produce coal without geological issues. The coal simply gave itself up. I didn't speak with the face Overman he wasn't one for small talk. I confirmed with the Control Room my plans for the shift and continued to make my rounds.

Travelling the various roadways allowed me to check the outbye districts for supplies including steel work, timber, mesh, struts, stonedust and not forgetting the ventilation bagging.

I was still having difficulty concentrating thinking of my new role. It was a matter of weeks till the end of the year. I was to start as Undermanager in the New Year. I contemplated how I would manage the place. The one thing I knew for certain keeping the place tidy was a must. It helped in keeping accidents to a minimum and reduced the time in prepping for the visits from HMI, Her Majesty's Inspectors whom I likened to Royalty. More to the point a good underground visit from them put you in the good books with the Manager.

The most important relationship would be with the Manager. He was the one I'd need to keep on side. He could make your life hell. I'd seen enough Undermanager's in the past fall by the wayside. Destroyed by the Manager if they hadn't been up to the mark. The verbal and at times physical abuse meted out was beyond anything I guess went on in other industries.

Over the years I'd witnessed Undermanager's under so much pressure they'd leave the industry. Others experienced mental breakdowns. Some moved sideways. Others continued in the role becoming sad and lonely figures ridiculed by the men.
I was never one to believe that a management position automatically gave you respect. A lot did, my view however it needed to be earned. You couldn't kid a pit mon.

"Hello Mick, hello Mick." Once more my thoughts were interrupted. I'd been walking out from the last development I'd planned to visit. The tannoy was at the meeting station just ahead of me.

"Hi Steve, Mick here."

"Could you give me a ring?" Whenever the Control Room asked for a call nine times out of ten it was never good news. It meant there was a problem a problem he only wanted me to hear.

"Hi Steve what's up?"

"Not good I'm afraid, there's been a runaway on 11's with a number of cables damaged."

"Fuck!" I looked at my watch, "Shite it's nearly five o'clock, only gives us an hour before the dayshift start to arrive."

"They've got all the lads with the electricians now pulling the damaged cables out. Another team have gone to fetch the spares from the crosscut shunt."

"Where's the face Overman?"

"In the maingate at the stageloader waiting for a call from you."

"Thanks." I dialled the number it was picked up immediately.

"Mick, it may not be as big a problem as we thought. A number of the lads have agreed to stop over we should be ready for when the dayshift get in." I listened his last comment something I wanted to hear. The decision I needed to make was whether I should go straight to him.

"Leave it with me I'll get it sorted there's no point you comin in."

He was right of course it would take me another forty-five minutes to reach the coal face. I was in a dilemma my head was telling me to go straight there, my heart was telling me different. I was tired. I'd promised the wife I'd attend our son's carol service.

"Are you sure?"

"Yeah mucker get yourself gone." Decision made.

Arriving back up the pit I made my way to the Control Room later than normal and provided my verbal report to the Deputy Manager. He took it well and readily accepted my explanation on the cable damage in W11's.

"And they'll be ready for the dayshift?"

"Yeah all under control." I left him and went for my bath.

Drying myself down I realised I was cutting it fine to get home on time. The doors to the baths flew open. It was the Manager's clerk.

"Mick you best get your gear back on. Manager wants you back underground."

"You don't think I'm going to fall for that do you?"

"I'm only doing as instructed and it ain't no joke seems there's more damaged cables than the night shift have let on. The face won't be starting up for another couple of hours."

This did get my attention *I knew I should have gone in to check I'd received a "going home" report I just wanted to believe it!*
"Well I've done my shift I'm going home. Now fuck off and let me finish getting changed."
"Don't shoot the messenger, I'm only passing on the instruction." The guy left. Bravado had now replaced common sense *I'll go and see the Manager myself.* As I finished getting ready my thoughts were interrupted once more. This time it was the Deputy Manager. He didn't look happy.

"Mick Manager wants you back underground." I looked at him. He turned his gaze away. I guessed the Manager had had words with him.
"You've got to be kiddin I've done twelve hours already plus I've got to get my lad to school."
"I think it would be in all our interests if you did as you were told." I stood up.
"I'll go see him myself because I ain't going back down."
"Don't say you weren't warned."

The Manager's office was at the end of a long corridor. Alongside the Deputy Managers. Reception to the left unoccupied at this time of the morning. I knocked on his door. No answer. I knocked again and followed up by turning the door handle. The door one of two opened into a long narrow office immediately ahead of me a large table. This was used by the Manager for his meetings. Beyond this at the far end of the room his desk. He was sat at the desk signing yesterday's reports.

A pipe hanging from the side of his mouth explained the smell of St Bruno in the air. I could hear the sound of footsteps and men chatting. The colliery baths were directly above his office. He didn't look up. Then silence. Just the sound of his fountain pen nib scratching against the paper.
"Manager excuse me, I'm told you want me to go back underground?" No response.
"Manager, I had no idea the damage would be as bad as the dayshift had suggested." No response.
"Manager……." This time he looked up removing the pipe his eyes glaring. They were angry eyes. He shouted.

"Get yourself back down the pit lad and sort out the fucking problem you've left for the dayshift. If you don't go then fuck off back down the road and don't ever bother fuckin coming back! Now fuck off out of my sight."

Without another word spoken I left his office. I got back up the pit later that day completing my first twenty-hour shift.

A week after the incident in W11's I received a call from the Control Room that the shearer on 11's was at a standstill. Electrical problems I wasn't making the same mistake again.

"I'm on my way."

Arriving at the district forty minutes later the maingate conveyor was still running. Every few yards I spotted shovel loads of fireclay on the belt. It normally carried a continuous stream of black coal. I guessed the face Overman had put some of the men on the maingate dint. I wasn't wrong two minutes later I could see ahead three cap lamps bobbing up and down.

"Hi Mick we guessed it was you."
"Morning lads all well?"
"Me and the lads have been talking we're guessing this place is jinxed."
"That may be true."
"Snuff Mick?" One of the men passed me a small round tin opened with the brown snuff exposed. "Hedges."
"Thanks, but I can't stop I need to get to the coal face, thanks anyway."

I continued inbye. *Jinxed they may have a point. The coal face was planned as the collieries big hitter having been supplied with a hundred and fifty tonnes of new equipment including Anderson shearer with extended arms allowing the cutting out of both gate roads, Dowty six leg powered supports, thirty-six-inch panzer and a brand spanking new stage loader. The advanced face had been operational for the last eighteen months each shear producing five hundred tonnes of coal.*

The target set by senior management was three shears per shift. It rarely achieved two plagued by equipment failure and geological problems particularly at the main gate end requiring roof bolting at the end of each shift. One of the face Overmen had been badly injured too crushed by a huge lump of stone now a cripple for life.

I could see the lights from the stage loader ahead the place was deadly silent. The clanking of the stage loader chain replaced by voices. Another team set the task of adding belt to the main gate loop the air clear of the continuous mist of dust. I spotted the face Deputy walking towards me.

"Mick hi; still no joy I'm afraid."
"Who's working on it?"
"Face electrician plus his outbye colleague."
"Where's the assistant engineer?"
"No sign. We tried calling him earlier but can't get hold of him."
"For fucks sake we've been stopped for over two hours......"

I was interrupted by the face chargehand over the tannoy.
"Right lads machine sorted let's have you all back on the job." There followed further conversations over the tannoy as the outbye belts were started up followed by the stage loader.
"Thank fuck for that."
"Are you coming onto the face Mick?"
"Yeah I need to make a call first and see where that cunt of an engineer has been hiding."

"Good luck with that it's the same with him every time we're on nights." The face Deputy left, I put a call through to the Control Room.
"Steve, have you tried his office?"
"Locked; no sign of him anywhere."
"Right leave that with me."

After my visit to the coal face I left the district via the return gate. Travelling up the main tunnels on the manriding conveyor now piled high with the black stuff.
"You're earlier than normal Mick." I'd arrived at the pit bottom having walked the main tunnel the loco had been busy shunting supplies.
"Yeah I need to see someone." The Onsetter signalled for the cage it was waiting just above the inset.
"I bet he's in for a round of fucks!" I entered the cage. *Not a truer word spoke.*
"See you tonight." Within minutes I was back at the pit top. I passed the Banksman my tally.

"Early Mick?"
"Yeah I need to find someone."
"So, I've heard." I said no more and headed to the lamproom. No one was about. I placed my oil lamp on the table outside the lamproom office and having removed my cap lamp and self-rescuer headed to the engineer's office.

The assistant engineer's offices one for the electrical team the other for the mechanics were adjacent to one another. The mechanics office door wide open; I popped my head in, it was empty. I turned towards the locked office and clenching my first banged on the door. No response. I placed my ear against the door and this time could hear the distinct sound of someone snoring. Now with both hands clenched I banged once more on the door.

"Wake up you; lazy bastard," I shouted for good measure I began kicking the base of the door too.
"Ah... ah... ah." I began to laugh.
The office door opened the assistant engineer stood one hand rubbing his back the other rubbing the sleep from his eyes.
"What the fuck is your game?"
"What do you mean?"
"Sleeping on the job; you lazy bastard."
"I've not been asleep I've been writing up my report."
"Fucking report; do know we've had a two-hour stoppage on W11's?"
"Nobody's told me."
"That's because you been locked up in here asleep."
"I wish you wouldn't keep saying I was asleep."

I reached forward and grabbed his overalls pulling him towards me.
"For fucks sake man you've been sleeping on the job and I'm going to make sure everyone knows. You lazy twat!"
"Prove it." I could see I was getting nowhere with our conversation and released him from my grasp and went towards the baths.

Once changed I headed towards the Control Room and started compiling my shift report. An hour later the Deputy Manager appeared his usual Players No 6 hanging from his mouth.
"Problems again on 11's I hear.........." The Control Room supervisor interrupted.
"It's the Manager for you." He passed the Deputy Manager the phone. Between the time taken to pass him the phone he had inhaled his fag only the ash remained. The colour had drained from his face.

"Will do." He replaced the phone. "He wants to see you now. Top shunt!"
"Me why?"
"Well I'm sure you'll know once you get there." *Fuck I bet that fucking engineer has complained about me grabbing him.*

Standing outside the Top Shunt head bowed I knocked. I reminisced for a moment; it was akin to seeing the Headmaster at school but worse far worse.

"Come," I went inside. The Manager was sat in his usual position signing reports and puffing on his pipe. Without looking up he asked.

"Now lad what happened last night?" He seemed very calm.

I described the incident from the previous night. I conveniently left out the bit about grabbing the engineer. He looked up.

"Go get yourself a cuppa lad. I'd like you back here in half an hour."

"Okay Boss."

Heading towards the canteen I guessed he wanted me at his morning meeting. The meeting normally started at eight o'clock attended by the senior team including the Deputy Manager, Mechanical and Electrical engineers and sometimes the Coal Prep Manager. The only person I'd had any real dealings with was the Deputy Manager. I liked him. I don't think he was comfortable in the presence of the Manager. Who was? The others I knew of but wasn't sure of their interaction with the Manager I'm sure I was going to find out.

Once in the canteen I asked one of the girls for a strong mug of tea,

"What do we owe the pleasure of your company Mick?" The canteen Manageress had come out personally to serve me.

"To see what I've been missing."

"I'll bet. What can I get you then?"

"Just a strong tea please."

I sat at one of the many empty tables. An hour previous the place would have been heaving. Dayshift ordering toast and bacon butties to take underground followed by the nightshift ordering a full English. The smell of bacon and sausage lingered in the air. A number of eggs still sizzling in the frying pan. Alongside huge thick slices of black pudding. One or two of the surface lads were still there.

I reflected on the previous night and the decisions I had taken. It was something I'd done ever since becoming a junior Manager. Satisfied with my recollection of events possibly with the exception of grabbing the engineer. I finished my drink and checked the canteen clock. Nearly eight; time to head back.

I knocked once again on the door. To say I was nervous was an understatement.

15

"Come," The others were already there sat either side of the meeting table. The Manager was still signing reports puffing on his pipe.

"Sit there lad." The Manager without looking up pointed with his pipe to the head of the table. I followed his instruction. The room remained silent. Except again for the sound of his fountain pen nib scratching his signature.

I looked across to the Deputy Manager. His face pale partly obscured by the smoke he exhaled from the cigarette he was holding. I was mesmerized by the amount of ash produced each time he drew on the cigarette. He caught me looking and smiled. His nervous smile.

Alongside him the Coal Prep Manager. For the short time I'd been in there he seemed to have slid down the chair. As if trying to hide. Opposite the two engineers. The Mechanical Engineer was visibly shaking. It certainly wasn't from the room temperature. If anything; I was getting warmer by the minute. The only person who seemed to be at ease was the Electrical Engineer. He had the habit of continually pulling the cuffs of his shirt from beneath his jacket. He eyed me suspiciously.

"Right gentlemen down to business." The Manager had stopped signing we all turned to face him. "Now lad tell us all about last night."

Once more I relayed the events of the previous evening. Including the confrontation with the assistant Electrical Engineer. It was at this point the Electrical Engineer interrupted.

"Is it true you manhandled my man?" Before I could answer the Manager raised his hand to me.

"Now lad you get yourself off home to bed." I needed no more encouragement. As fast as my legs could carry me, I left the office. No one else said a word. Once outside I stopped and put my ear to the door as the tirade commenced.

"Man, fuckin handled? I'd have thrown the cunt down the shaft."

"But, but……"

"Don't fuckin but, but me mister. You need to deal with that fucker and get him back on the tools." The Manager's voice grew louder each time he uttered the next sentence. Time, I left!

-

The following weekend my wife agreed that we go and look for a place to live. Reluctantly at first. However, she recognised the logistics of me doing a daily commute. Or staying away each week was far from ideal. Our two children James and Elizabeth though had other ideas.

"But Mum why do we have to go?"

"Because James it's your Dad's new job."

"But Mum me and Lizzie wanted to go for a walk today with Heidi." Heidi was the family's dog. Mum and James were in the kitchen. She'd just completed making a packed lunch for the journey.

"Don't worry about Heidi your Dad's been out first thing and taken her over the fields. Anyway, stop moaning we're going to Wales today and that's that. Where's your sister?"

I'd completed loading the car. I walked back into the house.

"Right car's packed, where's Lizzie?"

"She's having a poo on her potty." James replied. "Dad do we have to go?"

"Did you put the kid's wellies in?" Mum asked.

"No was I supposed to?"

"Don't worry I'll do it. The sandwiches and flask are there in that bag."

"Yes, son we need to look for a new house." I picked up the plastic bag.

"Sinished." Lizzie shouted from the living room. She was still learning how to pronounce the letter f.

"Mick can you sort Lizzie." It was an instruction not a request.

"Will do."

"But why Dad I like this house."

Ten minutes later we set off. We hadn't a set agenda or to be more accurate I'd decided we should just go. We had to start somewhere.

"Are we there yet?"

"Not yet darling soon though."

"There Mum I've seen another red car."

"Well done, now see how many green cars you can see." I looked in the rear-view mirror Lizzie was fast asleep. Satisfied our son was now occupied looking for green cars my wife turned to me.

"What's the plan then?"

"Plan what do you mean?"

"Where are you planning to start?"

"Are we there yet?" James asked again.

"Not long now."

"Start what?"

"For goodness sake, the reason we're driving to Wales."

"Just seen two Mum."

"Good boy keep counting."

She turned back to me. "I had assumed dear you had an idea where we'd be looking?" My wife had a good point; however, I hadn't given it any thought. I just wanted to get a general feel for the area.

"Yeah of course I have. First thing we'll head to the pit and then start driving around the surrounding area."

"Oh, right so you don't have a plan. No surprise there then. And by the way there's only two weeks left before Christmas I still haven't got your Mum and Dad anything. You'll need to take me into town tomorrow." I knew better than to argue.

Three quarters of an hour later we passed though Ffynnongroyw. I saw a sign for Gronant.

"Right once I've showed you where the pit is; we'll head to there." I nodded towards the road sign. No one answered they were all asleep. Five minutes later I saw the sign for the pit. I turned along a narrow country lane. Within a hundred yards a set of traffic lights where the road narrowed to a single track passing under a railway bridge. The lights were on red I stopped. I guess this was the route the coal wagons took to Fiddlers Ferry Power Station.

"We here then?" My wife asked yawning.

"Yes, dear just wanted to show you where I'll be working." The lights changed to green. I put the car in first and drove forward. Without warning a large white van appeared in front of us.

"For goodness sake!" My wife shouted. I did an emergency stop the sudden movement woke the kids.

"Are we there yet." I mumbled the phrase "dick head" under my breath. It was followed by a sharp blow from my wife's elbow in my ribs. The guy in the van was smiling greeting me with two fingers. I stared at him I was good at remembering faces.

"Yeah we're here now your Dad just showing us where he'll be working."

Once through; the road rose gently passing under huge electrical cables with signage indicating the high voltage, 33,000V. I drove on towards the car park. In the distance a number of glass fronted building which I assumed to be the offices. To the right a taller building behind which rose a set of headgear. I stopped the car.

"James that's where the men go underground."

"Can we go?"

"Looks as though you've been spotted" My wife indicated towards a gentleman walking towards the car. He was wearing boiler suit, NCB donkey jacket and white helmet. He walked with a limp. He stopped alongside my window which was down.

"Now what you be doin here?"

"Just havin a looksee." He spotted the kids and gave them a wave.

"Now this be private property boyo you shouldn't be on here without permission. You lost or something?"

"Go on tell em who you are." my wife whispered. Before I said anything, a large wagon appeared.

"Right you have a good day now. Just watch yourself goin under the bridge not a lot of drivers pay much attention to the lights." And with that he walked off.

We left and headed towards Gronant which looked bleak. Reaching the top of a short hill I spotted a house for sale. It was designed in a mock Tudor style.

"There's one. What do you think?"

"Dad I'm bored." My son responded.

"Darling won't be long now." My wife answered. "I don't believe Lizzie's a sleep again. Lizzie wake up." She didn't budge. "That means she'll be awake tonight." I drove on heading towards Prestatyn.

"Look there's another house for sale." This time no response. I continued to drive. Five minutes later.

"I'm hungry." Lizzie had woken up.

"Okay darling Mummy's made a packed lunch." She turned to me. "Think it's time we had a stop."

"We've only been to two places."

"Mum I'm bored." James added.

"I think you've had your answer."

"How about we go to the seaside for lunch? What about Rhyl?"

"No done that to death when I was younger."

"But they want to go by the sea."

"Conwy then."

"Too far. Don't forget we've come to look at houses."

We were now passing through Prestatyn I had an idea. I headed back to the A55. By the time we'd reached the signs for Abergele the wind had picked up.

"Mum I'm hungry."

"Mum when are we stopping?" Before my wife could answer I saw a sign with directions to the beach.

"We're here now kids. Look the sea." I brought the car to a stop on the pebbled beach. James looking out the window exclaimed.

"Is this where we'll be living Mum?"

"That has yet to be decided dear. Now take this." She passed him a sandwich. "Here's yours Lizzie."

"Thank you Mummy." My sandwich wrapped separately was thrown towards me. It landed in my lap.

"Thanks." I got no response. Not that I expected any.

"Mummy I don't like cheese." James having eaten his sandwich commented. I was distracted by the height of the waves as the sea whipped them ever more up in to a frenzy.

"Whatever you do don't open the door on your side James. You may get blown away.

"Here dear why don't you have your yogurt instead. You okay Lizzie?"

We continued to eat in silence for the next five minutes. I reached across for the flask.

"Mummy I feel sick." James advised as he opened the car door.

"No not that side James…." I shouted spilling my coffee in the process. The scene following happened so quickly. James having opened the door threw up just as a gust of wind flew off the top of a huge wave.

The contents of his stomach momentarily hanging in the air. Then…. Lizzie began to cry. "Mummy he's just been sick all over me." James began to cry too.

"It's not my fault."

"That's it we're going home." That was the end of our first house hunting visit.

-

The day after I'd been advised of my new promotion, I'd taken a call from my new Manager Ron Groves. I'd worked for Mr Groves before. At my first colliery. I liked him. He could be a miserable bastard at times when something went wrong. He wasn't much of a shouter. He certainly led by example. My first experience of a leader. He kindly congratulated me on my appointment and suggested I visit him at the colliery.

He suggested the weekend when he would be at work. Thought too it would be worthwhile if I brought Mrs Gibson.

"Why the hell would I want to waste my Saturday. We were only there last week. You do know it's Christmas in less than a week."

"For what it's worth it wasn't my idea. Ron Groves suggested it. You've met him before remember at one of the mining doo's."

"Work, work, work that's all you think of. Yes, I'll come, and I think I'll be having a word with him. You can arrange with your parents to look after the kids. Mum and Dad are still not happy with me about leaving Huyton."

So, we set off on the Saturday. Six days to be exact before Christmas Day. Mr Groves had suggested we keep the visit confidential. Ideally, I shouldn't speak with anyone on arrival. I duly obliged. We parked up as instructed outside of his office. He came out to meet us.
"Congratulations Mick. Welcome." We shook hands.
"Thanks Mr Groves. My wife whom you've met before."
"Hello Mrs Gibson. Good to see you again." He turned and we followed him into what must have been the reception area.
"This is Bronwen my secretary."
"Hi Bronwen." We shook hands. "And my wife Annie."
"Welcome to you both. How would you like a nice cuppa after your long journey?"
"Yes please." Bronwen's accent was quite lyrical and very Welsh.

We followed Mr Groves through a door directly behind Bronwen's desk. His office wasn't as big as my previous Managers. It did however feel warmer. A place I felt comfortable in. Maybe the fact that the far side of the room had windows along its full length. Allowing the winter sunshine to shine through. The centre of the room was taken up by a long wooden table with numerous chairs placed either side. A long sideboard was positioned to our right with a bowl of fruit. Either side a number of frames containing certificates. Each one seemed to refer to the colliery brass band. He caught me admiring the selection of fruit.
"Help yourself."
"I'm fine thanks Mr Groves."

His desk was at the far end of the room. Piled high with papers and reports. On one side a computer screen with keyboard. Ahead of us he pulled out two chairs. Placing them opposite his desk.
"Grab a pew why don't you." As we sat down Bronwen entered. This time through a side door off the main corridor. She was carrying a tray with our drinks.
"There you go. Enjoy." She left the room.
"How was your journey?"
"Not too bad thanks. A little busy before Queensferry but after that not a great deal of traffic. We took the coast road in. Dropping onto it from Hollywell."
"Yeah that's generally the way I come. I live near Chester." He then turned towards my wife. "And how's Mrs Gibson."

21

Here we go "Fine thank you."

"I know it must be hard moving to a new house and leaving family behind."
Get ready!

"Oh no. I fully understand this is Mick's job. He has to go where the work is."
I looked at my wife in disbelief. This wasn't the conversation we'd had on the
journey there. I think Mr Groves too knew how she really felt as he continued.

"Well Mick's a lucky man to have such an understanding wife. Mrs Groves
has never forgiven me from moving after my last job. Cried she did for almost
two years. It's not easy on you ladies. Something I don't think the Coal Board
ever consider. The upside though it's a lovely area. A beautiful place to bring up
your children. Plus, they get to learn a second language."

I couldn't believe what the Manager was saying. And being so open and honest
about it. It had the desired affect though. Mrs Gibson was smiling. Something
she hadn't done since we left the house. We spent the next half hour listening to
his plans for the pit. He was very passionate about the place. Complementary
too of the men that worked there. I sat and listened. Eventually I felt I needed to
ask a question.

"What time would you be expecting me to start my shift."

"For goodness sake Mick what sort of question is that? You're your own man,
you do exactly what you think is right. The time you start. The time you finish.
That's not for me to tell you." I was a little embarrassed. I looked towards my
wife. She was smiling. I didn't ask any more questions.

It was obvious he wanted me to make my own mark. It would be up to me to
manage the way I saw fit. The one bit of advice he did give me.

"Don't jump to any conclusions about the place or the men immediately you
arrive. They're a proud bunch. They've been through a lot of change with
plenty more to come. Give it a few months to get to know them."

"I will, thanks for the advice."

"Right I think I 've kept you long enough. You must have plenty of things to
do with it being so near to Christmas. I suppose Mick has plans for lunch?" My
wife smiled again.

"If he didn't, he will have now." I shifted uncomfortably in my chair. *That's
me told!*

"Right come on let me show you quickly around." We left the office through
the side door into the main corridor. Bronwen was sat at her desk.

"Thanks for the drinks Bronwen."

"My pleasure. See you soon." We followed the Manager along the corridor.
He pointed out the various offices on our right as we walked. I didn't take in
much of what he was saying. I was just too excited. I couldn't wait to start.

Towards the end of the corridor we reached a door. Passing through the door he stopped.

"And that's your office." The place was a complete shit hole. A large desk with two tables had been placed together. The desk, my desk, under the window whilst two tables placed perpendicular to it. A number of chairs had been placed opposite. Some wooden, some metal all shapes and sizes. The surface of the desks were littered with report books and copies of the latest Coal News. An in and out tray full of paperwork sat on my desk. The windows directly opposite to where we stood contained a surface layer of dust. Streams of sunlight shone through odd places where someone had wiped the glass clean. To the right of the desk stood two metal filing cabinets. One grey, one black. On top a number of unopened dust masks. To the left a coat stand. A donkey jacket with NCB hanging lopsided on it. The corner nearest to the door had a small table. On it a kettle, teapot, bowl of sugar and a number of mugs. Some with the remnants of tea and coffee.

There was a blackboard too. Someone had drawn a smiley face. Underneath the word *fuckoff* clearly seen. It didn't help that the walls were painted green. The look on my face must have said it all.

"Um, yeah I'll make sure it's cleaned up before you start." The Manager turned away mumbling something to himself. "Up there." He pointed to a set of stairs opposite. "The Control Room." Then pointing to his left. "Deployment and lamproom. Right well I'll bid you farewell and look forward to seeing you here next year. Merry Christmas."

"Thanks for seeing us today and Merry Christmas to you too."

"Yes, good to see you again. Merry Christmas." My wife added.

We left through a door opposite to the stairs and walked back to the car. My wife didn't say a word till we got inside.

"What time should I start Mr Groves?" She mimicked and began laughing. I joined in *she had a point*. Well at least that had brought a smile to her face.

-

3. 1988 The First Year

I'd done some research on the pit. Three shafts, only two used and an eight-hundred-metre-long Drift where the coal was transported from underground. It had been completed last year. Coal was produced from a single coal face using the retreat system of mining. Annual output was nearly six hundred thousand tonnes with a workforce of just over six hundred men. The panels of coal were blocked out using Dosco Dintheaders and supported by Hollybank arches or square work. I was well versed in using this method as the first pit I'd worked at had done the same.

To minimise production gaps the pit had been very successful at using Free Steered Vehicles or FSV's as they were known. These diesel operated vehicles were used mainly for supplying materials to the coal face and headings. Far more flexible than rope haulage I was advised. Where they came into to their own was on a face salvage and installation. I was yet to see that for myself.

There was even a pilot plant on site for converting coal to oil. Not dissimilar to that pioneered by the South Africans. The plans suggested converting two and a half tonnes of coal a day to a number of transport fuels; my thoughts were suddenly interrupted as a fox darted out from the undergrowth across the road in front of me. I'd been so deep in thought I hadn't noticed I was now In North Wales.

I was early so I decided to take the long route in via Mold. Passing by Connah's Quay, Flint, Bagillt, Greenfield, Mostyn and finally Ffynnongroyw.

The Manager had suggested I arrive at the pit about eight o'clock. That was the start of his morning meeting at which he'd introduce me to his senior team. After which I'd meet my team. It was now nearly six o'clock I wanted to get a feel for the place without anything stage managed.

Walking in through the double doors a number of men in their underground gear headed towards the lamproom. I breathed in. The unmistakable smell of pit. I'd recognise it anywhere. Nobody paid me any attention. I turned to the left I could hear shouting.

"I gave Gruffyd a clear instruction he was to get me a mine car of stonedust into the district on nights." The shouting came from the office next to mine. The office for the Zone A Undermanager. The underground districts had been divided into two. Zone B my district covered the greater area.

I looked through the open door and recognised the guy from my days at North Staffs Polytechnic Paul Taylor. He'd always reminded me of Rick Wakeman the keyboardist from the Yes. He looked different, still the same long blond hair but older, dark patches under his eyes. He looked towards me without recognition, moving forward he pushed the door closed.

"Well now I'm afraid Mr. Taylor Gruffyd never passed that onto me."

"It's not good enough Delwyn I've got a bloody inspector this morning." I assumed Delwyn to be the nightshift colliery Overman.

I continued into my office. The place was still a shithole. The only attempt to tidy the place up had been to stack the various reports in separate piles. The smell of tobacco hung in the air a layer of coal dust lying across the desks sat in the middle of the room. I walked in towards the large window behind the desk. It was still difficult to see out.

"Who the fuck are you boyo?"

I turned to see a short round gentleman in a blue boiler suit standing there. He was holding a half full bag of sugar. Before I could answer.

"Now hold on a minute I know who you are. You be the new Undermanager Mr. Gibson?" He was smiling as he said it.

"That would be me, but you can call me Mick."

"Now I'll give you some good advice stick with the mister. Manager likes that he's not happy with management being called by their Christian name. One of the many reasons your predecessor left. I'm Bleddyn your Colliery Overman for now anyway. Manager be pleased you're early guess your checking us out for yourself?"

"Something like that." I pondered his comment about him being the "Overman for now" but chose to ignore it. We shook hands.

"Tea?"

"Please."

He walked across to a small table in the corner of the room and switched on a dirty looking metal kettle.

"Bleddyn could you do me a big favour mate." Paul Taylor appeared at the door. He gave me a nod.

"I'm your mate now?" Bleddyn responded again with a cheeky smile.

"I need a mine car of stonedust first thing I've got an inspector coming. Delwyn was supposed to organise last night but it seems Gruffyd never passed on the message."

"Now I think your request needs passing on to the Zone B Undermanager." He turned towards me and then back to Paul. "Mr Taylor meet Mr Gibson." Paul offered his hand.

"Welcome to the madhouse."

"Good to meet you."

"Would that be okay then?"

"What?"

"The stonedust."

"Oh yeah fine." Without any instruction Bleddyn picked up the phone. "Osian take one of the stonedust mine cars and put it into the Zone A shunt.

"Thanks, I owe you one." Paul left the office.

For the next hour and a half Bleddyn took me through the plans as he understood for the pit. Coal was currently being produced from F42's in my district Zone B. It had a matter of months to run. Coal production would then start in Paul Taylor's section. The coal face there was still being installed and they had an inspector's visit that day hence the requirement for stonedust first thing. He explained alongside 42's was F43's. F stood for the seam Five Yard others included the Stone Coal, Two Yard, Three Yard, Durbog, Hard Five Quarter, Badger and the Bychton.

F43's another retreat face was still in the development stage although the return gate had been driven. Current activity centred around the main gate working three shifts with a Dosco Dintheader. There were a number of other drivages but the main one was heading towards a new area of coal at Strata Top in the Two Yard seam. From what plans he'd seen at least seven coal faces were planned.

"One of your first decisions will be my replacement."
"I guessed as much. Why you leaving?"
"Retiring more like it."
"You're not that old."
"Fifty actually my little legs won't be carrying my weight much longer." He pushed his chair back and pulled up a leg of his boiler suit exposing one of his knees. "See now how swollen they are." I wasn't surprised he was as wide as he was tall but kept that to myself.
"I've only just arrived."
"I'm good at weighing up people I think from what I've seen of you so far you'll just be fine. Anyway, Managers not agreed to it yet, so I'll be here for a few more months yet."

He continued to update me on my team. This included three development Overmen covering each of the three shifts, Osian, whom I'd meet later he was on shift plus Lewis and Evan. There was another Arfon he was used on supplies. The colliery Overmen covering the backshifts included Gruffyd on regular afternoons and Delwyn on regular nights. I recognised the names from earlier. Bleddyn's opposite number for Mr. Taylor was Dewi. The face Overmen alternated between each section dependant on the location of the coal face.

"Huw also known as Asyn, Alwyn and Hywel. They be the face Overmen now." The names just rolled off his tongue I was beginning to tire from so much information. He must have guessed as much.
"What time you seeing the Manager?"
"In about ten minutes he wants to introduce me to his team."

"Well I'll hang about here I need to pick up my breakfast. We'll go down when you've finished. Be careful of the Deputy Manager though bit of a sly one that boyo. I'm never sure about them Southerners..." Before he could finish the Manager walked into the office.

"You here already Mr. Gibson; see you've met Bleddyn?" Both Bleddyn and I stood up.
"Bora da." Bleddyn uttered as he stood.
"Good morning Mr. Groves; yeah he's been explaining the underground workings and the officials."
"Good. Well if we pop down to my office, I'll introduce you to my team. I've arranged for the engineers to be in here for eight thirty. Bleddyn if you like hang fire while I introduce the others and then you can both go down together."
"Sound like a plan Mr. Groves."

The Manager and I left and headed towards his office.
"I suppose he mentioned his retirement?"
"Yeah, one of the first things he said."
"Well he's in for a shock as he ain't going anytime soon!" As we walked along the corridor, he pointed out the various offices and their occupants.
"Personal manager Bill Hooper, Electrical Engineer Billy Blunt, Mechanical Engineer Gerry Tuffman, Deputy Manager Paul Adder and reception. My secretary Bronwen, whom you've met resides there. She's my protector." He winked as he said it. "And along there." He pointed towards the end of the corridor, "Conference room." He'd obviously forgotten we'd already had the tour before Christmas.

He turned to his left and entered his office. Three gentlemen were already seated around the large rectangular table. The bowl of uneaten fruit was still in place on the sideboard.
Each of the occupants rose in turn to shake my hand as the Manager introduced them.
"Paul Adder my Deputy Manager, Billy Blunt the Electrical engineer and last but not least Gerry Tuffman Mechanical engineer. We're expecting a replacement Assistant Manager at some point the previous incumbent has moved on. Take a seat."

They looked at me expectantly I felt obliged to give them a quick rundown of my career to date. All paid attention except for Paul Adder he seemed preoccupied continually playing with a ball point pen. They seemed friendly enough and suggested I would have no problem settling in. Part way through my introduction we were interrupted by the Personal Manager Bill Hooper who joined the meeting. The only question asked was by Gerry Tuffman inquiring as to whether I liked fishing.

"Thanks for that Mick, right if you don't mind Mr. Adder could you take the morning meeting. I want to take Mick to meet his team." I watched as Paul Adder jumped from his seat to sit in the Manager's chair. As we left his office, I overheard Gerry Tuffman speak to Billy Blunt.
"Manager seems to be taking an interest in the new guy."
"Yeah I hear Grovesey was his Manager at the first pit he worked."

Walking back along the corridor the Manager turned to me. "They're not a bad bunch that lot. Gerry's reason for asking you about the fishing is he does quite a bit himself always looking to sell on his catch. Make sure when you park up never outside his office. He has a nasty habit of spitting chewing tobacco out of the window."
"I'll remember that. Forgive me for saying but I couldn't believe how fast Mr. Adder jumped into your seat."
"Paul's eager for a Manager's role he'll get his chance soon enough."

Arriving back in my office the place was almost full including Bleddyn. The Manager again went on to introduce all those present. Zone B's Deputy Mechanical Engineer Denny Richards and his assistant Gethin, the Deputy Electrical Engineer Gregor George and his assistant Ifor. They too seemed a friendly bunch although I suspected Gethin hadn't taken to me immediately throughout the meeting he eyed me with suspicion. It may have had something to do with me spending a little too long looking at his right ear. Part of it was missing. There were a number of scars on that side of his face too. I was to find out later he'd been changing picks on the shearer some years previously and someone had accidently started it up.

After another half hour of general chit chat, I left to get changed. The Undermanager's baths entrance was directly opposite my office. Although known as the Undermanager's baths it was shared by the whole management team. Only the Manager had a private bathing area. The clean side lockers were immediately to the right as you went in two rows one above the other. The lockers were different to anything I'd seen before not dis-similar to those in a gym. Directly opposite a wooden bench with a full-length wall mirror to the right. I'd been given locker number S5 I assumed the S stood for staff.

I undressed and placed my clean clothes in the locker. I'd brought my own pit gear with me including my trusted jar of Vaseline. It always amused me the looks I received from some individuals whenever I extracted this from my locker. It was a must though for extracting the accumulated coal dust from around my eyes.

Opposite a door leading to the toilets. From there to the dirty side passing an open tiled area containing a dozen showers. Beyond which were the lockers, the conventional type exactly the same as previous mine's I'd worked at.
To avoid passing back through the clean side a further door led to the shaft side. Once changed I headed out. Turning off to the right towards the lamp room. Bleddyn was standing outside the entrance of the deployment centre.
   "Listen we've got a little time to spare. Let me show you the rest of the offices before we go down." Bleddyn suggested.
   "Good for me."

The complex I'd walked into contained the majority of offices for the support services and administration. On the right the Training Office beyond which a number of other offices unoccupied at the moment. Directly opposite the entrance a stairs leading to the Control Room. This was the communication centre for the underground workings, containing the switch board and tannoy system. A series of screens indicated the main trunk conveyors outside of the working heading and coal face. These could all be operated remotely through the MINOS system. An acronym for Mine Operating System. The same system monitored the ventilation too. Predominately methane and carbon monoxide. I hadn't appreciated there were Booster fans in Zone B. Whilst in there I was introduced to Idris. Bleddyn advised me he was the man to go to for pheasant. Outside of the pit he was a part time game keeper.

"Right think it's time we made a move underground." Back in the lamproom we picked up our cap lamps identified by the locker number. Placing it on my belt I went through my usual procedure. Checking the red wax seal was in place and the lamp actually worked both small and larger bulbs. Following which I turned towards the racks containing the self-rescuers.

Bleddyn was waiting for me by the lamp room office, leaning against a table containing a single oil lamp. It was already lit.
   "Mine I assume?"
   "Oes." I smiled. I'd need to get a Welsh phrase book to understand the words continually being used.
   I followed him out. Up and along a covered ramp towards No 3 shaft top. He pointed to a series of offices to our left.
   "Electrician's and fitters offices. Gethin and Ifor based there. The area outside with the tall desks and shelving the various reports are left there. I'll show you

when we get back up. You can do the signing of all the statutory reports first thing."

We continued forward. "Did he mention anything to you about me leaving?"

"Who?"

"The Manager."

"Why would he mention that?" Bleddyn smiled at my response. It would happen at some point. The Coal Board had already commenced a redundancy scheme for those fifty and over. Something known as EVRS. The Early Voluntary Retirement Scheme. The generous terms would I'd no doubt receive a good take up. At the time I hadn't envisaged the detrimental effect this would have on the industry.

"Bora da."

"Bora da Bleddyn. Welcome and good morning to you Mr Gibson." The Banksman greeted us both as we reached the shaft top. The two decked cage was in position with the mesh curtain raised and hung. Word was obviously out I'd started. The Banksman gave us the usual pat down. Searching for any items of contraband. We passed him our aluminium tally. I followed Bleddyn into the lower deck of the cage. Stepping in I was a little alarmed to see a sizeable gap between the pit top and cage floor. I looked down into the pitch darkness.

Out of habit I reached up and grabbed hold of the hand-rail running the length of the cage.

"Afraid of heights I see now?" I looked at Bleddyn. *Was it that obvious.*

"What makes you think that?" I answered.

"Have a good day gentlemen." The Banksman offered as he dropped the mesh gate. Stepping back, he retracted the keps then signalling to the Winder we were ready to go. Slowly at first the rope guides holding us steady. Picking up speed as we dropped further. Bleddyn reached into his pocket extracting a tin of snuff.

"Do you partake?"

"Please." I took a pinch. "Thanks." Bleddyn switched his cap lamp off. Now in complete darkness we picked up speed. Travelling in silence. The shaft was only three hundred and thirty six metres deep. The cold air whipping us as it passed by. The darkness interrupted as we passed an inset. The smell, damp, cold it was no different at any UK coal mine.

It hadn't always been like that. Particularly Monday morning dayshift. I remembered as a sixteen year old travelling down pit at the first place I worked. The old colliers faces as pale as anything I'd seen before. Ghostlike. Sat in the pit top cabin waiting for the cage. One or two coughing. Nothing like I'd heard before. A deep guttural cough it sounded hollow. Not that I knew then, but these guys must have had pneumoconiosis. When the cage arrived, we'd line up passing our tallies to the Banksman as we entered. Having been searched already by the Searcher in the airlock. Then dropping slowly at first into the depths below. Most of us still half asleep.

Silence suddenly broken by a fart.

"Tetley's." Followed by the sound of a further long drawn out fart.

"Greenall's." Laughter breaking out between one or two of the men. A further wet fart followed.

"Boddington's"

"You shit yourself Paddy?" More laughter.

"I wouldn't touch the stuff. Sooner take a mouthful of local canal." The smell was appalling.

"I'll take you down the belt line. Best if you see the face first." Bleddyn brought me back to the present.

"Yeah, good enough for me." The cage began to slow. Slithers of light from the Pit Bottom began to appear from beneath. The sound of escaping compressed air breaking the silence. It became louder. I shivered.

"Need to be getting you a Donkey jacket."

"I wouldn't say no to that. White one if possible."

"A Shaftman's jacket. I'll need to be havin a word with the Head Shaftsman James Runner. See what I can do now."

We stopped suddenly. The jolt taking me off balance. I tightened my grip on the handrail. Followed by the crashing sound of the steel platforms dropping to meet the cage floor.

"Morning gentlemen." The Onsetter greeted us both as he lifted the mesh gate. We walked out. "Bora da. Welcome to you Mr Gibson." I still couldn't get used to being greeted that way. I felt like my Dad."

"Morning."

We continued forward. I could smell the diesel loco up ahead followed by the gentle humming of its engine. The loco driver was stood alongside a single manriding carriage attached to the loco.

"Bora da Bleddyn."

"Bora da Ivor. This be the new Undermanager Mr Gibson."

"Bora da Mr Gibson, good to meet you."

"Good to meet you too Ivor." Ivor seemed a pleasant chap all four foot eight of him. We climbed into the carriage. In the footwell a number of old newspapers covered the floor. Bleddyn had obviously seen me looking.

"Could you act as the guard Bleddyn please. Tomos is inbye doing some shunting for the haulage lads."

"Oes. Could you make sure you clean the carriage out later."

"Da iawn."

Ivor hit his whistle twice. We set off with a jolt.
"Who's Tomos?" I asked.
"Another loco driver."
"I suppose we've got a George, Henry and Edward too?"
"That we have now." The joke seemed lost on Bleddyn, so I never pursued the subject.

We travelled in silence along the main tunnel. I took the opportunity to check the road as we travelled. Bags of stonedust had been laid out every twenty metres or so. This was good to see although a number lay as obstacles in front of the manholes in the side of the road. In places various lengths of heavy duty rail lay abandoned.
"What's with the rails lying about?"
"Spares in case they're needed."
"Oh right. Makes the place look little untidy though."
"I suppose they do but they save time if we have a problem. Do you know Mr Gibson you must be the tenth Undermanager I've worked for." He looked at me. "And I might be your last." Bleddyn smiled. It looked a hopeful smile.

Ten minutes later we began to slow. Signs ahead indicated the Alighting Station. We came to a halt against an area with a length of raised wooden platform. It was lit up. We climbed out. I rehung my oil lamp on my belt.
"Have a good day now gentlemen."
"Thanks Ivor we'll do our best." We walked forward about sixty metres to a cross junction. Bleddyn stopped. He pointed.
"This is known as the Two Way. Down there to our left is 45's leads to Motorway 3. The main FSV route for supplies. There's a lifting station at the far end. Ahead supply shunts and connection to the Access Road. To our right the main Meeting Station. We'll head off to the road towards the Two Yard manriding belt."
"Do you mind if we see what's in the shunts?"
"You're the boss."

I walked forward. There seemed to be a huge number of vehicles containing bags of stonedust. I was pleased to see one vehicle had bags of calcium sulphate.
"What's with all the stonedust?"
"We like to keep it handy if we have any visits."
"Wouldn't it be better stored in each of the districts?"
"Mr Adder likes it here."

"Okay." We moved back towards the Two Way Meeting Station. Bleddyn stopped to explain.

"Once the lads have gone underground, I phone through from the Deployment Centre to organise the men with the officials. They congregate here before moving inbye."

"Makes sense." We continued forward to a set of airdoors. I'd only walked a few yards. Clouds of dust rising into the air as I took each step. I looked towards the floor. It was covered in a fine layer at least six inches deep.

"Would it be possible to get some of the calcium sulphate spread Bleddyn."

"You're the boss."

Once though the doors we turned to our left. Bleddyn had reliably informed me the gradient of the tunnel was one in four. I was pleased to see the forty eight inch manriding belt.

"Any reason the belts still running Bleddyn."

"Guess they've forgotten to knock it off." The Boarding platform was accessed up a wooden ramp. Wooden grips running perpendicular across the ramp allowed ease of travel. I followed and stepped onto the belt. I lay forward supported by my hands and knees. The belt seemed fairly new.

"Only changed last week." He'd read my mind. Bleddyn ahead of me was neither stood upright nor lying down. His arse was the main feature. I assume if he'd have laid down, he may not have been able to get back up.

Within minutes we stood upright and walked down a centrally positioned Alighting Station.

"That was pleasant enough."

"I that it was now."

Once through another set of doors the cold air hit in addition to the noise of the conveyor belts. They were packed high with coal.

"42's doing her bit." I commented as we started to descend the arch roadway. Conveyor to our left and haulage system to our right.

"I that she is. This be Access 1. Three conveyors in total all within Mr Taylor's district." For a man about to retire Bleddyn travelled at some speed. I couldn't help but notice the poor state of the belt.

"Forty two inch, I guess, could do with replacing?"

"Mr Taylor thinks so too. And yes, it could. Mr Adder won't let him." Our conversation was suddenly interrupted by the ear piercing screeching of a damaged bottom roller. I stopped at the nearest lock out box and stopped the conveyor.

"What the fuck you doin now?"

"We can't walk pass that."

"You goin to be popular now."

"Never mind that the sooner we get it out the sooner we can start up." I put my back under the conveyor to lift the belt while Bleddyn removed the roller.

Bleddyn hadn't been wrong the tannoy suddenly burst into life.
"Lock out on Access 1. Who's got a lock out on Access 1." I assumed that to be the Control Room. I recognised Idris's voice.
"Who the fuck has stopped the belt. The machine is in the maingate."
"That be Ithel, face chargehand. You'll meet him later." In addition to the comments coming from the tannoy Bleddyn was providing his own commentary.
"Who's got Access 1 locked out?" Another voice I recognised.
"You've done it now. That be Mr Adder."
"Come on who's got the belt latched out?"

Bleddyn had now lifted the damaged roller out. No sooner had he done so he dropped it. "Fuckin hell man. That's hot. Come on let's get the belt goin again."
"Not till we've replaced it. I spotted some forty two inch rollers earlier. Let me just advise the Control Room what we're doin."
"I you do that now. I'm sure Mr Adder will be pleased with you. I'll get a roller." I walked across to the tannoy.
"Hello Control Room."
"Control Room here."
"Hi Idris, Mr Gibson here. I've got the belt locked out just changing a damaged roller." There followed a long silence.
"Hi Mr Gibson, Mr Adder here can you get a move on. The face is about to complete its third shear."
"Will do."
"It's our bonus you be effecting now."
"Can you believe the Undermanager stopping the belt now." A series of comments from nameless individuals then followed. I was tempted to respond but thought better of it. I looked up the brew. I could see Bleddyn heading back towards me. Roller sat on top of his right shoulder.
"We've got an Undermanager stopping production boyo. Wouldn't believe it now would you."

I recollected a previous time an Undermanager had responded to comments from the men. It had been at my first pit. I was at college completing the 2nd Class Certificate of Competency. A course covering mining legislation. The certificate was a requirement to become an Undermanager.
I'd been placed with one of two Undermanager's to gain some practical experience of the role. This guy was the smartest dressed Undermanager I'd had the pleasure to work for. He wore a cravat with his orange boiler suit and white

donkey jacket. A man's man always ready for a laugh and joke with the men. Happy to talk with anyone regardless of position.

Underground he'd walk with a stick, most officials carried one. Primarily used for taking samples of firedamp from roof areas into a bulb. The gas collected then inserted into the oil lamp to give a gas reading. I think with management however it became something of a fashion statement. I seem to remember being told it was to stop officials doing any physical work.

One of his many habits was his regular use of chewing tobacco. As he spat it out it would run down the side of his chin. Accompanied by the sound of him tutting. At the time, the Australian television series Skippy the Bush Kangaroo was on TV. Skippy too would make a similar sound each time his owner the Ranger whistled.

It hadn't taken long for him to gain the nick name "Skippy." The men were renowned for "piss taking" it was relentless regardless of a person's job or position. Whenever he entered an underground district the tannoy system came alive with the whistle or tutting sound followed by "Skippy's on his way in." The poor man believed the term Skippy was a sign of respect thinking they were shouting Skipper. I knew this to be true as he'd discussed it with me and one of the Colliery Overmen whilst making our way in one day.

As soon as he'd realized his mistake his anger knew no bounds. Constantly running across to each tannoy threatening whoever had made the comment One thing I was certain of. It wasn't going to happen to me.

"Come on get that fuckin lockout off." The commentary continued.
"You're goin to be popular now." Bleddyn commented as he reached me.
"Unfortunately, it comes with the job. Come on let's get that into position." We completed the change and I removed the lock out. There followed two further comments on the tannoy.
"Hello Mr Gibson. Could you give me a call when you get to a phone."
"Why now you don't want to be making an enemy of Mr Adder on your first day now." Bleddyn added. Followed by two further anonymous comments.
"You're in trouble now boyo."
"Wanker."
I walked across to the tannoy. "Will do Mr Adder."

We continued to descend the tunnel. I took note on the poor state of the belt. Numerous other top and bottom rollers too were in a poor state of repair. Below a light could be clearly seen bobbing up and down on the conveyor as the person approached.
"Bora da." He commented as he passed.

"Who's that? He's out early."

"One of the linesmen."

"Oh right. I'm guessing the belt is a recognised manrider."

"Yeah. All three are."

"Not in the best state, though are they?"

"Now that's not for you to worry about. Mr Taylor be the man in charge of them. You need to be havin a word with him now. I don't think Mr Adder will let him replace with new belt structure or belting for that matter. There's a couple of rolls of new belt on order." I was not impressed and made a mental note to speak with him when I got back up the pit.

We continued in silence. Although the intake air was cool and the air damp I soon began to perspire. The gentle throb of the belt passing over the rollers was soon surpassed by the sound of the second conveyor drive. There was something else too. A banging sound. It was coming from the tail end of Access 1. It became louder as I approached. Alongside I stopped and knelt down. I placed my hand against the side plate. It was red hot. Surplus grease lay against it and on the floor where it had fallen. The smell of hot oil clearly evident

"Bearings gone now. To be changed this weekend. Fitters keeping an eye on it. Plenty of grease." I heard Bleddyn shout above the noise. I nodded. We continued alongside Access 3 Bleddyn slowed till I'd caught up with him.

"Osian one of your Development Overmen will be at the bottom of the brew. I've asked him to meet us there. See what you think of him now. I believe he'd be the natural successor to me. A good man and knows his stuff. Men have a lot of respect for him they do."

"Okay."

Minutes later we reached the bottom. "That way Zone A." Bleddyn pointed to the left. "We be going off to the right. Heading towards the Five Yard." After a hundred yards Bleddyn stopped and pointed to a set of airdoors. "Return through there." As he finished the sentence I could clearly feel and hear a change in pressure. The airdoors we were stood opposite opened.

"Ah Osian. I wondered where you'd got to."

"Spot of bother with E2 now." Bleddyn turned towards me.

"E2 an FSV. Osian let me introduce you to our new Undermanager Mr Gibson." Osian walked towards us. He was carrying a stick. From the men and officials, I'd seen so far, he was quite a tall man. Perhaps six foot. He was wearing glasses perched on a very prominent nose. He had a warm smile. One of those faces you could take to instantly. However, his eyes portrayed something else. Like they were trying to read your mind.

36

"Bora da. Good to meet you Mr Gibson. I see you have had your first run in with our Deputy Manager."

"Shit!" I responded. "I was supposed to give him a call. Yes, good to meet you too Osian."

"There's a phone through there." He pointed to the doors still smiling. I turned towards Bleddyn.

"Go on I'll wait here."

Pulling open the first door the change of temperature was apparent. A blast of warm air hit me as did the loose floor dust as it rose into the air. The place was black as an ouzel. Some crystals and stonedust were needed. The wooden door as I released it didn't return to its original position. Its hinges seemed damaged as did the inbye side of the door. I made a mental note.

The phone was situated on the corner of an intersection. Luckily, there was a contact list pinned above the phone. Waiting for the phone to be answered I looked around the adjoining tunnels. Discarded arch legs, belt rollers and parts of what looked like belt chutes lay everywhere.

"Control Room."

"Hi Idris, is Mr Adder there please?"

"No, he's gone back to his office. Is that you Mr Gibson?"

"Sure is."

"Just a heads up. He's not in the best of moods."

"Thanks." I checked the number and called. It was answered immediately.

"Hello."

"Hi Mr Adder it's me Mick Gibson."

"Ah yes Mr Gibson. In future can we make sure you check with me before stopping our main coaling belts." I didn't answer immediately. If I saw a problem that needed sorting, I wouldn't be calling anybody to rectify it. That probably wasn't the answer to give so early in my tenure.

"Understood."

"Good." The line went dead. *Cheeky bastard.* I retraced my steps back to Bleddyn and Osian. They were both sat on an upturned cable drum.

"Fancy a pinch?"

"I go on. I don't mind if I do." I walked forward and removed a small amount. I ran it along the top of my hand. Then snorted it through either nostril.

"A professional I see." Osian commented smiling. "Fancy a chew."

"What is it?"

"My own concoction." He reached into his overalls and removed a round metal tin. He unclipped a penknife from his belt. He cut a short length of pigtail off. "Soaked in a ten year old malt."

"Thanks." I placed it in my mouth and began to chew.

"How did it go then?" Bleddyn asked. I used my tongue to place the chew on the side of my mouth.

"What?"

"Your conversation with the Deputy Manager." Before answering I chewed some more. I spat out the saliva produced in my well-rehearsed cowboy impersonation.

"He congratulated me in taking the time out to sort a problem." I caught sight of Bleddyn winking at Osian and smile.

"Osian." I asked. "Can you arrange to get some stonedust and crystals in on the haulage. We need to consolidate the floor dust between the doors and I'm guessing along the return too. I'd like a stack of stonedust on either side of the junction too."

"Will do."

"Oh, and next time the FSV drops supplies to the face can they load up with any scrap lying around." He nodded. "Thanks, Osian. Right Bleddyn we best get moving. Who's the face Overmen on shift today?"

"Oh, that be Alwyn."

"And Deputy?"

"Reece."

"Okay. Catch you later Osian."

We continued along the intake the rhythmic sound of the conveyor belt running alongside.

"This is where we save our little legs." Bleddyn pointed to a lit up area ahead. It was a Boarding platform. The distance between the top and bottom belt had been increased to create a bottom manrider. As we reached it, I noticed on the opposite side of the roadway a sub-station. Lit up with two large transformers and a number of electrical panels either side. A number of hessian bags lay across the top of the transformers. Bleddyn had seen me looking.

"Bloody electricians now. Nightshift." He entered the sub-station and removed the bags. No more was said we continued and climbed onto the conveyor. I wasn't satisfied with the condition of this belt either. The surface was badly worn. In places down to the thread beneath. After some two hundred yards further lights ahead indicated the Alighting station. Climbing off we continued on foot.

"Through there 42's return." Bleddyn pointed to another set of airdoors. Again, a number of upturned cable drums lay either side of the road.

"There's quite a few scrap items left lying around Bleddyn. Could do with a good clear up."

"I, prepping for 43's installation." It wasn't the answer I was expecting or wanting but decided not to pursue it. 43's was the next coal face. It would replace 42's as the pits main source of production.

Within three hundred metres we arrived at the top of the maingate. The ear piercing sound of banging. Large lumps of coal clattered into the metal chute. I walked forward to take a closer look.

"Just need to make a call." Bleddyn offered as he continued to the Meeting Station.

I peered inside the chute. Large lumps of coal were being thrown forward onto the front plate of the chute. Redirected through ninety degrees onto the top belt of the conveyor we'd just rode in on. The front plate continually rattling from the bombardment of coal. Swirls of dust engulfed the surrounding area. I looked for the dust suppression spray nozzle. There were two in the chute. One was damaged just hanging there. There was no hose attached. The other which I assumed to be the "live" one had a trickle of water dripping from the nozzle. I traced the hose to a small valve. It was turned off. I turned the handle through ninety degrees. I went back to see the result of my actions. A fine mist of water was now on view.

Having done so I stood back and took the opportunity to look under the gib end. There were two wipers in position. One had a strip of conveyor belt attached. Almost worn back to the metal. The other nothing just the metal with the belt rubbing against. Large mounds of slurry lay beneath, one almost touching the bottom belt. Not dissimilar to ant hills.

"You ready then?" Bleddyn appeared at my side.

"Yeah." I turned towards him. "The belt wipers are a lot to be desired. Could do with the fitters getting some neoprene ordered."

"None in the stores. I think Mr Adder has put the order on hold. Best you check with Denny."

"Denny?"

"Yeah Denny Richards. He be your Deputy Mechanical Engineer now."

"That's right I met him earlier."

"Bora da gentlemen." We both turned. "Hello Bleddyn and you must be our new Undermanager." If I thought Osian was tall this man was positively a giant. He also looked like the BFG. He had a very familiar sounding voice.

"Ah Alwyn bora da. Oes, this is Mr Gibson." I guessed that had been the call Bleddyn had just made. Alwyn offered his hand. I looked it was the size of a shovel.

"Good to meet you Alwyn."

"Welcome to the coal factory." He chuckled. *Yep I know who he sounds like –
Tommy bloody Cooper.* My thoughts were interrupted by the tannoy.

"Main gate belt slipping." Without hesitating Alwyn strode towards the drive
and then back towards the loop. He hit a button. The belt moved back. He
walked back towards the belt chute.

"Bloody water spray that be now. Who the hell has turned that on now?"

"I'm afraid that would be me." I offered. He answered once more with his
Tommy Cooper laugh.

"Bloody hell now here's me telling the Undermanager off on his first visit."

"Alwyn don't worry about that. You say it as it is."

"That be very refreshing Mr Gibson. I like that. You see the thing is the belt.
Well it's… how can I say it politely? Well it's… well it's shit you see. Shit,
shit, shit. The belt is that worn you can't wipe it now. If I had a pound for each
time, I'd told your predecessor I be a very rich man by now."

"What about the dust?"

"It'll put hairs on your chest." He chuckled once more. No more was said. We
continued forward towards the maingate end. Alwyn led the way providing me
with a running commentary of the coal faces operation. He pointed out, which I
had noticed earlier, the large lumps of coal.

"It's not just coal for the power stations. The larger lumps provide a domestic
product too. Welsh Dragon Trebles now. It's the nearest we've got to anthracite.
The Five Yard. Could burn your grate out it could." Bleddyn and I said nothing.

Looking up I saw to my dismay what I guessed to be the heavy stone dust
barrier. Bleddyn had obviously seem me looking.

"Alwyn what about the barrier now."

"Oes. I've arranged for more stonedust."

"You might want to check the shelves. Looks like they're off the light barrier."
I added. The place was a shithole. There'd been no attempt to maintain a tidy
workplace. The beam of my light lit up the first manhole. Again, before I could
say anything Bleddyn added.

"Get them to clear out the manholes too when they drop the stonedust off."

"Da iawn." In the distance I could hear the sound of the stageloader.

I guessed the shearer had left the maingate and was heading towards the return.
Alwyn read my mind.

"On its way up for the fourth shear. Mr Gibson one thing I need to warn you
on."

"And what would that be?"

"Ithel the Little, the chargeman!"

"Unusual name?"

"Oes, a little short in height but he's got a big gob. He can be a bit intimidating now."

"Thanks for the warning." We continued in silence. The noise of the stageloader grew louder.

I reflected on Alwyn's comment. I bet he'd never match up to the chargehand on the coal face I was face Overman at my last pit.

I recalled my previous Manager had sent for me. At the time I was employed as a Deputy. My main function, a Shotfirer for a team of contractors. We were in the process of constructing a maingate junction for an advance coal face. I'd been at the pit for six months. Arriving from my first colliery which had been closed. The 1984 Miners Strike had just come to an end. A little bored with my role I'd made a point of amusing myself by chasing guys illegally manriding the conveyor beneath where we were working.

I arrived outside the door of the "Top Shunt." He was sat at his desk smoking his pipe. Clouds of St Bruno hung in the air. The Deputy Manager was sat opposite. Not that I could see him clearly. He was smoking a Players No 6.

"Come in lad and take a seat." I did as instructed. They were both smiling. "Time to prove yourself lad." They were about to offer me a chance to become a face Overman. No big deal as I thought.

"The coal face is not producing its budgeted quota of coal. Operating on one shift per day all we're asking for are two shears. There's some geological problems at the maingate end..." The Deputy Manager began to tell me.

"The biggest issue is the lack of teamwork between the men. We believe you're the man to sort it out." The Manager added still smiling.

Lack of teamwork they explained further. The face team were made up of two distinct groups of men. Each with their own Chargehand. The face had produced coal on occasion through the strike with a small team. After the strike was over the size of the team was increased. The additional men came from a group referred to as "day oners'"" These men had gone on strike from day one and returned when the strike was called off a year later. I was to find out later the chargehand of this group was supposedly the cock of St. Helens. I was very pleased at being considered for the promotion. However, it was all very well being in charge of a team to deliver two shears per shift. But a team divided. Something I'd never done before; it would be a challenge certainly one I was up for.

The '84 Strike has caused a huge divide amongst the men. Something I suppose the Coal Board and Government had given little thought to. There were the day oners' and also the men who'd gone back in "dribs and drabs" before

41

the strike had ended. The term "scab" had been used to describe them. Not something I liked to hear. It was something we as junior management had been told to watch out for and deal with accordingly. How though do you deal with something you don't always see? An example I'd witnessed personally was a miner spitting on his tally before handing it to the Banksman prior to entering the cage. The Banksman being one of those returning to work before the strike ended. When asked if he wanted the action reporting and dealt with, he refused. He feared the repercussions. It was a sad state of affairs. The strike had turned working colleagues against one another. Father against son, brother against brother, neighbour against neighbour. I was to find out later that the Coal Board senior management saw this as an opportunity. An opportunity to gain control of the workforce directly by Management and not through the NUM. Something I bet those at Area level had never done themselves.

To date the coal face had been managed by a face Deputy assisted by two gate end Deputies. I was being added to the "management team." I arrived the following week and introduced to the face Deputy. The situation was far worse than I had imagined. I had one team that had worked through most of the strike. The majority being in the older age bracket. A further group who'd been on strike but had gone back early. And finally, the third group the day oners'.

The first two groups were happy to take instruction from me directly although any instruction given was continually questioned. Their way of checking my understanding and knowledge of the working of a coal face. Looking back on occasion I'd certainly been found wanting. The day oners' were something else. Any instruction given had to be given through the Chargehand. Something that I was trying to discourage. I was having to prove my worth on three fronts.

I needed to create a relationship with the men themselves. A change in my approach was required. This time I was having to give instruction on how we were to operate. No longer just barking instruction as to the rights and wrongs of how the men operated. Instruction was needed on how we would cut coal. I would need to work with those around me. Use their experience and knowledge to help in my decision making. It had to be my decision I couldn't afford to lose that. Above anything else it would be done safely. My role would be to measure and monitor. Using the information given to me be able to decide on a plan of action.

It was an uneasy relationship particularly with the Chargehands. I believed I had made progress with the men. However, that was about to change. As part of my management training I was mentored by the Areas General Manager. This required a regular monthly meeting at Anderton House to review my progress. Soon after being appointed Face Overman I attended one such meeting.

"Now lad I see the Manager has appointed you to Face Overman."

"That's correct."

"I hear they're quite a cantankerous group to say the least."

"You could say that."

"That's why I said it." He wasn't happy with my response. "Just remember we won the '84 strike the men need to understand Managers manage they do as instructed."

"Yeah I agree." I didn't actually agree. This wasn't the military. The way I saw it no one had won anything. The strike had been badly handled and created huge divisions in the industry. If anything, it required a period of calm reflection. A time to heal the wounds and build relationships.

"Next week when you get back to the pit. Pick out the biggest hairy arsed ripper and give him a good kicking. Create a walk out, Show 'em who's boss." I nodded in agreement. I wasn't sure I'd heard accurately his instruction.

"General Manager did I hear you right? You want me to cause a walkout."

"That's what I said lad. You got a problem with that?"

"No not at all."

Back at the pit the following week I reflected on the conversation with the General Manager. Surely he hadn't meant what he'd said. I must have misheard him. I put the whole episode out of my mind and continued as normal. I was hoping the conversation would be forgotten. That was until the Manager sent for me.

"How did your meeting go with the General Manager?"

"Okay I think. He seemed happy with the progress I was making."

"Did he ask you to do anything?" *Surely this can't be about the same subject.*

"Do'y mean the suggestion I get the men to walk out?"

"That was no suggestion lad. That was an instruction."

That night I gave some thought on the best way to tackle the instruction. I didn't really want to kick any of the rippers. They were all good lads. I'd built up a good relationship with them all. Physical violence would set me back in my task to develop a team. There was something I could do though. And I knew the person I could do it to.

The next day the face came to a stop. It was snap time. The twenty five minute break the men were allowed for lunch. Bang on eleven o'clock one of the shearer operators TT or given his full title Tommy Twat. A giant of a man. Ugly too. Put a latch on the AFC. He then lay on his back in the chock line with his helmet pulled over his face to take a twenty minute kip. Not today though. As soon as the stageloader came to a halt I approached the young lad operating it.

"Keep it running."

"But it's snap time."

"Keep it running. Today we're coaling through snap." The lad looked at me in disbelief.

"Has Ged agreed?"

"Never mind Ged. I'll sort that. Keep it running." I continued towards the coalface. The shearer was parked halfway up. I immediately saw TT alongside the red flashing light of the lock out. Crouching I continued forward. Perspiration dripping down my chest. I wasn't sure this was entirely due to physical exertion. As soon as I took the latch off I shouted into the tannoy.

"Start the panzer."

"It's snap time fuck off." Someone responded.

"Start the panzer that's an instruction." To confirm this, I kicked TT in his foot. It wasn't long before I got a reaction as he came to life. The pre alarm came on as the panzer chain kicked in.

"What the fuck.. Hey Gibson what the fuck do you think you're fuckin doin?" He shouted to make himself heard. By now TT was stood. He reached forward to try and grab me. He had little chance as I ducked to one side. He reached down on put the lock out back on.

"Get cutting we're coaling through snap." I shouted towards him. He lunged forward again. His size within the powered supports gave him little room to manoeuvre. I climbed onto the panzer.

"Come here you scouse twat." He climbed onto the panzer too. Not before I'd climbed back into the powered supports. He quickly realized there was no chance of grabbing me. Instead he reached for the tannoy. "Ged; Gibson's trying to make me cut through snap." As he made his comment I could see a light ahead making it's way down from the return end. Travelling at speed. I would need no introduction. He reached me.

"What the fuck do you think you're doin?"

"I want the lads coaling through snap."

"You don't give any instruction to my lads. That's my job."

"Sorry Ged I'm the Overman. They'll do as I say." Then I got the result I was looking. He shouted into the tannoy.

"Right Brother's we're out. It's a walk out everyone off. We're up pit."

"So, you're the man that wants to reduce my bonus!" My thoughts were suddenly interrupted as we reached the stage loader. I looked down. Obviously the Chargehand Ithel.

"Yes, that would be me." I laughed I bet he'd not expected that as an answer. I wasn't wrong he hesitated before answering. I continued and offered my hand. "Ithel good to meet you. Let me assure you that is certainly something I would not do. I want you to earn as much bonus as is possible. Your success is my success." This seemed to satisfy his concern and it made him feel important. He'd just told the Undermanager and got a result.

"Diolch yn fawr. That's good to hear. Bloody hell now." He looked beyond where I was standing. "Knock me down with a feather. Bleddyn's here too. We don't see much of you on the face nowadays. Bora da."

"Thanks for pointing that out in front of the Undermanager Ithel. I owe you." The exchange between the two was light-hearted enough. I guessed the three of them went back many years.

I sensed something had changed whilst we'd been stood chatting. The muffled sound of the stageloader had been replaced by the clunking, scraping of metal against metal. The young lad operating the stageloader shouted into the tannoy.

"Who's got a lockout on the face panzer?" The response was almost immediate.

"Breaking a lump at the maingate end."

"Bloody fuckin lumps. It's the bane of my life. All because the Manager wants lump coal." Ithel added.

"Now Ithel I've told you before. We get more money for the domestic product. Helps pay for your bonus now." Alwyn responded.

"Come on let's go and have a looksee." I offered. Ithel led followed by Alwyn. Bleddyn remained behind me. I sensed he saw the coal face as Alwyn's domain and was remaining quiet for the time being.

Underfoot the ground became soft and sloppy. I could see water dripping from one of the Victaulic pipes hanging from the square work. The clanking and banging of the stageloader continued beginning to be replaced by the methodical throbbing of the hydraulic pumps sited over the belt. Droplets of the creamy white fluid congealing on the outside of the tank. In places the colour turning to a yellowy mustard colour as it mixed with the coal dust. Its distinctive aroma filling my nostrils. An array of full and empty five gallon drums stood alongside. The place stunk of oil.We trudged forward the sound of the stageloader slowing. I guessed it had been stopped. Replaced by the hammering of the jigger pick blade ahead and the thud of handheld picks hitting the coal. I could feel droplets of perspiration running down my back. I counted four lights ahead the beams of light dancing around a very large lump of coal. We made our way onto the face.

"A crusher would be ideal but that would only defeat the object of the exercise." Alwyn commented. Three of the four face workers were taking it in turns with the jigger pick. The older of the group was holding the pick. Wearing shorts only. Beads of perspiration ran down his muscular body in places exposing his skin beneath.

"For fucks sakes lads, how many does it take to break a fuckin lump now." Ithel shouted out.

45

"You have a bloody go now if you think you can do any better now." The lad with the jigger shouted. Without hesitation Ithel leapt forward and grabbed the jigger. He considered the lump before placing the blade in position. We stood and watched as if in slow motion. A voice on the tannoy shouted.

"I've got some P4/5 coming we'll blast it." The next second the lump fragmented into pieces.

"Get the fuckin lock out off." Ithel again shouted and passed the jigger back. The men cleared the face panzer as the pre-alarm on the stage loader followed seconds later by the panzer.

"Right gentlemen I'll see you later. Need to make sure we get that fourth shear." Ithel left us and headed onto the face.

I walked back towards the stageloader and Bleddyn. Alwyn followed.

"Just a thought gents but why do you break the lump on the coal face?" I asked.

"If we let the lump get onto the stageloader it could catch under the metal platforms holding the panels and pumps. If that happens, we could be in big trouble." Alwyn responded.

"So why not break the lump before reaching there?"

"And how do you suggest we do that Mr Gibson?"

"Simple. Have the fitting department cut a couple of lengths of box bar to length and bolt to the side plates of the stageloader. Might help if you get them to weld some shearer picks to the bars. Then set your jigger pick up alongside and deploy one of the men to be on permanent "lump duty.""

"Worth a try." Bleddyn added smiling.

"It's not a perfect solution. I've used it before with some good results. Plus, if you can't break it just roll it off the chain." I made a note for myself in the pocketbook I carried. I was seeing too many problems just to make a mental note. Something I'd always done and used as a reference when compiling my list of things to do. Bleddyn on the other hand wrote nothing down he seemed to remember everything. I decided to leave out the bit how on one shift a huge lump of dirt got wedged under the bar. It broke off a number of the shearer picks. One managed to wedge under the chain and broke it. Cost us half a shift.

We continued back towards the coal face crossed over the metal bridge to the ribside. Once on the face the air temperature had increased significantly. The heat from the maingate drive combined with the heat emitted from the strata added to the discomfit. The three of us continued up towards the return end. Passing through the six legged two forty tonne powered supports was a struggle. They'd seen better days. Ithel had deployed two men from moving the chocks forward to cleaning the walking track. The original curtains on the back of the supports to prevent the waste flushing through had long since gone. Replaced now with pieces of old conveyor belt. The hydraulic bagging connecting each of the chocks hanging untidily as we passed through. I sensed Bleddyn falling behind and stopped.

"Alwyn just a mo." I shouted ahead. For a man as big as he was, he moved at an extraordinary pace.

"What's the matter Mr Gibson now. Am I travelling too fast for you?" He shouted in answer to me smiling.

"Yeah something like that." I turned to see Bleddyn steadily making his way towards us. I repositioned my oil lamp to the back of my belt. I guessed this was a route he rarely travelled. Hence the earlier comment from Ithel. It wasn't so much Bleddyn's size it was his width. No matter how many times he repositioned his self-rescuer and oil lamp it kept sliding to his side catching against the supports.

I turned towards the coal face. A steady stream of extracted coal passing by. The light from my cap lamp reflecting in places back from the coal seam. Seemingly devouring the beam of light. Beneath my feet I could feel the methodical throb from the hydraulic feed hoses. The lifeline for the powered supports. I turned through one hundred and eighty degrees to see huge lumps of coal lying in the waste. From memory the Five Yard seam was about ten foot thick. We were only taking six foot.

"Bloody waste it is now." Alwyn had reached me. He followed my gaze. "Chocks will only extend to five six. We've tried putting leg extensions in places now. Far from ideal. It's a good job we don't suffer with spon com. Pinch?" He offered me his tin of snuff.

"Thanks."

"Bloody hell Bleddyn you seem to be in a fine state." Bleddyn had reached us. He looked as though he'd been under a shower. Sweat pouring from every pore of his body. His boiler suit soaked through.

"Fuck off."

"I love you too man." Alwyn responded. "Mr Groves has promised a new set of supports for 43's. Should allow us to take an extra couple of feet." Having extracted a tiny amount of snuff I offered it to Bleddyn. He shook his head as he removed his oil lamp handing from the back of the chock. He sat down between the chocks.

"Watch your arse." I looked down. Alwyn was referring to a number of missing ram covers. "Wouldn't want that cute botty of yours getting squashed now." His Tommy Cooper laugh impersonation followed. The noise from the face panzer began to increase.

"That'll be them at the return end. On the bi-di." Alwyn commented as an explanation. "Four shears. That's a first for a long time. Must be you Mr Gibson bringing us luck."

"I'd like to think so." I looked down onto the empty panzer chain. I couldn't help but notice a number of bent flight bars. Bleddyn who'd now got his second wind commented.

"This weekend. I've got men on overtime to replace them." I nodded.

"Come on now best get moving now." Alwyn began. I looked towards the underside of the canopy. Painted in red I could just make out the number eighty eight. Not far now. From memory there were a hundred and thirty seven line chocks excluding those in the pack area. We continued forward. Within minutes I could see activity ahead.

We now moved from the chock track to the front of the chocks. The pans had been pushed over behind the shearer as it had advanced. Two men were working towards us bringing the chocks forward. We stopped once more to observe. The pair alternated bringing forward every other chock. I watched as he positioned himself within the confines of the chock. Facing the waste, he operated the controls positioned between the middle two legs. Pulling the lever to release the legs to drop the canopy. Suddenly engulfed in the dust this action created. I'd no doubt guess small lumps of coal falling down his back beneath his workwear. The light from his cap lamp hardly discernible. Quantities of mineral running forward from the waste area. And then as the chock was hauled forward on its base ram much of the waste material trickled back towards its original position. And then extending the legs once more to support the roof. We moved forward once more.

"Bora da." We exchanged niceties as we passed each of them. Once clear we passed back into the chock track. Ahead the rumble of the shearer as it moved back out of the return. The crunching of the coal as the shearer drums rotated and the tungsten carbide picks ripped into the coal. The sound from the panzer changing once more as it filled with the black stuff. We stopped once more to observe proceedings. The double ended ranger drum shearer edged ever closer. Water blasting out from behind each of the picks on the drum. The operator closest to us wore a full Perspex visor face mask. Small pieces of coal flew in all directions. He seemed to be using a length of wooden dowel to control the machine. Thick gloves too, to protect his hands. We each moved our bodies back between the middle legs to let the operator pass. He took the time to give me a nod and smile as he came alongside. The noise from the machine never ceased to excite me. The sheer power of the thing extracting mineral that had been stood for millions of years. Even back in the positions we had taken bits of coal flew out. I covered my face. The dust particle captured by the fine mist

48

spray. The second operator seemed out of position. I could see him grappling with the Bretby that had seemingly dropped out of its trough. The man moved back as a third person took over the responsibility of repositioning the nylon plastic protection for the shearer cable. It was Ithel.

Continuing into the return gate we bade farewell to Alwyn and thanked him for his time. We continued outwards to the Access road. By the time we reached the Two Way the afternoon shift had begun to arrive.

We arrived back on land. "I don't mind telling you Mr Gibson I don't want to be making a habit of getting up the pit late. Not at my age anyway."

"Sorry Bleddyn. Go get your bath." I continued in my black to the office. Nobody was about. I kicked my boots off and sat down to reflect on my first underground visit.

"How did it go?" Mr Groves asked as he walked into my office.

"Good thanks."

"What did you think of Ithel?"

"Quite a character. Reminds me of a little Jack Russel." The Manager started to laugh.

"Careful he doesn't hear you say that."

"I won't."

"Hear you stopped Access 1 to change a roller?" I nodded. "Good man. Standards I like that." It wasn't the answer I was expecting.

"How's the house hunting going?"

"Slow. There's just so many lovely places to choose from. We're spoilt for choice."

"I'll make it easy for you. I want you within a fifteen minute radius of the pit." That was me told then. It certainly ruled out any plans we had for Mold, Hawarden and Buckley.

I'd been advised by Paul Adder that weekend cover would be provided by himself and the Undermanager's. The roster therefore meant we'd be required to cover one in three weekends unless that is somebody was off. He was hopeful a new assistant Manager would be appointed in the not too distant future allowing us to go out to one in four. Cover would include being on site for the morning on both days. Thereafter "on call" in case of any emergencies.

In effect this meant being close to a land line. They'd agreed to invest in a more up to date system. Hopefully available by the end of the month. This would involve us being issued with a bleeper. Which we kept on our person over the weekend. If required the Control Room could call a set number. This would then send out a signal to the bleeper requiring an immediate phone call to the pit. I couldn't wait.

The Manager was on site every Saturday morning. As I was still in the process of house hunting, he suggested an overnight stay in a local hotel would be covered in my expenses. Towards the end of my first month it was my turn.

"I hear it's your weekend on Mr Gibson." Bleddyn and I were sat in my office having just returned from underground. Bleddyn was eating a bacon bap. I was still struggling being addressed as Mister.

"Bleddyn do me a favour. When we're alone could you call me Mick?"

"Oh, nac oes now. I've told you before Manager likes his team referred to in the proper way."

"Yeah I understand that, but he's not here."

"I know that Mr Gibson but what if I forget now?" He took another bite of his bap. Chewing it quickly he continued. "Far better we do it this way now." I could see I would get no further on this subject.

"Yeah with reference to your initial question I'll be working this weekend. Plan to stay over Saturday night and bring the family down to. Do a spot of house hunting."

"Where will you be stayin now?"

"Not decided yet. Not too far away and somewhere to keep the kids entertained."

"Why not try the Nant Hall."

"Is that the place on the road to Prestatyn?"

"The very same. Run by a famous person it is now." Pieces of the bap flew from his mouth as he was talking. Bleddyn loved a bap. One before we went underground and one when we returned. He was quite particular too. The morning bap contained bacon and sausage. His afternoon bacon only. Both covered in a lavish topping of sauce. I watched as he finished it. With the napkin he wiped the desk where the tomato ketchup had dropped. Then his chin. He continued. "You must have heard of the Abbots?"

"Family?"

"No not them although that would be quite something now wouldn't it. The Black Abbots. Russ Abbot owns the place with his missus. Worth a try. And they've got a kiddies playground outside." The conversation ended as the afternoon shift colliery Overman entered the office.

"Prynhawn da, Mr Gibson."

"Afternoon Gruffyd." He was holding a pen and sheet of paper.

"Now what will you be wanting to take in this afternoon?" Gruffyd's routine at the start of his shift was to take a list of supplies required to be taken inbye off the main tunnel. Before I could answer.

"Now let's start with two lots of Hollybanks for 43's…" I remained silent this was Bleddyn's territory.

I arrived home later that night.

"What the hell are we supposed to do whilst you're in work then?"

"You could take the kids into Prestatyn. I bet there's loads of thing they could do."

"Like what?"

"Oh, I don't know exactly but it is a holiday town. There must be amusement arcades stuff like that?"

"Yeah I'm sure a three and four year old will be thrilled to bits. Anyway, how are we expected to get there? You'll have the car."

"That won't be a problem there's a family run hotel very close to Prestatyn. The Nant Hall. It's that Tudor style building we've passed on a number of occasions." Mrs Gibson was far from convinced but went with it. She'd resigned herself to moving to a new house much against her better judgement.

"And what about the dog?"

"Mum and Dad have said they'll take Heidi."

Back in work the next day I booked a family room at the Nant Hall.

Saturday arrived. We'd packed a few things the night before. The journey was without incident mainly due to setting off early. The kids slept most of the way. We arrived at the hotel having agreed with Mr Groves I'd be at the pit about ten o'clock. The reception area was quite sparse. Each of the walls had large framed photographs of the Black Abbots. The only one I recognised was Russ Abbot.

"Bora da Mr and Mrs Gibson. You'll be in rooms twelve and eighteen." That wasn't the greeting I was expecting.

"Sorry I booked a family room."

"We don't have them now." My wife who'd now joined me added to the conversation.

"Are they adjoining rooms?"

"I'm sorry we don't have any of them either." She turned to me.

"Seems like a good start." I ignored the comment. I turned back to the receptionist.

"What's the sleeping arrangements?"

"How do you mean? The number of beds?"

"Yeah."

"Well you can have a double or two singles."

"Mummy I need a wee, wee." Little Lizzie joined the conversation.

"In a minute darling Daddy's just sorting out our rooms." I felt a tug on my arm. I looked down. James was looking up at me.

"Is Mummy in a mood with you Daddy?"

51

"No son. She's just excited we've come away for a couple days." I turned back to the receptionist. "We'll take the two double's please." The receptionist removed two keys from a rack on the back wall.

"We'll forward the bill onto the colliery."

"Oh, right thank you. Is Russ about?"

"Who?"

"Mummy I need a wee, wee." Lizzie again joining the conversation.

"Russ…."

"Are you coming or what?" My wife interrupted.

The remainder of the day didn't go much better. The Manager had suggested I bring the family with me. He allowed them to use the conference room. The room was ideal. The majority of it taken up by a large table the kids were able to sit around. My wife had brought with her a number of colouring books and crayons. The only instruction from the Manager was to keep the kids away from the trophy table. This was positioned at the far end of the room. It was covered in cups, plates and shields awarded to the colliery's brass band.

For the next couple of hours, I sat with the Manager discussing the future plans for the pit. By the time I'd returned to the family the kids had removed most of the trophies and placed them on the floor. James was using one of the cups as a helmet. The look on my wife's face said it all. The room must have been covered in a thin layer of dust. The kids' faces were smeared in coal dust, including their clothes. The Manager too recognised the situation for what it was. He made his excuses and left for home. Things got a little better later on when I took the kids for a walk through a mock tunnel on the surface. The Training Officer had kindly made them all, including my wife ID badges including photo's he'd taken with a Polaroid camera. Driving back to the hotel James was convinced he'd been underground.

"What's the plans for tonight then?" My wife asked as she attempted to clean the children up. We were now back in our hotel room.

"I've arranged dinner for six o'clock." I was interrupted by the phone. "Who could that be?" I walked across. "Hello. Yes, oh right I'll be down shortly."

"Who was it?" I hesitated before answering.

"Bleddyn."

"What does he want?"

"A pint!"

"A pint! What about us?"

"Oh, don't worry. I'll have a quick one just before dinner." I left and headed downstairs.

I joined Bleddyn at the bar.

"That's him there."

"Who?"

"Russ Abbot."

"Is it fuck."

"I bet you it is now. Just you wait and see." Bleddyn waved to the gentleman who'd just entered the bar. "Hi Russ." The guy looked over towards us. He didn't look happy. He walked across.

"Can I help you gentlemen?" Bleddyn thrust his hand forward.

"Just thought we'd say hello Russ."

"Why do you keep referring to me as Russ." I looked around I could sense other customers in the bar looking over in our direction.

"Russ Abbot?"

"No, I'm fuckin Lennie. Lennie fuckin Reynolds." The man walked off.

"What can I get you two fine gentlemen? I turned to face a young barmaid.

"Two pints of bitter please." I pointed to a sign Allbright Bitter. It was the only one on draught. Alongside of which displayed a further sign for Carlsberg lager. Bleddyn was somewhat subdued after his encounter with the Russ Abbot look a like.

"He was in the Black Abbots though." The barmaid offered as she poured the bitter. "Lennie and Russ never got on that well together hence his annoyance."

"Ah that explains the photos around the bar."

"Told you now didn't I." Bleddyn was with us again.

"Told me what?"

"He was in the Black Abbots." I decided not to pursue his illogical reasoning.

"That will be one pound ninety cariad."

"Get one for yourself."

"That's very kind of you sir. Diolch. I'll have a Pernod and black. Save it for later when I knock off."

"I assume you're still serving food?"

"Oes. Menus on the table. We serve till nine."

We headed over to the only large table in the room. It seated six. Having sat down Bleddyn began to tell me about the previous Undermanager and where he'd gone wrong in dealing with the men. "Too soft he was now. No respect. You have to earn it you see now…" He stopped talking and nodded in the direction behind me. I turned. It was my wife and two children.

"Hi. Come on over and say hello to Bleddyn." My wife smiled.

"Hello Bleddyn. I've heard so much about you."

"Sut mae Mrs Gibson." She looked at him quizzically. "I'm sorry cariad. Welsh for hello. Right what can I get you to drink?"

"I'll have half a lager and lime please. Do call me Annie."

"And the kids?" James and Lizzie said nothing.

"They'll both have an orange cordial please." As Bleddyn passed the children he ruffled the hair on each of them. Once out of ear shot.

"I thought you said he wasn't staying long."

"He isn't…"

"Same again Mr Gibson?" Bleddyn had returned to the table.

"Please." After he returned to the bar I received the Annie Gibson stare.

"You ordered yet?"

"No wasn't sure what you'd all want."

"Fish and chips. Plus, a portion of mushy peas.."

"There you go." As Bleddyn placed the drinks on the table he accidently spilt the pint of lager and lime.

"A pint. Well that's different."

"I'm sorry Mrs Gibson did you only want a half now?"

"Don't worry that'll be fine." He returned to the bar to pick up the two pints of bitter.

"Bloody pint and he's got the kids fresh orange. You know what Lizzies like when she has fresh orange." I knew full well what she meant, and they were in half pint glasses. The kids still hadn't said a word. Bleddyn had returned.

"Excuse me I 'm just going to order some food."

"I think I might join you. That's if you don't mind."

"No that's be fine." I responded without looking towards my wife.

When Bleddyn finally left it was gone ten. My wife had already gone up to bed with the kids. The evening had been an utter disaster in terms of family time. Bleddyn had done most of the talking. The kids didn't utter a word. My wife however spent most of the time kicking me under the table. If I thought that had been bad worse was to come. As predicted Lizzie was awake most of the night with diarrhoea. James added to the event with vomiting. When I returned to the hotel after work the following morning the three of them were waiting with bags packed. The plan to go house hunting had been abandoned and we returned home to Liverpool.

–

It wasn't until the following month my wife agreed we go house hunting again.

"Mick do me a favour. Can you get Lizzie's boots out of the car. Come here dear you're going to get wet feet walking around in your socks." We'd just arrived back home to Huyton from viewing a new housing development in Rhuddlan. It was about the sixth place we'd looked at. My wife still wasn't convinced about the move.

"They're not there love." I shouted to my wife. Lizzie appeared in the hallway.

"Daddy they're by the car."

"What do you mean you've left your boots by the car?"

"Daddy I took them off when we got in."

"I don't believe it Lizzie's left her boots outside the house in Rhuddlan!"

"The Care Bear boots? She's only had them a week."

"Tell me about it I paid a tenner for them."

"Could it be a sign?"

"What?"

"Mick Manager wants to see you." I was about to go underground with Bleddyn and the Zone A team. It was seven fifty.

"Fuck what for?"

"Never said."

"Bleddyn hold the cage for me I won't be long."

"Morning Mr. Groves you asked to see me?"

"Morning Mick. Remember the planned visit by the photographer from Coal News?"

"Yeah he was doing the article on the mini conveyor."

"I thought they'd cancel him as it's not yet operating but seems the slot has been kept and he's here tomorrow anyway. Might be best if you check out 43's district make sure you're ready, call it a dry run."

"Will do."

I left his office and headed towards the lamproom. *Well that fucks up my plans to visit Strata Top.* 43's was the new face development. The return gate had already been driven to the face line and the heading machine withdrawn for use at Strata Top. The main gate now two weeks behind schedule due to the number of stoppages requiring the use of methane drainage in the drivage.

The colliery was the only one in the Western Area operating with a single coal face. Production gaps were usually inevitable, however by using FSV's for transport instead of rope haulages face to face transfers could be completed in a matter of weeks. The success of this system relied on our ability to develop both gate roads in coal and of utmost importance turning from the gate roads onto the face line. On average it would take us just short of a two weeks to complete a turn and advance far enough to install the Lioness drive. Group Headquarters Technical Department believed this could be further improved to a matter of days by using a device called a "mini conveyor."

Unlike the current method of removing and then adding sections of the bridge conveyor suspended from a monorail. This device sat on the floor. As the Dintheader continued to form the entrance to the faceline it was the mini conveyor sections that were added without having to suspend them thus saving time. Our colliery had been chosen to trial this new piece of kit.

"Bora da Mr. Gibson."

"Bora da Dai, has Bleddyn gone?" Dai was the colliery Lampman.

"Said he'd be waitin at the pit head now."

"Thanks Dai."

"Hi Bleddyn where is everybody?"

"Mr. Blackhead sends his apologies. He's gone straight in seems the fluid coupling has blown on Access 1."

"Guess that's us fucked for a ride in then."

"Probably why he's giving an apology takin the loco and all that now."

An hour and a half later we entered 43's district via the intake. It was good to see the conveyor piled high with the black stuff. I spotted a light ahead walking towards us I guessed it was one of the beltman. Bleddyn had taken it on himself to introduce me to anyone we met underground. I was getting used to the fact that almost all the men we met were identified by the area they came from. So far I'd been introduced to Aled Flint and Dylan Denbigh.

"Bora da Rhys I'd like to introduce you to the new Undermanager Mr. Gibson."

"Mr. Gibson this is Rhys Llan." I shook hands with Rhys.

"Bora da Rhys let me guess you're from Llangollen?"

"Bora da Mr. Gibson no, actually Llandudno now."

"Oh, right my apologies," I looked towards Bleddyn. He had his head bowed I could just make out a smirk. "You're doin a great job along the belt line I haven't seen any spillage."

"Diolch yn fawr I try to stay on top of things now." I spotted a second light coming toward us. "This is my buddy Nefyn Shit." Somewhat taken aback I greeted Nefyn Shit. After some small talk both men moved on.

"Let me guess he lives somewhere a little unpleasant?"

"No actually his Dad use to empty the underground shit buckets his name was Nefyn Shit Senior."

"What? We've still got underground toilets?"

"Only Pit Bottom we don't tend to bother now."

I decided to leave the conversation at that.

"Right if you don't mine Bleddyn could we have a quick looksee in the return gate first."

Passing through the air doors I could hear the auxiliary fan up ahead. The sound increasing as we approached. I was surprised at the drop in temperature as we continued down the brew. There was a smell of staleness about the place. Sheets of old newspapers lying discarded either side of the roadway. The further we went the smell became more apparent. Bleddyn seemed oblivious to it. The roadway was holding up well with little if any roof distortion. There were a few place showing signs of floor lift. I stopped to make a note.

"Your always making notes Mr Gibson. I like that."

"Yep something I've always done. Helps me compile my action list when I get back up. Plus, it's good to keep a record of where I've been, who I've spoken to and any problems. You don't seem to have that problem. I see you carry a notebook. I've never seen you actually write in it." Bleddyn smiled and tapped the side of his helmet.

"All in here you see. Photographic memory. My teacher told me so now."

"Add this to your photographic memory. Stonedust. The place is as black as an ouzel."

"Already arranged now." We continued down. The further we went the quieter it became. Occasionally the stillness broken by air escaping from the ventilation ducting joints.

"Bleddyn what the fuck is that...." I stopped as the beam from my cap lamp captured a huge human turd ahead.

"Watch where you put your feet."

"For fucks sake Bleddyn."

"Oes I know I'll get the place cleaned out as soon as I have some men spare."

That seemed to end that subject. I could hear the sound of hammering up ahead. "We have a little problem with water ingress about halfway down. We've got a compressed air pump set up but it's quite temperamental now. Whatever you do make sure it's checked on a regular basis." I assumed from Bleddyn's comments he was preparing me for when he retired. "This'll be the main route for equipping the face." Ahead I could make out a person. Bleddyn stopped.

"Just a heads up Mr Gibson. The lad working on the pump is Dai. Dai Fingers good man. Ex contractor can do anything he's our fixer. Used to be a regular in the headings but suffers with dust. I try to keep him on any outbye work. Try not to look at his hands. Don't mention the state of them or we'll never get away now."

57

We continued down. The hammering stopped.

"Bora da Dai. How you doin boyo?"

"Bora da Bleddyn." Dai looked towards me.

"This is our new Undermanager Mr Gibson."

"How do you do Dai." I raised my right hand. I could feel clean air blowing against my face. Someone had slit the ventilation bagging at the pump site. Dai did likewise his grip excruciating. I looked towards his hand. I knew it was a hand because it was attached to his arm, however. Where were the fingers? I could see them but only parts of them. They were not full size fingers as I would have expected. He caught me looking. To deflect my embarrassment, I asked a question. "And why do they call you Dai Fingers?" I knew immediately it was the wrong thing to ask. Bleddyn who was stood to my right turned away. He was shaking his head.

"Well now you ask Mr Gibson. See this." He held up his right hand and wriggled the stump of his pinkie. "Lost this last year. One of the lads accidently dropped a steel girder on it. Put a claim in. Got five grand I did now." I shook my head to acknowledge his loss. "This bugger." He pointed with what was left of his index finger on his left hand to the ring finger on his right. "Deployed to the coal face I was. Not my usual place of work now. Some bad ground there was. I was timbering above a chock. Piece of dirt fell from the roof took it straight off. Fifteen grand for that now."

I watched as Bleddyn walked to the side of the road and sat down on the remnants of a chockwood stack. He extracted his tin of snuff. Dai Fingers was on a roll. The tip of his middle finger was missing. "I was holding a wooden prop. One of the lads was hammering a wedge above. Caught my finger he did. Just a black nail I thought. Got infected it did now. They had to remove it. Two and a half grand. I wasn't happy." I needed to say something.

"Not happy you'd lost it?"

"No, the two and half grand. I was expecting a lot more." He continued with the tale on his index finger and finally his thumb.

"Well there you go. Thanks for that Dai." I turned to Bleddyn. "You ready." Bleddyn shook his head and nodded back towards Dai. He was now holding up his left hand. Twenty minutes later I'd had the detail on those missing too.

"Thanks Dai good to meet you." Bleddyn was now back on his feet. We left Dai and continued down. "I know don't say anything. You were right."

"Now I wasn't about to say anything Mr Gibson. Looks like you'll be learning the hard way now."

"I never asked him what he was doin."

"Cleaning out the sump and replacing the filter on the bagging. Damaged by an FSV."

"What was with the red helmet?"

"Ex contractor Cemco. I mentioned it earlier. There's quite a few of the lads here. Stayed on after they completed the Drift. Most of them work in the headings, North side."

"Meant to ask. Who's the Deputy today?"

"That be Caerwyn. We may not see him as he's walking out the District's secondary means of access via the old stables."

"Stables as in horses?"

"The very same now. We'll have a wander over there at some point. Haven't been there in an age."

"Pit ponies! I've heard the tales. How long ago?"

"Must be late fifties, sixties well before my time now."

We finally reached the end of the road. Eight metres back the surveyors had painted a centreline on the roof bar. And on the mesh alongside the road.

"So hopefully that's we're we'll break through?"

"No hoping about it Mr Gibson now. My lads never fail." I smiled I liked his comment about them being his lads. For the short time I'd been here it was apparent it was very much a family pit. Out of curiosity I walked into the blind end. Removing the handheld methanometer I carried with me I raised it in the air. Pressing the button, I tipped the gauge towards me.

"Point five."

"Gas never normally a problem. As long as the lads keep up to date with the drainage.

"Good. Come on time we had a look at the maingate. Bleddyn checked his watch.

"I time is getting on now."

Once again we reached the compressed air pump. Dai had gone. I looked into the sump. What little water there was sucked into the filter. The gentle sound of the piston moving in and out on its strokes. The sound not dissimilar to that of a steam train in the sidings.

At the top of the return we turned left towards the airdoors. Just after we passed the fan I could smell diesel followed by the sound of an engine. I guessed it was one of the FSV's returning from the maingate. We waited not wanting to pass through the doors as the machine approached. The Free Steered Vehicles operated by a single person would normally have two men deployed per machine. The guy on foot ensuring the road ahead was clear and as now opening the airdoors for the machine to pass through.

The noise grew louder. I could feel the pressure as the inbye door was opened the machine passing through into the airlock. Much to my surprise and obviously to Bleddyn's too as I heard him use the word "oh fuck" which was somewhat surprising as I could count on one hand the number of times, he used any profanities. The doors nearest us burst open not completely just enough to expose the flat bed containing a pallet of stonedust and the cap lamp from the operator. *Good he'd arranged stonedust.*

"For fucks sake." I exclaimed. Now I understood why there always appeared to be damage on the wooden air doors. And why I often found some hanging from their hinges. The FSV was being used as a battering ram to open them. The FSV continued forward the doors opening further catching alongside the doors as it passed through. I heard Bleddyn shout above the noise of the engine. He moved forward through the swirls of dust due to the imbalance of the air pressure.

"What are you doin now Billy B." The machine came to a halt. Silence descended as he switched off the engine. The young lad was smiling.
"Bora da Bleddyn. How are you on this fine day now?"
"Never you mind how am I. What do you think your fuckin doin now." I walked across to join the conversation. By the look on Billy's face. One of shocked amusement. It was obvious to me this practice of opening air doors was regularly in use. Billy turned to me smiling.
"Bora da."
"Bora da Billy."
"This is our new Undermanager Mr Gibson." Bleddyn added.
"Good to meet you Mr Gibson."
"Likewise, Billy. What's with the B?"
"He's from Bagillt…" before Bleddyn finished the sentence he stopped interrupted by a second person whistling. Heading towards us he was closing the air doors.
"And this be Terry. Terry T from Talacre."

Terry walked towards me. "Ah you must be the new fuckin Undermanager Mr Gibson." He offered his hand smiling. I smiled back. I'd never known anything like it. All the officials and pit men I'd been introduced to always seemed to be smiling. Like most, other than Osian and Alwyn no one seemed to be taller than five foot.

"Hey boyo mind your language now. Have some respect." Terry T seemingly ignoring Bleddyn's comment.

"I wonder how long you'll fuckin last?" I was intrigued.

"Whatever do you mean by that Terry?"

"Well your predecessor only lasted three years. I reckon Paul Taylor will be gone soon enough. All down to that other fuckin crack pot Mr Adder." Bleddyn was uneasy with the conversation.

"Now listen here Terry T I'll be havin words with your uncle now I will. Remember it might be you gone soon if you keep damaging them air doors now."

"Whatever." Before I could add anything, Terry turned to Billy. "Come on mate let's get this load dropped off." The FSV engine exploded into life following Terry as he walked towards 43's return.

"I'm sorry about that Mr Gibson. He's a good lad really. Pity he's got such a big gob." Bleddyn turned back towards the lads and shouted. "I want those bags dropping every ten metres." Terry responded with a thumbs up without turning.

"Don't worry about that Bleddyn. I prefer someone who's open and honest with me. You've certainly got some characters here. Not frightened in coming forward. Who's his uncle?"

"Osian." We continued towards the entrance of the maingate. "Wait till you meet Baeddan. Baeddan the Boar."

"Who's that then?"

"The chargehand in the maingate."

Reaching the maingate the sound of extracted coal smashing into the chute. Spirals of fine dust rising through a top plate that was missing. I took a closer look. Good to see a water spray nozzle in place. However, its action was a lot to be desired. Just a constant dripping of water. I traced the hose back to the valve. It was turned off. Turning it on had the desired effect. A fine spray suddenly filling the chute. I stood back.

"Can't believe it. Just as we saw in 42's." I turned towards Bleddyn for an explanation. He pointed me in the direction of the bottom belt as it passed over the gib roller. Water was dripping from each of the bottom rollers. I went back towards the chute and took another look in. Not finding what I was looking for I followed the bottom belt to where it entered the Lioness drive. And there it was. Not where it should have been. It was lying discarded on the floor. Covered in wet dirt.

"I know what you be thinkin Mr Gibson. The lads have taken it off cause the metal damaging the stitches. As Alwyn mentioned the other day no neoprene. Nothing in the stores." Retrieving my pocketbook, I made a note. As I was writing the belt began to slip. Reluctantly I stepped forward and turned off the spray. We continued down towards the face of the heading. It was good to see Terry and Billy had already been in. Bags of stonedust laid out. We passed a couple of lads working on the belt structure. They were lifting it and rehanging with slings. Tracking the belt as they progressed. Bleddyn explained the need to keep the belt off the floor in case there was any build-up of dirt. In two separate places we passed timber spars and short wooden boards. I checked with Bleddyn and confirmed these were for the light and heavy stonedust barriers yet to be built.

The roadway as in the return was square work. No apparent distortion to any of the top bars. In places the dirt roof wasn't even in contact with the steel work. The mesh looked no different from the day it had been put in position. The tie bars were all over the place. Not the heavy duty ones I was used to seeing. These were classed as the wrap round. Secured in position with a seven pound hammer. The same as those used in the first pit I'd worked at. On the opposite side to the conveyor roughly every twenty metres an additional cut had been made to create a manhole. Bleddyn explained before the face went "live" he'd arrange for a Deputy to complete them to the desired standard using P4/5.

After another thirty minutes I spotted lights ahead. Three in total. One driving the Dosco Dintheader, one at the delivery end of the mini-conveyor and the third stood to the left hand side of the machine. I guessed he was the spotter. Checking sufficient ground had been cut for the legs. Previously heading teams had consisted of four men. British Coal's continuous drive to reduce cost had put paid to that. It looked as though they'd completed cutting. The cutting mat came to a standstill as the machine began backing up. It came to a halt. Two of the men walked back towards the conveyors tail end. They simultaneously bent down then stood. Now with a roof beam between them. They carried it forward. The third man from what I could make out had a leg hoisted on either shoulder. The last time I'd seen anyone do that was Billy Nelder at Cronton Colliery.

As we reached the Dintheader the roof beam had been placed in the lifting brackets on the cutting mat. "See what you make of this man." Bleddyn nudged me gently. He nodded in the direction of the guy who'd just dropped the legs to the floor. He was looking across towards us.
"Bora da Bleddyn. Who's that now?"
"This be our new Undermanager Baeddan. Mr Gibson." The man needed no invitation he disappeared under the bridge conveyor and rushed towards

me. Talk about invading my space. The man was huge he was looking down on me his face inches from mine. He was down to wearing vest and shorts sweat dripping down his chest. Around his neck a paper dust mask. And he was smiling.

"How do you do Mr Gibson now." He thrust his hand towards me. I could smell him. I wasn't sure if it was the clothes he was wearing or just BO. That was until he exhaled. I backed off a little. "I'm Baeddan."

"The Boar." Bleddyn added smiling. He obviously found the encounter amusing. Initially I moved back. I could see inside his mouth. Bits of food protruding from between his teeth. I guessed from his breakfast. Sausage and bacon. Although his face was blackened by coal dust he looked so pale. Possibly an albino.

Shaking his hand, I was relieved when he backed off a little. One of his team mates now joined us. "And this is Dai Denbigh. The other fella is Dai Dyserth." I shook hands with his colleague.

"How do you do lads. Good to meet you."

"You know we're due a new contract. We were promised isn't that right Bleddyn?"

"Now Baeddan, I'm sure Mr Gibson will sort that once he's had time to settle."

"Snuff Mr Gibson? Dai Denbigh offered." He was smiling. His protruding eyes the dominant feature of his face. Marty Feldman came to mind. He offered me an opened tin.

"Thanks Dai." I took a pinch. I inhaled as I passed it to each of my nostrils. *For fucks sake!* The snuff was stale. I looked towards Dai it was then I noticed the rim of his nose was dotted with tiny sores. Discarding the remainder of the snuff I remained straight faced.

The third member of the team hobbled towards us. "Hi Mis... Mis... Mist... Mister Gi... Gib... son. I'm Dai... Dai... Dy..."

"Of course, he knows who you are I've just fuckin told him." Baeddan interrupted.

"What's up with your leg?" I asked innocently.

"Fa... fa... fall. Ro... roo... roo."

"For fucks sake Dai we're goin to be here all day. Roof fall." Baeddan again added.

"Took us three hours to get him out now it did. Working in the Stone Coal." The other Dai now involved in the conversation. "Caerwyn our Deputy applied morphine he did. Broke off the tip of the needle in him now. It's still in him. Poor Caerwyn shakin like a leaf he was now."

"Is it fuck. They got the needle out." We all turned to Dai Dyserth to confirm the result.

"It… it… it's out n… n…now. Had t… t…t… go b… b… b… back to hospital. Nobody believed m…m…me."

"No Dai you know that's not true. The doctor wanted to get home for his tea now. He didn't have time for you to tell him now." Baeddan's comment caused all three to start laughing. It was infectious I joined in. The laughter died down only to start up again when Dai Denbigh added.

"Needed two stretcher's we did. One for Dai here and one for Caerwyn. After administering the morphine, he fainted he did." We began laughing again. I looked at each of these men. Their warmth and openness made me feel part of their world already. It was intoxicating.

"Right come on lads we've bonus to make." Baeddan shouted to his two colleagues.

"Before you go." Bleddyn interrupted. "We got a photographer here tomorrow. Make sure the place is kept tidy. Manager's asked for these photo's special now he has."

"I hope we get some taken of me and the lads."

"I'm sure you will." The lads continued forward to complete setting the support. Bleddyn followed. From behind I heard voices. I turned to see Gregor George accompanied by another person.

"Morning Gregor."

"Morning Mick, oops Mr Gibson." We both laughed.

"This is Roger Rhyll the heading electrician."

"Hi Roger. Let me guess. You live in the seaside town of the very name."

"No. I'm actually from Gronant." I made a mental note. Sometimes it was better to say nothing at all. What was that old adage *better sometimes to remain silent and look the fool. Than to open your mouth and confirm it.*

-

As soon as we arrived back on land, I put a call through to the store's manager Iolo Pyke. "Hi… yeah Mr Gibson here. Could you organise a couple of rolls of neoprene for Zone B. Yeah understand … no I'm happy with that. You want a note to confirm it? Consider it done. No, I'm not interested in what you've been told… Right yeah thanks."

Bleddyn had followed me into the office. "I hope you know what you're doin now. You don't want to be making an enemy of that man."

"I can assure you I don't want to be making an enemy of anyone. In answer to your first question I know exactly what I'm doin."

The following day the team assembled for the morning meeting. Denny Richards was first to arrive with Gethin.

"Now cock. Hope you not lookin to make trouble for yourself?"

"What would that be Denny?"

"You know fuckin well what I mean cock."

"I'm sure I do." The conversation ended as Gregor George and Ifor entered. "Right lads what have you got for me…" Twenty minutes later the meeting was over. Everybody left to go and get changed. I stood ready to leave as the door opened.

"Now Mick how's it goin?" He closed the door behind him.

"Good thanks Mr Adder. Well impressed with what I've seen so far. Still got to walk the Drift yet but hoping to arrange with Denny." The visit had come sooner than I thought. But I knew it had to happen.

"Iolo tells me you've ordered some neoprene?"

"Yep that's true."

"You know I'm trying to keep control on costs?"

"I hadn't been told but I can understand why."

"Well that includes ordering items without my permission."

"Right. My apologies I didn't understand procedure. Are you okay if I order it then?"

"No, I've put a stop to it."

"Right you've cancelled my order…" I stopped as the office door opened. It was Bleddyn.

"Oh, sorry now gentlemen." He looked towards me and guessed what was taking place. "I'll see you in the lamproom now." He closed the door.

"Could I have that in writing then?"

"Have what in writing?"

"The fact you've cancelled my order."

"Mr Gibson. I'm the last person you need to be making an enemy of."

"I can assure you Mr Adder that is not my intention." There was no response he looked towards me. I returned his stare. Then without another word spoken he turned and left. By the end of the week I was informed the neoprene had arrived.

-

As planned the following day the photographer arrived, I escorted him into 43's maingate. Bleddyn had gone to check on the eighteen inch pipes we were laying in M1. The guy had been very accommodating and suggested we get a number of team shots too. I promised the lads I'd get them a copy.

Two weeks later I received a call from the Manager he'd asked to see me.

"Afternoon Mr. Groves." I greeted the Manager as I walked into his office.

"You wanted to see me?" Larry Llewelyn was there too. I'd noticed how the Safety Engineer always seemed to be with the Manager."

"I did; those photos arrived today. The one's taken in 43's maingate."

"Any good?"

"You tell me they're on the table; take a seat. Thanks Larry we'll speak further later." Larry smiled towards me before leaving.

I did as instructed opposite a pile of large black and white photos. I was quite excited I knew some of the photos were of me. I'd never been photographed underground before. I took the pile and begin flicking through them one by one. A number of them contained shots of the Dosco Dintheader and the bridge conveyor. Each of those had the operator in position Baeddan the Boar. Plenty showed the roadway surrounded by the Hollybank arches connected by the wrap around tie bars. Some stonedust we'd spread before he started taking photo's was evident.

I looked up towards the Manager he was staring at me he seemed to have something on his mind. It was a little unnerving. I needed to say something.

"That one of Baeddan on the machine you can see me hiding in the background." I laughed again looking towards the Manager. He continued to stare. "Wow that's a good one with me, Baeddan, the two Dai's and Gregor with his electrician Roger." I continued there were twenty in total. "Not bad I'd say Mr. Groves." This was his cue to move forward and sit opposite me. He reached across and picked up the pile.

"Not bad you say well let me tell you what I think." He started to review each one quicker than I had as if shuffling a pack of cards.

"This one of the bridge conveyor the hydraulic hoses and cables are hanging all over the place it looks like the bottom of a snake pit. There's mesh lying loose under the conveyor with a seven pound hammer propped up against it. Tie bars, bolts lying everywhere. You've even left the centre line string up with coal hanging from it. There's no evidence of stonedust being spread." His voices getting louder and louder. Finishing his comment, the photo was skimmed into the air.

"This one of Baeddan on the machine; he's made no attempt to clean the top there's even a five gallon drum of hydraulic fluid sat in full view." The second photograph followed the trajectory of the first.

"Why would I want a team photo of you all?" No further comment that was launched too. "The ventilation bagging is all over the place no attempt made to straighten it out. Liftin brackets attached to the steel supports and that venturi hanging doin nothing. You standing writing in your book did you want to be on stage? Scattered bags of unopened stonedust."

The tirade continued for a full five minutes. *I guess you're not happy then Boss?* I kept this thought to myself. When he'd finished, I knelt down and started to collect the photographs. I went to place them on the table.

"Don't leave them there I never want to see them again they're a complete joke. Take them with you. Make sure next time I ask for photographs to be taken the place is adequately prepared first. Now get out my sight." I guessed it was time to leave.

Waiting outside next to Bronwen's desk was my colleague Paul Taylor. "I see he's started on you now. Not sure I can take anymore." I was somewhat taken aback by his comment. Not fully aware of what he meant. I smiled as he entered the Manager's office. I looked across to Bronwen. She'd obviously heard what had just been said. Without a word she raised her eyebrows and continued typing.

–

After the initial fuck up with the FSV getting bogged down in 43's return due to the compressed air pump being turned off. The place had flooded. Things were now back on track. The face line drivage was ahead of target and looked as though we'd complete before the end of the month. Three weeks ahead of schedule. This was excellent news. There was the potential to avoid the usual six week production gap. The lads had done an excellent job. Baeddan would certainly get his completion bonus.

Instead of the usual face to face transfer of equipment from F42's to F43's the Manager had secured an agreement with the Area Director to purchase a new set of powered supports and face panzer. Just as Alwyn the Face Overman had mentioned previously. Once the face line had holed through to the return gate, we could start the installation. The existing equipment on F42's would still be salvaged and transported to Zone A. For their next coal face S61. There was a possibility by manning up to three shifts seven days per week we could complete the installation in two weeks. A record.

We'd still need to remove the stage loader and shearer. With the right preparation I estimated it would take us no more than a week to dismantle, transport and re-assemble. The maingate belt slinging had been completed to the required standard. The drive would need replacing to a bigger size. My greatest satisfaction was the Manager was happy. If there was one thing I'd learnt above all else as an Undermanager you keep the Manager happy.

–

"Mr. Groves you've asked to see me?" The Manager was at his desk.

"Yeah come in Mick, take a seat." He was smiling. There was a further knock on his office door. Gerry Tuffman popped his head in.

"You've asked to see me Gaffer?"

"Yeah come in we're just about to make a start, just waiting on Mr Adder."

"Shall I sort you some drinks Mr Groves?" Bronwen had entered through the door behind her desk. I was still getting used to the fact that the Manager's office could be accessed through three doors.

"Ron, sorry I'm late you haven't started, yet have you?" the Deputy Manager eased himself past Bronwen. She grimaced as he entered. There was no love lost between these two. I could never understand why he always called the Manager by his first name. I assume he got a kick out of it. And to highlight his position above anybody else. The Manager never seemed to mind though.

"Please Bronwen if you would be so kind." Bronwen took our orders and left.

"Right gentlemen I'm told the equipment for 43's is now available to view. At the Dowty plant near Gloucester. A place called Ashchurch actually." Paul Adder had yet to sit down. He was toying with the bowl of fruit on the sideboard. The Manager stopped and waited for him to sit.

"They've created a mock-up with the pans allowing us to take some measurements." I must have looked unsure. The Manager looked directly at me "It'll enable you to position the maingate end in its exact position. Allowing your men to continue laying the pan line."

The fact Mr Groves had to explain this to me seemed to amuse Paul Adder. He shook his head as he peeled a tangerine. Gerry gave me a nudge.

"Watch and see young man. You're with the A team now." I smiled.

"Can't wait."

Mr Groves continued. "I can't emphasise enough the importance of this installation being completed on time. I've given my personal assurance to the Area Director the maximum production gap we'll have will be a week." I nodded in agreement I understood his comment to be an instruction.

"Ron you could be setting yourself up for a fall."

"And why would that be Paul?" Before he could reply Bronwen entered the room.

"Tea gentleman. Yours I believe was the coffee Mr. Gibson?"

"Yeah, thanks Bronwen."

"I asked for coffee too." Paul added.

"I'm awfully sori I've made you tea." Bronwen looked towards me and winked. "Plus, one sugar."

"I don't have sugar."

"Oops that's right you only have sugar in coffee I'd clean forgot now." This time her comment was followed by a smile. "Let me get you another." I looked across to Paul he didn't look happy.

"Thanks, Bron." The Manager hadn't taken any notice of the conversation taking place he'd been watching his computer screen. Connected via the control room and using some software known as MINOS he'd been monitoring the conveyor belts. "Think you've got a problem with the x-cut belt Mr Gibson."

"Yeah fully aware. The lads were deployed first thing to clean out the drive. Looks as though the wiper was missing. I've got a fitter refitting it."

Mr Groves looked towards Gerry and shook his head. "Yep I'm aware Gaffer I've got the Deputy Engineers to check all the conveyors first thing. Now we've got some neoprene in the stores." He looked at me and winked. Mr Adder made no comment.

"Okay then. Right Paul you were saying about a fall?"

"Yeah Ron it's a tall order can we rely on the FSV fleet to remain fully operational during the install. We've only got the two supplying 43's."

"Mr Gibson's got that covered, would you like to explain?" I nodded.

"Yeah I'm moving one of the bigger machines out of Motorway 3 this weekend. It'll give us some spare capacity."

"How come I'm unaware of it?"

"Only decided this morning after a conversation with the engineers. Seems we've got a part dismantled FSV in the Motorway 3 garage. Denny has ordered the parts we need. Looking to rebuild over the weekend."

"It would have been nice to be told." I looked at the man had he not listened to my comment. I sensed the Manager looking towards me. I returned his gaze he was shaking his head. "Where's my bloody coffee? Do you have to do everything around here?" With that Paul got up and left the room.

"Don't take any notice. He's a bit tetchy this morning after finding out he never got the Manager's job at Parkside. Anyway, as I was saying one-week max production gap."

"Yeah got that loud and clear Mr. Groves."

"I'd also like you to arrange cutting in the developments over the weekend. I want to have additional coal stocks to supplement 43's during start up."

"What about the overtime budget? Mr. Adder has insisted we reduce where we can."

"Don't worry about that I'll speak with him."

I turned towards Gerry. He hadn't said a word. He was holding a clay pipe packing it with tobacco.
"Don't you dare Mr. Tuffman."
"I wouldn't dream of it Gaffer. Won't be lighting up till I get in my office,"
"Such a filthy habit." I was intrigued not fully understanding the Manager's comment.
"It's chewing tobacco. Our Mr. Tuffman after he's finished chewing the stuff leaves it to dry out. Then smokes it."
"I like to think of it as fully recyclable."
"Word of advice. Never park outside his office window." I'm sure he'd mentioned this to me before.
"Where do you think he spits?"
"Now, now Mr. Groves any gobbin I do goes straight in the spittoon."
"Bloody hell I wondered what that was in your office."

"Right think we need to make a move."
"Why when are we going?" I asked
"No time like the present. We'll take my motor."
"I was planning on checking that x-cut conveyor."
"I'm sure Bleddyn will sort that for you." The Manager added.
"Okay give me a minute while I get my jacket and notebook."

I left through the far door passing Bronwen's desk.
"How you settling in Mick?"
"All good thanks Bronwen, just put a deposit down on a house too."
"That is good news. Close by?"
"Rhuddlan actually not far from Billy Blunt."
"Mrs Gibson okay with everything?"
"Getting there. Not happy about moving from Liverpool. Sorry I need to make a move I'm off with Gerry to Gloucester."
"Just you be careful of our Mr. Adder now." She smiled. I left her and continued down the corridor.

"Mick, you got a minute." I'd just passed the Deputy's Manager's office. I stopped and retraced my steps.
"I'm in a little bit of a hurry I'm afraid. Off to Dowty with Gerry."
"Won't take a mo. Could you close the door behind you?"
"I don't like surprises Mick."
"Sorry?"
"Your comment about the FSV I should have been consulted first."

"Why?"

"Just because." For what liked seemed an eternity we stared at each other.

"Okay understood." *See what you think of this.* "By the way, the Manager has told me to forget any restriction on weekend overtime. He wants the developments operating each shift. Seven days a week." *It wasn't exactly what he'd said but it had the desired effect.*

"We'll see about that."

"Please let me know if there's a change of plan." He didn't answer.

He jumped out of his seat brushed passed me. Heading straight up to the Manager's office. I took a look at his desk. There was still no sign of his coffee.

—

The journey down to Gloucester took just over two and a half hours. Gerry was good company. He suggested I should come across to his place in Mold one night for dinner. He was a keen fisherman. More recently he'd been trying his hand at using ley lines. Again, suggesting I should join him one afternoon with the kids. Like Billy Blunt he'd previously worked at Haig Colliery. The Manager there I'd previously worked for too. We laughed at some of his antics particularly his dislike of engineers. I mentioned the time I'd gone up to the management suite to visit the Ventilation department. The Manager's office was at the end of the corridor. I arrived to see his door open with the Mechanical Engineer in somewhat of a rush. He was followed by the Manager's foot. Another occasion I was working with one of the fitters. We'd been sent to salvage a tailend roller for one of the heading conveyors. Walking along an outbye road the fitter with me caught sight of somebody ahead. They were taking a dump. His lamp picked out the guys white arse. "Seen that face somewhere before." He shouted laughing. To our astonishment the Manager turned to face us.

"Come on lads keep moving." We did as instructed without uttering another word.

Once we arrived at Dowty I was introduced to the Sales Manager and one of his reps. After a quick coffee and biscuit, we went out onto the yard. The weather was dull and overcast. It had just started to rain. A very fine rain. The type you don't feel too bad in. Until ten minutes later you're soaked to the skin. I hoped we wouldn't be too long.

We headed over to a line of AFC pans. As Mr. Groves had said both the tail end and maingate drive were in position. Gerry was brandishing a tape measure. He headed over to the maingate end with the Sales manager.

"I'll get you the position to lay the first pan." Gerry shouted over to me.

"Okay, I'm just going over to look at the chocks."

"I'll come with you." The sales rep responded.

The supports were in two areas. One containing the gleaming white canopies and the other the bases each with the four brass coloured metal legs sitting proud. In total I guessed some two hundred tonnes of metal supports.

"How much?"

"How much what?" the rep responded.

"For this equipment,"

"About a quarter of a million pounds worth."

"Bloody hell you wouldn't believe it."

"That's nothing. In our top yard we've got a set of supports worth at least five million pounds going to one of the big Lancashire pits. Bickershaw I believe."

"Yeah I've heard mention something about a heavy-duty installation taking place in the Plodder seam. A mate of mine from college is Undermanager there. What about those?" I'd spotted two assembled chocks at the far end. We walked across.

"Yeah this is what they'll look like when fully assembled."

They looked impressive set to a height of six foot I clambered underneath the first. The extended part of the leg positioned and fixed to the main canopy in welded cups. Secured with a one-inch steel bolt. The base was about eight inches deep. The main ram covered over with inch plate to avoid trapping the operator's foot. The back canopy was metal too concertinaed to rise and fall with the main canopy. I thought back to 42's coal face where they used strips of belting to avoid the waste flushing into the chock track. The hoses or bagging as they were often referred to still had the outer coat of white paint. These would contain the hydraulic fluid for pressurising the chocks once in-situ.

I tapped my pockets. "Shit!" I looked across to Gerry. "Here borrow mine."

"Oh, right thanks." The rep passed me his tape measure. "I need to get measurements to build a wooden scale model of the chock. Need to make sure there's no surprises when transporting them to site. I'm guessing we'll transport the canopies separate."

I'd already planned the position for a building station at the top of 43's return. Here we'd attach the canopy to the base before transporting to site on the FSV. The rep must have read my mind.

"You moving them onto the faceline with FSV's?"

"Certainly am."

"Yeah always good to plan ahead. The packhole chock canopies are over there." I looked across to where he was pointing.

"We'll never get those in the cage. They'll need slinging." I added that to my list. To meet with the Head Shaftsman when I got back. Once I'd taken all the measurements needed, I passed the tape back to the rep.

"Right fella you ready?" Gerry shouted across.

"Yeah all good here Gerry." We said our farewells and set off on the journey back to North Wales. After an hour of travel, we stopped for a bite to eat. I had my regulation fish and chips and a pint of Guinness. Gerry chose the steak and ale pie. With a Guinness too.

"You'll need this." Gerry passed me a slip of paper. "That's the distance from the centreline of the maingate to position the first pan."

"Thanks, I'll guard it with my life." I responded laughing.

Once back on the road traffic had been particularly heavy. This time it took us over three hours to get back. I asked Gerry if he'd wanted me to give him a spell at driving. He didn't take me up on my offer and was quite happy to drive. It was just after six pm when we drove onto the pit yard.

"Looks as though the gaffer's still here." I looked across to where the Manager's car was parked. No sign of Paul Adder's car though.

"Can only mean one thing we got trouble!"

Back in the office I called the Control Room. The coal face F42's had been stood for an hour.

"The cross-cut belt I supposedly cleaned out this morning." I listened. "For fucks sake!" The words had barely left my mouth when the Manager walked in. I looked towards him shaking my head. I covered the mouthpiece of the handset. "I arranged to get it cleaned out this morning."

"I know you did. Obviously not complete?"

"Thanks Lewis." I put the phone back down.

"If you want a job doin. Do it yourself." I began to walk out of the office.

"Where you goin?"

"To sort it."

"But you've only just got back." I didn't respond. I continued to the baths. The missus wasn't going to be happy. I hadn't planned on staying over tonight. The one thing I wasn't goin to let happen again. If there's a problem I needed to see it for myself!

Two hours later I was back up the pit. The face was coaling again. Now on its second shear. I walked into my office. I'd need to call the missus and explain. I'd only just sat down when the Manager appeared.

"Mr Groves what you still doin here?"

"Waitin for you. All sorted now?"

"Yep. Looks as though they'd just done enough this morning to get the belt running. Hadn't cleaned the drive out completely. I'll pick up with Bleddyn tomorrow. New wipers fitted though."

"Well done. I'm off now thanks for sorting. Never let yourself be criticised for not making a decision. Better to decide on the information you have than not make a decision at all. See you tomorrow." And with that he left.

I made a mental note of his comment. Sound advice. I liked that. I put a call though to my wife. Funny though she didn't see it the same way as the Manager had done.

-

"James he's busy, you can't just barge in."

"You watch me. I don't even make an appointment to see the Manager."

I could hear the conversation taking place outside my office. I'd just finished signing the days reports. I was about to get up the door flew open.

"Ah Mick good to finally meet you." I was confronted by a miniature James Robertson Justice. He was wearing a blue boiler suit and a white donkey jacket.

"Sorry Mr. Gibson I did warn him."

"No problem Bleddyn I've finished signing." By the time I'd stood the man was alongside me. He raised his right hand. I took it.

"James Runner, Head Shaftsman."

"Just the man. I was hoping to meet you." I got the impression this man made his own decisions. Ignoring my comment, he continued.

"One thing you need to know about me." Behind him Bleddyn was imitating a sawing action across his arm.

"Cross me and it will be like losing your right arm." I smiled.

"Okay and understood I'll make sure I remember, particularly as I'm right handed." He smiled in return. I took to the man instantly another character to add to my list.

Without invitation he sat down. Bleddyn now facing the kettle in the corner asked. "Drink gentlemen?"

For the next half hour James filled me in on his background. He was also a member of the Rhyl lifeboat team. As he knew I had kids he suggested I bring them to an open day they would be having in a couple of weeks. He also thought it was a good idea if I were to accompany him on a shaft inspection. Heights were not my thing. I changed the subject as I passed him a slip of paper.

"I guess these will need slinging." He took a look at the measurements.

"43's packhole chock canopies?"

"The very same."

"What about the line chocks?"

"They'll be fine."

"I think that's my decision to make." I noticed Bleddyn lower his head as he supressed a chuckle. I passed him a further slip of paper.

"Yep. They'll be fine. Right if there's nothing else I need to be making a move." He stood and offered his hand once more.

"I think Mick, me and you will get on just fine."

"I think so too James. One other thing. Any chance you can get me one of those." I pointed to his white donkey jacket.

"Mick, I have to tell you there's only a select few allowed these." I remained silent. "I'll see what I can do. Paul Adder put a stop to ordering anymore." He smiled. "After he'd received his. Your mate next door never received one."

"See what you can do James it would be much appreciated." He left.

"Tell you what Mr Gibson." I turned to Bleddyn. "You be settling in here just fine. You mark my words now."

–

Following the visit to Dowty I'd arranged with Denny to have a scaled wooden version of the new chocks constructed by the joiners. Just the base we'd agreed to transport the canopies separately. Once off the main loco tunnel we found a number of areas where height and width became a problem. Bleddyn set the two trackmen Llew and Gordon to carry out remedial works. Mainly floor dints and dropping the track.

Within a week of my visit the pans began to arrive. These were shipped underground and offloaded in 43's crosscut either side of the doors. The spill plates were transported separately. Not ideal as we'd be handling them twice. We couldn't afford to tie up the flats we were transporting them on. Our approach had been to get ahead as much as we could. Once the faceline was complete we could start the install without delay.

The chocks followed soon after. We'd constructed a building station at the top of the return gate. Denny's number two Gethin had offered good advice on its construction. A number of heavy-duty steel rebars were inserted in the roof. Attached to which lengths of four by three RSJ's. Two sets of compressed air lifting blocks were then positioned. With the required lifting chains the canopy once offloaded was lifted allowing the base of the chock to be positioned underneath. The completed chock was then lifted once more by a third set of lifting blocks. Transported along the girders to the storage area ten metres further inbye. Each time an FSV arrived with a further chock base the completed chock was taken and stored in the return road. All the FSV's used had been installed with hydraulic winches to assist in dragging the chock onto its flatbed. On average the men were building between four and five chocks a day. Depending who was on shift.

With coaling taking place at weekends the faceline broke through two weeks ahead of schedule. I'd been on hand with Denny and Gethin to witness the breakthrough in 43's return. A mesh barrier had been put in place by the Deputy to avoid anyone getting too close. During my time in the pit I'd been on hand to witness many of these events. Even now the excitement of the occasion was still palpable.

"Here it comes lad." Denny shouted to no one particular. Gethin and I said nothing. The noise of the cutting mat was deafening. Pieces of dirt and dust fell from the roof the closer it got. The side of the tunnel began to vibrate. A lump of coal flew out from a position it had been in for millions of years. Then another and another. Chinks of light then appearing from the faceline. The cutter picks on the mat catching the wire mesh. A number of picks caught the side of a Hollybank arches. Sparks flew. The Dosco driver pulling back before any further damage was done. Pieces of coal flew in all directions. The dust made it hard to see other than the beams of the cap lamps dancing in all directions.

We moved back to avoid being hit by the airborne lumps of coal. The driver now taking a series of sweeping actions as he enlarged the breakthrough. Each pass by the cutting mat exposed the heading team on the face line. And then it was over the machine backed off. Deadly silence. We walked forward the mesh made it look like a cage. The heading team chargehand stepped forward and thrust a banana towards me.

"Look lads we've accidently broken into the Welsh Mountain Zoo!" It was followed by hoots of laughter from all sides. I noted the breakthrough had been exactly on centre. I was pleased.

Once all the congratulations were done, the team secured the roof and sides. It didn't take long. Everyone aware time was of the essence. The heading team had repositioned the power cable into a recently installed panel in the return gate. They continued to track the Dintheader out. It was required for another development in the Two Yard. The Deputy had set the back-up men to start removing the ventilation bagging after which they would drop the auxiliary fans from both gates and load up. I was pleased to see everything was being followed up as per the plan we'd agreed at our recent section meetings. I made a note to get the faceline stonedusted. I was sure Bleddyn had that covered. The silence was exacerbated as both auxiliary fans were switched off. The three of us continued towards the maingate end

Arriving there it was good to see the linesman. He was hanging the strings for positioning the first AFC pan. We'd planned to start moving the pans onto the faceline on the noon shift. Denny stopped and turned to me.

"Now cock if I arrange with the night shift to get a couple of fitters here will the maingate end be here ready for build?"

"Yeah certainly will Denny. First run in this afternoon with the FSV will be the pans. I've got a separate team fetching the maingate drive down the intake. Following which we'll lay out the Stageloader."

"You want to watch we don't overload ourselves with tackle."

"Don't worry we'll make sure it's spaced out."

"What bout shearer?"

"Fuckin hell Denny do you think we're fuckin stupid?"

"You don't want me to answer that do you cock?"

"Mick, don't forget the roof bolts." Gethin was pointing towards the roof.

"Useful as additional lifting points for the shearer build."

"Good point." I noted Gethin's comment.

"And a couple of cans of phosphate ester."

"Come in Mr. Gibson, Mr. Gibson." The tannoy outbye of where we were standing burst into life.

"Bet that'll be the Manager wanting an update."

"No that'll be Adder. Mark my words." I walked up to answer the call. "Hi control."

"Could you give the Deputy Manager a call Mr. Gibson. Says it's quite important."

"Will do Ellis." I waited till Denny and Gethin caught back up with me.

"You got a problem with him lad?"

"Not so much of a problem. Just think he's a lazy twat. Claims he knows what's going on underground, but he rarely gets down himself. As soon as I tell him we've broken through he'll be straight in to see the Manager. Like he'd done it."

"I wouldn't let it get to you. He thinks his current role is below him. Thinks he should be the Manager. Ay up is that Gregor and Ifor?" We looked outbye to see two lamps approaching.

They were measuring up for additional armoured cable for the panels that would be mounted on the Stageloader. All five of us stopped for a catch up and to confirm the plan over the coming days. Everyone was conversant with what had to be done. We'd spent many hours in my office planning for the installation. I found it useful to have these additional conversations on the job. There was always the chance we'd missed something. As this was my first face installation as Undermanager I was keen it ran smoothly.

"I've arranged for the face signalling cables to be offloaded in the x-cut. We'll throw them on the truck as and when required." Ifor added to our discussion.

"What about the Bretby?"

"It's in a mine car at pit bottom I'll arrange to have it moved in next week."

"Now cock have you forgotten something?"

"Oh shit. Adder! Right lads I'll catch you later." I'd got so engrossed in our conversation I'd completely forgot to call the Deputy Manager. I continued walking up the return gate to the x-cut. The nearest telephone was at the bottom of the access road how would explain the delay in returning the call.

"Hello Mr. Adder." I began panting.

"Hello is that you Mick?"

Panting louder "Yeah it's me sorry for the delay in calling you back. I couldn't find a fuckin phone that works."

"Oh, right not to worry. I was just checkin the breakthrough happened without incident."

Still panting "Yeah all good and smack on centre."

"Excellent thanks for getting back to me, speak later." *That seemed to work I'll remember that for future reference.*

Once back up the pit Bleddyn had given the work instruction to the noon shift. He was standing in the deployment centre as I walked through from the lamproom.

"Mr. Gibson all okay?"

"Yeah thanks Bleddyn we seem to have gotten off to a good start. How far did the lads get the Dintheader?

"They've made excellent progress and got it onto the x-cut. As planned, we'll start moving the pans this afternoon. And yes, before you ask, I kept a couple of the supply lads on to spread some stonedust along the face line between shifts."

"Excellent, right I think I'll go straight for a bath ready for the overtime meeting."

"Okay now and by the way the Electrical Engineer was after you earlier on."

"Billy Blunt what did he want?"

"Didn't say." I left Bleddyn and headed towards the showers. Just as I was passing my office the phone rang.

"Hello, Undermanager here."

"Twat!" I recognised his voice immediately.

"Billy how nice to hear from you too."

"Never mind that. What about the shite you fed to Adder? I've had to send two electricians to check all the phones in the 43's area when both you and I know there was fuck all wrong with them."

"Sorry mate maybe a bit of a misunderstanding!"

"Don't fuckin mate me. I owe you one." And with that the phone line went dead. I went for my bath.

I'd been at my desk five minutes when the phone rang. "Undermanager here…
what? Can't be. You've got to be fuckin kiddin. I'm on my way."

"What's up." Bleddyn asked as he walked into the office.

"Afternoon shift reckon there's no room to fit the maingate end. The first pan
is in the wrong position."

"That can't be the case. You measured the position at Dowty?"

"Not me exactly I'll need to check." I wasted no more time and headed
underground. Two hours later I arrived back in my office. Both the Manager
and Gerry greeted me.

"Is it true then?"

"Yep we've had to remove a pan. We'll need to replace it sometime in the
future." The Manager and I turned to Gerry for an explanation.

"I knew it. I should never have let the Sales Director hold that end of the tape."

Within three weeks F43's face installation was complete even with the fuck up.
Other than testing the electrics and running up the various pieces of equipment
we were ready to go. It had been a fantastic effort by all concerned. The men,
the officials, and my team even considering Gerry's measurements. It was my
first face installation as Undermanager. It had been completed a week earlier
than expected. Mr Groves was happy too which was good.

I arrived into work at five thirty on the day we'd planned to start shearing. To
avoid any surprises we'd agreed the nightshift would take the first shear off and
test the system. I walked into my office. Bleddyn was still in the deployment
centre. My nightshift Development Overman was sat waiting.

"Good morning Lewis." I greeted him as I sat down. A mug of black coffee
was waiting too. One of Bleddyn's first tasks. I was excited this was the day.

"How did it go last night?" He stared back at me. He was still in his black no
obvious indication on his face. He leaned forward towards me.

"Okay, now" *Okay*, Lewis was never one for showing emotion, his answer
could mean anything, the cage has fallen down the shaft, a roof fall on the face,
an inrush of water had flooded the developments. I try to be more specific.

"How did the shearing go?"

"It didn't now." It wasn't the answer I was expecting.

"It didn't fuckin what now?" I could feel the blood rush to my face. Saliva
flying from my mouth as the decibels began to rise. "And you're tellin me
everything is fuckin okay?"

He looked at me with disbelief "We had a slight electrical problem." He didn't
seem to grasp the enormity of the situation.

"I'm not interested in the slight problem. Tell me what stopped you producing the coal last night?" I'd given up any attempt to drink my coffee. Patches of it lay over the desk. Each time I slammed my fist down added to that discharged from my mouth.

"An electrical problem on the shearer was the only delay we had. It wouldn't start now."

My anger starts to subside. His answer wasn't ideal. I'd made a promise to the Manager we'd start last night.

"Why didn't you say earlier I wouldn't have lost my temper?" Lewis's expression still hadn't changed. "Has the Deputy Electrical Engineer been advised?"

"No, I don't think so." He senses blame is to be apportioned elsewhere. For the first time he sits back he looks more relaxed.

I reach for the land line.

"Elis give Gregor George a call. Tell him to get his fuckin arse in here now." I scream into the receiver.

Having completed my grilling of Lewis on the other non-productive parts of the shift I suggest he goes for a bath. As he leaves the office Bleddyn walks in. It seems he'd delayed his entrance until I'd been made aware of last night. He confirms my suspicion when he looks towards Lewis.

"See ya tomorrow Lewis." He turns towards me. "Bora da Mr Gibson."

"Morning Bleddyn."

Bleddyn was carrying a white paper bag. It contains his usual white toasted bap. The contents of which include four rashes of bacon, two pork sausages, and two fried eggs. All coated in a thick layer of tomato ketch up. He places the bag onto the desk. In his other hand he's carrying a pint of milk. He reaches across for my depleted mug of coffee and asks smiling.

"Same again?"

"Please." He walks across to the table in the corner of the office and switches the kettle on. He places the milk down alongside an already opened two pound bag of sugar. He makes no attempt to empty the contents of my mug. He simply adds two teaspoons of instant coffee. Having stirred it he places it on my desk. He sits down.

"Suppose you've heard the news from 43s?"

"That I have now. I'm sure it will be sorted shortly now."

"How are we fixed everywhere else?"

"All good." whether there are problems or not he wouldn't tell he'd just get on and resolve them. He reminds of one of the Colour Sergeants at Rorke's Drift although the red tunic would have problems buttoning up at the front. He'd never admit to having a problem as in his world it would be admitting defeat, something he'd never do.

He gets back up and heads towards the table in the corner with his mug of tea. He proceeds to add spoons of sugar. I lose count of the number. He sits back down and takes a mouthful of his tea. He turns his attention to the egg and bacon bap. He rips the bag along one side and flattens with one hand pulling the now exposed bap towards himself. This allows any pieces of the bap or its contents to be caught on a clean surface. He raises the bap towards his mouth.

Taking a mouthful, the tomato ketchup oozes out. Falling on his chin. He uses his right hand to wipe the surplus and licks it off. He takes another bite. This charade is played out every morning.

My next appointment at seven o'clock is with the Deputy Manager. Here I report on the previous days performance. I use the time available to confirm with Bleddyn our preparedness for the oncoming shift.

"How are we for materials in the headings this morning?" Bleddyn still eating attempts to finish devouring the mouthful of food. Unable to help himself he answers before he's finished.

"We've only got one pack of mesh left in the Durbog headings. There's more at the end of the road so shouldn't be a problem." Small pieces of bacon and egg fly from his mouth falling on the desk. He reaches across to pick them up looking to me for a response; I say nothing. He takes another bite.

"Did we complete setting the two arches in overtime in the North heading or was it three?" He looks across attempting a response.

"Three," he answers nearly choking. He reaches across and takes a mouthful of tea. He waits looking towards me expectantly I smile. I've enough information to compile my report for the Deputy Manager.

The report I provide verbally but I always produce my notes in the form of bullet points. These I later file for future reference. Something I'd learned long ago as sometimes people forget or choose to forget what they've been told. I keep a diary too. Listing the places, I've visited underground. Useful if there's ever a mishap and I need to explain where I've visited.

The report is predominately my excuses for poor performance and not achieving set targets. In both the headings and on the coal face. I'm under no illusion that there's anything good to report. As the saying goes *you're only as good as your last job.*

Once dayshift had arrived at the Two Way Meeting Station the dayshift development Overman called Bleddyn to agree where the men are to be deployed. Priority is given to the coal face as that is where the bulk of the coal is produced. It could be seen as a contradiction as without the development headings achieving the required yardage it may affect the replacement coal face being ready on time. I'd completely forgotten my earlier conversation with the Control Room and my message for the Deputy Electrical Engineer. As Bleddyn finished his conversation my office door flew open with a bang. As it hit the adjacent wall. It knocked a five pound fire extinguisher off its bracket. Causing Bleddyn to jump. The contents of his mug splash onto the desk.

"You fuckin scouse twat!" Standing in the doorway was Gregor George. Gregor is forty five years old, although he looks much older. Age being a mining thing – we all looked older than we were. He stood approximately four and a half foot, beginning to bald on top. But adequately covered by his Bobby Charlton quiff. Eyebrows Dennis Healy would be proud of and sideburns reminiscent of Stewart Granger in King Solomon's Mines. His most redeeming feature by far are the hairs protruding from either nostril. Akin to someone having forced a cork up either nostril.

I chose to ignore this interruption and continued to discuss the forthcoming day's activities with Bleddyn. Bleddyn however was not of the same opinion.
"You ignorant twat I'm talking to you!"
"What about the bad ground towards the tailgate have you arranged additional timber."
"I'm fucking talking to you!" The decibels begin to rise. Bleddyn is alternating his gaze between each of us. No doubt wondering who is the craziest. The colour had drained from his face. He'd given up any further attempt to finish his tea. Fortunately, he'd finished eating his bap.
"You shitty arsed fuckin scouse bastard, you'll listen to me if it's the last fuckin thing you do."
"Yeah I'd have a word with the surface foreman and arrange some extra wagons." I realize at this point I may have gone too far as Gregor reaches with both hands to pick up a metal tubular chair. He holds it above his head and screams.
"You scouse bastard," bringing it crashing down onto the table in front of me. Bleddyn I guess is considering his options for escape, through the door behind Gregor or out of a window behind me.

I smile which under the circumstances was not the best thing to do. Gregor raised the chair once more but this time aiming at me; halfway through its downward motion releasing it. I dive to my right whilst at the same time parrying the chair away from my body. My action inadvertently sends it in the direction of Bleddyn. Ready for the situation to deteriorate he has planned his next move. For a man of his size he springs from his chair instinctively diving to the floor. Landing with ease he jumps up and runs out of the door without looking back.

It's now time for me to protect myself I jump up and throw my arms around his shoulders. My intention to get him out of my office; I find however this was easier said than done. The man was rather good on his feet and took me longer than expected to get him to the door. By which time the Training Officer and others had rushed in to view the commotion. Not before we'd knocked over the table containing the kettle and other tea making facilities. The altercation was soon over.

"What the hell is wrong with you?" I ask.
"Fuck off." Gregor responded as he turned and walked away. I found out later Elis in the Control Room had delivered my earlier comment verbatim. Gregor had only been lying in bed next to his wife. An hour a half later at eight o'clock we go underground together as if nothing had ever happened.

For the first week after the face started up I visit each day. The place was performing as expected. I took the opportunity thereafter to visit the other areas of my section. The place was like a rabbit warren. It also gave me the opportunity to meet the men. By week two however Bleddyn was showing a little concern with regards to the waste.
"What's the problem? It'll drop when it's good and ready."
"I don't think you understand now Mr Gibson. The Five Yard seam is overlain by sandstone. If it doesn't cave in soon weight will be thrown forward now onto those nice new chocks. I've seen a whole new faceline collapse under the weight when that waste doesn't fall."
"What do you suggest?"
"May have to make it drop." I knew where he was going with this. I'd heard of it before. Using powder to bring the roof down. An idea but not the best it could have consequences.
"Tell you what. Let's pop in there this morning and have a looksee."

We arrived into 43's district just after ten. Rhys Llan and Aled Flint were the first to greet us. They were carrying chock timber down towards the maingate.
"Morning lads."
"Bora da Mr Gibson, Bleddyn."
"Have you seen Alwyn?" I asked.
"Sori Mr Gibson." Bleddyn interrupted. "Face Overman today is young Hywel. Alwyn is at rehearsals with Flint choir."
"I didn't know he sung in the choir."

"Oh, oes and what a lovely voice he has. He's been likened to Aled Jones now." I smiled. That was something I had to hear.

"Bora da gentlemen." Hywel appeared.

"Bora da Hywel."

"Rather timely your visit today. We've got some concerns with the waste. Roof beginning to break up in front of the chock canopies."

"Come on then let's go and have a looksee." I turned towards Bleddyn.

"If you don't mind Mister Gibson I'll give the lamproom a call. Get them to put a note on Asyn's lamp for the afternoon Face Deputy to pick up some dets." I was hoping it wouldn't come to that, but it sounded like we had little choice. I nodded and continued towards the face with Hywel.

Arriving at the maingate end we clambered onto the face. Ithel and two of his men were there. Stood with their backs to us. Looking into the waste. I followed their gaze.

"Bora da lads." Ithel turned towards me.

"Not good Mr Gibson. Look now it stretches for miles." Ithel's comment was a little exaggerated. The white sandstone sedimentary rock standing firm. Our cap lamps picking out and reflecting the minute quartz particles. The space between roof and floor seemed to go on for ever. One of the facemen stood next to Ithel commented.

"I remember some years ago in a similar situation the waste hanging like this. When it finally dropped flattened the face it did now. Collapsed the supports. We were using props and bars then. Luckily, it was between shifts."

"I. Remember Melvin Jones telling me. He was the Deputy that day. Heard a loud crack he did now just before it dropped."

From the waste as if in answer to Ithel's comment we heard a loud bang. "Like that?" I asked jokingly.

"For fucks sake!" As Ithel uttered his comment his two mates disappeared. Off like hares escaping a hound. "Fuckin run now." Ithel joined them. I couldn't see Hywel. I guessed he'd followed the other two. And then it happened as if in slow motion. A blast of warm dust laden air swept from the waste engulfing the face line. The power of it knocked me onto my back. The rumble of the rock hitting the ground sounded like thunder but much worse. I struggled to breath as the dust entered my throat and nose. Placing my hands over my face I turned to face the floor. It seemed to go on forever. And then silence. Complete and total silence. I had my eyes closed. For what seemed like an eternity I lay there.

"Mr Gibson, Mr Gibson you okay now?" I couldn't answer immediately. It was Bleddyn accompanied by Hywel. I lifted myself up. I still couldn't see.

The tannoy system suddenly burst into like. "Hello Hywel, hello Hywel." In the background the sound of alarms clearly heard in the control room. "You got a problem in there? All the methane alarms have gone off outbye of the return." Someone at the stage loader answered. "It's okay Lewis now. Waste has finally dropped."

"Thanks, got that." I was now back on my feet.

"Guess we won't be needin those dets!" I responded.

"Mick you've got to see it to believe it."

"Denny I'm busy."

"You'll lose out; yon fella next door will have it."

"And?"

"You'll regret it. All your Christmas's come at once. Undermanager's dreams come true."

"And why would that be?"

"Well for starters you're always bloody moaning you haven't got enough men. The time you lose preparing for a visit. You'll be getting Brownie points big time. And don't forget the arse kicking you got recently off Mr. Groves when that photographer visited 43's."

I'd just come up the pit, Denny had spent all day in the surface workshops.

"You've got nothing to lose the lad's set it up outside the workshop he's waiting for us now." Reluctantly I rose from my chair I'd finish signing the reports later.

"Come on then let's see what all the excitement is about. Tell you what though let's go the long way round I want to check on the supplies the guys have loaded for the afternoon shift."

Leaving my office, we entered the main car park and headed towards the stores office. It was a warm sunny spring day. To our right the old harbour moorings where the coal boats used to load up in days gone by. It was a magical scene the sun reflecting off the sea's surface blinding our vision. The sea birds breaking cover as we walked forward. Hard to believe this was the scene above ground while three hundred metres below the lads were working in the dirt and dust extracting coal. My mood lightened.

"Denny did I ever tell you the time we had a visit from the General Manager? He and the Manager had come to see F43's after we'd completed the installation. I was feeling quite pleased with myself. We'd completed the installation early. Exceeding the Manager's expectations. The General Manager had asked me how things were with the family since we'd moved to Wales. The weekend before I'd taken the kids down to the river Clwyd. Wanted to give the missus a break. It was a Sunday. I was stood with them with our wellies on. The kids with their fishing nets trying to catch the tiddlers. It was a day very much like today warm, sunny with a slight breeze running in from the coast. I remember looking up to take in my surroundings. The Clwydian mountains to my right, to the left a 14th Century church and directly ahead the 13th Century castle built by old Long Shanks. I responded by telling him it was like being on holiday. I didn't give it much thought at the time although I do recall him looking towards the Manager and raising an eyebrow." I looked towards Denny to check he was still listening.

"After I got up the pit later that day Mr. Groves sent for me. I went along to his office ready for praise and acknowledgement of what we'd achieved but do you know what I got the biggest bollocking ever. He told me I wasn't here on holiday I was here to work. And if I ever made a comment like that again I've be going on one permanent holiday." I turned again towards Denny. Up to that point he hadn't made any comment.

"I cock you've told me that tale before."
"For fuck's sake Denny why didn't you stop me from waffling on?"
"You seemed to be enjoying your recollection of the event. I thought I'd just let you continue." Our conversation was interrupted as a plume of white dust rose from the side of the workshops followed by a number of cheers.
"Looks like they've started without us."

We were greeted by Denny's assistant, Gethin and two lads from the workshops. One of them quite short in height. They were standing around a five-gallon hydraulic fluid drum connected to a length of inch compressed air bagging attached to the bottom of the drum. Gethin was holding a three-inch hose connected to the other side. Stonedust was being projected into the air for a height of at least twenty feet.
"Bloody hell I'd have to have seen it to believe it," Denny shouted above the noise. We both walked forward to the other three.

"Undermanager this is Rick, Little Rick to his mates." I leaned forward and shook his hand. He had the gentlest of handshakes.
"Hello Rick."
"How do you do now Mr Gibson. I hope you like it now." The other guy had wandered off to switch off the supply of compressed air. "If you look I've welded in the bottom a small venturi. Like you use underground for dispersing firedamp." Gethin gave Little Rick a pat on the back.
"Such a simple but effective idea now."
"Can I get the lads to take it down this afternoon and give it a try."

86

"Of course, you can Mr Gibson. I'm sure it will do the job now."

"Thanks Rick, I'll let you know how it goes. Thanks again. Unfortunately, I need to keep moving. Overtime meeting shortly"

"Bloody hell is that time already cock. I'll walk across with you." Denny added. Shaking hands with Rick and Gethin we headed back to the office.

"Denny, don't forget I need a couple of lads for the PPM's Saturday." Gethin shouted after us.

"Oright cock." We continued walking. "I meant to mention. Gethin suggested we get together with the wives at the weekend and go for a bite to eat. You up for it?"

"Sounds like a plan. Let me check with the missus and see how we're fixed for a babysitter."

"Haven't asked you in a while. Are things any better with Mrs Gibson settling in?"

"Do'y know what Den I'm not sure she'll ever really settle."

"Not being funny with ya lad. Need to get a bit tougher. Show her who's boss..."

Returning home that night I'd had plenty to think of from the day's events. There had to be a better way of dealing with Paul Adder. He seemed to block anything I was trying to do. He always wanted control.

"Hi kids where's Mum." James and Elizabeth were sat in front of the TV watching Scooby Doo. Without turning James replied.

"She's in a mood Dad. Upstairs she's been crying again."

"Okay I'll go and have a chat with her. You two okay then?" I didn't receive an answer other than Elizabeth turning to her brother and saying.

"Told you he was the baddy." She was pointing at the screen. A police officer had removed a mask off some ugly guy. Velma, Daphne, Scooby, Shaggy, and Fred looked on. Scooby making that funny noise when they've discovered the truth. Followed by "scooby, scooby doo..."

My wife was sitting on the bed looking at some old photos. She looked towards me as I entered the room. Her eyes were red and bloodshot.

"You okay?"

"No, I'm not."

"What's up?"

"You know what. This whole situation. Been on the phone today to Mum. Dad's got worse and I'm here. I can't offer any help."

"Listen we'll go down at the weekend." She seemed not to hear.

"I went into Prestatyn today for my blusher. Boots in Huyton always had my colour. Not in this one horse town though. They'd never heard of Elizabeth Arden. Said she didn't work there! Until I explained it was the name of a brand.

The next delivery of make-up would be at the end of the month. Everything in the shops seems so expensive. Mick I want to go home." She began to cry.

"Come on now." Sobbing she continued to explain how bad she felt.
"I take the kids to school. Come home. Take the dog out and then nothing. All on my own. Till it's time to pick the kids up again. I'm still young I need a life. I can't do this anymore."
I'd been warned of days like this both by the Manager and Denny. Denny had suggested it had taken his wife two years to accept the move. Which was a little discouraging as it meant there was still eighteen months to go. We'd arranged a night out at the kids school's PTA Barn Dance. Even that hadn't gone down too well after Denny's missus had suggested to my wife "*a good man, a good man. I ask ye, it's easier finding Dobbie horse shit.*"
"Come on it'll be fine. Denny's suggested we go for a meal at the weekend. I'll go and make a cuppa. We'll have a chat when the kids go to bed."

Later that evening we sat down. "As I said before we'll leave early Saturday morning. We could even stay overnight."
"What about the dog?" The phone began to ring. That's all I needed. I looked towards her apologetically. "It's no good looking at me. It'll be for you. The bloody pit as always."

I climbed out the chair without responding. What could I say. I walked into the hallway.
"Hello. Oh, hi Gruffyd. Right you've sorted now. How the hell did that happen. Okay speak again later. By the way, any feedback on Rick's duster? Excellent." I put the phone down and walked back into the room. "Problem on the face…"
"Mick I'm not interested." She got up and walked back out into the kitchen. My mind wandered back to the conversation with Denny earlier. We needed to be firm with our wives. In his words "don't take any shit cock. Show her who's boss."

I went upstairs into our bedroom. From the bottom of the wardrobe I pulled out a suitcase. I'd had enough. It was bad enough dealing with what I had at work let alone coming home to this as well. With both hands I grabbed a bundle of her clothes, still on the hangers and thrust them into the case.
Without zipping it up I took it downstairs. My wife had sat down to watch Dallas. I threw the bag onto the floor. "If you're not happy then go on go!" The silence that followed was broken by Sue Ellen giving JR a mouthful. I realized I'd gone too far from the change in my wife's eyes. They seemed to switch. I'd seen that look before.

She jumped up and reached towards the fireplace. I needed no further encouragement. I ran from the room and up the stairs. Mrs Gibson in hot pursuit accompanied by the poker in her right hand. Taking the stairs two steps at a time I just made it into out bedroom. I closed the door and placed all my weight behind it. What followed was a little disconcerting to say the least. She gently tapped the door with the poker. Obviously not wanting to wake the kids. How considerate gently whispering. "You'll have to sleep at some point, and I'll be waiting."

So much for me trying to show who's boss. Thanks for the advice Denny.

Wednesday was generally the day we had the overtime meeting chaired by the Deputy Manager. This weekend we'd planned quite a bit of work in the North Headings. I wanted to be sure of all the facts around what we'd be doing I'd arranged to go with Bleddyn and visit the place. The only tunnels in Zone B where the development wasn't in coal. Due to an upthrow fault we were using drill and fire to regain access to the Two Yard coal seam. Setting sixteen by seventeen foot arches on a gradient of one in four we estimated a drivage of some forty metres in stone. The lads in the heading were mostly ex Cemco contractors. Well versed in the drill and fire technique.

The overtime meeting was one of the few meetings where I never had complete control of the outcome. It was I suppose quite an adversarial event. The Deputy Manager having the final say on what was allowed. The one thing you never did as Undermanager was go in unprepared. Paul Adder liked to dominate. This being one of the few places he could. I didn't like that.

The work we were looking to carry out on the Saturday and Sunday was to remove belt structure in a tunnel we used as a dumping ground for the extracted stone. Rather than being sent out on the conveyor belts up the Drift to the surface it was simply redirected into a disused tunnel. A conveyor suspended from the roof took the dirt to the far end where a plough removed it. Depositing on the ground below. As the dirt built up the conveyor return end was simply shortened off and the plough repositioned further outbye. A track mounted Hausherr bucket was then used to compact the material to the roof. Ideally to avoid the build-up of methane as the ventilation ducting was retracted.

After checking the inbye shunts for supplies Bleddyn and I continued inbye to our destination.

"Any reason why we store the dirt underground Bleddyn?"

"Coal Prep couldn't handle it now. Whole place came to a grinding halt. Lost a day's production underground. Manager want very happy. Sulked for a whole week if I remember. Blamed your predecessor he did now. One of many occasions. Suppose that's why he left. I think it was mutual." I nodded.

"Think it best if we go see the lads now." Good bunch of lads they be now."
We arrived at the entrance of the district. The Meeting Station looked quite
impressive all neat and tidy. We continued forward on the flat. The conveyor to
our right was stood idle. After a hundred yards the brew began to climb. A
mound of hessian sandbags piled up with the shotfiring cable reel to our left.
The Beethoven 100 Shot Exploder was hanging from an electrical cable hanger
secured to the mesh, pigtails cable suspended. At this point I could hear the
unmistakable sound of the percussive drills. The closer we got the hammer
action of the drilling becoming louder and louder. I reached up and pulled down
on my ear protectors. I turned to see Bleddyn had done the same.

In the distance I could see the heading team. Not clearly, they were shrouded
in a light mist of dust and water spray. I counted three of them. Two holding on
to the drilling machines suspended on the extendable legs. A number of hoses
trailing from each with its own yellow oil bottle. Even at that distance I could
smell the mineral oil mixed with the dust laden air. One man was stood away
from his machine. It was still operating at least eight feet off the ground. Very
impressive. I'd seen it done once before whilst I was training at Bold colliery. A
fourth person who I assumed to be the shotfirer was stood looking into a half
cut mine car. He looked up as he saw us approaching. It was Edwin, better
known as VG. We arrived at the tailend of the conveyor. Over which sat a metal
chute. The tailend protected by an inch thick plate of steel.

Above the din of the three drill machines VG greeted us both. "Bora da
gentlemen." The noise was excruciating. Without looking at the persons mouth
I wouldn't have understood what they were saying.
"Bora da Edwin. How are you?"
"Good thank you Mr Gibson. Nice to see you've brought our Bleddyn in to see
us." Edwin's comment referencing Bleddyn was due to the family connection.
They were cousins. My eyes unintentionally wandered over Edwin's distorted
features. From what Bleddyn had told me the accident to his face had happened
at a colliery near Wrexham, Llay Main. Edwin had been a shotfirer on the coal
face. They'd operated with a stable at the maingate end. He'd been in a rush as
the shearer approached. Rather than retreat to the requisite distance he'd
positioned himself between the chocks before firing. Rumour had it his
damaged eye was only found on the following noon shift. Falling from the
canopy of a chock as it was moved in.

I was staring which I knew to be wrong. The side of his face didn't actually
look too bad. More like severe acne. It was only when he removed his ear
protector. There was no ear to protect. I assumed that's how he'd received his

nickname VG. The part that caught my closest attention was where his eye should have been. The skin from the eyelid had been pulled over the empty socket. Behind it however was movement. Each time his good eye moved in a direction the missing eye did likewise. It was fascinating or so I though. He repositioned the ear protector as he caught me looking. "Just finishing off the last few holes and we'll be ready to charge." As he finished the sentence the last of the machines became silent.

Embarrassed I turned away. I pointed to the side ranters. At least ten metres back from the face. I regretted the action immediately. "We'll move them in later. Lads moved them back to avoid any damage." Pointing to the roof, "same with the horseheads." These too were well away from the face of the heading.

"Ready VG." One of the three men shouted. I guessed it was Larry. He was the chargehand.

"Sorry gents." Edwin stood. "Want to get this fired off and cleaned up before the noonshift arrive." We following him to the half cut mine car. It was painted red. Either side painted in white the words *Powder Cart.* Lying alongside was the det pouch. Open already. Each det colour coded. He must have been checking as we arrived. Pinned to the side was a signed copy of the Manager's Scheme of Transit.

The heading team walked towards us. Each carrying a drilling machine with the leg still attached. They all wore red helmets. Tom, Rick, and Larry. I smiled you couldn't make it up. Larry as usual wasn't wearing any ear protection.

"Morning lads. Larry where's your ear defenders?"

"Bora da Mr Gibson." Tom and Rick responded. Larry smiled. He hadn't heard a word I'd said.

"I see you've brought old Bleddyn in with you." Tom continued.

"Hey. Less of the old ye cheeky fucker. You're not too big for me to give you a good hiding now." They all laughed. Tom and Rick having put the drill machines to one side grabbed two canisters of explosive in each hand and walked back to the face of the heading. Each canister containing the regulation five pound of explosive. Edwin followed them with his det pouch.

"Hold it Rick." Bleddyn shouted. The pouch he was carrying hadn't been secured. The short narrow brown paper sticks of P1 explosive left a trail as they fell. "We don't want to be blowing up the Undermanager now do we." Rick retraced his steps as he retrieved the sticks. Larry offered his hand. "Good to see you Mr Gibson but if you don't mind now we have our target to keep."

"Good to see you too Larry. Where's your ear defenders. I've told you before."

"Eh?"

"Ear defenders

"More like your bonus." Bleddyn added.

"I that too now." Larry reached forward he too grabbed four canisters of explosive. The dets half second delay – indicated by the colour of the leading wires red and yellow – a plastic tag attached to the wire indicating the delay period numbered one to ten, total delay of five seconds. They'd drilled a total of forty holes using the Wedge cut pattern. They left one of the drill rods in one of the holes to indicate its angle.

The lads were busy I didn't want to delay them. I followed them to the face of the heading. The Eimco bucket had been lowered they'd be using that to climb on when charging the trimmers. Before firing they'd track it back towards the tail end of the belt leaving the bucket in the raised position. I turned to Bleddyn pointing to some handmade stemming standing on the side. I shook my head. These lads preferred the old ways. Making up their own stemming by adding water to the soft dirt. It created a soft firm clay. Boxes of sand stemming were available. As too were the new water ampoules. These guys were the professionals and preferred the old ways. Who was I to comment they'd been doing this for years. I'd also seen a scraper at the meeting station not that I'd ever seen it used. Each firing cleared enough ground for two arches.

I watched as Edwin primed each stick. Placing it into the hole with the detonator leading. Followed by two further sticks of P1. Then using the wooden ramming rod to push the explosives to the end of the hole. He then moved onto the next. Leaving the lads to stem up. I smiled. I guessed if I hadn't been there all four would have mucked in together placing the explosives into each hole. I turned to Bleddyn it was time we made a move back to land.

-

As we left the North heading Bleddyn suggested we try a different route out to pit bottom. It would help me get to know all the areas currently ventilated in Zone B. The route would take us through the old stables. He'd mentioned it previously about there being such a place. It was only after a conversation I'd had with Dai in the lamproom. As a lad he'd looked after the pit's ponies. A task given to most of the young lads when they started in the pit. He explained how the use of horses was ended towards the end of 1960's. Those left were put out to pasture in the fields surrounding the entrance to the mine.

"So, this is it?" We'd arrived, I'd guessed not that the area looked anything like a conventional stable. The individual units had no stable door. The giveaway were the troughs where I assumed they were given food and water. Against the side of the roadway hay nets still in place. I counted at least fifteen individual stalls.

"I'm told there was a total of four separate stables. There was about sixty horses kept underground. Me coming from Llay Main I'm not sure of all the detail. Dai in the lamproom used to look after them."

"Yeah he mentioned it to me." In the distance I heard the repeated sound of a dull thud. "What the hell was that?"

"North heading."

"Of course. The delay sounds a lot closer than half a second."

I moved into one of the stalls to take a closer look. "Bloody hell Bleddyn look there's a name plate still in place. Dick."

"I now. I think Dai's Dad used one called Turpin."

"Now you're taking the piss."

"I kid you not Mr Gibson. Why ever would I want to do that now?"

"They weren't kept down here all the time were they?"

"No shut down during the annual holidays taken to the surface they were now. Most anyway. Had to keep their eyes covered as you can imagine."

"What a sad life."

"It wasn't all bad. Some lived to be twenty years old."

"Were any injured?"

"I guess so. I'm not aware of any incidents myself. Although I 've heard stories of how the lads had to get the dead pony out of the pit. Had to break their legs to get them on the vehicles in one piece now."

"Oh dear, that's sad."

"There's even tales of ponies saving men from injury. Dai's Dad when he worked here claimed Turpin stopped him dead one day in a newly formed roadway. Dragging wooden props to the coal face it was. The days when miners had their own stint and operated on piece work. Well before PLA came into being. No matter what he tried it wouldn't budge. Then without warning the side came in it did." I stood listening to the tale being recounted by Bleddyn. Took me back to when I first started in the pit. Listening to the stories from the old pit men including many from Poland and Germany who'd been through the Second World War.

"That's a rather smart looking box. What was it used for?"

"Cartridges for killing horses."

"What? Tell me you're kiddin."

"I kid you not Mr Gibson. Never seen it used but we had apparatus for killing them if badly injured." The thought of it was upsetting I changed the subject.

"What are those for?" I pointed to what looked like a number of miniature arches."

"Manhole arches. We've used them on the main tunnel and to create a rat run behind number three shaft."

"What are they doin here?"

"No reason. Just left them here in case we ever need them. You never know what they'll come in handy for."

"Come on best get a move on or we'll be late for the overtime meeting."

-

"I'm just nipping out to the canteen for some snap. Do you want anything now?"

"No thanks Bleddyn fine thanks."

"The overtime list is on the desk. Don't forget meetings at two. Mr Adder is quite particular we get there on time."

"Yeah seen it I'll have a check through." I was attending my first overtime that afternoon. Bleddyn had suggest he accompany me.

My mind drifted back to the first time I'd experienced overtime at a mine. It was the first place I worked at. A Sunday morning. Seven till one. Treble time as against a Saturday when it was double time. As a "traveller." The role was to accompany a Deputy during his inspection of the underground districts. It was stipulated that a traveller remain a certain distance behind the Deputy. This was to ensure if the Deputy walked into an area containing gas, the traveller could raise the alarm.

One particular shift a team of heading men had been coaling. They'd been given a set target of four yards or four sets of square work to complete. Once done they could head off home. The practice of "job and knock" was used extensively as an incentive during those days. Coal at the time was wound to the surface in a series of mine cars. As it was the weekend coal winding very rarely took place. Any coal or dirt that was mined was stored in a series of underground bunkers. The bunkers being fed by a number of conveyors. At that time none of the underground conveyors could be operated remotely. A person was required at each transfer point to stop and start the conveyor.

As one of the transfer point attendants had been taken ill they requested my help in manning up the place he'd vacated. That transfer point was C1. One of three conveyors passing through the wettest parts of the mine. The C stood for the seam area passed through. Crombouke. C1 was situated at the end of a dip which narrowed as it turned off in a separate direction. Here was the tailend of the next conveyor C2. Because of the reduced area the ventilation velocity increased. Standing there with the air passing through was quite uncomfortable.

To avoid the transfer point attendant getting wet. A manhole had been hewn out of the surrounding coal. The roof and sides supported by wooden slats and

94

covered in hessian sandbags, A bench had been installed alongside the tannoy and white metal box below which protruded a stubby metal pull/push handle. By underground standards it was probably the most comfortable transfer point anywhere in the pit. The downside however was the stopping opposite. The stopping one of two sealed off an old disused district. Three years previously a methane explosion had occurred killing a Deputy and electrician. Many of the younger lads said they'd seen the ghost of the Deputy passing the manhole his oil lamp hanging from his side.

I tried to put the thought out of my mind as I climbed in to take up my position. I hung my safety lamp at the edge of the entrance. The oil lamp unlike that carried by the Deputy was not a relighter. As the outbye conveyor was running I started C1. And that was it. All I had to do was ensure the outbye belt was running. If it stopped I used the tannoy to advise the Control Room. I made myself comfortable positioning the plastic bag containing my snap I hung it from the roof. Although comfortable the downside of the manholes position was very little ventilation entered the enclosed area. Within minutes I began to feel tired.

Sat in the upright position it hadn't taken long before I fell into a deep sleep. I could see the deputy walking towards me smiling. He looked a friendly sort of chap. However, as he came closer I could see both of his eyes were missing. The sight of this caused me to stir. I was in that place where you're half awake and half asleep. My eyes began slowly taking in the surrounding area. I saw my bag of snap moving of its own accord. I could feel movement on my thighs and chest. Tiny feet running in all directions. The more I regained consciousness the more apparent the feeling became. The sound of the tannoy and voices shouting "number three bunker is stopped. Number three bunker is stopped." The voices becoming louder and louder.

Now fully awake my anxiety level was exaggerated when I realized my snapping was under attack from at least four moggies. A further six were on me as the crumbs fell from my sandwiches onto my body. The shock of it caused me to jump and flick the creatures in all directions. The squeals of indignation echoing from each as they scurried from my reach. The upside though as I jumped from the manhole was to see coal pilling up in the chute of my conveyor and spilling onto the tailend of C2.

That was some years ago now. I picked up the list Bleddyn had left. A knock at the door caused me to look up. It was Paul Taylor.
"You ready?"
"What?"

"Overtime meeting it's nearly two."

"Oh yeah I'm ready just waiting for Bleddyn we'll meet him there." I climbed out of the chair and followed Paul along the corridor.

A small group were already assembled outside the Deputy Manager's office. My two colleagues Denny and Gregor plus their opposite numbers in Zone A. Dafydd Jones the Deputy Electrical Engineer and Owain Jones the Deputy Mechanical Engineer.

"Oright cock?"

"I all good thanks Denny." I replied.

"Have ye got list cock?"

"Certainly have."

The Deputy Manager's office was situated alongside the main entrance to the management suite. I heard the swing doors to the entrance open.

"Not started then?" Bleddyn asked no one in particular. Gregor however offered an answer.

"No Bled. It's one rule for him and another for us."

"For fucks sake Gregor keep your voice down." Dafydd responded.

"Will I fuck. I get here in the dark and by the time this charade has finished I'll be goin home in the dark."

"Fuck me Gregor you're in a right one."

"You'd be the same if you'd just found out there's no armoured cable in the stores. It stops us doing a move up in the North this weekend."

"That's if he gives you the shifts cock." Denny offered.

I stood listening to the comments from my colleagues. I sensed a nervousness as they waited. I guessed the overtime meeting was not as straight forward as I'd imagined. At the last pit you could never get all the overtime slots filled.

"What's the hold up anyway?"

"Manager's in there with him." Dafydd responded to Paul. Then without warning the door opened. It was the Manager. He said nothing. One by one we walked in. Paul Adder was sat eyeing each one of us as we entered. I was somewhat taken aback by the small table opposite his desk. There were six chairs three either side. Bleddyn was the last person to enter.

"You may want to get another chair Bled."

"Bled you take mine I'll get another." I offered as I stood up.

I quickly made my way into reception. Bronwen was sat at her desk. She was typing.

"Mind if I borrow a chair."

"Help yourself Cariad. Just as long as I get it back now." She responded without taking her eyes off whatever she was writing. Making my way back in the meeting had already started. I placed the chair at the head of the table directly opposite Paul Adder.

"Access haulage three lads Sat and Sun days." Paul Taylor asked.

"No. Man up between shift during the week." Mr Adder responded.

"Two men on back up in 61's headings Saturday dayshift and afternoons."

"No." *Gosh this looks fun* My colleagues all sat heads down facing the table in front. All accept Gregor. I guessed he was about to say something.

"Access 2 Saturday morning. three men replacing damaged stitches."

"No. Do it between shifts. Time and a half is better than double." Adder's comment brought Gregor into the conversation.

"For fucks sake Mr Adder, we go through the same shite every week. Why don't you just tell us how many shifts are available without wasting everybody's time." I caught Denny giving him a gentle nudge in the side.

Paul Adder completely ignored Gregor's comment. "Next." Paul Taylor continued.

"Two men and one electrician salvaging DAC cable."

"No. Do it in the week." Dafydd looked towards him.

"Mr Adder if we don't salvage the cable we'll have no comms in 61's headings."

"One man and an electrician then."

"Thank you.". The conversation continued for a further ten minutes.

"Right Zone B." Bleddyn began reading from our list. He got the same reaction as Paul Taylor had received. However, he never faltered and continued reading.

"Two men and two electricians Saturday morning moving panels in for the North headings."

"No in the week. Between shifts." Of all the requests I knew this would be the most contentious. Gregor had commented on it at our morning meeting. I wasn't wrong.

"We don't have the staff between shifts. I use the electricians on the coal face."

"Next." Gregor's response completely ignored. Bleddyn looked towards me. I swear I could feel the tension in the room rise. From my own personal experience with Gregor I knew what he was capable of.

"We'll extend during the shift." I offered. Bleddyn looked at me as though I'd lost the plot.

"Stop the drivage?" He asked.

"If we can't get the men to do it between shifts and there's no weekend work I don't see any alternative. In fact, I'll give the Deputy a call straight after this." All eyes were now on me. All except Paul Adder. Silence descended. Slowly ever so slowly Paul Adder raised his head.

"Gentlemen could you give me a minute please. I'd like to speak with Mr Gibson in private." The room emptied in seconds. Bleddyn remained seated.

"You too please Bleddyn." He looked towards me. I nodded. He left. Adder waited until the door was shut.

"Let me be clear Mr Gibson I'm going to give you the benefit of the doubt. I'm in charge here. I give the instruction. You're relatively new so perhaps your unaware of protocol." I heard enough shite already without listening to this. It was time to put the man straight.

"Mr Adder forgive me for interrupting. Zone B is under my fuckin jurisdiction. I'm responsible as the Undermanager for what happens. That is and unless the Regulations have changed since we've been sat here. If I deem fit to stop the drivage that is my prerogative. My measure will be achieving the target as set out in the Action Programme. Like it or lump it no overtime this weekend the drivage stops this afternoon." Once more silence. He was staring at me. Wanting to say something but not sure what to say. Without warning the office door opened.

"You two okay?" It was the Manager.

"Yeah all good thanks Ron."

"Why's everyone else stood outside?" Without waiting for an answer, he ushered everyone in. The meeting only lasted another five minutes and I got the shifts requested for the weekend work.

–

"Have you decided who'll be replacing me now?"

"No not yet but I've got a fair idea." Afternoon shift had just gone underground. Bleddyn and I were sat in the office.

"You do know Mr Groves will expect you to appoint Arfon. He worked for him at Bersham he did now. He's his little blue eyed boyo." I'd already guessed as much. Arfon was never going to be my choice. He didn't carry the gravitas required for the job. I also didn't believe some of the long standing Point men completely trusted him.

"You're a nosey bugger Bleddyn but I'm not planning on appointing Arfon."

"Must be Evan you're thinking of then?"

"Bleddyn can you give it a rest. I haven't decided yet." He seemed not to hear. I was enjoying the banter with him though.

"The majority of the officials will be expecting Osian. They see him as my natural replacement. Next in line so to speak. They all have a lot of respect for him they do now. I know they're not keen on Evan." Bleddyn was not telling me anything I didn't know. It was something I planned to take up with Osian personally. Our conversation ended as the dayshift arrived up the pit.

The following week I got my chance with Osian. I was in the office and he'd arrived early for the afternoon shift. Bleddyn was still underground.
"Prynhawn da Mr Gibson."
"Oh, hi Osian. Good afternoon to you too. Do us a favour. Close the door please"
"Da iawn. Must be important now."
"Sort of. I wanted to get your thoughts on something."
"Let me guess now. Bleddyn's replacement." I smiled this guy was bright. He seemed to know everything that was going on. He certainly would have made a good replacement. "Not me and certainly not that little fucker Arfon. Evan would be my best bet."
"Thanks, Osian I'm glad we sorted that out with no fuss."

-

There was no leaving doo planned for Bleddyn something he'd specifically asked us not to do. I'd enjoyed my time with him. We'd been together just seven months. I'd learnt plenty. The two of us were sat in my office. Dayshift had gone home. The afternoon lads hard at it underground.
"Mind how you go now. I hope things work out for you what with the way the industry is heading."
"Sorry, Bleddyn whatever do you mean?"
"A mate of mine, ex Undermanager at Llay Main was tellin me over a pint at the weekend that the number of mines has dropped from before the '84-'85 strike from one hundred and sixty nine to eighty six."
"I can't believe that. I mean when I joined in '75 there was over two hundred and forty."
"And the number of employees has dropped from one hundred and thirty nine thousand to less than half. Sixty nine thousand actually."
"Sorry I find that hard to believe."

-

"Come on kids you go in the water first I'll follow."
"No Dad you get in you always make us go in first." Before I knew it, someone had pushed me into the sea.
"Mick, Mick wake up phone." I dragged myself reluctantly from my slumber. Since we'd gotten back from Majorca, I'd dreamt about our holiday most nights.

"What, what's up?"

"Phone, quick before it wakes the kids up." I jumped up and rushed down to the hallway. *I really need to get one of those mobile one's for around the house.*

"Down, down no jumping up Sophie." Our cocker spaniel had come to greet me as I reached the hallway. I sat on the floor and let her lick my face. Our previous dog Heidi had died the year before.

"Hello."

"Mick sorry to bother you. We've had a fall on the face. Been stopped about an hour now Hywel reckons it could be another two before we get going."

"Anyone hurt?"

"Think it caught the shearer operator unawares but more of a shock than physical injury."

"Okay, tell Hywel I'm on my way I'll be there shortly. Make sure there's a loco waiting for me." I checked my watch two am, another four hours before the dayshift would arrive.

Within ten minutes I was on my way. I'd locked the dog in the kitchen, the kids hadn't woken. By the time I'd got back upstairs Mrs. Gibson was asleep. At that time in the morning the roads were empty. I watched my speed travelling through Meliden as I'd been cautioned once before. Within fifteen minutes I'd arrived. Not bothering to go into the office I headed straight for the baths. Changed I picked up my tallies. There was no one about in the lamproom, however my cap lamp, rescuer and oil lamp had been placed on a table outside the office. How thoughtful.

I headed towards the No 3 downcast shaft. The two decked cage was in position. The chain mesh gate lifted and secure.

"Bloody hell Mr. Gibson now that didn't take long." It was the Banksman. I passed him my silver tally.

"Yeah no one about at this time of the morning." I walked into the cage and dropped the mesh gate myself.

"Have a gooden. Wela i chi."

"Thanks." I then heard the keps retracted with a thud.

Within seconds I was dropping at a rate of knots. The cold damp fresh smell of the intake air greeted me as I descended. I shivered; I was in complete darkness. Out of nowhere a flash of light. I'd passed the first inset leading to the older part of the mine. Then the second. The cage passed with a whoosh of air. Within minutes the cage began to slow. The sound of leaking compressed air becoming louder.

The cage stopped, air hissing all around then the deafening sound of metal on metal as the platforms were dropped.

"Your carriage awaits you Mr. Gibson!" It was the Onsetter he'd got to the gate before me and lifted the mesh.

"Thanks." By carriage he'd meant the loco. It was positioned some ten yards away. Closer than the designated manrider station. I could see the driver he was stood. He waved I waved back. It looked like Tomos. I walked quickly towards the vehicle and climbed onboard. Tomos tooted his whistle twice and we were off.

I was sat sideways on feeling quite uncomfortable being rather warm and inhaling the nitrous oxides emitted from the loco's exhaust. The lights from pit bottom became fainter in the distance as we travelled at speed along the main loco tunnel. I lolled about in my confined space to the rhythmic bouncing of the loco body against the rails. I began to drift back to sleep once more. The memory of the sun on my back from the recent holiday still playing on my mind. My body still clean and refreshed from the days spent with the kids in the sea. Now enclosed by my dirty smelly overalls.

The loco came to a sudden stop. My past thoughts extinguished as reality hit me once more. We'd arrived at the alighting station. I climbed out and for the first time switched on my cap lamp. Placing it in position on my helmet and fixing it to the clasp at the rear.

"Thanks, Tomos."

"You have a good shift now Mr Gibson. Wela I chi."

"You know more than me Tomos I wasn't planning on spending a full shift in there." I walked quickly passing through the Two Way Meeting Station towards the 1 in 4 Durbog manrider. The conveyor was running as I turned the corner towards the getting on platform. There was no taking it away from these guys everything was in place to get me to 43's post haste.

Alighting the conveyor after two hundred yards I headed towards the airdoors leading me to the Access Road. Grateful for the cold intake air that hit me as soon as I passed through the last door. I was now fully awake and began to walk quickly down the 1 in 4 brew. The forty eight inch Access conveyors to my left, three in total continued to send a trickle of the black stuff from the development heading from Zone A. The area for the next coal face 61's? It wasn't long before I'd built up a sweat. It began to trickle down my chest. It was another twenty minutes before I reached the tail end of Access 3. Turning to my right I passed under the gib of the two-way manriding conveyor. I followed the belt line for another thirty yards before jumping on to continue my journey. Riding the conveyor, I began to cool. It wasn't long before a shiver ran down my back.

Twenty minutes later I'd arrived at the return end of the coal face. The place was littered with supplies. Chock wood, split bars, six foot wooden props, six by two mesh panels and three by three RSJ's. The regulation bundles of wooden dowels and boxes of resin lay close to the snicket.

"Bora da Mr Gibson. Hope you didn't leave the missus unfulfilled, did you now?"

"Now Hugh that's no way to speak to the Undermanager. He's only upset Mr Gibson cause his next-door neighbour is probably giving his missus what he can't."

"Gents I can assure you my missus is sound asleep sex would be the last thing on her mind. Anyway, enough about my sex life where's Hywel?"

"I'll give you one guess where our Face Overman is."

"Up the hole doing what he does best!"

"Hugh send that next run of chock wood down." A voice shouted out from the face tannoy. Hugh reached across.

"Will do boyo." He released the lockout button and hit the signal twice. Immediately the pre-starter alarm on the AFC rang out. The chock wood was already loaded on the pans.

"Catch you guys later." I'd begun to perspire again I could feel the sweat dripping down the front of my shirt.

I headed down towards the fall area. Within minutes I could see lights ahead.

"For fucks sake!"

"Grab the lad." The commotion ahead was evident as I approached. The four lights I could see were suddenly joined by one dropping from above.

"Fuckin gas. Get me some more slack on the bagging and reposition the air mover."

"Bora da Mr Gibson."

"Hi lads." I could see Hywel lying flat out beyond the first two facemen. He seemed dazed but uninjured.

"You okay Hywel." He sat up as one of the men passed him a bottle of drinking water.

"Yeah my fault. There's a thick layer of methane we'd been diluting with the air mover. I should have moved it closer." The sound of the panzer came to an abrupt halt.

"Timber's here lads."

"Go'n have a minute in the maingate." I suggested to Hywel.

"No, I'll be fine." He attempted to lift himself in the confined space between the chocks. Still dazed through lack of oxygen he sat down again.

"Well sit there for a minute at least."

I walked forward and climbed onto the pans to look above the chock canopies. They'd done an excellent job on the timbering. The three by three RSJ's laid perpendicular across three sets of chocks. Covering a ten-foot area back from the coal face. The highest point at least eight foot. There was one more chock stack to build.

"Now then Mr Gibson if you don't mind could you start passing me that there chock wood." Hanging my oil lamp on the nearest support I duly obliged.

"Hello Hywel, hello Hywel. Any idea when we'll be coaling again?" He leaned forward to the nearest tannoy.

"Shouldn't be long now say another thirty minutes." I wasn't so sure.

"Hywel if you don't mind me suggesting."

"Yeah?"

"I noticed the dowels and resin in the return road. Why not get some in before you start up?"

"What about coaling? We've not completed a full shear yet."

"I'd sooner spend the time now getting it right. There's no guarantee those coal tops will stay up. I'm guessing the dowels would do the job."

"What about Adder?"

"Let me worry about him. He seems to have lost interest in what's happening underground whilst Grovesey's away. Can't get him out of the office. Oh, and see if you can get the lads to stay on and make a proper job of it."

"Will do, you heading off then?"

"Yeah I'll see if I can get a couple of hours sleep and come in later. Any idea where Delwyn is?"

"He'll be back on top now. Don't tend to see him if there's a cavity to pack!"

Arriving back at the pit later that morning I headed straight to the Control Room. The coal face was in good order and on to its third shear. Hywel and the team had obviously done a good job. I decided to pop in and see Paul Adder. I wasn't planning on going back underground as I had an appointment with the new Coal Prep Manager Lyn Garvey at two. He was going to show me around the plant. Something I knew little of. I headed up to the Manager's office. Bronwen was at her desk.

"Hello you, is he in?"

"Well now you wouldn't be expectin him to be underground?" I laughed. "He's on the phone to Mr. Groves giving him an update I'm sure he won't mind you going in."

Paul was sat with his legs outstretched on the Manager's desk. The phone handset was cradled under his chin. He was peeling a tangerine.

"Yeah Ron we lost the best part of a shift. Coal tops down exposing a cavity I thought it best the lads complete the timbering and put some dowels in before we start up." He gestured towards me to take a seat. "My decision paid off we're on the third shear now. I'm guessing well have done five by the end of the shift."

I sat expressionless *the cheeky bastard listening to him you'd think he'd been there himself. Come to think of it had he been underground at all over the last two weeks?*

"You're coming in at the weekend? I wouldn't bother have the full two weeks off. It'll still be the same Monday." We sat for what seemed like an eternity staring at one another. "Okay see you then enjoy what's left of your holiday." He replaced the receiver.

"Where is he?"
"Betws-y-Coed, goes every year."
"Just thought I'd pop in and give you an update from last night but seems you have all the detail."
"Yeah I had a chat with Evan before he went down. You not going under today?"
"No, I'm with the Coal Prep Manager guy Lyn. He's showing me around the plant." I couldn't resist asking him. "What about you? Are you underground today?"
"I wish. I'm with the surveyors most of the day reviewing plans for the coal faces in the Two Yard at Strata Top. There's a possibility of seven in total." He popped a segment of the tangerine into his mouth.
"Right I'll be off then."

"I suppose you heard him telling Mr. Groves how busy he's been." Bronwen offered as I closed the Manager's door. "The only activity he's involved with is drinking coffee. I'm worn out making him drinks."
"Not to worry Cariad, the boss will be back Monday everything will be back to normal."
"Thank goodness."
"See you later." I headed towards the baths. Even though I wasn't going underground from what I'd seen of the Coal Prep Plant I was better in my pit gear.

–

Walking across towards the Plant I spotted James Runner. He waved.
"Bora da Mick could I have a word?" The question from James meant he was. Whether I wanted to or not." I walked towards him
"Morning James, what can I do for you on this fine day?"
"This weekend there's a high spring tide." I waited for further explanation.

"I'll need some of your lads to bag the top of No. 2 shaft."

"Why?"

"There's the possibility of flooding the pit bottom."

"Sorry James I'm still not with you. And what the hell is a high spring tide?"

"Exactly what it says something to do with the alignment of the sun and moon. Anyway, I'm no fuckin astrologer we get them a few times a month. Normally there's no problem but the lads down at the lifeboat station have warned me this will be big! Happened a few years back and we ended up floodin the pit bottom taking out all the electrics. I've already arranged with the surface foreman to bag along the estuary road."

"Okay I'll take your word for it. I'll ask Gruffyd to sort some lads for you this afternoon."

"Diolch. Where you off to?"

"Coal Prep meeting up with Lyn Garvey."

"Something else I meant to ask you. Next week the emergency winder will be on site. Something we're required to practice on once a year. I'm planning on using it in No. 2 shaft. Kill two birds with one stone so to speak it'll allow us to carry out a shaft inspection."

"Why do you need the emergency winder for that."

"No cage. The winder was removed just as you arrived here in eighty-eight. The reason I ask, do you fancy a go in the kibble with me?"

I hesitated for a moment.

"You're not scared of heights, are you?" I'd waited too long before answering James was grinning.

"Am I fuck!"

"You up for it then?"

"Count me in."

The emergency winder arrived as planned. It had travelled across from the Mines Rescue Station. It was a huge white mobile crane. An area to the side of the shaft marked out for it to be positioned. The base then secured to the ground. By the time I arrived I was feeling a little apprehensive. I couldn't back out now.

Arriving at the shaft side the bullet shaped kibble was in position. Large enough to accommodate us both.

"I thought you used a gong for signalling?" I'd seen James previously holding the device at the No3 Shaft.

"Nah, don't need it here. Shaft's not as deep Walkie Talkie will be fine. That is unless the battery runs out!"

"What?"

"Don't worry our procedures cover that. If we haven't spoken to anyone for at least twenty minutes they send a search party out." I wasn't sure what good a search party would do or if James were taking the piss. I decided not to pursue the conversation. James suggested we both face outwards as part way down the shaft there was a kink in the wall.

"If the kibble were to catch the side of it there's the potential for it to tip. We'd be thrown out."

"You've got to be fuckin jokin?"

"Oh, I wouldn't joke about thing like that. You're not frightened, are you?"

"Me no!"

"You just seemed a little hesitant getting into the cage. Any way not to worry I'll give you a shout as we approach the kink. If you're nearest to the wall it'll be just a matter of pushing the cage away from the side."

The whole conversation was making me feel uneasy and as, yet I hadn't looked down. When I finally did there was nothing to see. The beam from my lamp seemed lost in the expanse of darkness. I was surprised to see the shaft wall was constructed from segments of cast iron.

"I didn't realise the shaft wall was made from metal." James had his back to me. Holding his cap lamp, he was examining a length of drop pipe attached to a water garland.

"Yeah, the Mostyn Colliery Company when sinking the No 1 shaft sometime in the 1880's had to abandon it due flooding. After it was dewatered the cast iron tubbing was installed." James raised the Walkie Talkie.

"Stop winder, stop please." We came to an immediate stop alongside the tubbing. "There's two types of tubbing - English and German. Here you can see the flanges and reinforcing ribs are external. They contain no bolts. They rely on wedging the segments together. Whereas the German tubbing everything is internal, and they use bolts."

"Which is best?"

"Do I really need to answer that?" I smiled. "Winder continue the descent same speed."

"So, the No 1 and 2 shafts were the first be sunk?" I regretted the question as soon as I'd asked it. James seemed not to notice.

"Yep this shaft is six hundred and thirty feet deep and 9 foot wide. Upcast obviously. The cast iron tubbing was used through the superficial deposits, thereafter the walls are lined with brick."

"What about No 1?"

"About the same depth although that's fifteen feet wide. Used to be the downcast before No 3 was sunk. The lining the same as this."

"You may as well tell me about No3. I seem to remember some men were killed during the sinking?"

"That would have been before your time."

"Yeah some six years. Studied the incident during my time at college."

"They were using the Caisson method. Basically, an enclosed pressurised cabin. A break in the surrounding strata caused an inrush. Six of the poor bastards drowned. Two of which I think they got out alive but died later."

"Sad. I bet not many know that when travelling through the shaft."

"True. No3 is a thousand feet deep and eighteen feet wide. Lining again with cast iron tubbing but this time the brickwork was replaced by concrete.... Mick get ready to push kibble away from the side. Mick now..." I'd been so engrossed listening to James I hadn't noticed the approaching bend in the shaft. I looked down.

"For fucks sake.. what do you want me to do." The beam of my cap lamp shining on the bottom of the kibble which was now sat on the brickwork. We were still descending. This time not down the shaft the kibble itself was moving from its vertical position towards horizontal. I could feel James behind me trying to manoeuvre his body.

"Mick fuckin hell shove the fuckin thing before we get thrown out. Winder, winder stop. Stop now." The fear that had been with me at that point subsided. My survival instinct kicked in. Lowering myself to a kneeling position I pushed against the brickwork. Nothing. The position of the kibble to shaft wall was now lying at approximately sixty degrees. I hadn't taken much notice of James talking with the winder. I guessed he was arranging to raise the kibble. I pushed once more.

Success. The kibble once released swung across the shaft. From one side to the other. Complete silence.

"Winder, stop, winder stop." Still swinging from side to side the kibble ceased moving upwards. "Well Mr Gibson that was a first for me."

"Surprisingly, Mr Runner it was a first for me too and hopefully the last." As I was speaking I looked across to the offending brickwork. Even now the bend was not obvious. I guessed the main indication would be the narrowing distance between kibble and brickwork as you descended.

"Shall we continue?"

"Please do." We completed the examination without any further incident. It wasn't till I reached the surface I noticed my overalls were wet through. It certainly wasn't due to any external water.

-

Towards the end of the year we were seeing more and more visits from Government Ministers. Something I always enjoyed. It was pleasing to hear the comments from people who'd never been underground before. It was a chance to "show off" the excellent work the lads were doing. In addition, it was always nice to see the Deputy Manager underground escorting the various dignitaries. To hear his comments on what we'd done, how we'd done it and the reasons for. The common theme of the visits from comments I overheard were all about cost and the need to reduce it. Something to be fair Paul Adder had made abundantly clear from the day I'd started.

It was no surprise that some weeks later British Coal began to run a series of seminars on taking cost out of the business. For the Undermanager's in the Western Area this took place at Kemble Training Centre in Stoke-on-Trent.

The underlying theme was to increase productivity whilst reducing cost. This included Undermanager's creating and using ad hoc contracts for various pieces of work. Revisiting old districts and salvaging equipment. Particularly electric cables, rails, belt structure and pipework.

Improvements in the use of new technology and a greater emphasis on the use of heavy duty equipment became the norm. Face team numbers were drastically reduced as was the drive to increase the use of retreat mining. Three man heading teams became the standard throughout the UK.

The creation of the "Superpit" where separate collieries connected underground. Within the Western Area Bickershaw became a "Complex" connected to Parsonage and Golborne. In Staffordshire Hem Heath was connected to Florence to become the Trentham Complex, use made of one Coal Prep Plant to handle all the mineral mined from underground. Older less productive pits were closed. There was little the NUM could do. The biggest drive was the reduction in manpower. EVRS was extended.

By the end of my first year as Undermanager the number of operating pits had dropped from ninety four to eighty six. The workforce had reduced from seventy five thousand to sixty nine thousand. With little impact if any on production eighty six million tonnes of coal down to eighty four million tonnes. I hadn't realized it at the time but when I'd first joined the industry in 1975 the figures were even more astounding. Two hundred and forty one pits, a workforce of two hundred and fifty two thousand producing one hundred and seventeen million tonnes of coal.

"I don't believe it Denny. The only day we pick to walk the full length of the Drift we have a break down on the face."

"I know cock, just one of those things."

"What about a spare Universal coupling? According to Control we're having to send out to the manufacturer."

"Tell me about it cock. I mentioned it to Gerry last week. Problem is cock it's a new type of coupling."

"Oil filled?"

"No cock these are water with a fuseable plug tha knows."

"Hello Mr Gibson, hello Mr Gibson. Can you give Control a ring?"

"What the fuck now? Where's the nearest phone Den?"

"Probably tailend cock." I walked across to the tannoy. "Hi Lewis give us a mo. I'll call you as soon as I reach a phone."

"Thanks Mr Gibson." As soon as we reached the phone, I made the call.

"Yeah on my way now Lewis. How long has he been there? Okay. I see. We're on our way. Yeah Denny's with me."

"Denny you're not going to believe this. The Managers on the face. Making his way up to the tail end. He wants us both in there pronto." I put a further call through to the Face Overman Asyn. He confirmed the culprit had been a lump of dirt jamming behind the cutter.

Forty-five minutes later Denny and I entered 43's return gate. Denny had been chunnering on for the best part of that time. I hadn't taken much in as I was trying to have my excuse ready for the Manager when we arrived. Regardless that I couldn't prevent the lump of dirt I was still at fault. Something I accepted as the Undermanager of the only production face at the pit. What I'd have to explain was why we hadn't any spares at the pit. My thoughts were finally interrupted once more by Denny.

"It's times like this cock when we need to stick together. Gethin is on site he'll have made a start to get the old one off. Hopefully, the replacement will be here early afternoon. I'd make sure there's a loco on standby to fetch it straight in."

"Thanks for those words of wisdom Den but how come there's no spare at the pit."

"Ah, bit of confusion there cock. Gerry thought I'd ordered one and I thought he ordered one."

"For fucks sake. Did you guys never learn anything from Gerry I've got hold of the wrong end of the tape?"

We'd now reached the snicket. We lowered our heads to continue towards the return end. Rising once more I could see Mr. Groves. He had a face on him like a smacked arse. He didn't look happy.

"Mr Gibson a word please." He gestured for me to follow as he walked down the face. I turned to Denny, but he'd gone. So much for sticking together. As soon as we'd entered the face, he'd remained crouched grabbing an adjustable and joined the other two fitters and Gethin at the return end. Reluctantly I followed the Manager. Once we were out of earshot the onslaught began.

"How the fuckin hell do we end up in a position with no spare coupling in the district?" I stood there and took it. "Have you got nothing to say?"

"It seems that..."

"It seems what?" Obviously frustrated he was tapping his stick on the panzer.

"It seems that one had been on order but..." The tapping became louder.

"I don't want excuses." He was right of course. No excuse whatsoever could magic up a replacement coupling. I said no more. "Make sure you keep the noon shift over cutting." And that was the last thing he said.

I continued down to the main gate. Asyn was at the stageloader.

"You okay Mr Gibson?"

"Yeah thanks Asyn. Any news?"

"Oes coupling arrived about ten minutes ago now. Gruffyd is getting it loaded now."

"Excellent. Who's Overman on this afternoon?"

"Hywel."

"If I don't see him ask him to get the lads to stay over and coal until the nightshift arrive."

"I thought the Deputy Manager had stopped all the overtime?"

"And I've just started it again."

We got coaling again by two o'clock. With the overtime we made up for any lost production. Which was good news. However, I knew what to expect tomorrow from Paul Adder!

–

"Bring the kids with you."

"I'll check with the missus and let you know."

"I'll be there anyway about two on the opposite side to the old landing stage."

"Okay thanks hopefully see you later."

It was Saturday morning. My weekend on. Gerry had called in to pick up some gates the joiners had made. He planned to do some fishing later. By fishing he meant retrieving ley lines he'd positioned earlier that morning.

After he'd left I called Mrs. Gibson.

"Never mind fishing I need to go shopping. I can't get anything I want from the local shops you're going to have to take me into Rhyl."

"What can't you get?"

"My foundation."

"Your what?"

110

"Never mind you wouldn't understand. It's make-up. Something I could pick up in Liverpool any shop I walked into but not in this god forsaken hole. I don't know how people survive here. Plus, the kids are bored."

"I thought you were all off on a walk today."

"We did. I let them take their bikes down to that river whatever it's called."

"Clwyd"

"Who?"

"The River Clwyd."

"Whatever, we took some bread to feed the ducks but these two enormous swans appeared. Your daughter, you know what she's like with animals. Tried to feed it. Bit her finger she's been crying ever since and wants you." I smiled as I listened it always amused me how they were my kids whenever anything went wrong. "Anyway, you need to get home you promised we'd move here for a better life. All you seem to do is work."

She had a point this was my third weekend on the trot. It was supposed to be one in three; however, the face installation was behind schedule I felt obliged to be there.

"Okay get the kids ready I'll make a move shortly."

I arrived home and took them all into Rhyl. As a treat we called into McDonalds.

"What we doin after Dad?"

"Best ask your Mum. We could go and watch someone I know at work fishing."

"That sounds cool Dad, can we?" Mrs. Gibson now in a far better mood that we'd found a shop that sold Elizabeth Arden agreed.

"Will they need wellies?"

"No, I wouldn't think so plastic sandals should be good enough. We'll be walking on sand."

We arrived back at the pit half an hour later than planned. Gerry had suggested I take my car towards the stores area and then onto a narrow dirt track running alongside the estuary. I spotted his car ahead I parked up alongside.

"That's a funny colour for sand." I spotted Gerry bending over what I assumed to be the ley lines. The tide was out.

"We'll be fine come on let's go." My wife didn't look convinced. A slight breeze carried the sweet smell of the sea. We clambered down the embankment onto the floor of the estuary. Our son was the first to slip over in the tidal mud. The smell of the sea replaced by the salty muds staleness.

"I did ask you if we needed wellies, didn't I?"

"Ah, ah, Mum Dad!" Lizzie was next to fall.

"For goodness sake this is ridiculous. The kids have only been here five minutes and they're already black as an ouzel."

"Hello there." I hadn't spotted Gerry walking across to us he was dragging a large polythene bag. He was wearing a pair of waders. There was movement in the bag.

"No wellies?" I turned smiling having received the death stare from my wife.

"No, my fault, I guess. Can I introduce you to Annie my wife and the kids James and Elizabeth?"

"Good to meet you all. Right Dad if you could take this plastic bag and haul it on to the embankment, I'll take your missus and the kids to check out the other lines."

I did as instructed. Gerry took each of the kid's hands and walked back out towards the sea. The glimmer of the sun onto the wet mud made it difficult to see.

"Just follow me Mum and place your feet in my footprints save you from slipping." I avoided looking at my wife. Gerry was asking her about our new house. I heard him mention something about a clematis. "A Montana would look lovely over your front porch. Comes into flower every May. Beautiful purple flowers."

I hauled the bag up the bank. For the first time I got a closer look at the catch. I recognised them immediately. Flatties or to give them their actual name plaice. They were attempting to breath. Mouths opening and closing creating. Taking imaginary gulps of water to pass through their gills Through the condensation on the inside of the bag their eyes staring. It was sad to see but they were only fish. Leaving the bag close to the cars I headed back to the others.

Gerry had part filled another bag when I reached them, he was showing the kids how to remove the hook from the fish's mouth.

"Once out just drop them in the bag like so." He looked towards me. "Not as much as I thought today but still plenty to go around." The fish he placed in the bag was flapping wildly. My wife was looking away.

"It's so cruel to watch."

"You won't be saying that later when you're having it with chips. Plenty salt and vinegar."

"Well I can assure you I won't be chopping any of those." My wife replied once more giving me the stare. Ten minutes later we arrived back at the cars. Without any further incident. Gerry had laid sheets of newspaper on the floor of my hatchback's boot. One by one he placed the fish on their bellies.

"One for Dad, one for Mum and one each for you two." The kids had climbed into the car. Kneeling on the back seat they watched Gerry. They were fascinated.

"Gerry they're still alive."

"Not for much longer. Right if you don't mind, I need to be making a move I've got deliveries to make around my village. See you tomorrow Mick?"

I could sense my wife looking at me.

"No not planning on I'll see you Monday."

Once Gerry had left, we headed for home. The kids remained on the back seat watching the fish.

"Dad the fish are still moving."

"The biggest one keeps opening and closing its mouth."

"I think Mum's one is dead." The commentary from the kids continued till we reached home.

"And don't think your chopping them in my kitchen."

"Well where do you suggest?"

"Outside; use the old camping table. You two get in and wash your hands." I waited till they'd all gone inside the house. Wrapping the four fish together in the newspaper I carried them around the side of the house and placed them on the ground.

"Phone for you it's the pit would you believe." My wife shouted from the back door. Leaving the fish, I went inside. The call was from Osian; he'd called to update me on the end of shift report. In total we'd transported another six powered supports it had been a good shift.

"Will you be here in the morning?"

"Not planning to be."

"Probably for the best now. You're spending quite a bit of time here if you're not careful you'll come home one day, and the missus will be gone. I've seen it so many times with previous Undermanager's."

"Thanks for the advice Osian see you next week." Placing the phone down I walked back towards the kitchen. My wife was preparing dinner.

"What are you doing I was going to cook the fish later."

"I somehow don't think so."

"What do you mean?"

"The kids have got other ideas see for yourself." She pointed to the kitchen door.

Outside the kids were looking into one of my home brew fermenting buckets. Our son was holding a plastic jar with the words "table salt" emblazoned on the side. He looked up.

113

"Dad they're still alive we've put them in water and added some salt."

"We can't kill them now Dad it would be so cruel. I think I'll become a vegetarian." His sister added.

I walked over and looked into the bucket. Sure, enough they were all moving around at the bottom of the bucket even Mums had returned from the dead.

"Well what do you plan on doing with them?" My wife asked standing at the kitchen door.

"Let's take them back to the river." Lizzie added.

"I'm not sure they'll survive in fresh water."

"Don't be daft the river leads to the sea. Of course, they'll be okay."

"Anyway, they were out of the water for a long time."

"They look okay to me."

"They might have brain damage." I was running out of ideas to save the situation.

"Why don't you both go with your Dad and put them back." The situation was now well and truly lost. I looked at my wife. She responded with the "I told you so" smile.

Ten minutes later myself and the kids were back in the car. The river was a five-minute drive. Both of them took up the same position on the rear seat. Looking at the fish happily swimming around in the fermenting bucket.

"Dad, where should we let them go?"

"I thought we'd go down towards the rocks, water's a lot deeper there."

"Good I don't want to go by the bridge in case those bad swans are about."

Once at our destination the kids passed me the fish one by one and as Gerry had done passing comment.

"That's your one Dad." My son passed me the larger one I placed it gently into the water. We watched as it swam a short distance then settled on to the riverbed.

"This is yours James." Again, it followed the actions of the first fish.

"And yours Lizzie." Then finally Mums. As I held it, we all said goodbye.

"Look Dad she's blowing you a kiss." I looked closer and sure enough its mouth was once more opening and closing. She even winked at me.

"Well time we got back home."

The following Monday I didn't see Gerry till the afternoon I was sat in my office discussing results from the dayshift with my team.

"What were they like then Mick?" Gerry had popped his head around the corner of the open door. I heard him before I saw him the office was clouded by cigarette smoke.

"Oh, hi Gerry I'll speak with you later you wouldn't believe the carry on….."

Christmas arrived. Sat in my office I contemplated what we'd achieved over the first year. My thoughts suddenly interrupted by the Manager entering.

"There you go." He passed me a bottle of Bell's whisky.

"Wow, thanks Mr Groves."

"Merry Christmas to you." I shook his hand.

"I get all the staff a bottle each year." I couldn't resist.

"And Bronwen?"

"No, she likes Courvoisier." He smiled. "You do know we're having a get together in my office shortly?"

"Yeah Billy Blunt mentioned it yesterday," He'd even arranged for his missus to bring us in this morning. Just in case.

"Three o'clock see you then."

"Thanks again Mr Groves will do."

Just before three Denny arrived outside my office. "You ready cock?"

"I certainly am. Where's Gregor?"

"He'll be in there already. He and Dafydd been in a meeting with Billy Blunt all day."

"Any excuse not to go underground."

"Aye you're not wrong there cock. What about yon mon next door he not comin."

"Paul no. Says it's not his scene. Got something on at home."

Arriving in the Manager's office Gerry Tuffman was in full flow. Paul Adder laughing at whatever he'd just said. Ron Groves was sat at his desk. He winked at me as I walked in. He was holding what I assumed to be a glass of white wine. Gerry looked towards us.

"And here's number eight and nine." I looked for who else was in the room. Billy Blunt, Gregor, Dafydd Jones, Owain Jones. Me and Denny obviously bringing the group to nine in total. As I went to close the door Larry Llewelyn joined us. "And finally, number ten." I looked towards Gerry for an explanation. "The ten most powerful men in North Wales!"

By five o'clock having consumed four bottles of Bell's whiskey between us no one was making any sense. I occasionally glanced at Mr Groves. He was watching us all and joining in the laughter. However, his glass of white wine seemed untouched. We began to toast one another on any subject. It didn't matter.

"I raise a toast to 43's having less mechanical delays than 42's" We all raised our glasses and shouted "Hear, hear."

"I raise a toast to the least electrical delays ever." Billy followed Gerry's announcement. "Hear, hear."

"I raise a glass to the least number of times Mr Adder has been underground this year." Gerry was on a role. Some of us still not completely pissed looked towards Paul. I guessed he hadn't heard Gerry's comment because he was the first to shout "hear, hear."

Then to our surprise and delight Mr Groves shouted.

"I raise a toast to not holding the right end of the tape." That without doubt got the biggest laugh.

Thereafter we stopped to recover from the laughing. Without warning there was a knock on the office door. No one said anything just staring. The door opened slowly at first. Standing there was Mrs Gibson, Mrs Blunt, and Uncle John.

"Come on in." The Manager announced. "Just who we've been waiting for." He jumped from his seat and lead the three guests to their seat.

It was time to leave or so I thought. My wife had said nothing I think due to the state we were all in. The Manager returned to his seat and announced.

"And now for our little surprise to our new recruit. Over to you Billy. I turned towards Billy. No one else did they seemed to know what was coming.

"Right gentlemen after me." I was now the centre of attention as they began to sing.

"Pen blwydd Hapus…" How the hell did they know my birthday. I guessed by the smile on his face. *I owe you one.*

-

4. 1989 A New Colliery Manager

The announcement that Paul Taylor was to resign came as no surprise. I hadn't had much interaction with him. He kept himself to himself and seemed a really nice person. Too nice to be an Undermanager. Within weeks a replacement arrived suggesting his departure was expected. I recalled the conversation from last year outside the Manager's office. The day I'd received my first "bollocking" as Undermanager from Mr Groves.

The new guy Kelvin Blackhead had his work cut out. He'd arrived during the time S61's coal face was in full production. I say in production. Coal from the Stone Coal a four and a half metre thick seam was problematic to say the least. The cutting horizon was difficult to maintain. If the coal tops left were too thin roof falls became a regular feature. Too thick the tops would drop out anyway. The strata above, shale, was friable at the best of times. Without coal tops it was impossible to maintain. I'd spent some time in their myself just after Paul had left. I guessed this had been the final straw.

Kelvin was usually underground by the time I arrived and still there as I left. Things however began to improve as they always did. He began to surface at a more reasonable time.

"Hi Mick."

"Hi Kelvin, blimey you're up early mate." He'd just walked into my office still in his black.

"Do you mind if I have a word?"

"Yeah, come in take a seat." No sooner had he taken a seat.

"Now how are my favourite Undermanager's in the whole wide world?"

"Storm how nice. We're both good thank you. Mr Blackhead is just about to have a private word with me." Storm was the canteen Manageress. As soon as I'd made the comment Storm immediately stopped fluttering her eyelids.

"Aw I'm sooo sorry to disturb you both now. Just wondering if I can get you boys a drink?"

"Thanks Storm I'll have a coffee."

"What about you Mr Blackhead." The fluttering eyelids had started again.

"Same please Storm. One sugar."

"Not as sweet as Mr Gibson then he doesn't have sugar but loves his blue Penguins. Isn't that right Mr Gibson now?"

"Yeah sure is." She blew me an imaginary kiss and left us.

"She's got it bad for you."

"I can assure you that is far from the case. There's a new Coal Prep Manager."

"Llyn Garvey?"

"No, he's recently moved over to the Liquefaction Plant. Producing oil from coal I'm led to believe. No, the new fella. Not sure of his name. They refer to him as Muscles; I'm yet to meet him. Anyway, I've not seen much of you how's it goin?"

"Wasn't what I expected. Talk about being thrown in at the deep end. We seem to have got to grips with the tops now. Manager seems happy. He's been in a couple of times. Tell you what though the other fella's yet to show up."

"Paul Adder don't hold your breath. Spends most of his time in the office. Not sure what the fuck he gets up to. Other than thinking of excuses why we can't spend money. You've not been to an overtime meeting yet. It's an experience to say the least."

"There you go now boys." Storm had returned with our mugs of coffee.

"Thanks, Storm very kind of you."

"And for you Mr Gibson a little treat. A blue Penguin."

"Where's my treat?" Kelvin asked.

"Now what sort of a treat would you like me to give you?"

"A Penguin?"

"Sorry now all out of Penguins. I could give you something else if you wanted."

"Thanks Storm that'll be all now." She smiled again and I got my imaginary kiss and left.

"What did you want a word about?"

"It's my car."

"The new white escort? Very nice."

"Well it was."

"What do you mean?"

"There's started to appear brown stains over the bonnet. The lads tell me it's the seagulls. But I've never seen dark brown bird shit. Someone suggested it was curry takeaways discarded on the seafront by the holiday makers. Reckon the gulls love a curry."

"Where abouts are you parking?" Kelvin pointed towards the far end of the cars parked outside the offices. I stood to take a look. I saw his car immediately. Directly under the window of Gerry Tuffman's office.

"Yeah not the best of parking specs…"

-

"I'll tell you what Mick, this place is going to produce some coal."

"I do hope so Mr Groves. Strata Top is the place to be. I was up in the surveyors office yesterday afternoon looking over the plans. Seven coal faces I counted."

"Yep after this T3's, T4's. 5's, 6, 7 and 8. Just a pity the panels weren't longer." I was walking with the Manager along the return of the recently completed T2 retreat face panel of coal. Three hundred and twenty metres of seven foot Two Yard coal.

We said little as we walked. He didn't do small talk. The place was eerily quiet. I was pleased he was happy. The Hollybank arches standing proud under the glare of our cap lamps. Each leg sat on a wooden block. The wrap round struts positioned perfectly. Two on either leg with two on the main roof beam each lying close to the two inch bolts securing the legs in position. Six by two mesh straddled across the beams and the legs. The only item that looked out of place were the odd cable hangers no longer required. He stopped and shook his head.

"The place is perfect. No weight whatsoever on the steel. I bet you could remove half of what the lads have put up it wouldn't make any difference."

"True." I answered. He had a point. The conditions were perfect.

The thirty six inch conveyor belt was still in position. Its line perfect as far as the eye could see. We planned to start removing it later that week. The thirty inch ventilation bagging which had hung above it during the development already salvaged. Transported to the T3 development.

On the opposite side of the conveyor the three inch Victaulic water pipes and six inch Carlton compressed air range. Each range hung separately on pipe chain. Below the narrow cable connecting the tannoy system. My light caught the green and white, fluorescent manhole sign. A little further in the distance the red and white hydrant sign. The place positively glowed. The use of Little Rick's duster had played a huge part in ensuring the stone dust covered the roof and sides. What little had fallen had covered the floor. The picture reminded me of a snowfall. The sight first thing of a morning before the surface has been affected by movement.

"How long did it take to turn?" We'd reached the end of the return. Now standing at the entrance to the one hundred and seventy five metre face line.

"Three days. Three days to complete the turn and advance ten metres."

"Previously it would have taken a week probably longer just to complete the turn." I nodded. "The mini conveyor must have been a huge help?" *Fuck not that subject again. The mini conveyor had been the bane of my life.*

"It certainly was Mr Groves." I returned his stare. He was eyeing me suspiciously. He'd obviously guessed what had really happened. I'd often wonder why Llewelyn Larry spent so much time in here.

"Pity we hadn't got the Coal News photographer here to take some shots." He was still staring at me. I tried to avoid any further eye contact.

The fact was if the lads had used it as intended we'd probably still be here now. Trying to complete the turn. Parts of it were okay. Particularly the gib conveyor. We could attach to the back of the machine. It allowed the extracted coal to be dumped on the floor. Using a mini Eimco bucket the coal was then tipped onto the floor mounted conveyor suspended over the main conveyor. I'd spent time with the lads on it. It couldn't be used as intended. However, we had achieved the result as planned.

For the eighteen months I'd been Undermanager the one thing I'd learnt above all else was the benefit of teamwork and forward planning. No matter what the project. We'd spend hours discussing how we'd approach a task. I'd involve my officials, engineers and when appropriate the lads who'd have to carry out the work. It was a "no brainer" the skill set available was unbelievable and certainly one I put to good effect. It was days like today where I got my reward. Seeing the Manager happy was good enough for me.

"Where is it anyway?"
"What?
"The mini-conveyor."
"Oh, on the cross-cut ready for T3's."
"Come on let's keep moving." He was smiling once more. I guess he knew exactly what we'd done. He'd made his point. We continued along the faceline.

I'd never seen the Manager in this mood before. I can only describe it as melancholy. It was as if he were reflecting what he'd achieved and now leaving behind. Something I couldn't put my finger on. However, the following week all was revealed. I was to see exactly what had been on his mind...

-

"Hi Bronwen, is it true then?"
"Unfortunately, yes, did you want to see him?"
"Yeah if I may, the rumours are rife, I just wanted to hear it from the horse's mouth so to speak. I'd already guessed."
"Whatever do you mean?"
"Underground last week. We had a walk around T2's; I knew then something was about to happen."
"Fingers crossed you know who doesn't get it."
"Yeah must admit he seems chirpier than normal."

Mr Groves was smiling as I entered. An unusual occurrence unless he had wind. He couldn't contain his excitement. He recognised it was a poisoned chalice particularly regards the new heavy duty coal face in the Plodder seam. I believed this was his first "big" pit, a complex too. In effect it was three pits if you included Parsonage and Golborne. All the coal came to the surface at Bickershaw.

His final comment as he left was a little concerning.
"I'm not sure how long we've all got."
"What do you mean?"
"I've just seen the latest figures for this year. The number of collieries in the UK stands at seventy three with a workforce of fifty six thousand. You look after yourself."

-

Mr Adder became the acting Manager. We assumed interviews would take place for a replacement. He seemed a different person. He was now in the role he'd always believed was his. In fact, it was a pleasure to work for him. He let us get on with what we had to do without interference. He'd even backed off on his stance with overtime.

The morning meeting unusually went without a hitch. Only Gregor had a beef about some armoured cables that should have been moved inbye with the haulage lads. I was feeling lucky as the planned inspectors visit that morning had been cancelled. There'd been an incident at Parkside colliery. Something to do with a runaway. The details were sketchy.

"For fucks sake Gregor I'll arrange to get them moved in this morning. I think the lads got mixed up with the Jumbo cables."

"That's a shit excuse. For starters they're about four times the diameter plus the 3.3kv are coloured blue and the 6.6kv are yellow."

"Fuckin hell Gregor keep your hair on."

"That's rich coming from you." Evan regretted his comment immediately. His comment lightened the mood, and everyone began to laugh. "If you lot don't stop smoking I ain't attended anymore of these meetings." Gregor had a point. Denny had just lit up a Hamlet and had passed one to me. Evan was puffin away on his Players No 6. A cloud of smoke hung over the desk. "If our Lord had wanted us to smoke he'd have put a chimney up our arse."

"I that's a fair point cock."

"Listen lads try and keep from falling now we've got a new acting Manager."

"I cock; let's just hope he doesn't get it permanently."

"That's not a very nice thing to say."

"You wait and see. He's as nice as pie at the moment. Give him a few weeks."

"Morning Billy." I shouted. Billy Blunt had just passed the office but made no comment.

"Miserable bastard what's up with him?" Denny added.

"The electrical inspector's here today off to Zone A. He's never any different when we have a visit. And it's his birthday."

"For fuck's sake. How old is he?" Forty-four I think."

"Fuck he's getting on."

"Hey watch what you're sayin."

"You'll get there one day."

"Whatever. Anyone in a rush this morning?" I looked around the room. Nobody seemed to be. Shaking their heads to confirm. I had an idea and I owed him one from last year. I picked up the phone. "Storm hi, you okay? Good, listen you couldn't do me a favour could you? No not that. Have you any cakes left ideally one that hasn't been cut into. A lemon sponge. That would be ideal.

Could you pop some candles in it too and take it to Kelvin's office? Excellent see you in a mo."

"Gibson what the fuck are you up to?"

"I want to bring some joy to birthday boy. Gregor see that eight-foot drill rod in the corner?"

"Yeah."

"Are you able to lift it?"

"Cheeky bastard of course I can."

"Well if you pick it up and pretend to hit me with it."

"Don't tempt me."

"No not yet. Wait till we've got the cake." I picked up the phone once more. "Hi Dewi is Kelvin there? Hi mate I'm attempting to bring some joy into Mr Blunt's life. It's his birthday today and think we should celebrate it. You up for it. Great and yeah, all your team too. Storms on her way round now with a cake. If you guys could light the candles and fetch it round as soon as you hear us singing. See you in a mo."

I looked round the room Denny, Gregor and Ifor were smiling. Gethin was shakin his head.

"You guys are fuckin nuts." Five minutes later Storm arrived.

"Right now, I've done a requested. What you doin now?"

"Storm, it's Billy's birthday today and we'd like to give him a surprise. Could you pop along to his office and tell him he needs to come here immediately as Gregor is about to kill the Undermanager."

"Oh yes, this should be fun."

"Right lads close the door, give it a few seconds and let's go!"

Gregor who was already holding the rod lifted it as if to swing it towards my head. It brought back memories. "Gibson you're a fuckin twat I'm goin to kill you."

"Gregor nooo." Ifor added. Followed by Denny.

"No Gregor you'll kill him, don't do it!" Gethin joined in too.

"For fucks sake." The door to the office was thrown open as Billy Blunt rushed in.

"Gregor nooo." Billy's face was ashen. In unison we began to sing "Penblwydd Hapus…." Kelvin then appeared with his team at the door holding aloft the lemon sponge. The four candles flickering …. "You shower of fuckin shits." Billy shouted out to no one in particular although I guessed his anger was aimed at me. He left my office as quickly as he'd entered it.

Denny turned towards me. "Nowt, as strange as folk. There's just no pleasing some fuckin folk cock!"

Sadly, for Mr Adder he never got the Manager's job. Bronwen had kept us updated. She seemed to be the only delighted person when the news broke. The guy who got the job was a Mr Maurice Adam. He was from South Wales. We assumed that must be a positive sign. The first indication came with the name change on the Manager's office door *Colliery Manager - Mr M Adman.*

"He wants fuckin what?" I turned towards Denny Richards in disbelief.

"Afraid so cock, Gerry Tuffman mentioned it to me this morning after he came out of the morning meeting. He wants you, me, Gregor and James Runner to be one of the teams carrying out the inspection."

"Me? I haven't got the time."

"Bloody hell Mick it's only once a month."

"It ain't my job for starters plus the fact you and the shaftsman do it anyway."

"Seems the new Manager has a different view on safety he's even making Gerry and Phil Blunt carry out an inspection too. Only they'll do it every six months."

"What about soft lad next door?"

"The shafts don't come under his remit just you."

"We'll see about that I'll see the man myself."

"You do cock don't shoot messenger just thought I'd mention it."

"Okay thanks," Denny left the office. I sat there contemplating what he'd just told me. I'd been in the emergency winder in No 2 shaft but that was a one off. There were two things in life I was never comfortable with; one confined spaces, a little odd for someone who worked underground and two heights. Worse still how the fuck would we all fit on the top of the cage?

Later that morning Kelvin and I were sat in Mr Adder's office. He was back to his usual self. His mood seemed to have darkened. We guessed he was going through some form of depression.

"You've exceeded the overtime budget on the face and it's only Wednesday."

"Well it's your call Mr. Adder. I needed the lads to stay over to timber the maingate end, prep it for the dayshift."

"Are we cuttin then? The last piece of information I'd received from the control room is there's more timbering to be done."

"Exactly my point; imagine how much more there would be if we hadn't have kept them on."

"The Manager has been very explicit he wants underground overtime reducing......" He suddenly stopped talking as his phone rang.

Kelvin turned towards me. "Have you met him yet?"

"The new guy, no I plan to pop in before we go underground and introduce myself. What about you?"

"Spoke with him yesterday I thought I recognised him the first time he passed the office. I met in Hobart House when I was secretary for the Manchester Geological Mining Society. From what I remember very approachable. A really nice guy. Think we should get on well with him. Quite funny how he refers to everyone as laddie…" Our conversation interrupted as Mr Adder slammed the phone down.

"That fuckin man. How did he ever get the job?" I guessed who he was referring to.

After I'd finished my session with Mr Adder I went along to the Manager's office. Too early yet for Bronwen I knocked. No answer. I knocked again. No answer. I decided to go in just as he appeared from the door leading to the Manager's shower room. He had the look of a very young Jack Nicholson. He was must have only been about five foot. Not a good sign in my experience.

"Ah good morning Mr. Adman sorry to bother you so early in the day, have you a minute?"

"Come in laddie grab a seat. I was planning to come and see you today anyway. What can I do for ti?" I noticed his lips had some sort of cream on them. He was still rubbing them as he approached his desk. He placed a small tube on the desk.

"I'm told you want me to accompany the Deputy Engineers and the Shaftsman on a monthly shaft inspection?"

"I that's right laddie" For the first time I noticed the intensity of his eyes. I felt hypnotised paralysed by his glassy stare. He continued rubbing the substance on his lips. I stared back his eyes seemed lifeless like I was looking into his soul. I must be imagining it Kelvin tells me he's okay. Still staring he reaches across for the tube which I now realize is Zovirax.

"And why would that be?"

"Because I say so laddie." *Those eyes really do look menacing think it's time I fucked off.*

"That'll do for me, good to meet you Mr. Adman."

"Good to meet you too Mick, might see you later I'm off underground to visit the coal face with Mr. Blackhead"

"Okay thanks." I left his office with mixed emotions. Closing the door, I stood in the corridor. I turned to see the nameplate once more *Colliery Manager Mr M Adman.*

I quickly made my way to the baths. Already behind schedule. I didn't want to be late and miss the underground manrider. Arriving at the shaft top I was met by Kelvin, our two Colliery Overmen Evan and Dewi, and the two Deputy Mechanical Engineers Denny and Zone A's Owain Jones.

"Where's Gregor?" I asked Denny.

"Seems that Billy has kept him and Dafydd Jones on the surface for a debrief on the Manager's morning meeting."

"For fucks sake any excuse to stay on land." Kelvin laughed at my comment.

"Did he see you then? What did you think?"

"Yeah I popped in for a mo, wants me to accompany Denny, Gregor and James Runner on a monthly inspection of the shafts."

"I mean do you think we'll get on with him?"

"Not sure yet early days." I couldn't get the look of his eyes off my mind.

"On that point I've arranged with James for a first inspection tomorrow." Denny interrupted.

"Yeah that should be fine."

"He's coming in today on his first underground visit, 61's face." Kelvin continued.

"That should be fun."

The double decked cage arrived at the top of the shaft.

"Right gentlemen" the Banksman lifted the cage gates and beckoned us forward. After patting us down he held out his hand to collect our tallies. The six of us clambered in saying little more as the cage gate dropped shut, each of us consumed in our own thoughts.

"You off with the golfing lads later Kelvin," the silence broken by Owain.

"Yeah that's the plan. Just me and Dafydd. Probably come out with the Manager, looks as though the weather will hold."

As we descended darkness replaced the light. Interrupted as we passed the lights of the various insets flashing by with the smell of the underground workings becoming more apparent as we dropped. Then the sudden deceleration as the winder applied his brakes slowing the cage to an almost standstill as it entered the metal "L" shaped guides. We came to a final stop followed by the dropping of the platforms. The sound of the hissing compressed air ringing in our ears. Each of us turning on our cap lamps clipping to the back of our helmets.

The manrider was some fifty yards from where we exited the cage. The sound of the loco clearly heard. Its methodical hum recognisable. Puffing out the deadly nitrous oxides. It's attached to a single bogie subdivided into four separate compartments. We walked towards the manrider kicking the dust beneath our feet causing it to rise in the cold air.

"Bora da gentlemen," we're greeted by Ivor the driver and his guard Tomos.

"Morning lads, do me a favour when you get back out. Could you move those old sleepers next to the manhole nearest pit bottom and get a bit of stone dust spread."

"Will do Mr. Gibson."

"Have we got a visitor today then?" Tomos added.

"Yeah our new Manager Mr. Adman is paying us a visit."

"Anywhere special now?"

"Yeah he's going to see Mr. Blackhead on 61's face."

"Should I get a run of stonedust in for him do you think?"

"Might be best, you can ask him yourself he's just behind me."

Myself, Denny and Evan climb into the front carriage.

"What's he like then the new guy?" Evan asks. "Kelvin tells me they've met before and seems okay." I shrug my shoulders.

"You don't agree?"

"Early days yet let's wait and see." I had my doubts there was something about those eyes.

Later that day back in the office. "Bloody hell man I've never known anything like it now."

"What's up?" I ask as Osian enters the office.

"Next door they're running round like headless chickens now. The new Manager's still on the coal face laying into everyone."

"That can't be right. I'm told he's such a nice chap." I respond smiling. We continue to discuss the plans for afternoon shift and the men are available.

"Why the hell doesn't someone answer that fucking phone?" The constant ringing noise from next doors office is starting to distract me.

"They're too bloody frightened now. Might be the Manager."

"You got to be kiddin me I can't listen to that." I jump from my seat and head towards Kelvin's office. I'm met by Asyn, the Face Overman, Dewi and Gruffyd. Each sat staring at the phone as it continues to ring.

"Gents what the fuck's up? Can't one of you answer the fuckin phone for fucks sake."

"It'll be him."

"Who?" I ask as I reach across for the handset. The three of them jump up and run from the room.

"If it's for me I've gone to get changed." Gruffyd shouts fighting his two colleagues to be first out of the door.

"Hello Mick Gibson here." There follows a long silence. I can hear breathing.

"Hello anyone there?" I ask again. "Hello......" I hear some movement.

"Mr. Gibson, Manager here can you put the afternoon Overman on…"

"Oh hello Mr. Adman I'm afraid you've just missed Gruffyd he's gone to get changed." I'm sure I detect a growling noise. "Hello Mr. Adman are you still there………." Again, no answer but this time he hangs up. "Charming" I respond to no one in particular and head back to my office.

Next morning, I arrived at the pit for five thirty and discover Kelvin was already underground. Of late he hadn't been arriving to the office until six thirty. The fact he's already underground is a surprise as I know from my conversation with Delwyn he never got to the surface until early hours. "Guess he didn't get to play golf then?" I ask Dewi as I pass the Zone A office. Dewi is sat in Kelvin's chair reading some paperwork. He's got a Players number six hanging from his mouth. By the look of the ashtray in front of him it's not his first. He doesn't answer.

I continue towards my office. I'm not in any rush this morning. It's the day of my shaft inspection.

"Where's Denny and Gregor this morning?"

"Sorry Evan should have mentioned it yesterday. I've cancelled the morning meeting. Off on a shaft inspection first thing."

"Bloody hell seems to be a regular feature now. It was only last month you were down No 2."

"I can assure you it's not of my doing."

"Right then I'll see you later."

We'd agreed to meet at the shaft top at eight thirty to give the eight o'clock riders a chance to get down. By the time I arrived Denny and James were waiting with harnesses on.

"There you go Mick you've got the newest." James passed me the harness he was holding.

"Suppose Denny's got the extra-large."

"Cheeky fucker. If you want to know cock they're all one size. Adjust to fit." The harness wasn't dissimilar to a waistcoat with the addition of a crotchet cover. A number of straps in place to secure it once on attached to a series of small chains. These were attached to a thicker longer chain with a snap hook on the end. I looked at it not sure how it was supposed to put it on.

"Best drop it on the floor Mick and step into it." James could see my dilemma. Doing as he suggested I pulled it up placing my arms through the respective position but struggled to secure it.

"Come here cock let me show you." Embarrassed I walked across to Denny. "Who got you ready this morning cock? Missus." I said nothing.

I'd finally got the thing in position when I noticed the Manager walking up the ramp towards the shaft. He was walking rather quick. Behind him in tow were Billy and Gerry. Nobody seemed to be in a good mood. By the look on Billy's face they'd obviously received a round of fucks.

"Morning gentlemen." I received no further response as the Manager turned to Billy Blunt.

"Where's Mr Adder?" Before Billy answered the Deputy Manager appeared. He was struggling to get his oil lamp onto his belt. Gerry had started a conversation with Denny and James.

"Morning Mr Adder." He didn't look happy.

"Mick can you make sure we've got a ride in." *Yeah good morning to you too Mick. Ignorant fucker.*

"But of course. It would be my pleasure." I walked across to the nearest phone to arrange. No more was said. I stood and watched the four of them walk into the cage. The atmosphere I could only describe as icy. The Banksman dropped the mesh gate and stood back to signal the Winder. Keps withdrawn the cage disappeared almost immediately.

"There goes a happy bunch. Where they off to?" James enquired.

"I'm guessing 61's."

"Poor old Blackhead. He's in for some fun." James walked across to the Banksman. "Anyway, Denny where the fuck is Gregor I thought he was with us today?"

"Fraid not cock. Seems Billy's keeping him on land to arrange for some extra cables for 61's."

"61's! Where the fuck's Dafydd?"

"Golfing. Playing with Osian at Meliden Golf Club."

"Besides spending time on land and playing golf that's all those fuckers tend to do. I'll tell you what Denny if I had my time again that's what I'd train to be. An Electrical Engineer."

"Doubt if cock. You'd find it boring."

"Rights gents if we could pay attention." James moved towards the shaft top. He was holding a metal plate and the accompanying gong. I hadn't noticed but the Banksman had positioned the top of the cage level to the surface. "What I suggest is I'll get on first followed by Denny. Once we've secured our harnesses Mick can follow. All okay with that."

"Yeah." I responded. Denny nodded. Moving my tongue around the inside of my mouth I was as dry as a bone. Without warning James used the gong to hit the metal plate. The noise caused me to jump. He looked at me smiling.

"Just checking it still works." He was taking the piss and obviously knew how I was feeling. I guessed over the next few hours the two of them would make the most of my discomfort. "Just to confirm Mr Banksman." He hit the plate twice. "To lower." Then once. "To stop. And finally." He hit it a further three times. "To raise." James was loving the attention even the Banksman was laughing. "Now before we get in let's point out a few things to you." He turned to the cage. "The chains attached to the cage are attached to what is called a distribution plate. That in turn is attached to the detaching hook and finally the rope cape. I guess you already know what happens if we overwind?" I nodded. He remained silent. He was expecting a reply.

"The detaching hook allows the cage to detach in the arrestors in the event of an overwind."

"Good. Let's make a start shall we."

James stepped gingerly onto the cage top dropping the metal plate and gong by his feet. He secured the chain from his harness to the D link attaching the four chains from the top of the cage to the winding rope. Denny followed carrying out the same procedure. It was now my turn. I'd already planned how I would overcome my first obstacle. That was the gap between the side of the cage and land. The distance was at least twelve inches. I stepped forward without looking down. My heart was pounding. Perspiration ran down the front of my chest. I was on. My first reaction was to grab hold of the nearest two chains securing the cage to the winding rope.

"Now cock tha av to let go of chain to secure harness." I hadn't noticed but guessed I'd not moved since stepping on. Reluctantly I released one hand and took the clasp attached to the harness chain. I clamped it in position.

"Mick you'll have to place it higher than that. Just in case you fall off the top. Less distance to travel." James added. Like I needed to hear that. It reminded me of an incident at my last pit. The shaftsmen had been securing a new pipe system to the shaft wall. The brackets retaining the pipes had sheared causing a number of pips to fall down the shaft. Fortunately, no one had been injured but one of the shaftsmen had fallen from the cage and been left dangling in the shaft for a number of hours. He never worked again.

I did as James suggested and returned to securing both hands on the chains above the cage. James hit the plate twice we began to descend. I shivered. I was cold. It didn't help my shirt was soaked through. The freshness of the downcast air was more obvious on the outside of the cage. As we slowly descended the surface light became less and less. Our cap lamps came into focus.

"Now Mick if you don't mind I think it may be well worthwhile just pointing a few things out." I guessed this would be coming. He hit the gong. We came to an immediate stop. "Do you fully understand the function of a shaft?"

"Ventilation and transport."

"Correct. Plus, there's three other jobs…." He waited but I thought best if he continued. "Signalling, power both electrical and compressed air. Pumping from the sump."

"Hold on a minute James. What about water and methane drainage."

"There endeth the first lesson. For fucks sake cock can we get move on." Denny was getting restless. James responded with a further two hits with the gong. We began to descend once more.

"No 3 Shaft was sunk in 1952 using the Caisson Method, six men killed."

"James we've had this conversation before." He seemed not to listen.

"Depth three hundred and thirty six metres with a winding depth of three hundred and fifteen metres." I smiled. The last time he'd given me this information it had been in Imperial measure. The day we'd nearly tipped the kibble in No 2 shaft.

"Three hundred and fifteen and a half to be exact cock." James again took no notice of Denny's comment. He was on transmit.

"Diameter five point five metres. Used originally for mineral transport and occasional manriding. That was until the Drift had come into operation. Two cages with two decks per cage. Capacity twenty four men per deck. Cage guides as you can see rope." I guessed what was coming next. I'd spotted the cast iron tubbing.

"There's two types of tubbing - English and German. Here you can see the flanges and reinforcing ribs are external. They contain no bolts. They rely on wedging the segments together."

"Whereas the German tubbing everything is internal, and they use bolts." I interrupted.

"Well done Mick I'm impressed. We'll make a shaftsman of you yet."

"Will that include the white donkey jacket you keep promising me?"

"I was saving it until we'd completed the inspection you'll have it the afternoon."

James reached down and picked up the plate. He hit it once. The sound vibrated around the walls of the shaft. The cage stopped just below the tubbing. He removed the cap lamp from his helmet and shone it onto the shaft side.

"There Denny. See how it's started to break away." I looked across but couldn't see anything different.

"Where cock? I canna see a thing."

"Watch your feet." James used his right foot to lift a wooden platform running the length of the cage nearest to the shaft wall. I hadn't noticed until that point. Pushing it beyond ninety degrees it fell horizontally in line with the cage top. Retained by three hinges spaced equally along its length. The width of it added another three feet to the width of the cage top. I watched in horror as the two of them stepped onto the hinged platform.

"I see it now cock. What plan to do?" Denny asked as he touched the shaft side.

"Plan to remove the patches effected over the annual holidays. Should only take us a week."

"Nightshift?"

"Nah. Days. The lads can use No1 shaft. I've agreed it already with Mr Adder." Up to this point I hadn't said anything. The two of them stood on a wooden platform astride of the cage. The conversation however required comment.

"Don't you think it should have been agreed with me James. As I'm on the inspection?"

"Yeah. Sorry Mick. This was before you arrived. Do you want to have a look yourself? You'll need to unclip your harness and reattach this side."

"No, I'm fine I'll leave it to you two experts."

"Do us a favour cock. Can you pass me thommer." I guessed the hammer was somewhere on the cage top but couldn't see it.

"Whereabouts?" I turned to Denny. He was once more in deep conversation with James. I was sure I detected them both smiling.

"In corner cock, tuther side." I shone my cap lamp to the far corner of the cage top. I spotted the wooden handle immediately. It was out of my reach.

"How the fuck am I supposed to get that." Neither of them responded.

Slowly I lowered myself onto the cage top. Once more I could feel my heart pounding. I crawled tentatively towards it. Perspiration again began to fall from my chest. Once I was in arms reach I stretched across. Manging to draw it closer with my fingertips. Still on all fours I retraced my way back. Finally, in position I lifted myself back up. I hadn't up to this point noticed both of my colleagues had turned to watch my progress.

"Don't think we'll be needin it now cock." They were both smiling.

"You pair of bastards!"

An hour later we'd completed my first full shaft inspection including the sump. To say I was relieved was an understatement. Arriving in my office James had been true to his word. Laid across the back of my chair was a cellophane bag containing a white donkey jacket. There was also a note. Paul Adder had been in touch. He wouldn't make it up the pit in time to chair the overtime meeting. It would be left to me. Things unsurprisingly weren't going too well with their visit to 61's. Rumours began to circulate that my counterpart Mr Blackhead had walked out of the district and currently uncontactable.

The overtime attendees included Denny, Gregor and Owain. It was the shortest overtime meeting we'd ever attended. I was under no illusion that what we'd agreed collectively would be changed as soon as the Deputy Manager got his hands on the list. Such was life.

Paul Adder had finally got his wish he became Manager at one of the few remaining Lancashire pits. I wasn't sure who was happier. Paul himself or the

131

Manager. It was obvious to us all the relationship had been strained from day one. We heard some weeks later on Paul's first trip underground, he'd caught one of the men asleep on the coalface. Using his stick to poke the guy and then asking him. "Do you know who I am?" He got the inevitable reply. "Don't know who you are cock?"
Without moving grabbed his stick and broke it in half. The faceworker was sacked on the spot. Followed by the underground workforce walking out.

A week later he was reinstated, and the men returned to work. We all readily agreed perhaps it hadn't been such a bad thing if Mr Adder continued to manage from the surface.

"You met him yet?"

"Who? Do me a favour." I passed Kelvin my flannel having smothered it with soap. He took it from me and began to scrub my back. We were alone in the management baths.

"The new Deputy Manager, Tony Douglas."

"Yeah. He popped in the office this morning to say hello. Seems okay. Terrible cough though continually trying to clear his throat."

"One of his many redeeming features. I've worked with him before. Hard work though. Not sure how he'll manage Maurice."

"If I were a rich mon, iddle, diddle, diddle, diddy, do."

"Shut up Denny." I shouted.

"All day long I'd diddle, diddy, do... Don't tell me to shut up ye daft cunt." Denny had come into the baths. As usual singing out of tune.

"We'll soon find out. Think the Manager's attending this afternoons overtime meeting. Can you do mine." Kelvin passed my flannel back with his sponge."

He turned and I began to clean his back.

"If I ruled ta world...."

"Denny will you shut the fuck up."

"What's up cock not into thold classics? Thope thive put me two fitters on shearer maintenance Sat mon?" By now Denny had also stripped naked. Turning the shower on next to me he handed me his flannel. "Here cock do me the thonours."

"For fucks sake Denny overtime meeting's in ten minutes I've not had chance to clean myself yet." I replied laughing.

Arriving in the Deputy Manager's office I'm joined by Denny and Kelvin. Gregor, Dafydd and Owain having arrived earlier. The new guy Mr Douglas is sat at the head of the table. He's holding a white porcelain mug. To his right a half full bottle of Tizer. The meeting now takes place at two o'clock on a Thursday afternoon. Not Wednesday as it was when Paul Adder had been in charge. We're all in our clean having bathed earlier. Except for the engineers who like to use the meeting as an excuse to stay on the surface. Denny being the exception today. Each of us armed with the relevant paperwork supplied by the Overman and Assistant Engineers listing the jobs and men required. Kelvin leans across and whispers.

"Tizer the Appetizer." I smile "It's a change from his usual Irn-Bru." I point to the corner of the office where there's a pile of empties. No wonder the guy suffers with wind he interrupts my thoughts with a loud burp.

"Right let's start with Zone A. Mr Blackhead."

"I'll need three men Saturday and Sunday dayshift to complete transporting supplies into the main and tailgate for 62's."

"You can have two."

"I need three."

"Why?"

"One on the engine and two travelling with the vehicle."

"Three then"

"Thanks"

"Saturday dayshift only."

"For fucks sake! Remember what happened last week after we ran out of chock wood in the tailgate, the Manager wasn't best pleased." I smile the Manager is our secret weapon when it comes to requests. It doesn't look as though it's working this week as the only response made is another loud burp.

"Is that it?"

"Don't be daft I've only just started. Two lads Saturday and Sunday extending water pipes in the main and tail gates."

"Why can't you do that in the week?"

"No men. If you remember all the spare PLA men you've told us to use manning the headings for D28's. And before you ask the supply lads are used as back up dragging supplies in."

"Saturday dayshift only I'm not paying treble time to extend pipes."

"Well we'll only get half the work done then won't we?"

After a short silence there's no response. I look towards my team and shake my head. We went through this same drama with Mr Adder too. Must be something they teach you when becoming Deputy Manager. What they never seem to get is the additional cost. Using additional overtime in the week to complete the unfinished jobs from the weekend. The silence is broken by a further loud burp. I look towards Mr Douglas wondering if he burps during the Manager's morning meeting.

"Six men Saturday morning for a panel move up."

"Plus, two electricians," Dafydd adds.

"Why two electricians?"

"One at the rear of the panel train and one at the front as they move in."

"You can have one,"

"Remember what happened last time when they pulled in before removing the cable from the panel. They stretched it we had to change a cable with the consequence of the face delayed starting up."

"One."

"Don't say you haven't been warned." Dafydd replied shaking his head.

Mr Douglas responds with a cough and then another. The phlegm in his throat has begun to move. He attempts to bring it into his mouth. He looks surprised. He turns to his left then right. Undecided where it will be deposited. Finally turning towards the window behind him. Without warning the door to his office is flung open with a bang.

"What the fuck have I told ti Mr Douglas about the fucking overtime budget? Do you not understand? When I tell you to fuckin reduce the fuckin thing!"

The Manager has made a surprise appearance. It causes us all to jump. I look towards him, his eyes wild with anger, saliva drips from his mouth. He's now waving his fist.

"What have I told you, heh? Are you fuckin incompetent of following a simple fuckin instruction?"

I turn back towards Mr Douglas. He's staring at the Manager. Eyes unblinking his skin colour now ashen. I watch as his Adam's apple bobs uncontrollably with the inevitable consequence.

"Have you got nothing to fuckin say?" He attempts to answer. His mouth now empty.

"I, I, I......." The Manager leaves. We remain silent. The remainder of the meeting continues without any further distraction.

-

Next morning, I head off to attend the morning meeting with the Deputy Manager at seven twenty. He's very insistent we attend on time. I had second slot. Kelvin had been in since seven ten. I've never really understood his requirement for punctuality as my colleague always exceeds his allotted slot. I didn't complain. I had the enjoyment of listening to his list of excuses for the poor performance the previous day. As Undermanager neither one of us is under any illusion that we ever have a good day.

"Why have they only set four arches in the Durbog headings last night?"

"Because.........."

"I don't want any excuses."

"I'm not going to give you any excuses if you'll let me fuckin answer."

"Go on then tell me."

"We had a problem with the only FSV........."

"I knew it!"

"For fucks sake will you let me answer?"

"I've already spoken to the nightshift Overman... what's his name?"

"Delwyn." I added trying to be helpful.

"Well why the fuck are you asking me?" Kelvin looked towards me shaking his head.

The same pattern of questioning was repeated each morning with us both. I had a degree of sympathy with Mr Douglas. He was only protecting himself before he in turn reported to the Manager. His only means of defence was to have the correct answers to any questions raised. That's assuming he raised the right question. We had by now all got used to Mr Adman's approach.

Kelvin leaves the room. One of the first rules I've learnt as Undermanager when facing the Deputy Manager is to be positive in the answers you give. Don't give him any opportunity to dissect your argument. Allowing him to interrupt when you're in full flow must be avoided at all cost.

If there's been an issue underground learn to put the blame elsewhere as far from your door as possible. Safer to blame the electricians failing that the mechanics. The electricians see themselves as coal mining royalty.

Never, ever blame your own men. As the saying goes "there are no bad soldiers, only bad officers." Something quoted by Napoleon I believe.

Ideally give a detailed technical excuse, you may not know what you're talking about, but you can be certain he won't either. Alternatively, if you don't have an answer play on your emotions.

I remember one such occasion. I was a Face Overman on nightshift at my last pit. Each morning on reaching the surface reporting to the Deputy Manager in the Control Room. The room sited just off the passage from pit top to the baths. He used to wait for the nightshift there. Regulation fag in hand.

Our target each night was to complete three shears from the coalface. This was achieved on a regular basis. My face Deputy would lead the way from the shaft top to Control Room. Allowing him to gain the praise each morning. One night however we'd completely failed. One of those shifts when time completely escapes you, delay after delay. I found myself leading the way this morning. I hadn't even come up with a script on what I would say. It's times like this when improvisation takes over.

"Mick what the fuck..."

"What the fuck! I'll tell what the fuck…" I threw my helmet onto the floor and began to throw my arms in the air. "Electricians shit'em. It's one thing after another. If it's not the shearer it's the AFC. To add insult to injury a lockout appeared on the stageloader. Find it? Could they fuck. An hour I tell ye a fuckin hour to sort. And then the hydraulic pump packs in. Takes the fitter forty minutes to make a start. He's been working on the return Eimco bucket." I take a breath. Both the face Deputy and Deputy Manager are transfixed. I continue.

"Then the outbye belt wouldn't start. Electrical problem again. Had to take the lads off the face." I looked towards the Deputy. He's now wondering where he'd been when all this was happening.

"Mick, Mick.." The Deputy Manager attempts to interrupt. "For fucks sake Mick okay, I get it. You've had a bad shift. It happens.."
"Bad shift you say, bad fuckin shift."
"Okay go and get a bath." I stop gesticulating. Retrieve my helmet. The silence is deafening.
"Thank you.."

"Right Mick." Mr Douglas brings me back to the present.
"Good morning Mr Douglas. I'll start with…." His phone began to ring. He never answered it immediately. He was staring at it. We both knew who it would be. Decision made he coughed to clear his throat. He took hold of the handset slowly placing it against his ear.
"Hello." I could hear shouting and screaming. "Yeah. Yeah. I certainly will." The shouting and screaming continued. "Yep Mr Adman I certainly will." Then silence. He put the phone back down.
"Mick we'll catch up later. Something I need to do."
I didn't complain. I just got up and left. They were the kind of morning meetings I loved the best.

-

"Phone" My wife shouted from the kitchen. I'd just sat down with a glass of malt to watch the evening news. It seemed Margaret Thatcher hadn't secured sufficient votes in the Tory leadership challenge. I was feeling quite relaxed after a reasonable shift salvaging chocks from the coal face.
"Can't you get it?"
"Why? It'll be for you anyway." I looked at my watch. *A little early for the afternoon report* I walked into the hall whiskey in hand. I lifted the phone just as a further commotion broke out on the television. I turned having placed the handset to my ear. I took a sip of the malt.
"Mr Gibson apologies a little earlier than normal bit of a problem I'm afraid."

On the television the BBC reporter John Sargent was updating the viewers on the latest development when the doors to the building behind him opened Thatcher appeared.

"62's coal face has been gassed out for most of the afternoon we've only managed to move the cutter sixty yards."

"Thanks, Gruffyd not good but why are you telling me?" I took another sip of the malt. Different to my normal tipple it had been on offer at Leo's the supermarket. "Where's Blackhead?"

The reporter had been joined by the Prime Minister advising him she would be contesting the second round.

"On his way with both of his Deputy Engineers and before you ask Mr. Adman has asked that you, Denny and Gregor make your way in too."

Thatcher was now being interviewed. "What the fuck for?" I put the malt down.

"Just said he wanted you all there by the time he got in."

"Thanks, Gruffyd if he asks tell him I wasn't in." I put the phone down and went back into the living room. Thatcher was now in full flow. The phone began to ring again.

"Gruffyd?"

"No, it's me. You heard?"

"Yeah Denny but I ain't goin in I'm busy."

"Mick don't be daft lad he's even got Douglas there too. Might be best if you do but say fuck all."

I listened to Denny he was always good for advice particularly when it concerned the Manager. I said nothing I was thinking.

"What's that noise?" I responded.

"What noise?"

"Clippety clop."

"Oh, that's the missus with her high heels on the floorboards. She thought by removing the carpet while I was out, we'd get another. I've put her straight though."

"You best get me a replacement." I heard Mrs Richards shout in the background.

"What you goin to do then cock?"

"Don't suppose I've got much choice, see you there." As I replaced the phone my wife walked into the room.

"Well who would have believed," She was looking at the television. Thatcher was still being interviewed by John Sargent.

"Sorry love I'll have to go back in."

"But you've been drinking."

"No choice I'm afraid Manager wants us all back in."

"If you don't mind me saying you're drinking almost every night lately."

"I'll be fine, see you later."

I grabbed my jacket and car keys *she was right though a malt each night helped me unwind.* On the journey in I reflected further on her comment.

The Undermanager never believes he has a problem with drink. It's evident to those around him but not him. My first encounter was during my time as a face Overman on a coal face that was continually susceptible to geological problems, a euphemism to cover a whole multitude of sins.

My Undermanager had asked me to call him when I finished my afternoon shift. Generally, we arrived up the pit at half past eight. However, I'd stayed behind with the men to carry out some roof bolting. Prepping the face for the dayshift. Production on the face took place on days and afternoons. Although late I decided to call him anyway.

"I don't know why you're bothering lad. You'll never get any sense out of him." I'd asked the nightshift Colliery Overman for his contact details.

"What do you mean?"

"You just won't, I never do." He passed me a notebook with a number of contact numbers for the colliery Management team. "He hits the bottle about six." I chose to ignore his comment and dialled his number. I listened, waiting for an answer. "Told you it was a waste of time," the Colliery Overman made a final comment as he left to get changed. Then finally......

"Ello?"

"Hello Undermanager, it's me you asked me to call when I got up. Sorry it's late."

"Ello?"

"Undermanager it's me Mick. You asked me to call when I got up the pit we've secured the maingate end with some roof bolts."

"Ello?" I removed the handset staring at it shaking my head.

"Told you it would be a waste of time." The Colliery Overman had reappeared before going underground.

Some weeks later the geological conditions on the coal face had improved. The Manager had decided to increase the collieries production by putting the face on three shifts. Two weeks in we had a further roof fall at the maingate end. The coal face had been stopped for most of the shift timbering. The Manager wasn't best pleased having spoken personally to me over the phone.

He'd instructed me to stop over and prepare for the oncoming nightshift. I agreed without argument.

I'd stayed on with half a dozen men to timber the fall area. I'd checked my watch ten thirty; nightshift would be on their way in. Probably bottom of the manrider by now.

"Colin how are we fixed?" The tannoy system suddenly came to life. I was at the top end of the face. I'd been checking what timber we had left so I could arrange with the haulage team priority for the first run. *Sounds like the Undermanager what's he doing in the Control Room?* I scrambled to the nearest tannoy.

"Hello Undermanager it's me Mick."

"Colin will we be ready for the nightshift?"

"Undermanager it's me Mick, Colin is on dayshift." I've detected his slurring of words. I continue down the face towards the maingate end whilst the Undermanager continues his one sided conversation with the dayshift face Overman.

By the time I reach the men they've stopped working to listen to his comments over the tannoy system.

"Pissed as a fart."

"Come on lads let's finish up here and make our way out."

"Colin, how long before we're shearing again." I don't respond and assist the men to complete the timbering.

"Do I need to make my way down to you?"

Timbering complete we made our way out to the manrider. It's about half an hours travelling time. The nightshift Face Overman and his team are at the meeting station when we arrive at the outbye end of the maingate.

He walks across to me out of earshot of the men.

"Do me a favour make sure he doesn't come down the pit?"

"What state is he in?"

"Not good, he was in the Control Room when I came on shift. I'm guessing the Manager's given him a bollocking and told him to get it sorted." I continue to give my opposite number a shift handover.

"Anyway, you get yourself gone you'll be meeting yourself coming back if you don't get a move on." I didn't need any further encouragement time was pressing.

"Good luck see you tomorrow." My men had already left.

Twenty minutes later I arrive at the manriding station.

"Come on fella."

"Haven't you got a home to go to?" My men are sat on the carriages waiting to go.

"I'm coming." I notice a light in the distance moving from side to side.

"Who the fucks that?" the driver of the manrider shouts out.

"Oi what the fuck do ye think ye doing?" The cap lamp is getting closer. I then see the oil lamp and hear the sound of a walking stick. *Fuck it can't be!*

I laughed. At least I wasn't that bad or was I? There was an occasion just after I'd finished for our annual Summer holiday. Probably when I was at my worse state "demob happy."

I lay in bed awake on a Saturday morning later than normal but still before my wife and kids. Lying there I was unable to recollect the events from the previous evening. It wasn't long before my wife was awake too.

"I think you've surpassed yourself this time."

"Sorry what do you mean?"

"I mean your behaviour is disgusting and particularly in front of the kids."

"What? What the hell do you mean?"

"Well darling after you'd consumed half a bottle of the whiskey Mum bought you, you fell asleep. No surprises there then as that's all you seem to do when you get home."

"Sorry about that, it's just a hazard of the job."

"Me and the kids took little notice as we're well used to it now. Then without warning you jumped up and headed to the hallway. I assumed you'd gone to the loo until I heard the fridge door open." At that time, in the hall cloakroom there was an old fridge freezer. We used for the kids soft drinks and my beer.

"This was quickly followed by the sound of a hose being discharged into the fridge. The kids went out to see what the commotion was about. That's when I heard them giggling and shouting.

"Quick Mum Dad's weeing into the fridge.*"

"You're joking me?"

"And why would I do that? Go and look for yourself I had to remove the carpet. I threw it out. You'll need to remove it before the neighbours see."

"I don't believe it and why will the neighbours see?"

"Because dear the carpet soaked in piss is on the front lawn!"

Needing no further explanation, I jumped up out of bed and went to the window in the front spare bedroom. Sure enough................

"Bloody hell I'm here already." I shout out aloud. I'd been that busy daydreaming. I'd arrived at the pit lane. I indicated and slowed down. *I wonder what delight the next few hours have in store for me.* Driving onto the main car park I spot the Manager's office lit up. I can see clearly all those assembled. Only Denny turned in my direction. *Oops I'm last to arrive.* I could see

Blackhead and his team, Denny and Gregor, the Deputy Manager, and the Manager. He was pacing up and down his office. I could only guess why. I was glad I'd taken Denny's advice.

I parked up and headed straight to the Manager's office. I knocked on the door. Without waiting for an answer, I walked straight in. Ready to offer my apology. There was no need.

"So good of you to join us Mr Gibson." I nodded towards the Manager. He was stood at his desk. "Right gentlemen please take a seat." Kelvin and his team sat one side of the table. Myself, Denny, and Gregor the other. Mr Douglas looking paler than normal. He took a seat at the far end of the table. Rather ominous I thought. Well away from the Manager. All eyes were fixed on the Manager.

"You're all well aware by now how I expect to be kept appraised if a problem arises." He looked at us individually. Ensuring he had our attention. He did. "Well?" I don't think any of us thought his comment was a question. "I'll ask you again. Do you?" His comment a little louder this time. Followed by "Well do you?"

"Yes, Mr Adman." We answered collectively. Other than Mr Douglas. He said nothing. He was staring at the table. Not a good sign. The whole incident was surreal. Memories of school came flooding back. For the first time I began to relax. Whatever was coming wouldn't be aimed at me or my team. I now understood I was an observer. I intended to enjoy the poor bastard who was about to get a good and proper arse reamering. I guessed I knew who it would be. By the look and colour of his face he knew too.

"Why was I not informed of the gas problem on 62's?" No one answered. I looked around the table at each of my colleagues expressions. Poor Dafydd looked as though he was about to start crying. "Will someone answer the fuckin question."

Kelvin coughed to clear his throat. "You were." Nobody moved. We knew what was coming next.

"I was fuckin what?"

"I left a note on your desk and Mr Douglas's. You were obviously off site. Mr Douglas was still underground. I had to pick my lad up from cubs." I looked towards Kelvin. *Cheeky bastard. You'd arranged to play golf with Dafydd and Osian.* I knew that for a fact. "I'd planned to come back later to see how Gruffyd and the team were getting on." I had to give it to Kelvin. He was so convincing. Either side of me both Denny and Gregor relaxed. They too now recognised Zone B were in the clear.

"Is this fuckin true Mr Douglas?" The question was followed by the Manager's clenched fist hitting his desk. The force of which caused the handset of the land line to dislodge. "Well????" The Deputy Manager attempted to answer. I say answer his first response was a series of coughs. I just hoped it wasn't followed up by a burp.

"I, I, I…" As hard as he tried the sentence he was trying to convey to the Manager wouldn't form. By this time, we were all looking at him. Our attention suddenly distracted by a knock on the door. It was Gruffyd.
"Anyone fancy a cuppa? I've got kettle on."
"Answer the fuckin question!" We all jumped. The Manager hadn't taken his eyes off Mr Douglas. Gruffyd's head suddenly disappearing from view. I guessed the Manager's comment had answered his question.

How strange at time's like this how much enjoyment we get from seeing a colleague in distress. I reflected. We must all have a touch of sadism in us. "Mr Douglas I'm still waiting for an answer." The Deputy Manager for the first time raised his eyes from the table to look directly at the Manager. His eyes looked glazed. His mouth continued to move but again no words came forth. At this point I began to feel sorry for the man. At the end of the day there's only so much pain you can watch others inflict on a colleague.
"Could I suggest this may have been a slight oversight." I offered. Perhaps it hadn't been the best move I'd ever made. My comment caused the Manager to jump from and seat. Screaming he shouted.
"Out, out get out of my fuckin office. Now fuck off the lot of you!" We needed no more encouragement. We left. All accept for Mr Douglas.

–

5. 1990 Right 1st Time

The new Assistant Group Director Larry Button began to take a real interest in what we as Undermanager's were up to introducing regular meetings which he chaired. The man was from the South Yorkshire region. Colleagues from there had suggested he was a tough task master but fair. The, meeting referred to as the Progress and Efficiency meeting held monthly. We'd discuss all manner of subjects production targets, development progress, delay analysis, safety, cost, FSV performance, planning and overtime. One of his focus areas was development progress even at the expense of production from the coal face. I always liked to prepare.

"Finally tell Delwyn to make sure T3 headings are manned up. I've got a Progress and Efficiency meeting tomorrow with Button. I've got enough explaining to do without any further lack of progress in there."
"Should I get him to phone you?"

"No need even if he leaves the face short man up T3."

"Got you gaffer, you on a promise tonight then?"

"No," I laughed at Gruffyd's comment, "I need to get the dog out for a quick walk before I call it a day."

"No problems enjoy." The call ended. Ten minutes later I was out walking along the River Clwyd; Mrs Gibson was curled up on the sofa watching Dallas. Mentally I began to prepare for tomorrow's meeting. The Manager had pre warned me that Button would visit T3's before the meeting.

Before bed I'd need to check my figures for the coal drivages for both T3's and the H5/4. T3's was the next panel of coal to replace T2 and although behind target it was gradually catching up to where it should be. The H5/4 could be described as the strategic drivages accessing additional reserves of coal in this seam. After the last visit when I's had my arse kicked for redeploying men to the coal face I'd kept a diary in which I recorded where and when the drivages hadn't been manned up. My book of excuses became very useful and something I had to thank my latest Manager for. He tended to give instructions and when the shit hit the fan forget he'd given them. Bless, but I suppose that's one of the advantages of being a Manager.

Next morning, I was up at five without having a particular good sleep. One of the problems I had if prepping for work the next day it remained in my head. So much so that I'd dream I was in work and last night we'd completed three shears off the face. It was a good dream and put me in a good frame of mind. However, driving into work, I felt I'd done a shift already.

"You did fuckin what?"

"I did exactly as I was told Mr. Gibson."

"Delwyn I gave a clear fuckin instruction to man the headings."

"The Manager told me to man the face we needed the coal."

"For fucks sake I gave a clear instruction. Why didn't you phone me?"

"Gruffyd said you were out with the dog."

"And?"

"But the Manager said…" I could see I was getting nowhere with Delwyn. I spotted my development Overman lurking outside the office door.

"Lewis get your fuckin arse in here. Why didn't you call me?"

"You never asked me Mr. Gibson now."

"Lewis I'd given clear instruction to man up T3's"

"Delwyn told me to put the men on the face we were short of men to pull the chocks in." I turned to Delwyn.

"The Manager told me to man up the coal face." He responded shrugging his shoulders. I was getting nowhere with either of them. There were things to do and I'd wasted enough time already. I stopped myself and very calmly said to them both.

"Gentlemen next time there's a change to any instruction I give please, please call me."

"Even if it's an instruction from the Manager?" Delwyn asked.

"Yeah even then."

"Even if you're out walking the dog. Lewis added.

"Yes, even then!"

"What if......."

"No fuckin more please I couldn't be any clearer.." I stood shaking my arms in the air. It had the desired effect they both ran from the office.

At eight o'clock I headed towards the pit top. The meeting with the Deputy Manager had been short. Any visit from the Assistant Group Director had the desired effect. He would be visiting Mr. Blackhead in Zone A. Anything to keep him away from the Manager.

Once underground Evan and I split up, he would check on the supply situation and arrange to cover any shortfall. I would head into T3's and have a quick recee before the visit. I'd meet Mr Button and the Manager at the entrance to Zone B. I was quite pleased with what I saw. At least the nightshift had used the stone dusting machine to good effect. The roadways looked as though there'd been a fresh fall of snow. To add to the scene the haulage lads had stacked a further pile of stonedust bags at the meeting station.

"Hello Mr Gibson, hello Mr. Gibson." The tannoy system rang out. I moved across to the side of the roadway.

"Hi Control Room."

"Mr. Gibson the Manager has asked me to let you know he and Mr. Button will be heading towards the pit top shortly."

"Thanks Idris, make sure the loco lad knows."

"Already sorted."

"Thank you." *Hmm starting a little earlier than normal must have something else on.* I turned and began to make my way to Strata Top.

"Mr. Gibson." I turned to see the District Deputy walking towards me.

"Everything to your satisfaction?"

"Yeah looking okay thanks Caerwyn, just going out to meet them now."

"You okay?"

"Certainly am. We've already set two and the lads have just started cutting for the third."

"Nice one. Don't worry about meeting us we'll see you on the way round. I'll catch you later."

I left Caerwyn and headed out to the top of the Durbog manriding conveyor. I didn't have to wait long. In the distance I saw two cap lamps bobbing up and down as they travelled along the conveyor. One by one they clambered onto the wooden platform.

"Mr Gibson good morning to you. Hope you're well?"

"Good morning Mr. Button, Manager all good thanks."

"Bit earlier than normal as I've been called to a meeting at Gadbrook Park with the Director. Still time for a quick visit though and our meeting later."

"Good I'm looking forward to it" *Like fuck I was.* We moved off towards the air doors leading to T3's district with me leading the way.

"Just a minute gents I've got a stone in my boot." Mr. Button shouted. We stopped the Manager walked across to me.

"Laddie that pile of debris is still at the bottom of the manrider I want it fuckin well gone!"

"Will do Mr. Adman."

The remainder of the visit around T3 went with out a hitch. Other than when Mr Button asked me a direct question once we arrived in T3's maingate.

"Mick."

"Yes, Mr Button?"

"Are you manning these developments continually?" I looked towards the Manager. He was standing alongside the Assistant Group Director. He was smiling. Not a kind smile.

"That's the instruction I've been given by Mr Adman." The answer I'd given hadn't been a lie, but it certainly wasn't the truth. Particularly if he were to find out about last night.

"Good. It's so important the developments take priority over the coal face." The Manager was still smiling. "Wouldn't want any production gaps now would we?"

"No Mr Button. Not at all." An hour and a half later I was bathed and back in the office.

"Hi Mick, they're ready to see you now."

"Thanks, Bronwen, on my way." Replacing the phone, I grabbed my notebook and pen. Evan and Osian were sat either side avoiding any eye contact.

"Wish me luck Gents."

"I, good luck Mick. Can't believe he didn't ask about T3's being on stop last night."

"Like I was at fault? No, he'll get it between the eyes if he starts."

"Mick, Osian is right keep your fuckin gob shut. Denny mentioned the last time you were summoned." Evan added with a chuckle. I climbed out of my chair and left.

"Go straight in Cariad, tea?"

"Think I'll have a coffee please Bronwen."

"Good luck."

"Thanks."

They we're both sat to the left of the long meeting room table. In deep conversation initially.

"Ah Mick come on in and take a seat." Mr Button seemed to be leading the conversation. I sat immediately opposite the two of them.

"Good visit today Mick."

"Thanks..." There was a knock on the door. Bronwen entered with my coffee. "Thanks, Bronwen."

"Just referring back to our conversation underground."

"Yes." *Oh, fuck not T3's again.* The Manager hadn't said a word. Only offering his glassy eyed stare.

"You must ensure the developments are manned at all times. Even at the expense of the coal face.

I nodded and switched my gaze to the manager. Expressionless still. *If he hadn't have got involved last night and Del had stuck to the plan.* Again, I said nothing. Without any warning he suddenly changed the subject.

"Mr Adman has concerns on the attitude amongst you and the officials in Zone B. There's a tension within the office and one creating a very aggressive approach amongst your team. *For fucks sake talk about kettle calling the pot black!*

"How do you communicate to your team?"

"On a daily basis?"

"No, I was thinking more on how you update your team on performance."

"I have a weekly section meeting."

"And when does that take place?"

"Usually Wednesday afternoon when we get up the pit. If we have a face transfer or salvage, I'd run that as a separate meeting."

"And who would attend?"

"My team. The Deputy Engineers, their assistants, my Colliery Overman and the Development or Face Overman."

"And what do you discuss?"

I explained how the weekly section meeting operated. We'd touch on production and development targets. The detail on these areas usually happened at shift change. This would include delays and where we could improve. Gregor would add any electrical installation that were required including move ups.

146

Denny and Gethin giving advance warning on any major maintenance required on face or heading equipment. I paused for breath.

"Yeah just as I thought. You're trying to cover too many areas in too little a time. I was thinking more of a standard agenda to include such things as – delay analysis, FSV performance, cost saving initiatives, development progress compared to the pits Action Programme, a review and application of Group Technical Instructions." I continued to listen but his comments although admirable made little sense. In an ideal world yeah great but this was here! My mind began to wonder. I really needed to talk with Gruffyd on additional timber for the face. I hope Evan remembers. I was on auto pilot up until he turned to the Manager. It was his prompt to add to our conversation.

"What we're thinking Mick is if you were to take a full day out each week. Arrange with Storm and her team to fetch bacon baps, teas and coffees and later in the day finish off with sandwiches." He stopped talking and looked to me for a reaction. Unusually I was speechless. *Take a full day on the surface, bacon baps, drinks? Had they both been smoking dope? I couldn't even spend time at home with the family without him calling. Demanding I get back to the pit. Only last week we'd just sat down in our clean for the weekly section meeting. One of the development heading became gassed out. Adman was underground. After his call we followed suit.* I came back to the present. They were both looking at me.

"Yeah but…"
"No buts Mick." I couldn't believe my eyes the Manager was smiling. "Make it happen."
"And we're going to arrange a team building weekend for you and your team." Mr Button added.
"A what?"
"Team building. A weekend away from the pit. Get to know one another better." I wasn't sure what to say. I just sat and stared at them both.
"Ever heard of TQM? Total Quality Management."
"No."
"We'll talk more of that later."

Returning to my office I replayed in my mind what had just been said.
"You okay Mick?"
"Yeah I'm good thanks Evan."
"You don't look good." Osian added. I wasn't sure I should tell my two senior officials what I'd been told. *Oh, what the hell!*

"We're going on a team building weekend." I avoided mentioning the weekly session in my office. I would see how the next few days panned out. I didn't want to excite Osian. He loved a bacon bap.

-

The drive to take cost out of the business continued unabated. What we didn't know at the time British Coal had begun to review new methods of work. These new methods included greater use of roof bolting.

Before I'd arrived, roof bolting had been used as a supplementary support on face salvages. Proving its worth in the number of reduced shifts to salvage a coal face. Further trials at Betws and Ellington collieries with experts from the USA determined a number of important facts, namely:

- Relation of hole size to bolt diameter
- The superiority of polyester resins to water extended resins
- The importance of drill bit type and wet drilling to provide hole straightness and cleanliness

Towards the end of the 1980's a number of senior Western Area management visited Australia. The visit concluded:

- Australian mining conditions compared favourably with those in the UK
- Many roadways in Australia were supported purely with bolts
- Where a roadway was unable to be supported purely by bolts it was deemed uneconomic to mine
- The Australian techniques could prove beneficial in the UK

"What's the meeting about?"
"No idea. I believe there's some guys here from Staffordshire House. Douglas mentioned something about new methods of work."
"I see he's asked Evan and Dewi to be there too."
"Yeah they've just gone for a bath."
"Best not be late." Kelvin and I headed off for a shower.

Twenty minutes later all four of us arrived at the conference room. The Manager's team were already there. Douglas, Blunt, and Ken John the newly appointed Mechanical engineer. My good friend Gerry Tuffman had decided to take early retirement. In his words this was now a young man's game. I felt his reasoning was a load of bollocks. It was more to do with Adman being on his case.

The room had been laid out with a number of chairs facing a white screen. The overhead projector was positioned opposite.

"Help yourself to teas and coffee's lads."
"Thanks Mr Douglas."
"Mick go easy on those biscuits. They're the Managers favourites."

148

"I wouldn't dare." As I responded the door opened. In walked the Manager followed by two gentlemen. They looked important. I didn't recognise either. The Manager was carrying a folder. I assumed containing the acetates for his presentation. He walked straight to the front of the room placing the folder alongside the overhead.

"Right everybody if we could make a start." He introduced the two gentlemen, both Geotechnical specialists in the Technical Department. I didn't quite catch their names. One of them was exceptionally tall. They were there to take questions after the Manager had completed his presentation.

For the next thirty minutes the Manager explained how we would trial roofbolting along T6's maingate development. For the first fifteen metres we'd continue on conventional supports sixteen by nine foot square work. Then dropping down to fourteen foot bars on seven foot four inch legs. This time alternating with rockbolts through something called a Celstrap. This he described as a steel metal plate with holes in. The handheld machine we'd be using for drilling and inserting the rockbolts was referred to as a Wombat. It had an extendable leg. What else would we have expected it to be called? The equipment was from Australia after all. This would continue for the next fifty metres with a monitoring station installed every twenty metres.

The next stage would see the proportion of Celstraps to conventional supports increased two to one again for another fifty metres. A further monitoring station would be included. We'd been asked to keep any questions to the end of the presentation. It seemed the Manager didn't want any interruptions to his rehearsed presentation. I however couldn't help but spoil his fun.
"Sorry Mr Adman, what do you mean by monitoring station?"
"What?" He looked towards me, eyes glaring. Kelvin alongside me whispered.
"You're fucked now fella." I gave him a dig with my elbow and continued.
"You've mentioned monitoring stations on two occasions now. What are they?" As expected, the faint sound of a growl could be heard. None of the management team seemed put out, well used to his antics by now. It seemed however to unsettle the smaller of the Geotechnical experts.
"We have an acetate with the detail Mr Adman. I think it's near the back of the folder." Poor man he wasn't to know what was to come next. Eyes blazing the Manager's attention was redirected from me.
"I know full fuckin well where the slide is. As I've already said we'll take questions at the end." Billy Blunt turned towards me shaking his head.
"Cunt."
"Thanks Billy."

"If I may continue." As expected, he'd lost his train of thought and took a little time before he continued. "Thereafter all further support will be provided by the rockbolts with the addition of wooden legs attached to the Celstraps."

"What the fuck! I can't see the lads being very happy with that now." Dewi blurted out. "You want the lads to stop setting steel and work under bolts?"

"Exactly." The glare had returned.

"Sori I can't see that happening now. It'll be too dangerous. What happens when the strata above start to move heh? There'll be nothing to hold it back." It was good to see the Manager's anger being directed elsewhere. The interruption caused the others in the room to begin talking to themselves. I turned to Kelvin.

"What the fucks up with him. T6's is in Zone fuckin B not A." Kelvin raised a hand.

"Mr Adman, are we likely to carry out any of this in Zone A?"

"Too deep. Strata Top is the ideal place to trial it. Dewi let me be clear the pit has to cut cost, and this is a way of doing it. If we don't, we may not have a long term future. Let me be very clear about that."

The taller of the Geotechnical experts jumped out of his seat. He was holding a Yellow pages, two in fact one with a series of short bolts in position. He took the opportunity to demonstrate the rigidity of the book and how it would be supported by the coal pillars. The Manager took the opportunity to sit down. The Geotechnical experts then presented a series of slides showing the monitoring stations and use of the sonic extensometer and strain gauge bolt. A further slide depicted a series of arrows and the direction of the in-situ stress. We would learn that the national trend for the major horizontal stress direction was roughly NW-SE.

After the meeting Mr Douglas advised me that one of the haulage lads had been appointed as our Rockbolting specialist – a nice enough lad called Noah. He would be trained by the Group's experts and become our own in house expert.

Over the following weeks he carried out a series of "teach ins" with the heading teams advising on the importance of the correct depth of hole drilled, correct drill bit, keeping the Wombat drilling apparatus fully operational. The benefit to me was that any issues raised regards drilling could be referred directly to Noah.

One of the shifts seemed to have a problem with bolts falling out of the hole after the insertion of the resin capsules and the spinning of the bolt. Even after waiting the stipulated time of thirty seconds the bolts continued to drop out of the hole. We assumed we'd received a faulty batch of the fast and slow resin. However, it was later proven a number of the team members were colour blind.

The green resin capsule was being inserted before the red. It also helped explain why there'd been an increase in the use of the slower set resin.

Two weeks into the start of the drivages I went into T6's maingate with Evan to see for myself the bolted only roadway.

"Bora da Mr Gibson and you too Evan."

"Bora da, Terry how's it going?" Terry was one of the chargehands. A capable lad. When I first arrived, he'd been one of the FSV drivers.

"The lads are a little concerned working under the bolts alone, but I suppose we'll get used."

"Come on then let's have a look." We continued forward. It was my first time too. Although I wasn't about to say anything, I was a little apprehensive myself. Fourteen years working underground and for the first time walking along a road with no steel above my head. Evan turned to me.

"It's a little unnerving don't you think now?"

"No, we'll be fine." I'm not sure my bravado even convinced Evan.

The heading team had been reduced to three. A further cost cutting exercise that had originally began under our previous Manager Mr Groves. One of the lads was operating the Dosco Dintheader. He lifted the cutting mat on which a celstrap had been placed to the roof. Hanging in cantilever were two lengths of six-foot rectangular mesh attached to its neighbour with a series of metal springs. I couldn't help myself by shouting out.

"Make sure it's on centre." Terry laughed pointing to two lengths of string from which hung small lumps of coal ten yards back.

"Wouldn't have it any other way." He raised his cap lamp to indicate the chalk mark above the newly suspended celstrap. The centre of the celstrap identified by hole three. It lay perfectly below it.

Terry and his colleague then drilled holes, using the Wombat, for the number two and number one bolt. Having inserted the resin and pushing the bolt into the hole. Thereafter spinning the rockbolt to secure the celstrap to the roof. The final act was to attach a wooden leg with clamps to the celstrap. Lowering the cutting mat, the machine was withdrawn to allow drilling of holes three, four and five and bolts inserted. Followed by the positioning of the leg. Terry moved back towards us whilst his two colleagues positioned the side straps. This time using a hydraulic drilling machine attached to the Dintheader. Glass fibre bolts on the faceside and steel on the ribside.

"Very impressive Terry and the time taken to do it much improved. Only one thing though."

"Before you say it, waste of fuckin time!"

"What is?"

"The fuckin arm we're supposed to put the celstrap in."

"You read my mind."

"What would be good if we could extend the cutting distance beyond the 2.1m and be able to set two straps."

"I've no doubt that will be next but not just yet."

Our conversation was interrupted by the commotion coming from behind although I could smell it before it arrived. One of the FSV's had arrived with a pack of supplies. The smell of diesel filled the roadway. One of the initiatives brought in by Noah included a full pack of supplies sufficient for ten metres advance. There was sufficient room on the flat bed to get two packs. It had been a good move. Very rare for any of the headings to be on stop waiting for supplies. Beyond the FSV I could see the deputy, Caerwyn.

"Go on ask him to come over."

"Why?"

"He's frightened to fuckin death he won't come under the bolts only as far as the steel work."

"How does he do his inspection and check for gas." As we were talking, we moved to one side as two of the lads dragged a 30" length of ventilation bagging forward. "I hope that's not for my benefit Terry?"

"As if!"

"I don't fuckin believe this." Evan commented to no one in particular and walked towards Caerwyn. "Caerwyn get over here now."

"Sori fraid I can't now Evan I've a report to write." And with that he turned tail and ran off.

"Well I've seen it all now."

"That's why we struggle to get cover at the weekends. Many of the officials are avoiding T6's."

"I think when we get back up the pit, I need to have a conversation with the NACODS reps."

"Leave it with me I'll arrange it now."

That afternoon Evan and I sat with Osian and Dewi.

"The thing is gents how can we get the men to work in the heading if some of the Deputies won't."

"You can't very well force them now."

"No, I'd agree but there are the issues of falsifying the reports."

"Whatever do you mean? Who's been falsifying the reports."

"Well how the hell does he do his pre-shift."

"Nightshift, two hours before the commencement of the shift."

"Okay, let's say that's true. What about a mid-shift?"

"Not required. According to the Manager's and Officials Regs, 1956, 12(1) if men are continuously in the district since the last preceding pre-shift inspection, it's sufficient to do an inspection at intervals not exceeding eight hours."

"Bollocks, that only refers to the pre-shift inspection. Regulation 15(1) and (4) dictates you must make at least two inspections during the shift. During an inspection he needs to test for gas, examine the state of the ventilation and the state of the roof and sides. You can't do that from a distance. Anyway, just out of interest have either of you two been in T6's?"

"It's not my section."

"Fair point Dewi."

"Osian?"

"Well, err, err I haven't yet found the need."

"For fucks sake Osian you're the fuckin Development Overman!"

By September we'd reached the faceline position and began to turn off at ninety degrees. Without the free-standing supports affecting the length of the machine we had been able to turn and create a five-metre stub end within four shifts. Three days later we'd opened up enough ground to install the Lioness conveyor.

"Have you done the list?" I asked walking into to my office. Evan looked up.

"Yeah all done gaffer I've heard the visit with the Manager didn't go too well?"

"Understatement of the year mate he's gone ape. You'll need to add extra shifts for the FSV lads and haulage. The chocks are beginning to pile up at the lifting station and we need to move them across to T6's face line before Monday." No more was said Evan duly noting my comments.

We were part way through the chock salvage of T5's coal face. T3's chocks were still in situ. The plan was to move these later to D28's. Unlike previous salvages when we built chock stacks to replace the extracted powered support; this time we'd position the first two extracted supports in line with the coal face perpendicular to the supports still in place. Each time a support was lowered it pulled itself forward using the main ram attached to a steel bolt secured in the coal face. Thereafter the FSV, used its on board ram to manoeuvre the support onto its flatbed. The two perpendicular supports were then individually pulled forward allowing the ground behind to collapse.

Unfortunately, the nightshift in an attempt to speed things up decided to remove three supports before supporting the ground causing a roof fall in front of the two perpendicular chocks. For the first time in the pits history we were attempting to avoid a production gap. Coal was currently being extracted from S64's in Zone A, however due to numerous geological problems we'd not been achieving production targets.

Visits to T6's coal face were now becoming a regular feature particularly by senior staff from British Coal. I was often prewarned by the behaviour of the Manager. He became a nicer person during the days before the visit. The interest shown on the visits concerned the maingate and the area supported only by roof bolts.

The colliery was now part of the newly formed North West Group based at Northard House, Gadbrook Park, Northwich. Staffordshire House was still operating but rumours abounded the building was about to be sold. Just as had happened with Anderton House some years before. Now replaced by a housing estate.

For the visit I would meet the Manager and his visitors at the top of the Durbog Manrider and lead the group into Strata Top. They included the newly appointed Technical Director of British Coal, the North West Group's General Manager who was about to retire and his replacement. I was good with remembering faces. His replacement I'd met before but wasn't sure where. Once they'd all alighted the conveyor belt introductions were made. Thereafter I generally kept my distance. By distance there was no set measurement. It was more to do with the look I received from the Manager.

There was an uneasiness within the pit at that time and I've no doubt elsewhere too. The industry had gone through some major changes. Including increased productivity and cost savings on a scale never seen before. Particularly in the reduction of manpower. I was hoping to learn more today without getting "too close."

"Gentlemen I can with absolute certainty confirm the Chairman's commitment to the industry. He's a pitman through and through. It doesn't sit easy with him when he took on the role there were one hundred and ten operating collieries producing ninety million tonnes of coal with a workforce of ninety thousand. By the end of this year we're estimating sixty five collieries, forty nine thousand employees producing seventy three million tonnes. For someone with little time left as Chairman he wants to see the industry left in good shape." The Technical Director commented.
"When does he finish?" The Group General Manager asked
"End of the year."
"Do we know his replacement yet?"
"I have an idea. He's from outside the industry but he seems a decent chap. He too wants the industry to survive."

The Manager hadn't said anything up to this point. I backed off a little as we continued down T6's maingate. I'd gone on a little too far at this point and missed most of what they were now saying. They stopped beneath one of the tell tales hanging from the roof. I retraced my footsteps and just caught the tail end of a further comment from the Technical Director.

"The Government is hell bent on destroying the industry. Many still blame us for Heath's demise and she's never forgiven us for the first so called turn." Quiet laughter broke out amongst the group.

"As you can see gentlemen." The Manager shone his cap lamp on the tell-tale. "No movement none whatsoever."

"Remarkable truly remarkable."

"This has to be the place. None better in the Group."

"But will the Board release the capital?"

"I don't see they have much choice. We keep being told how good the Australians and Americans are at producing coal. Using their technology and methods of work I can't see them refusing."

"Can I just add lest we forget. We keep talking about their technology and methods of work. Don't forget this is how the British coal mining industry were producing coal back in the fifties.

"I true very true Technical Director."

We didn't continue onto the face. After looking at some further tell-tales we made our way back out to the T7 headings. Little more was said other than nodding in agreement after the Manager had commented.

"After here we've got that narrow panel of coal T8's. T4's would be my suggestion."

"The panel you showed us on the plan Mr Adman before we came down."

"Yeah. I can show you were that is."

"No, I think I've seen enough. Time is of the essence. I'm due to attend a capex meeting in Hobart House later today with my counterpart. I wouldn't want to see this little project rejected."

And that was it visit over. They said their farewells and headed off. One of the shortest visits I'd had to date.

I made my way back to T4's. *I wonder what they had planned for here?*
"Well I think we should do as we did last time with the chocks." I was sat in my office with the team. Evan, Osian, Denny, Gethin, Gregor and Ifor.

"Could we make sure this time we leave some room for my lads to get in and replace the redline."

"Sure Gregor, just a mo." The phone was ringing. "He's done what? And he wants to see me there now. He's got to be joking. I'll speak with him myself. He's nowhere near a phone. Okay leave it with me." I replaced the handset.

Everyone sat around the table looked towards me. Denny was the first to speak.

"What does the daft fucker want now cock?"

"That was Control. The Manager's put a lockout on the main crosscut belt. He's stopped the inbye developments and wants the men to clean out the tailend and drive. He's waiting to see me on site." Nobody spoke for a moment; Gregor broke the silence.

"For fucks sake. How does he expect us to plan ahead. Every time we have a fuckin meeting he interrupts. Where's his sidekick Mr Douglas."

"On his way. He's on 62's with Blackhead." The office door opened.

"You know the Manager's havin a dickie he wants to see you now."

"Yeah, got it Billy on my way."

"Good job you never got changed."

"Something I've learnt along the way. Anyway, I need to make a move. I'll catch you guys later."

"I'm coming with you."

"Gethin there's no need, you stay here and finish the meeting. Evan will chair in my absence."

"If there's a problem with the belt I need to be there."

Forty minutes later we arrived. I heard the Manager before I saw him. He was using his stick to smash a lump of coal on the belt whilst at the same time screaming at Mr Douglas. "I've fuckin told them all to keep the fuckin barrel ends clean. How many times have I warned you all on the possibility of a fire? Hey how many times? Does no fucker listen to me?" Mr Douglas said nothing.

I waited as Gethin went on ahead. Mr Douglas started to speak. Before he could utter a word the Manager turned on him again. "How many fuckin times?" He spotted me watching. I walked forward. I was about to ask him what a barrel end was but thought better of it.

"Right Mr Gibson, so good of you to join us. Follow me." He walked towards the drive. The Deputy Manager gave me a nod and drew his hand across his mouth. Indicating an imaginary zip. We followed him around to the gib end, the front of the chute was missing. He began jabbing his stick. "Where's the fuckin wiper laddie where?" We hadn't quite judged our position correctly as he turned suddenly. To avoid contact I backed off and trod on Mr Douglas's foot.

"Sorry." I offered.

"Sorry I'll give you fuckin sorry." The Manager assumed I was talking to him. He now stood at the back of the gib once more jabbing with his stick. "A wiper with no fuckin neoprene! Some fucker has used belting." We said nothing. "There should be at least two wipers. He was now pointing at the bottom belt above the tailend.

Without warning he marched off at pace towards the tailend. We followed. Up ahead the heading lads were walking towards us. Terry the chargehand was leading. "Morning Mr Adman." He received no response raising his eyebrows as he saw me. I stopped.

"Hi Terry how many lads have you got?"

"There's eight of us in total. I've pulled the lads off the transfer point too. I've left two at the tailend of the crosscut belt with two cleaning out our belt. Me and these three are making our way to the drive."

"Good I'll catch you later." He whispered as he left.

"Mick look on the positive side. It won't be just you getting an arse reamering." I smiled and hurried forward to catch the other two.

Up ahead I could hear the Manager screaming once more at Mr Douglas.

"I know there's a plough in place, but the neoprene has worn down. The metal is sitting on the conveyor. It'll damage the fuckin belt." Once more he started to thrash the belt with his stick. Gethin appeared and leaned across towards me.

"There's been no neoprene in the stores for the last two weeks. According to Iolo the last two orders for the stuff have been quashed."

"Thanks, Gethin. Could you get your lads on afters to check if there's anything we can salvage from T5's."

"Will do."

"You may as well make your way back to land I'll catch you later. Oh, and thanks for coming back in with me." Gethin nodded and walked off.

I turned back towards the Manager. Mr Douglas was taking a hammering. "You fuckin imbecile." As much as I was enjoying the spectacle, I was beginning to feel sorry for him.

"Mr Adman, I've arranged to get some neoprene salvaged. We'll have it fitted before the afternoon shift commence." It had the desired effect he stopped and looked directly at me.

"I'll leave it with you laddie. But be warned if I ever, ever find another conveyor in your district without adequate wipers and ploughs you'll be for the high jump." Mr Douglas was once more doing his imaginary zip demo.

"Loud and clear Mister."

The Manager turned and walked out towards the Access conveyor followed by Mr Douglas. I let them get some ten yards away before adding.

"The reason there's no neoprene on the belts is because we haven't got any. There's nothing in the stores. Some other fuckin imbecile cancelled the order." His aim with his stick had not been particularly accurate. I'd had plenty of time to duck as it came hurtling over my helmet.

The episode had given us all a salutary lesson. From then on, all conveyors had the necessary wipers and ploughs. It had immediate results with less conveyor stoppages, less spillage and less preparation time was required whenever we had a visit from HMI. Each morning at our meeting with Mr Douglas, Kelvin and I provided an update on each conveyor. For the next few weeks things quietened down. I was able to hold my section meeting without interruption. I'd also made provision to take Osian off shift. He had no complaint. I'd decided to use him as my belt supremo to ensure that all future installations and those already operated remained at the highest standard.

"Mr Gibson, I saw the strangest thing happen today."

"Now what would that be Osian?"

"Well would you believe I was about to pass through the airdoors at Strata Top and noticed some scrap that needed moving. I stopped to make a note when I saw someone the other side of the doors acting suspiciously."

"Suddenly become our new underground detective, have we now?" Evan who was sat opposite added laughing.

"It was only the Manager. He'd put a newspaper near to the tailend of the crosscut conveyor and placed a lump of coal on it."

"What a twat. After all the work we've done he's still trying to catch us out. He can't find any shit build up anywhere so he's planting his own to see if we notice it."

"Now Mick you can't be certain of that."

"I'll lay you a pound to a pinch of shit he's up to no good. What have you done with it?" Osian reached inside his overalls.

"Here, I wasn't about to leave it lying there, now was I? And particularly as it was the Sun. I know how you Scouser's feel about that daily."

"True I wouldn't wipe my arse on it. But could you do me a favour?"

"What?"

"Put it back but this time move it to a different position. Thereafter each time we know he's been into my end move it to another position. Let's play the cunt at his own game."

"Now Mr Gibson you're playing with fire there. Watch you don't get burnt."

"I won't but keep it to us the less others know the better."

A week later as the Manager passed my office, he popped his head in.
"Hello Mr Adman."
"Be careful laddie, be very careful."
"Why, whatever do you mean?" There was no further reply just a smile.
Although I'd asked Osian to keep our little game to ourselves things were about to change. Travelling out one afternoon he'd bumped into the Face Overman Asyn.
"What are you doin?"
"What does it look like now? Just following the instruction from the Undermanager."
Osian went on to explain what I'd arranged. Asyn being Asyn liked a bit of fun too. Particularly as he was from Wrexham. He began to move the newspaper to a different position at the end of each shift on leaving the district.

"What the fuck!" I looked up after Evan's comment. Standing at the entrance to my office was Asyn. He looked like something out of Ghostbusters. White from head to toe. It looked as though he'd fallen into a vat of stonedust.
"Called me a goat he did and then a sheep!"
"Who did? You best sit down." The lad didn't seem himself, completely stressed out. It was so unlike him.
"I got caught I did now." Asyn was visibly trembling.
"What the fuck are you on about?" I asked. Before he could answer. Osian walked into the office. Laughing uncontrollably.
"You poor fucker I saw it all." Still laughing he began to shake his head. "I was the other side of the airdoors. I was with Caerwyn. We heard him shouting. I opened the hatch ever so slightly. He picked up half a bag of stonedust he did now." Both Evan and I sat waiting for the punch line.
"It's not funny now Osian." Asyn began.
"Funny? It was fuckin hilarious now."
"Osian could you please tell us what has happened."
"The Manager caught old Asyn here moving the newspaper…" He began laughing once more. "Emptied the bag of stonedust over his head he did now."

–

"Not a bad shift for a change, I won't need a call from Delwyn tonight."
"Oh, before I forget we managed to get the two hundred metres of type eight to the top of the Access road."
"Thanks, Gruffyd can you ask Delwyn to unload at the back of Access 1 loop."
"Yeah let me write that down on my list. You expecting trouble?"
"You could say that; the shite we salvaged is down to the thread. There's at least a hundred metres needs changing now and before we bring the lads in to vulcanise."

"It never ceases to amaze Mr. Gibson when we talk about reducing cost; it always becomes more expensive in the long run."

"You know that, and I know that pity the grownups weren't as intelligent."

"Right lovely talking to you but must go. Don't want to keep the Manager waiting."

"How is the lovely man on his nightly call?"

"Do'y know I was only saying to one of the lads in Control the other day he seems to have changed. No more ranting and raving over the phone if there's a problem. He now goes quiet and I'm sure he starts to growl."

I laugh. "Well good luck with that, speak tomorrow."

"Thanks, and goodnight Mr. Gibson you have a good evening now."

I replaced the phone making a note to add beltmen to the overtime list for the weekend. Fingers crossed it lasts till then. Perhaps I might indulge in a spot of malt before I retire.

"I'll be back about one."

"Where you off to?"

"I'm meeting up with Denny at the Tavern for a spot of lunch…."

"Mick, Mick the phone."

"What?" I wake with a start I was about to leave the office in Chester, I was just telling my secretary my plan for the afternoon. It takes me a few seconds to gather my thoughts.

"Can't you hear me? The phone you'd best get it before the kids wake up."

"Yeah, yeah I'm going." I check the clock on the bedside table *half fuckin one.* I'd been asleep for just over two hours. Having a recurring dream that I worked in Chester.

"We need one in the bedroom."

"What?"

"A phone and on your side." I say no more and grab my dressing gown. Sophie the dog began to bark as I head down the stairs to find Gizmo the cat scratching at the front door.

"Ello?"

"Mr Gibson; Access 1's broke we're full in the bunkers face is on stand."

"For fucks sake. What have we done on the face?"

"Nearly one and half shears. I've called the belt lads they're on the way in."

"All three?"

"Yeah."

"Where's the type eight?"

"Fortunately, just offloaded it as you'd asked."

"Thanks, Delwyn I'll be there shortly."

Back upstairs the missus has gone back to sleep I quickly dress. The kids are flat out. Downstairs I let the dog out for a quick pee the cat seemed to have disappeared again. Within ten minutes I'm driving towards the pit. The roads are empty, almost, as I brake to let a vixen run across the road. The pit is only a fifteen-minute drive away. I'm glad I restricted myself to the one glass of malt. My mind begins to race through a mental check list of the things we'd need to do. The one thing I had forgotten to ask Delwyn if he'd called the Manager. I'll check that later.

Having parked the car I head straight to the baths and change. Before heading to the lamproom I retrieve a tin of snuff and pack of chewing tobacco from my office. No. 3 pit top is empty save for the Banksman.

"Poor you Mr. Gibson, no peace for the wicked!" I nod and pass him my tally. He drops the mesh gate. Removing the keps he signals to the winder. The cage slowly moves downwards before picking up speed. The darkness and cold close in around me. Within minutes I'm at the pit bottom the sound of leaking compressed air increases as the cage platforms are dropped.

"Loco ready Mr. Gibson." The Onsetter greets me as he lifts the cage gate.

I walk quickly forward along the loco track. The humming of the diesel engine louder as I approach. The loco looks out of place and lonely without the attached carriages. Tomos acknowledges my arrival with the wave of a hand. He climbs into the front of the engine. I do likewise at the rear. The smell of the diesel fumes is further exaggerated and quite uncomfortable until we start to move, and the surrounding air dilutes it. I check my watch *not bad going from receiving the phone call to getting on the loco three quarters of an hour.*

Delwyn met me at the top of the Access road. For the first time I see activity. Cap lamps bobbing up and down.

"Sorry about this but thought you should know."

"Not a problem you did the right thing." I extract my tin of snuff and offer it to him before taking a pinch myself.

"Should have asked earlier did you…….."

"Yeah both of them Manager and Mr Douglas no answer from either."

"Good, thanks how we fixed here then?"

"I've pulled most of the lads off the face clearing coal off the belt leaving a couple in the maingate preparing a move out. I've put two others with Gareth and Owen securing the belt below the break. Managed to use the chockwood still under the belt and the lashing chains. Tecwyn is with the fitter removing the sprag clutch off the drive."

The lads were well versed in changing the belt. The new type eight suspended at the back of the loop. They'd already attached to the existing belt. Reversing the belt and pulling on the top belt using the return rope of the Access haulage.

"Mr Gibson."

"Hi Tecwyn."

"We could do with putting the full two hundred metres in. We've identified another bad length behind the original."

"Have you checked with Delwyn?"

"He said check with you. Probably means we won't get coaling again this shift."

"Yeah do it. Let's get it ready for the dayshift. Do me a favour though Tec. Any decent lengths keep to one side for the developments."

"Will do."

And that was it the rest of the shift was spent changing the belt. We did better than expected completed by five thirty Delwyn kept the facemen over. Another half a shear was better than nothing or so I thought.

By the time I'd got back to land the dayshift had already arrived. So too had the Deputy Manager. He was waiting for me in the office.

"Mick how we looking?"

"All sorted. All we'll need this weekend are the lads for vulcanising."

"How come you changed the full two hundred metres?"

"We found another length that needed changing. Thought it best we do it all at once."

"Yeah maybe so but we've hardly done any shearing."

"I think two shears and changing two hundred metres of belt ain't bad for a shift. Don't you?"

"Doesn't matter what I think. How do you think the Manager's going to take it?"

"To be honest with you Mr Douglas I don't give two fucks. I made a decision and that's it." He nodded. Not that he agreed with my comment. I knew where he was coming from. Confirmed by the look of fear in his eyes. He'd obviously spotted the Manager's car coming onto the yard.

"Right I need to go and get changed. I'm with Mr Blackhead first thing. Havin a look at repositioning 18's pumps." And with that he was gone.

I sat down. Evan had left me a coffee. I grabbed a Hamlet from the drawer and lit up. The phone rang.

"Hello… No, I think he's in the baths… Who's after him?" Did I need to ask. "I'll let him know." No sooner had I put the phone down when Delwyn appeared. He didn't look happy.

"Would you believe it now."

"What's up Del?"

"That bloody Mr Douglas just passed him going to the pithead now. Manager's trying to get hold of him. Now he's asking for me."

"Listen if it helps just tell him it was me that made you put the two hundred metres in. Don't take any shit." I began to laugh.

"I don't think this is any laughing matter Mr Gibson. I don't need all this hassle at work now. I've got enough going on at home."

"Why what's up?"

"It's my wife. She's having an operation on her feet. Won't be able to walk for a week the doc reckons."

"Tell that to the Manager. I'm sure he'll go easy on you. He's a very understanding man he is."

"There you go again Mr Gibson taking the piss..." The phone rang.

"Hello... He certainly is. He's on his way. Yeah I'll pop in when you're done. Mr Douglas.. underground I believe something to do with 18'pumps." I moved the phone away from my ear. "Will do. I'll let Denny and Gregor know too." I replaced the handset. Delwyn's colour pale at the best of times had gone a shade paler. "He's waiting." Delwyn left. I sat back to reflect on this being my third Christmas at Point how time flies. In spite of the constant bollocking we received on a regular basis I enjoyed it still. I then put a call through to Denny and Gregor.

"Now listen cock you know we're in for a pasting. Can we just try and take it without antagonising him. In other words, keep yer fuckin gob shut. Seems you and the lads had a good shift last night..."

"He might be wishing us a Merry Christmas." Gregor interrupted. Before I could comment Delwyn poked his head through the door.

"All yours." Poor old Delwyn he looked even paler than he did before he went in.

We entered the office. The Manager was sat at the large table in the middle of the room. Storm was there too. She'd placed a tray in front of him.

"There you go Mr Adman. I know it's a little early in the day for your Christmas dinner. However, Bronwen tells me you're off to Group and won't be around for the rest of the day. Enjoy,"

"Diolch Storm I'll try my best." She winked at us as she left the office.

We sat opposite the Manager. My colleagues either side. His plate was piled high with turkey, stuffing, roast potatoes, and a variety of veg. The sprouts were enormous.

"Right now. What have you got to say for yourselves?" I could feel Denny nudge my leg. "Well?" He began to eat, and then the onslaught of abuse began. After each comment he took a mouthful of food. Denny and Gregor tried to answer. He wasn't on receive just transmit the abuse continued.

"And in spite of you and your pathetic fuckin performance we still manage to produce coal." He then placed the largest of the sprouts into his mouth. I waited till he started to chew. I'd decided at this point to add my thoughts.

"My fuckin performance what about you and your pathetic fuckin ability to demotivate your management team." I hear Denny groan. The Manager's eyes widen followed by an inaudible sound. Followed by chewed sprout. We dive to take cover as he begins to choke. Recovering he starts to spew out the contents of his mouth.

"Out, out… get out of my fuckin sight." We needed no further encouragement.

-

For the short time Mr Adman had become Manager we began to see a number of changes within the business. We assumed to was to make us more efficient. It became a time of constant change. During which we saw the introduction of consultants. It was a time of cost cutting, becoming more efficient and increasing productivity. I'd experienced something similar at the last pit I'd worked at, so the idea was not new. The consultants would visit us underground to see how we operated. Thereafter gaining our thoughts on areas for improvement. This was followed by a series of seminars. Presenting our ideas on how we could improve day to day working. Even at that time I found it strange how money would be spent on consultants using ideas presented to them by the management and the workforce.

The term team building became common place. The concept of these improvement was covered by a further term Total Quality. The Assistant Group Director Operations was the sponsor for this new initiative. The programme was called Total Quality Mining a derivative of Total Quality Management. Providing concepts and ideas to make the colliery more efficient by reducing cost and improving productivity. Its basic principle Quality was to continually satisfy customer requirements. Total Quality was to achieve Quality at the lowest cost and would require everyone's commitment.

The consultant appointed was a young chap ex Undermanager which I supposed helped. Over the coming weeks we'd go underground together. I think he was surprised how involved I got in the detail of what we did. It was an opportunity to get an understanding of exactly what was meant by Total Quality. Not just the theory but in practice. He claimed this approach was about getting it right "First Time." A phrase we began to hear quite often. He suggested this approach wasn't just about achieving a target it was about making sure what we did was right. No shortcuts. If it took longer to complete a task to get it right – so be it.

He would often ask my thoughts on the Manager. Something I managed to avoid answering. I certainly had some. Those thoughts, I kept to myself unless with my colleagues. Often in the Undermanager's baths our private enclave we shared our thoughts. Not before a thorough search was made of every nook and cranny. There was always someone who'd provide feedback to him. Criticism of the Manager was a no, no. This was the man who controlled your destiny, your life. It would be suicidal to be openly critical. However, as the young consultant would often confirm. Honesty was needed for this to work. I wasn't convinced.

Later in the programme we were introduced to management workshops where discussion became ever more open. At these sessions we'd split into small groups and discuss our view of Total Quality Mining. Even to the point where we offered reasons why the programme would not work or the perceived barriers to its implementation. At the opening Total Quality Workshop, the consultant running the programme made it perfectly clear that the Manager was away from the pit. Anything discussed at the forum was between us, discussion must be open and honest, hold nothing back. In his words call "a spade a spade."

I was cynical. I remember some years previous as an up and coming management trainee on a residential course being told the same thing. This was often done whilst we were at the bar during the evening. The Staff Manager hovering around our group watching us sink pint after pint. He would pick his victim with the cunning of a fox.
"Now my little management trainee how's it going with you?"
"Okay thankyou Staff Manager."
"What are your thoughts on the Coal Board's policy towards industrial relations? I'd appreciate an honest answer." This was before the 1984 strike my personal view they were shite. I wasn't about to share that with him. For those foolish enough to give an honest opinion they were never seen or heard of again. Stalinism was supposedly a Soviet curse.

And then without warning towards the end of 1990 PA Consultants disappeared without trace never to be seen again … or so we thought.

-

6. 1991 A New System of Work

As I'd done throughout all of my career I'd taken note of the senior people I'd worked for. Mr Adman had been no exception. His stance on all matters relating to health and safety was admirable. Although I did question his commitment to this if it were to affect production. Something I would need to understand better. Part of this approach was to confirm the various parts of the mine visited. I'd always kept a diary not detailed but sufficient to know what I'd been up to. To these daily notes I now added my underground visits.

Additionally, my approach in dealing with the men and officials. I'd believe I was firm but also fair. What I'd never considered before was the feelings of the person I was dealing with. I hadn't suddenly gone all "soft" however a constant barrage of abuse and insult to an individual did have consequences. Having been on the receiving end of it for nearly eighteen months now I'd altered my approach. Going that "extra mile" for the pit I now put on the back burner. No matter how hard I tried the Manager would always find fault. Now when I saw an opportunity to improve a situation I would leave it. Until such time I received a "bollocking." After that I would react.

With this knowledge I tried to better my management skills with those that I took charge of. I began to listen more. To better understand a situation for what it was. Not just barking orders and expect them to be carried out. Ron Groves had always lead from the front. He never distanced himself from a problem. He got involved. It became a team problem. Not one individuals.

I was beginning to better understand the man's behaviour. He wasn't the nut case we'd all assumed. Something must have happened in a past life. To create the person, he had become. His aggression was a way of hiding his insecurities. He was using anger as a defence mechanism. Denny had a far simpler view. Instead of being breast fed as a youngster he reckoned his mother gave him raw meat to chew on.

My thoughts were abruptly interrupted as the manrider came to a sudden halt. The braking of the loco caused the individual carriages to clash together.
"For fucks sake cock I weren't expecting that."
"That's cause you need to get underground more Denny."
"Or at least pay attention in the morning meeting." Gregor added.
"Damaged rail Denny. Manager on his way out yesterday picked it up. The lads are changing before he comes back in today. I'm guessing he'd check it. Come on it's a walk from here in."

Climbing out of the carriage I looked ahead. Evan was walking toward us.

"Almost done Mr Gibson. If you wait a further ten minutes we'll be up and running now."

"Thanks Evan but I think we'll keep movin. Manager wants to meet me and Denny at the GMT."

"Checkin up on the chock loading arrangements then?"

"Yep, not satisfied we've got everything in place. I mean what'll this be I reckon it'll be Zone B's fifth face installation since he's been here."

"Does he not trust us or what?"

"He trusts no one! Do me a favour though Evan just make sure you have a good tidy up when you're done and spread a bit of stonedust too."

"Will do."

"Oh, I meant to ask have we got lads on roof repairs in the Access road?"

"Yeah. Tom, Rick and Larry."

"Excellent. Come on Denny best be making a move. Where's Gregor?"

"Gone on ahead cock. He said he's meeting up with Ifor in T6's."

T6's at Strata Top was still in production. Our next coal face was in the Durbog D28's. Originally part of Zone A we'd inherited it to allow our colleagues in Zone A to concentrate their efforts in the Stone Coal and the two new drivages in the Hard Five Quarter. I think the Manager recognised our experience in the face to face transfers. And as the chocks for D28's were coming from T3's logic seemed to suggest this was the best way forward. The logic even extended to adding the Access Road to Zone B too.

Once Denny and I arrived at the GMT we had a good look around.

"Everything seems in fine fettle Mick."

"Yeah I agree but you can bet soft lad finds something amiss."

"It's just to keep you on your toes lad. I guess we'll know soon enough."
We both sat down on two upturned empty cable drums.

"Snuff cock?"

"Cheers Denny." No sooner had I inhaled the brown powder up each nostril the phone began to ring. It was Evan.

"Hi. Yep I wouldn't have expected anything else. Thanks for the heads up. Yeah were waiting for them now. Oh, is he. Catch you later."

I sat down again.

"Everythink oright cock?"

"As expected he stopped the loco to check the rail had been changed. He's got Tony Douglas with him and your mate Clark Michaels."

"For fucks sake that's more work for me then."

"Reckons Douglas doesn't look very happy."

"I'll bet he's had it up the arse cause you've put a stop to manriding on Access 1."

"Tough tits. Until he gets me the replacement type 8 it's a fuckin walk up."

Ten minutes later I felt the change in air pressure and then the slamming of the airdoors on the crosscut. Before long three sets of lights came into view. As usual the Manager was leading.

"Good morning Mr Adman what a pleasure to see you so early in the day." I don't know what it was I just couldn't help myself. My opening comment was bound to wind him up. I was given confirmation as Douglas began shaking his head frantically.

"Good morning Mick pleased to see you're on form today." He was smiling as he said it. His eyes were the giveaway though. I guessed replacing the damaged rail hadn't helped. "Right laddie explain your plans here."

For the next five minutes I took him through our plans once the chocks from T3's arrived at the GMT. Where we'd store them before loading onto the low cut flats and take them to the bottom of the Access and then off to the East towards D28's district.

"Another compressed air hoist wouldn't go amiss there." Clark Michaels interrupted pointing up towards the already established lifting framework. Two hoists already in position. I ignored his comment and continued.

"Between the usual run of heading supplies we're planning to transport at least nine per day minimum." The Manager had listened intently. I guessed trying to find a weakness to the plan. There was none. The team and I had planned this meticulously over many weeks.

"Wouldn't it be easier and quicker to send the canopies separate to the bases?" I know he knew the answer. He was testing I had everything covered.

"Double handling lifting off and putting back on. No, it'll take too long. Denny had a mock framework set up." Denny nodded. "There's only one area on the Access road where we'll need to do small re-rip. We've got lads on it again today. Six arches in total. They'll have that completed by this Thursday."

"Well laddie you seem to have this covered. You any questions Mr Douglas?" The Deputy Manager who up until this point had been staring into space turned abruptly and attempted to clear his throat.

"Have you sorted the problem with manriding on Access 1 and replaced the damaged stitching's?" I looked at him. *Are you for fuckin real?*

"Mr Douglas it isn't just the stitching. We need replacement belt. Which I believe isn't here till tomorrow. So, no there's still no manriding on Access 1."

"Can you get your beltmen to confirm the position."

"Why? I just told you the situation."

"Just fuckin do it laddie!" Bless the spell had been broken and there was me thinking we'd got off to a good start. How wrong was I.

We continued down the Access Road. The Manager making a point to stop at each drive and check the wipers and dirt build up between the rollers. It was an action we'd all witnessed many times. I'd taken the added precaution to get Delwyn on nightshift to deploy two men on overtime to each drive. He didn't find anything. Which I found quite amusing and was certainly not expecting any pat on the back. He spoke little as we travelled down the one in four brew.

Each time we passed a tannoy someone began to meow. At first I thought I was hearing things. That was until I distinctively heard someone shout.

"The cat's on his way in." The Manager seemed not to notice although when I looked across to Denny he smiled.

Thirty minutes later we reached 28's maingate. It seemed I had been the only one to keep up with the Manager. He stopped and turned towards me.

"Remember Mick no matter what Mr Douglas tells you. Use as much overtime as you want. Seven days a week if required. I want this face ready before 6's finishes."

"Yep. Understood." I assumed his comment in isolation from the Deputy Manager allowed him to continue his tirade of abuse at his morning meeting each time the overtime budget was exceeded.

Ten minutes later the five of us were on 28's faceline. The Dosco Dintheader had yet to be tracked back. The Manager seemed pleased with what he saw. He was stood on the opposite side of the bridge conveyor to me. The call on the tannoy would soon change that.

"Hello Mr Gibson. Mr Gibson."

"Hi Control Room."

"Belt lads have just been on. Access 1 is still condemned. If anything, two of the five stitches have gotten worse."

"Thanks control understood." I turned towards the group. "Looks as though it's a walk boys." I'd hardly finished the sentence as the Manager rushed towards me. Conveniently the bridge conveyor separated us.

"I'm goin to drop ti laddie." He screamed whilst at the same time waving his fist in the air. Well this was a first. A Colliery Manager threatening to drop the Undermanager. I looked towards him whilst keeping a neutral look on my face. My three colleagues looked on in disbelief. For me it was no surprise. The tension had been building ever since he'd checked the rail on the loco tunnel. My quandary was what would be my next move. Should I take him on? I had no

169

doubt I would give him a good arse kicking. Or is that what he was looking for? Because it wouldn't certainly mean my dismissal. Was knocking this cunt out worth it?

"Now Mr Adman I don't think there's a need for that." Bless I couldn't believe Mr Douglas was attempting to intervene.
"Keep out of this laddie if you know what's good for you." He needed no more persuasion. He stepped back. Even with the smattering of coal dust on his face I could see the colour had drained from his face. I continued to stare him out without making any comment.

Without a further word spoken he stormed off. Quickly followed by Douglas and Michaels.
"Well cock that went well." That certainly was the understatement of the day.
"I thought I did quite well Denny."
"What that you never hit him?"
"Well that as well. Come on let's fuck off. We've got the overtime meeting to get to. Oh, one other thing. What was with all the meowing over the tannoy?"
"Have you not heard cock. The Manager's nickname is the cat."
"Why?"
"No idea lad." We left it at that and continued up the Access.

I hadn't realized it at the time but the other three hadn't gone directly out. It was only whilst Denny and I were walking up Access 1 three lights passed us. Denny stopped. "Well would you believe that. A Manager, a Deputy Manager and a Mechanical Engineer illegally manriding!!"

Back on the surface Evan and Osian were sat in the office.
"There you go Mick. I've filled in most of what we'll need for the weekend." Evan passed me the overtime sheet.
"Thanks."
"How did your visit go with the Manager?"
"Usual shite." Osian began to laugh. "What's up with you then?"
"I don't know whether you noticed some fucker meowing on the tannoy?"
"Yeah heard it again today. Denny reckons the lads have given the Manager the nickname cat. Not sure why. I'd never class him as a pussy."
"Fuck all to do with pussy. It's a fuckin acronym." Evan interrupted.
"What the fuck is an acronym?" Osian asked.
"The letters stand for Crazy Aggressive Twat!"

The following week we received a call HMI would be visiting T6's face. It gave us three days in which to prepare. There wasn't much prep required other than moving the stonedust barriers outbye in the maingate. We just needed to ensure timbering and roof bolting at the maingate was kept up to date. The maingate was passing over the pillar edge of some old workings in the Durbog seam below. The roof for the last ten metres towards the maingate end had become very friable. We were having to "nurse" the face line through the area. The consequences of this meant production had almost halved for the last week. Which as you could imagine hadn't put Mr Adman in the best of moods.

The industry was experiencing a number of changes particularly on the marketing front. Ever since the end of the '84 strike pressure on the indigenous supply of coal had increased. In part due to the fall in demand at home from the so called "heavy industries," ship building and steel making. The increase in nuclear generation and an area where the Western Area was particularly vulnerable imported coal. Fiddlers Ferry Power Station where most of our coal was sent. Imported coal, we were told, was produced at a lower cost per tonne and it's quality superior to what we produced. Particularly the chlorine content.

We were advised on all these matters on the regular management updates we received each week. A new measure on cost had been introduced and that was the cost per giga joule. In its simplest form the cost per heat content of the coal produced. We'd relied so long on the demand from the CEGB and what had been termed the "Joint Understanding," They guaranteed to take an annual tonnage from the Coal Board. In 1987/88 that amounted to some seventy six million tonnes. However, that too was no longer the case. Last year the power generator had been privatised with the formation of Powergen, National Power and the National Grid. Now with a requirement to satisfy their shareholders with a regular dividend they too had their own demands. Top of the list was to cut cost. In effect look for alternative fuels to provide cheaper electricity.

All good stuff to hear and in later years to reflect upon but at that moment my number one priority was to get the coal face ready for the Inspector's visit today.

"For fucks sake Delwyn why aren't you timbering and bolting between shifts?"

"Instruction from the Manager now."

"But I was very clear Del. It's been the same for the last week and a half."

"Manager come on the phone he did. Told me to keep the lads shearin now. Reckons the quicker we get over the pillar edge the better it will be now."

"What about stonedusting?"

"As requested. Main tunnel, Durbog manrider and GMT. Haulage lads stayed on to complete both gates and the crosscut."

"28's?"

"Oes little bit of gas now but we've managed to get the Dintheader halfway up the return. Oh, forgot to mention quite a bit of gas found at the T2 and T5 stoppings. Deputy has hung some additional brattice cloth."

"Good we shouldn't be goin there I don't think. T3's?"

"Two chocks. They're on with the third between shifts."

"How many does that leave us at the GMT?"

"I checked myself I did now. Nine in total."

"How many down the Access?"

"Another three."

"Good. T7's?"

"Three apiece. Lads in the maingate on half a bone to get the fourth."

"Thanks Del. Oh by the way I see Mr Blackheads car was here when I arrived, problems?"

"S64's maingate machine bogged down. Done nothing all night."

"Oh, poor Mr Blackhead. Right thanks Del speak with you tonight. Let's hope the maingate end holds up."

"I shouldn't be a problem now. Wela i chi." The speed at which Delwyn left my office should have given me a clue to what was coming next.

"Mick bad news I'm afraid." Evan appeared he'd just returned from the deployment centre. My phone began to ring.

"Just a sec Evan. Hi. What? For fucks sake." I replaced the receiver.

"Yep I was just coming to tell you. Maingate's in again. Hywel reckons at least ten foot now!"

"Nearest timber?"

"About fifty chockwood in the return. Plenty three be three's. Nearest after that one mine car full on GMT. Plenty pit bottom."

"For fucks sake. You getting them moved in?"

"Therein lies the next problem. Loco's derailed halfway along the tunnel."

The rest of the day never got any better. Due to the loco, the Inspector arrived in the district late. His first visit was to the T5 stopping. Picking up four per cent on his methanometer. Arriving in T6's there was a gas build up at the return end. In part due to an FSV carrying the third powered support off T3's damaging the crosscut airdoors. And then as he passed through the fall area a stone fell from the roof and hit the Manager on his hand. The face Deputy duly bandaging. I was hoping they'd go to the surface straight after. Not so. He continued to find fault. The Manager's Support Rules at the maingate were missing. The icing on the cake though were the heavy barriers two of which were completely empty of stonedust. I left my visitors at the outbye end of the return having been suitably chastised. Having been described as a complete waste of fucking time and not worthy of my position. The Inspector had stood by listening. I was sure I detected him smiling. After they left I headed back to the face. I was later joined by Mr Douglas.

We arrived back up the pit at half six that night. Waiting for us was the Manager. Not as you might imagine to say thanks for all the hard work. No just another round of fucks before we left. Accusing us both of double standards. One consolation however as I was driving away from the car park was seeing Mr Blackhead's car still in the same position as it was first thing this morning.

Arriving back into work the next morning and despite all of the nightshift's efforts the maingate end had fallen in again. As soon as the dayshift had gone in I went to get changed. Within ten minutes I was at the pit top.

"Bora da Mr Gibson." The Banksman offered as I entered the cage. "Have a good day now."

"Thanks." Evan had remained on the surface he would chase up the supplies. Staying with them until they'd arrived in the District. Chockwood, split bars, three be three's and a mine car full of resin and wooden dowels. Osian had been given the task of finding anything he could along the outbye roads to keep us going until the additional supplies arrived.

I travelled to the fall area directly via the maingate. The belts were all on stand. Arriving at the stage loader Hywel was standing there with no helmet, head back the face Deputy Owen was trickling water into his left eye.

"What's up?"

"Oh, nothing now just a bit of dirt now. Owen here just clearing it out."

"How we looking on the face?"

"Reckon another hour and we'll have the timbering complete. I've also got three of the lads using that Christmas tree bit you sent in."

"Right for the forepoling?"

"Oes. Only thing though the compressed air drilling machine has seized. Sent one of the lads to get Dai Finger's machine. Having to use the hydraulic machine. Absolute shite. Nearly took Ithel's arm off."

The phone on the panels began to ring. It was the Control Room advising us the Manager was on his way in.

"That's all we fuckin need. Another fuckin Manager. No disrespect Mr Gibson." Hywel commented laughing replacing his helmet. "Come on let's see how the lads are getting on." Before going onto the face, I went across to check the position of the AFC sprocket. Something I did on a regular basis ever since the maingate end had become fast on F43's. I even gone as far as introducing an additional requirement on the Face Overman's report. A measure of the distance of the centre line of the sprocket to that of the road.

173

They'd done an excellent job. The cavity was over an area spanning six chocks. A total of eight three by three's had been used. Four over each set of three chocks. Above which they'd built seven chockwood stacks. I estimated to a height of eight foot. A number of split bars had been used to prevent stones falling between the chocks. Two of the nine foot three by three's forepoles were now in position. Approximately four foot of each sticking out of the hole, directly opposite chock numbers two and four. The third which the lads were still drilling for was opposite chock six. The shearer was sat waiting at chock fifteen. Hywel planned to bring the shearer into the maingate without pushing over behind. Once cut out the shearer would move back to its original position. This allowing the pans to be pushed over in the fall area. Chocks two, four and six then lowered and advanced. Allowing the front of the chock canopy to support the exposed forepoles. Once complete the remainder of the bottom end chocks to be advanced and a second shear taken.

The plan worked for me. Just waiting now for the lads to position the last forepole. Twenty minutes later the last three by three was carried onto the face and placed in the hole.

I grabbed one of a number of shovels lying between the chocks. I could see in the distance the flickering of the red light on the lockout box. I climbed over onto the face pans. Using the shovel, I scraped the cut face towards the floor. Satisfied I walked along the pans towards the shearer and repeated the action. Happy with what I'd seen I climbed back over the spill plates into the chock opposite. My timing was perfect.

"Take the latch off the panzer."
"Start the stage loader."
"Latch still on."
"Is it fuck I've taken it off."
"Latch still on." Hywel scrambled to the nearest tannoy.
"For fucks sake Bryn where about on the face?"
"It's not on the face. It's on the stageloader."
"Why didn't you fuckin say!"
"I just have. Hold on clear now." I was sat in chock twelve as the shearer kicked in the drums began to rotate. Water from the sprays caught me as the shearer advanced. The crunching of the coal becoming louder as the tungsten carbide picks cut deeper into the seam. Still no sign of the Manager. I check my watch. *Should have been here by now. Perhaps he's had second thoughts.* The shearer begins to pass me. I push myself into the middle legs as Ithel and his colleague move alongside. The noise of the machine and coal flying in all directions.

I followed the machine down as it cut into the main gate. Shear complete the machine began to withdraw to its original position. I watched as the operator using a short length of wooden dowel pushed against one of the brass buttons on the control block. The silence of the hydraulics operating the machine only becoming apparent as the cowl surrounding the drum began to lift. Slowly at first then having reached its halfway position dropping with a thud onto the floor. It seemed a long time ago when the operators had to wedge chock wood against the cowl to get it to move. The machine began to haul itself back towards the return.

I realised something was wrong when we heard the sound of the return disc cutting into coal as it moved back up the face. Hywel was first to turn.

"Who the fuck? Who's pushed over behind the machine?" Next a chock was lowered just above the fall area. I looked towards the lowered chock as it advanced. The operator unrecognisable as the collapse of the roof brought down the coal tops. His lamp shone through the dust. I'd recognise that face anywhere. The Manager. He must have entered the District through the return. What the fuck is he doing?

The lads on the shearer instinctively reversed the machine back. The Manager recognising his mistake lowered the chock to push it back. Again, a further shower of debris falls from the roof. He then attempted to pull the pans back. The unmistakable ping as one of the connecting bolts is sheared could clearly be heard. He'd been on site less than five minutes. Brought the roof in after we've spent all morning timbering. And to add insult to injury he'd parted the pans. I remained motionless as he headed towards me. I wasn't sure what to expect. An apology perhaps?

"Well laddie if you didn't have a problem before you've certainly got one now." He continued down towards the maingate end without a word to anyone.

"Prynhawn da Mr Adman." Hywel received no answer.

Hywel was beside himself. "Well I never. What sort of a man is he Mr Gibson. I'm glad I don't have to deal with him on a regular basis. I do feel sorry for you and Mr Blackhead." No more was said. Two hours later we'd completed the additional timbering.

"See you later Hywel."

"Give us a mo Mr Gibson I'll come out with you now. It's nearly time. The lads will stop over and attempt to get the shearer back to the return now."

"I'm not going straight out. I want to pop into T3's see how the salvage is going."

"Don't be too long now. You've got that lovely wife to go home to now. You be spending too much time here now. Evan tells me you've done three weekends on the run."

"You can't do too much for a good firm Hywel." I responded laughing. He did have a point though. One which Mrs Gibson would agree whole heartedly with.

I continued back out of the maingate. Once on the cross level I turned off to the left passing the stoppings for what had been T5's face. Now salvaged and sealed off. Chocks on T3's were ex 43's the ones from Dowty we'd purchased when I first started as Undermanager. We had a number of problems over the last week. Predominately due to weight on the face line having left it for three months before attempting to salvage the supports. We'd done the usual by positioning roof bolts, celstraps and mesh over the last ten shears. In addition, the coal face had been bolting and meshed too. The proximity of the adjacent worked panel T2 and T5 directly opposite had contributed too.

I wasn't too late getting back up the pit. Having deposited my lamp, I headed towards my office. "Have you heard?" Kelvin shouted towards me from his office. I walked in. "Douglas has just informed me weekend's we'll be doubling up!"

"What?"

"Yeah, one of the senior team will be on site each time we're on shift."

"For fuck's sake. None of them have a clue when they're here in the week!"

–

Two weeks after the incident in T6's. "Mick, before you sit down the Manager wants to see you." I'd just walked into my office from arriving on the surface.

"Did he say why?"

"No but he seemed in a jovial mood."

"Jovial? The fucker doesn't know the meaning of the word. Right I'll get a quick bath and pop in to see our lord and master."

"Fraid not. He was quite insistent as soon as you got up." Evan replied smiling.

"Okay, make sure there's a coffee ready when I get back."

Heading towards his office I bumped into Billy Blunt.

"Oh, Mick I was on the way to see you."

"Sorry Billy, gaffer's after me."

"Not a problem just to let you know the electrical inspector will be paying us a visit Thursday. He's planning on going to T3's salvage."

"Why there? Still pulling chocks off the face not much in the way of electrical gear to see."

"Who am I to question the reasons why. Just letting you know."

"Okay thanks, we'll be ready." There wouldn't be much to do in the way of prep work. Perhaps a little stone dusting.

"Hi Bronwen, his lordship has asked to see me."

"Hello you. How's Mrs Gibson and the kids?"

"All good thanks. Although the missus is finding it hard to adapt to the ways of the country life. She's a city girl at heart!"

"She'll get used to it. Anyway, you can go straight in now. Would you like a drink?"

"No thanks. I'm not planning to be too long."

"He's in a good mood actually."

"I'm sure I can change that!"

Knocking on the door I walked in. The room was empty for a second before the door to the Manager's bathroom opened.

"Ah Mick please come in." The man was smiling which was a little unnerving. He was rubbing Zovirax along his bottom lip. "Take a seat." I looked round for the seat cover. I was still in my black. "Don't worry about that." I sat down.

"Your tea Mr Adman." Bronwen walked in.

"Would you like a drink Mick?"

"Already asked him Mr. Adman." She placed it on his desk and left. He took a sip his eyes hadn't left me since I'd walked into the room.

"You know Mick you remind me so much of me."

"Is that good or bad?" I regretted saying it as soon as I'd finished. He never replied at first just continued to stare.

"Depends which way you look at it." There followed a long silence. I continued to meet his stare. "Any way the reason I've asked to see you is about a very, very important visit we have from a senior member of British Coal." He waited to let his comment sink in. I wasn't particularly concerned as of recent we seemed to be getting our fair share of visitors.

"The Deputy Chairman in a little over a weeks' time."

"Wow that's got to be good news?" He ignored my comment.

"I want ti." He pointed at me which was somewhat surprising being the only person in the room. "To make sure we have an excellent visit, something special. Something he'll remember!"

"I'm sure we can sort that."

"Make sure you do." I took this comment as nothing more than a threat to my very existence.

"I assume T6's face?"

"Yeah and he may want to see the developments." His phone rang. "Ah hello, yes I'm aware. Next month I'm told." As he listened, he waved a hand at me. Our conversation was over. I needed no further encouragement.

Outside his office Bronwen was listening to her phone. She placed her hand over the mouthpiece and whispered to me "Chairman's office." She showed no sign of embarrassment listening to the Managers call. I smiled and continued on my way. As I walked along the corridor, I recalled the first time I'd seen the Deputy Chairman. He was then the Area Director for the Western Area. I was working on the haulage at Cronton Colliery between my time at college. He'd turned to the then Manager Ron Groves and his Deputy. "Gentlemen this just won't do. There's no management control of those men they seem to do what they want." I readily agreed who if anyone could manage the Scouser's? Apart from his comment I remember looking at the size of his hands. They were like shovels. Huge!

At the end of the corridor smoke was billowing from the open doorway of my office. I walked in. Osian was sat puffing on his pipe one of the office phones cradled under his chin. He nodded an acknowledgement. Evan sat opposite was talking to Asyn one of the Face Overmen. Both had cigarettes poking from their mouths. I sat down and decided to join them. Reaching into my desk draw I extracted a Hamlet cigar from the pack. I lit it. It would have been cheaper to sit there and inhale the passive smoke. Visibility wasn't good. I stood and opened both windows. It was a glorious Spring afternoon. I sat back down.

"You best tell him yourself Asyn." Evan turned towards me. "Might be heading for more trouble on T6's!"
"Mr Gibson I was just tellin Evan here that the coal seam is thinin. If we keep extracting the same height of coal, we'll reduce the coal tops and you know what that could mean?" As he was speaking, he'd raised his right hand above his eyes. The sun from outside was shining directly into his face.
"At ease Asyn."
"What now?"
"Doesn't matter. Thanks for reporting the situation we'll have a looksee tomorrow. Have you taken any additional precautions?"
"I left a couple of the lads positioning some wooden dowels between shifts."
"Good man, go and get a bath."

"You know those fuckers next door have nicked the last mine car of stonedust off the inbye shunt." Osian had finished his phone conversation.
"Don't worry boyo I'll get Gruffyd to send another one down." I sat listening and inhaling on my cigar.

178

"Hi boys." I looked towards the office doorway. It was Storm the canteen manageress. She was holding a tray containing the Manager's lunch.

"Now Cariad fancy sitting on this?" Osian was leaning back on his chair. He was rubbing an enlarged lump between his legs. For some reason he always seemed to get an erection at this time of the day.

"Oh, get away with you Osian you dirty old bugger." She replied laughing and continued on her way.

"You could do with getting those blinds fixed." Evan had turned towards me. He was shielding his eyes.

"Yeah I've mentioned it to Denny. By the way I've been meaning to ask what sort of name is Asyn?"

"It's not his real name. It's Welsh for donkey."

"He's got a huge cock!" Osian added. He was still rubbing his own.

"Well you wouldn't believe. He only looks about three stone wet through."

"I true. Rumour has it he passes out each time he gets a hard on!"

"Talking of cocks, what was the Manager after?" Evan changed the subject.

"We've got a big visit week after next from Hobart House. None other than the Deputy Chairman."

The following day after the early shift had gone underground Evan and I reviewed the underground plan for the mine. We were planning the best route to get our VIP to the coal face ideally without him having to walk any great distance.

Pit bottom was easy we'd bring the loco and a single manriding carriage as close as possible to the shaft side.

"Make sure we order some white paint and whitewash for the pit bottom." Evan noted down my comment. "We'll need to check height for the loco to get as close as we can to the Two Way Meeting Station, again plenty of stonedust. Could do with Denny making us some more of those Rick's Dusters. We can mention it to him at our morning meeting. The Durbog manriding conveyor needs new belt."

"I'll make sure we have a man at the top of the manrider to stop the conveyor once they arrive at the top. Just make sure they all get on together."

"Yeah good point. Might be best if I meet them at the Two Way."

"Morning gents." It was Denny and Gethin soon followed by Gregor and Ifor. Gregor was carrying a mug of tea.

"This place fuckin stinks of nicotine."

"Good point Gregor." Evan responded as he lit up another Players No 6.

"Filthy fuckin habit."

179

"Right gents now we've got that out of the way. You'll be aware by now of our VIP visit?"

"Why is it always Zone B never those fuckers next door?"

"I've always assumed it's because the Manager wants to create a good impression."

"Don't kid yourself. It's only because we've got the coal face."

"Right me and Evan here plan to walk the route this morning. You guys are welcome to join us."

"Count me in cock."

"Me too boyo."

Bronwen had been on holiday when the Deputy Chairman's secretary had called the pit to confirm his visit. The call had been taken by a temp. She had mistakenly put the time for the visit at ten o'clock when actually it should have been nine. He had to get back to Hobart House later that afternoon for a meeting with the Board and the Government's new Energy Secretary. The consequences of this meant the underground visit would commence an hour earlier at nine thirty.

When the Deputy Chairman arrived, the Manager was in his bathroom taking a shit. It had been left to Bronwen to cover the absence. She was sat at her desk when the chauffeured Limousine appeared.

"Good morning sir, what a pleasure to meet you again."

"Ah Bronwen, how nice to see you too. Must be five years since we last met. I'm guessing that would have been at Bersham Colliery?"

"That's correct Mr Groves was the Manager at the time."

"That's right. I was with Ron at Bickershaw last week. He's got a hell of a job on there."

"I'm sure he'll manage. He's the best I've worked for."

"Quite right. That's why we put him there."

Bronwen led the DC into Adman's office.

"Oh, he's not here at the moment, shall I get you a tea or coffee?"

"A quick tea would be fine. I'm on a tight schedule today need to be away at one. Hence the early start." Bronwen realized immediately the time in the diary had been a mistake.

"Right let me get you that cuppa." At that moment Maurice Adman walked in from his bathroom.

"DC how good to see you. Traffic is obviously good you must be an hour early?"

"No, I was always going to be arriving at nine o'clock." As soon as Bronwen got outside she put a call through to the Control Room.

180

Back underground I'd been walking the route we planned to take. Evan had gone in ahead to check on the coal face. One of the three loco's we had stood out. Looking splendid in its new lick of white paint. As I passed it, I touched the paint work. However, there was no sign of the manriding carriage. I walked towards the garage. My concern soon abated as I saw it. I could see a set of orange overalls moving alongside it.

"George?"

"Bora da Mr. Gibson it's me Tomos."

"Sorry Tomos Bora da to you too. Everything okay?"

Tomos stood up alongside the carriage he was holding a hessian sack covered in paint. As I approached him the smell of paint became very apparent.

"Bloody Henry on nightshift decided to give the inside of the carriage another coat of paint now. He's only used gloss I'm giving it a wipe over now."

"I'm sure it will be fine. Make sure the rider is at pit bottom for half ten. I'll catch you later."

I continued along the main tunnel. I could see where the lads had stonedusted, not that it made much difference. Even with Rick's duster it would be difficult to reach the top of the arches. Each of the manholes however had, had a good dusting. Ahead I noticed a couple of lights, whoever it was seemed to be working on the side of the road.

"Morning lads."

"Morning Mr Gibson."

"What you up to?"

"Just changing one of the tannoy's. There's been a leak from a joint in the water range. All the comms inbye from here are down. The phones are still working though."

Back on land. "Well Maurice think we could make a move"

"Certainly, we're a little early though?" Bronwen walked back into the room and caught the last comment. As she retrieved the cups and saucers, she gave Maurice a nod to confirm she'd advised the Control Room on the change of plan.

"The sooner we make a move the better. I wouldn't want to be late for the Energy Secretary. He's giving an update and the Government's plans for the industry. Talking with the Chairman yesterday it looks as though we'll be down to fifty pits by the end of the year and still producing seventy three million tonnes. That's the forecast anyway. We just need to confirm the contracts with PowerGen and National Power to ensure we maintain a semblance of an industry. My big concern is the threat from gas."

"I would have thought our biggest threat would be from foreign imports?"

"Don't kid yourself the recently privatised generators are on a dash for gas. Bloody hell Maurice what's that smell?"

Upstairs in the Control Room. "Hello Mr Gibson, hello Mr Gibson can you give me a call as soon as poss." He turned to his colleague.
"That's not like Mick he usually responds immediately."
"Hello Control. He won't hear you the inbye tannoy's are down. Best you give him a call."
"Thanks, Tomos I'll put a call through to T6's."

I continued on my way to the new alighting station for the manrider. It had moved inbye by a further twenty yards after the lads removed a number of bent arches. The Two Way looked splendid with the additional layer of stonedust. The inbye supply shunts had been emptied as requested. I continued through the newly painted double set of airdoors.
"Bora da Mr Gibson," The greeting took me by surprise. It was one of the haulage lads, Keith. He was to remain in the vicinity just in case we had any problems with the belt manrider.
"Morning Keith. Just remember don't let the Manager see you."
"Will do." I continued towards the conveyor it was running.
"Mr. Gibson I thought you was meeting them off the manrider?"
"Yeah I am. I'm just checkin the route up to 6's maingate."

I continued towards the Strata Top. The faces here although no records had been broken as yet had provided a consistent level of production. Unlike my poor colleague Mr Blackhead working the Stone Coal seam which had its fair share of geological problems. I didn't want to tempt fate but to date T6's had been the most problematic. The coal seam had thinned towards the maingate end requiring us to leave additional coal tops. Between shifts we'd introduced a regime of roof bolting with wooden dowels.

I was interrupted from my thoughts from the continuous ringing of the phone at the top of T6's maingate. Without realising it I'd passed the T7 developments.
"Hello."
"Mr Gibson, thank fuck!"
"Idris what's up?" The man sounded quite stressed.
"I've been trying to get hold of you for the last twenty minutes. The Manager and the DC have gone underground early. The tannoy's are out of action."
"For fucks sake. Not again! Don't worry I'll leave now. Make sure you let Evan and the guys on the face know."
"Will do. I'm awfully sorry Mr Gibson."

"Don't worry it's not your fault. It's those fuckin electricians. Why they couldn't repair the tannoy on the night shift?"

Ending the call, I quickened my pace. I'd forgotten to ask the exact time they'd descended the shaft. I guessed they'd still be on the manrider. Still time for me to get to the bottom of the manrider conveyor. I'd specifically asked Gregor at the morning meeting were we ready for the visit. To add insult to injury his boss had called a meeting. They'd all be sat there now in his office supping tea.

I arrived at the top of the manriding conveyor. Still no sign of the visitors. Usually I'd meet them there, but the Manager had suggested I meet them as soon as they got off the loco. I continued down the one in four brew. Halfway down I realized my mistake. Ahead of me the unmistakable outline of two cap lamps bobbing up and down. I stopped immediately recognising the profile of the lead rider. I could already feel the intensity of those eyes burning a hole through my body.

"Morning." I received no response not that I had expected one. The DC then passed me. He was lying flat out on the conveyor. *Fuck who's going to stop it before he reaches the top.*

Checking the Manager wasn't looking I clambered onto the conveyor. Slowly with head stooped I walked towards the DC. The lights ahead indicated the alighting station. I reached across and tugged on the green line. The conveyor slowed just as the Manager had reached the wooden platform. *Thank fuck for that!* When it came to a final standstill the Manager got to his feet followed by the DC. I followed, *for fucks sake, I don't believe it.* Both the Manager and DC looked as though they were wearing prison garbs. The unmistaken outline of the manrider back rests clearly visible across the back of their donkey jackets.

Striding purposely forward I introduced myself to the DC. The Manager had said nothing up to this point. The DC's hands were exactly as I remembered them and his grip unbelievably strong. Guessed he must have worked out.

"Nice to see you're ready for my visit Mr Gibson."

"We try our best DC."

"I think what he means Mr Gibson is the lack of preparedness." With that the Manager walked off followed by the DC. I followed behind not included in any further conversation.

We reached the meeting station at the top of the maingate.

"Could we have a moment Mr Adman. I need to retie my boot lace."

"Of cause DC whenever you're ready." DC moved across to the timber bench. The Manager ushered me to one side.

"I don't want any more fuck ups laddie or you're for the high jump." I didn't answer there was no point. Momentarily I was tempted and advise him if they'd got the DC's arrival time right perhaps things would have gone to plan. The phone began to ring.

"Hi Evan yeah we're here now. The plan is to head into the maingate first. Where's the shearer? Excellent that works for me." The shearer was halfway along the face heading towards the maingate end. We'd planned to avoid taking our visitor pass the shearer near the maingate just in case! "Yeah best if you just stay ahead of us pre-warn everyone."

"That's me done." DC announced.

"See you shortly." I replaced the handset and began to lead them towards the maingate.

"Mr Gibson change of plan. I want to show DC T8's return gate and what little effect T5 has had on it." *Fuck.* Once more I followed rather than lead.

Having shown DC T8's return road and lack of any signs of deformation we headed off down T6's return gate. This time I lead the way. Behind me the two were in deep conversation. I slowed to see if I could hear anything of significance. DC seemed to be doing most of the talking.

"Maurice to have any chance you have to cut costs. Productivity is where it should be. Do whatever it takes. We need to play for time. You're one of a number of pits on the so called vulnerable list. If we can get through the next twelve months there's a chance. I've got our Technical Department looking at new technologies and methods of work that will assist in taking cost out. The Government have appointed some mining consultants from the States. They'll be visiting here at some point. From what I've heard conditions at Strata Top are ideal. The report from the Technical Director last year was very encouraging."

Ahead of me I could see a light. I guessed it was Evan which was a concern. He was supposed to be keeping ahead of us. I quickened my pace. Any conversation we were to have needed to be out of earshot of the other too.

"Problems I guess?"

"Just a bit. Maingate's fell up."

"For fucks sake."

"Yeah. Worse I've seen."

"Meaning what?"

"Walkway through the bottom six chocks blocked…"

"Hi Evan how are you today?"

"Bora da Mr Adman."

"Let me introduce you to the DC. DC this is Evan. He's Mr Gibson's Colliery Overman." The DC offered his hand.

"Good to meet you Evan."

"You too DC."

"Problems I guess?" Evan and I exchanged glances. Surely he hadn't heard our conversation. "Don't look so worried. I've been there myself remember. Started out as a haulage hand."

With that in mind Evan went on to explain what had happened at the maingate end. I was surprised how well the DC took it. Not for the Manager, however. He walked off initially kicking the ground. I think he was finding it hard to join in on the conversation. He returned eventually only to offer me the deadly stare whilst tapping his stick on the ground. It wasn't as if I'd planned the fall. But I guess that's what Undermanager's were there for. A good arse kicking when things went tits up.

"Come on then let's make a move. I need to be back on the surface in an hour." I took the lead followed by DC then the Manager. Evan brought up the rear.

By the time we reached the fall area two of the facemen were on the shovel cleaning out the walkway. Two were above the chocks timbering. Whilst another two were on the faceside passing the chockwood to those timbering. There was no way through. We'd have to climb onto the panzer. I turned to advise those behind me. To my surprise the DC had already made the decision. Soon followed by the Manager and Evan.

"Morning lads."

"Bora da Mr Gibson. You don't fancy giving us a lift up here now do you." It was Ithel. As always leading from the front. He looked down from above the chock.

"I'll be with you later no doubt."

"Good morning gentlemen." I hadn't noticed the DC. He'd climbed onto the spill plate and with his head above the chock canopy looking into the cavity.

"Sorry lads this is the DC. On a visit with the Manager this morning."

"Oes we know. You don't fancy coming up here and giving us a hand do you now?"

"Any other time yes. Unfortunately, I've a meeting to attend. A meeting with an outcome that will affect us all."

"You just make sure you keep us open now. We're not into all these bribes, oh sori you call them incentives to close the pits." I found it hard to believe the conversation my lads were having with the DC of British Coal. By the look on his face he seemed to be enjoying it. I couldn't say that for the Manager though.

We continued on our way. Once at the stage loader I turned to the Manager.

"Mr Adman if you're okay might be best if I stay with the lads to get this sorted." I wasn't sure how he was going to react. The look on his face wasn't helping either. Then, quite unexpectedly.

"I'm sure the Manager and I will find our way out. I've enjoyed my visit today Mr Gibson. After a disastrous start its gone well." I couldn't believe my ears. I nodded in response. "One piece of advice I will give though." He held out his hand to bid me farewell. "If you're going to paint the manrider carriage do it in plenty of time. Helps the paint dry."

"Thank you, I will." I replied smiling. The Manager said nothing.

I arrived back up the pit at six that evening. I'd left Asyn and his team shearing. No sign of the Manager which I took as a positive. I'd no doubt he would give me his feedback tomorrow. I was to later find out that when they arrived at pit bottom Tomos had yet to pull the manriding carriage out of the garage. When finally, he did in full view of the Manager and DC he'd got into a little bit of a flap. Not securing the loco to the manrider carriage correctly he'd set off and within yards they'd disconnected. The Manager and DC had remained motionless. He'd travelled along the tunnel a further twenty yards before realizing his mistake. No wonder we'd got off to a bad start. On the upside we'd certainly given him a visit to remember.

-

"How's your day been?"

"Do'y know, it hasn't been bad at all. Mainly due to those two keeping off my back." Kelvin and I were in the baths having just come up the pit together.

"Do me a favour Mick." He handed me his sponge. As I started to clean his back the sound of coughing interrupted our conversation. "Talk of the devil."

"Do me a favour Kelvin."

"What?"

"Lean against the tiles and shove your arse out towards me."

"What the fuck for?"

"I'm going to pretend to shag you when Douglas enters. It'll teach him to disturb when we're having a shower." Kelvin began to laugh.

"Don't get any ideas though."

"On that you can be certain. Some groaning would add to the scene. Just pretend I'm Dafydd."

"Fuckin hell Mick you don't ask for much."

We took up our positions. Kelvin placed both arms up against the tiled wall. He laid his head onto the tiles too. I placed either hand on his hips and leant forward. The coughing became louder. As he came around the short dividing wall opposite the bath entrance Kelvin began to groan as I commenced my pelvic thrusts.

There then followed a scream from Douglas. "For fucks sake. What the fuck are you two doin?" The look of shock and horror on Tony Douglas's face was a delight to see.

I pulled away from Kelvin. Pleased to see no evidence of an erection. We both turned to face him. The colour had drained from his face. He had a hand across his mouth. I assumed to catch the phlegm. Unfortunately, the resident lump of mucus was swallowed again. I think his was gagging and ready to throw up.

"Sorry Tony, what's up?" We both played our parts to perfection. It was as if what the Deputy Manager had witnessed was a regular occurrence. We waited as he began to take a series of deep breaths. Finally recovered he began to speak. Eyeing us both with suspicion "I've come to give you the news." I think he was still having problems breathing.

"Come on man spit it out, oops forgive the pun." He ignored my comment and continued.

"He's leaving. Got another job in Staffordshire at the Complex." His comment certainly got our attention as we both knew who he was referring to.

"Your kiddin, tell me your kiddin." Kelvin seemed quite excited. I wasn't so sure.

"Who's his replacement?" I just hoped it wasn't him.

"Paul Adder." Fuck I wasn't sure if I'd have been happier with Mr Douglas.

"Fuckin hell when?"

"End of week. The guy at the Complex has been sacked and Adder's managed to close his pit!"

"That's the end of my team building weekend!"

Mr Adman's leaving doo was better attended than I thought. Since hearing the news, I reflected on the time he'd been the Manager. It went without saying he'd been an absolute twat. However, having said that he'd certainly taught me a lot. And that I would be grateful for. I would use what I'd learnt going forward. We'd had a whip round buying him a nice bottle of malt. The highlight however had to be the book. The Assistant Manager Tommy Oldham had chosen it specially. *How to Win Friends and Influence People.*

A week later Paul Adder was back. Pretty low key and no big announcement. The biggest change was with Bronwen. She decided to call it a day.

"He's not in Mick. Gone to pick up his new company car."

"I've come to see you. Wish you all the best with your retirement."

"Retirement! I wish. No, I'm about to do something I've wanted to do for years."

187

"And what would that be?"

"I'm opening my own little B&B in Betws-y-Coed."

"How wonderful. You've got a place then."

"Yeah it came up last year. I made them an offer, but they wanted more. Called me back last month they did now. We agreed a deal."

"Nothing to do with the other fella coming back?" She smiled. She didn't need to say anymore. "I bet if there was a vacancy at Bickershaw you'd be there like a shot."

"Do'y know Mick your probably right. I've become good friends with the family we still keep in touch."

"How is he?"

"He's got a lot on. And travelling each day. Mrs Groves before he took the job on made it very clear she wasn't moving again. Oh, there he is now." I turned to see the Manager park up his brand new top of the range Ford Granada.

"Right I'll make a move."

"Catch up again before you go."

–

Now Paul Adder had returned a calmness descended on the senior team. Tony Douglas was more relaxed. Still nuts and still suffering with his phlegm but certainly relaxed. It seemed quite obvious over those first few weeks. For me, the daily interaction with men and officials continued as normal. Maurice Adman's legacy lived on. However, two instances were to occur in my office highlighting a problem I never realized we had. Both fortunately witnessed by the new Manager.

The first concerned Mr Blackhead. Not known for any displays of aggression. Not that we in Zone B had witnessed anything first-hand. In fact, we saw little of Kelvin during Mr Adman's tenure. Most of his time was spent underground from first thing in the morning till late at night. Overtime meetings he'd rarely attend. Sending his Colliery Overman Dewi in his place.

"Well go on. There fuckin take it. Take it, take it fuckin all." Kelvin still in his black dropped a bag of stonedust onto the meeting table in my office. Evan and I were sat at my desk putting the final touches to our overtime sheet. Together we looked at Kelvin. We said nothing. I certainly hadn't seen him like this before. "You twats can take everything see if I care." As he finished his second rant. The Manager unexpectedly walked in.

"Afternoon all."

"Afternoon Mr Adder." I responded, followed by Evan.

"Prynhawn da Mr Adder."

"I've had enough of this shite." Kelvin added and walked back out to his own office.

"Perhaps I'll come back later." Paul Adder followed Kelvin out.

We later discovered off Dewi that a minecar of stonedust Zone A had ordered that morning had inadvertently been taken along to 45's and offloaded at Motorway 3 lifting station. The lads believed they'd transported a minecar of chockwood. One of the surface lads thought he'd be helpful and load the half full car with chockwood burying the stonedust beneath. The reason Kelvin had been so upset was a visit from HMI the following day. I found it hard to believe that after all this time he hadn't learnt to keep a stockpile of the stuff inbye ready for such visits. Evan arranged with Dewi the return that afternoon.

The second occurred at shift change the following day. Again, in my office between two of my face Deputies, Reece and Owen.

"You fuckin cunt you." Owen had just arrived on shift.

"Don't you fuckin call me a cunt now. You fuckin cunt." He was providing his end of shift report to Osian. Osian was sat to my right with Evan to my left.

"You're the fuckin cunt now you are." This time Owen's comment was followed by him pushing Reece in the chest. I sat speechless it was like watching something from the playground.

"Nac oes, now hold it you two now." Osian reached up to part the two.

"Afternoon all." Owen and Reece backed away from one another. Osian sat back down.

"Prynhawn da Mr Adder." They all responded in unison.

"Mr Gibson when you get a mo could you pop down to my office. Nothing urgent."

"Will do." I responded. Smiling he turned and left. "What the fucks up with you two? I don't need the Manager seeing you two carry on like that." Owen was first to respond.

"He told me yesterday he'd left men on half a bone timbering the maingate. Which they fuckin didn't. Took my lads an hour before we could start cutting."

I walked down to the Manager's office. It was strange seeing Lizzy sat there. I'd always come to expect Bronwen.

"He's expecting you Mick. Go straight in. Would you like a drink?"

"Thanks Lizzy. Coffee please black, remember no sugar."

Mr Adder was sat at his desk. Feet up shoes removed. He was reading the Financial Times. "Take a seat." He offered without looking up. "Bloody hell would you believe we're down to fifty pits and still producing seventy three million tonnes."

"No, I hadn't realized." I hadn't given much thought to anything of late. Other than making sure T7's was ready for start-up and we got D28's in a position for salvage. "You asked to see me?"

"I certainly did. Drink?"

"Lizzy's on the case." Right on que Lizzy walked in with our drinks. I tasted it before she left. She'd put sugar in again. She smiled at me and gave the thumbs up sign. I returned her smile.

"How are you Mick?"

"Good thanks."

"You?"

"Oh, I'm fine. However, it's you and your team I'm concerned with." He waited a moment before continuing. "The tension in your office which I've witnessed on a number of occasions since being back, it's palpable." *Now there's a word I don't often hear at the pit. He must have picked it up in the FT. He'd become an avid reader since being back.* The look on my face must have suggested I didn't know what the word meant. "I'm referring to the atmosphere. It's so intense."

"Yeah see what mean. Might be to do with the T7's starting up."

"No, I think it's more than that. I've noticed it too with Kelvin and Zone A. I think it's time you all had a break."

"A break. I think there's too much going on to be having a break."

"Yeah I understand that. What I mean is a re-energising of the team spirit that was so obvious when I was here. Let's get it reinvigorated." I wasn't sure how to respond. Thought it best if I kept my gob shut and listened.

"Initially you and your team. Officials and the engineers. Thereafter the lads. Get you all away on a team building weekend. I think Mr Adman mentioned it before he left. He mentioned it in his handover note. Throw in a free bar. It'll give everyone a chance to reflect, reassess relationships, understand one another better." I wasn't sure I was quite understood what he meant. "You don't seem convinced?" I wasn't actually. Two and a half years of Mr Adman had changed us all in one way or another. "Week after next. I've arranged a session for you and the team to spend the weekend in a country house, Hope, Derbyshire with Impact Development Training Group." He passed me a single A4 sheet of paper. "Leaving on the Friday at two o'clock a coach will take you there. Twenty in total. I'll leave it to you to choose the participants. Include Denny, Gregor, Gethin and Ifor plus the new electrical assistant Baldwin. Probably better suited to the younger officials although I would include Evan." He stopped whilst I read what he'd passed me.

The paper was entitled Objectives and consisted of eight bullet points:

- To review and re-evaluate the role of the Zone B team and individuals in it.
- To examine individual skills within the team.
- To create a culture in the team that provides proper support and encouragement to each member.
- To agree a strategy for managing Zone B's relationship and reputation with the rest of the teams at the pit.
- To identify specific actions to continue the development of the team
- To identify what you need from Paul Adder and the rest of the senior team to help Zone B perform better.
- To explore how this team makes decisions
- To develop critical reviewing techniques (such as feedback) that focus on performance (rather than personality)

I'd finished reading and looked towards the Manager *what a load of shite.*
"Yeah looks good certainly what we need." For the first time in my career I began to wonder what part of the brain was removed to become a Manager nowadays.
"Good, I'm glad you agree."

And that was it. The following week we went. Stopping off at Buxton on the way for a pie and a pint. Denny was in his element. And what a thoroughly enjoyable time we had. Between abseiling, which I wasn't particularly keen on, rock climbing and potholing. We even had a go at orienteering. This however was ended fairly quickly as we kept getting lost. The highlight had to be when each of us were blind folded. Two team were formed. Each member of the team had to assist their colleague when passing through or over a series of obstacles. What the Impact Development Training Group had not planned on was during the exercise when the two groups came into close proximity of one another. Members on the opposite team threw punches at the opposing team. Other than a couple of black eyes and split lips no one seemed to mind.

Team spirit kicked in on the Saturday night when Reece and Owen were caught snogging two of the local girls. That in itself shouldn't have been a problem. Except they were both married to brothers. Both farmers and ex rugby union players. The brothers had second thoughts on rectifying the situation when facing a number of miners protecting their colleague. The benefits of the weekend away were for all to see when we got back. Interruptions in the office ceased. If somebody wanted to speak the term "excuse me was used." Where

191

inadvertently somebody was interrupted it was followed quickly by a "sori." Osian thought we'd all gone soft. However, two weeks later we were back to our normal aggressive selves. Well at least Mr Adder had tried.

Nearly twelve months to the day after the DC's visit we received another VIP visit. This Time from Group. The newly appointed Group Director who'd I'd met the first time and a new Operations Director. I was advised Larry Button had moved on. Taken a senior position with one of the big mining contractors. The Manager requested I meet them at the usual place. Top of the Durbog manrider.

"Morning Gentlemen."

"Morning Mick." Mr Adder turned towards the two visitors. "Can I introduce the Group Director who you've met previously I'm told." Which I had and after that visit I remembered where I'd seen him before. During my two week stay at the Vache in Chalfont St Giles. "And the Group's new Operations Director Phil Fowler."

"Good to meet you gentlemen." Pleasantries complete we moved on.

The Manager had requested we visit T7's retreat panel. The panel now fully developed but yet to be installed had been driven using our old faithful Dosco Dint Headers, but this time wholly supported by roof bolts. The trial for roof bolting in T6's had only included the maingate and faceline. Due to its success any development taking place at Strata Top was wholly supported by roof bolts. Free standing square work was resigned to the past. To my surprise Mr Adder was happy for me to stay with the Directors and join in conversation.

"I remember it well Mr Adder. The last time we visited with Mr Adman was during the trials. Obviously, you must be pleased with the results. In fact, looking at it you begin to wonder if it needs any support at all." I winced at the thought of it. More so making a comment to Paul Adder he was already considering using shorter bolts he'd need no further encouragement.

"My thoughts entirely Group Director." He responded giving me a glance. To be fair the place did look rather special particularly after the lads had given it a thorough stone dusting with Rick's Duster.

"What were you using for drilling Mick?" Mr Fowler asked walking across to the side of the road and placing his hand on one of the fibre glass dowels.

"Wombats. That's a one point eight metre, nineteen millimetre fibre glass dowel. On the rib side." I pointed to the opposite side of the road. "Same length but this time a twenty two millimetre steel rebar." He nodded his head to acknowledge my comments. Shining his lamp towards the roof area I continued.

"Celstrap supported by two point four metre by twenty two millimetre steel rebar."

"What about the resin." I wasn't sure if he was really interested or just testing my knowledge. Having had that many visits to the area he wasn't going to find me wanting there.

"Twenty five millimetre diameter Australian type Cemfix. For the roof, a four hundred and fifty millimetre fast set plus an eight hundred millimetre slow set. The sides two hundred and twenty five millimetre fast set and then another eight hundred millimetre slow set."

"Full column?"

"Would you have it any other way." I responded. He began to laugh. A sense of humour I liked that.

We continued the full circuit of the district. We never bumped into another soul. There was some discussion as to when we planned to start the face installation. The chocks would be transported off the adjacent panel T6's. Production planned for the following month. Currently the main production for the pit was D28's. I think they seemed pleased we had a plan in place. What seemed to excite the Group Director the more he saw was the perfect conditions we walked through. The conversation moving onto the various stresses surrounding the excavation. They began to discuss the major, minor, and vertical stresses. Adder pointing out that the gate roads had been driven in line with the major stress. I seemed to recall from the presentation last year given by Adman and the Group's Technical Department this was the best direction. It was at this point I'd switched off and just listened. We had enough stress of our own to start worrying about geological stresses.

"Right Mick, let's just have a minute here." The Manager shouted towards me. We'd arrived at T4's maingate. Ever since the visit the previous year when I'd met the Deputy Chairman rumours had abounded on the future of the T4 panel of coal. The drivages had yet to start to develop the panel although this was now imminent. The first five metres had been driven. The electricians as was the norm were using the place as a dumping ground. A number of empty armoured cable drums lay upturned, I made a note to get the place cleared out.

"Well I'm advised the Capex has been agreed." The Group Director commented as he sat on one of the upturned drums,

"Excellent news" the Manager responded.

"This is the place then?" Phil Fowler added.

"The very same three and a half million pounds agreed." I was intrigued. I moved a little closer.

"Before any order is placed there's one final hurdle."

"Hello Mr Gibson, Mr Gibson." The tannoy along the crosscut rang out. *Fuck.* The Manager and his visitors seemed not to hear.

"Don't tell me. Those bloody consultants the Government have brought in." Phil Fowler responded to the Group Director's comment.

"Hello Mr Gibson." *For fucks sake.*

"Yep the very same." And that was the last of the conversation I was to hear. The Control Room were advising me the belt lads had seen a bad stitching on Access 1. They wanted me to check if it was okay to continue running and repair it between shifts. D28's was on its third shear. The best run we'd had for some time.

"Hi Control. Tell the lads I'm on the way." I made my way back to the other three.

"Sorry gents. Little bit of a problem I'll need to leave you."

"Not to worry. Good to meet you. I'm sure we'll see you again soon."

-

One of the regular Group meetings that took place with the Colliery Management was the Quarterly Accountability meeting. As Undermanager I was never involved at this level. The team attending consisted of the Colliery Manager, Deputy Manager, Accountant, Assistant Manager and Safety Engineer.

The Group staff attending included Group Director, Assistant Group Director Operations, Assistance Group Director Personnel, Group Technical Services, Group Electrical Engineer and Group Mechanical Engineer. The results for the previous month would be reviewed. This included the profit/loss account, production, and safety.

Arriving on the surface I headed towards my office a little later than usual, so far it had been a pretty shit day. Another roof fall on the coal face which had delayed production for two hours and one of the T4's intake heading had been gassed out. Little did I know things were about to get worse.

Walking into my office Evan acknowledges my presence as he replaced the land line.

"Manager's just been on needs a quick chat."

"Fuck I suppose it's about the face, are they still shearing?"

"Yeah last time I spoke with them they were up at the tail gate just turning the cowls over and heading back towards the main."

"Good their second shear I'll pop in the shower first."

"He's specifically asked you go straight in when you get up the pit."

"What's the rush?" Evan shook his head.

"Not a clue."

"Oh well get the kettle on I shouldn't be too long."

"Mick"

"Mr Adder"

"As you're aware the Larry Llewelyn is away on holiday."

"Yeah."

"And as you'll be aware we have the Accountability on Wednesday at Trentham."

"Yeah.," *Not sure why he'd sharing this information with me. I'm the Undermanager and Undermanager's don't attend such meetings. For one we're far too way down the pecking order.* There followed a short silence. Unsure of what to say next I added. "Can't you get him back in for the day?"

"If you'll let me finish,"

"Sorry."

"Highly unlikely him returning from the South of France for one day." The Manager was now smiling he was saving the best till the last. "I'd like you to come along and present his report."

"What me?" I found it hard to believe what I was hearing. "Me..?" I was trying to think of a reason why I couldn't go. "I've got my weekly team meeting on Wednesday and…….."

"I'm sure your team can run that without you. I wouldn't worry too much you know how much the Group Director likes you. All you have to do is present some overheads explaining how we've reduced accidents over the last month. The overheads have already been completed by Larry before he left. The figures and statistics look very impressive."

If I wasn't worried before I certainly was now. Statistics and figures were never my strong point. I was expected to present all this in front of the Group Director and his team.

"There on the desk in front of you contains all the information you'll need." He pointed towards a blue folder. "Take it home have a read. If you have any questions let me know. Make sure though you emphasise the reduction to the slip, stumbling and falling accidents. With the recent introduction of the new high ankle boots. He'll see it as money well spent. And not forgetting the mandatory introduction of safety glasses. The figures show a marked reduction in eye injuries."

"Anything else?"

"No that's it for now, happy reading." Happy was not a word I'd use to describe how I felt at that moment. I picked up the folder.

Returning to my office I sat down. My mug of coffee was waiting. Reaching into the desk drawer I removing my pack of Hamlet cigars.

"I thought you were packing those in. It's not that bad is it?" Evan commented.

"I'll let you know after Wednesday."

"Right if you don't mind I'm going for a bath."

"Thanks Evan." I lit up and to contemplate the conversation I'd just had with the Manager.

The two new initiatives introduced by British Coal had followed the introduction of ear defenders last year. In reality the idea that things had improved was far from the truth. Slip, stumbling and falling incidents in my opinion had actually increased since the introduction of eye protection. The plastic safety glasses often steaming up whenever any physical activity took place. Causing individuals to walk into objects they would ordinarily walk around and trip over objects they would normally step over.

To avoid reporting such incidents those involved were encouraged to return to work. They were placed on "light work" normally on the surface. This reduced the number of plus three day accidents. Staff working in the lamproom and baths increased tenfold. Even the Personal Manager had a team of new recruits. The upside however was the increase in underground productivity.

Later that night at home I began to rehearse my safety presentation. In front of my wife and two young children. They all look suitably bored. I held up each acetate paper without the benefit of the overhead projector. Sat in the dining room we'd just had dinner.

"Dad," my son asked.

"Yeah?"

"The new boots you've mentioned do they have studs like football boots?"

"No."

"Why?"

"Because they're not football boots."

"Okay, sorry Dad."

"Dad," my daughter asked.

"Yeah?"

"What colour frames do the safety glasses have?"

"You can have either yellow or blue."

"What about black?"

"I suppose so."

"And pink?" I've hardly begun as the interruptions come thick and fast. I look towards my wife for help.

"Don't look at me. You've got us all sat here like idiots listening to facts and figures we don't understand. They're only children and I've certainly got better things to do with my time."

"Hold on dear that's a little harsh. I only want to practice what I'm going to say on Wednesday. I want to be prepared."

"Well go and prepare in front of someone else!" And with that she and the children disappeared into the living room to watch Coronation Street.

I put my head in my hands and wonder if any of it is worthwhile. Presenting facts and figures I don't understand and worse I don't find one bit interesting. My thoughts are interrupted as the phone rings in the hall. My wife answers and shouts to me.

"You'll never believe it; it's for you the pit!"

The following morning as I prepare to go underground I bump into the Colliery Accountant Cuthbert Sum. He's smoking his regulation Marlboro. Cuthbert had only been with us for six months. His role was another initiative introduced by British Coal. The drive to make each colliery become financially self-sufficient no longer merely cost centres. He was an extremely nice gentlemen he personified the word cool. The canteen girls couldn't get enough of him. The fact he looked Italian may have helped too.

"Hi Mick."

"Hello Cuthbert what brings you so close to the shaft? Are you planning an underground visit?"

"Don't be silly not my scene. I'll leave that to you guys. Real men. No, the Manager mentioned you're attending tomorrow's accountability meeting. You're presenting the Safety Engineer's report." *The man now has my full attention as I'm unsure why he's so interested.*

"And?" The cage was ready to board.

"I'm not sure the figures are correct." He responds with a chuckle.

"All aboard," the Banksman shouts to no one particular.

"What? The figures aren't correct?"

"That's about the sum total of it. I've checked them again and I'm afraid they're not providing the information described."

"What do you mean?"

"Well actually…" he chuckles once more. "The trend depicted is incorrect."

"Are you comin cock." Denny shouted. He and Gregor were accompanying me to the coal face.

"I don't fuckin believe it… Listen I need to go underground I'll pop round to see you later." *That's all I need the day before I attend the group accountability and the presentation I've been given is inaccurate.*

Six hours later back on the surface I head straight to Cuthbert's office. He's sat inhaling on his Marlboro.

"It's as I thought the figures presented are misrepresented in the graph."

"What does that mean?"

"I'm afraid," another chuckle, "the trend presented is factually wrong."

"Yes, I know you mentioned that earlier but what does that mean? Does it matter if the downward trend is not as dramatic as shown?"

"Therein lies the problem...." He pauses for affect, "there's no downward trend it actually rises."

"But it can't"

"But it does."

I stand there gaping at the man. *I'm due to stand in front of the Group Director at tomorrow's accountability meeting presenting facts and figures showing the opposite to what I'll be telling them.*

"Mick are you okay? You look a little under the weather."

"Yeah just fuckin great. Thanks for the heads up" I leave Cuthbert and make my way to the baths.

Having showered I return to my office; my spirits lifted a little. Denny having advised me the problem we'd had earlier with the shearer had been sorted. The phone rings.

"Mick?"

"Hi Mr Adder."

"Cuthbert tells me your presentation on the accident statistics is inaccurate?"

"Yeah afraid so." *My fuckin presentation it's been prepared by Larry fuckin Llewelyn the Safety Engineer sat somewhere in the south of France drinking fuckin red wine. Probably laughing his cock off that he won't have to present.*

"What do you plan to do about it?" *Absolutely fuckin nothing.*

"I'm working on it now actually."

"Good I wouldn't want you to be presenting inaccurate information to the Group Director. You certainly don't want to put our colliery in a bad light. Certainly not after the introduction of these new initiatives. You never know what difference it will make."

Fuckin unbelievable this is now my problem; the Manager once more has absolved himself of any ownership of my fuckin problem.

"Sorry Mr Adder what do you mean when you say what difference it will make?"

"You'll never know."

"I know you've said that but what difference will it make?"

"You'll never know I'll leave it with you." The line went dead.

Well he's made that perfectly clear, I'm still to present the data but if there's any come back that'll be on me and the Safety Engineer. The art of being blameless, let the shit hit the fan open the umbrella and let everybody else catch it.

I put any further planning of the conveyor installation in T4's to one side. *What the hell am I going to do. I'm shit at presenting facts and figures and graphs? No chance.* I reach for my pack of Hamlet. I then have what can only be described as an epiphany.

Some months ago, I'd presented my monthly performance report to Tony Douglas. The report provided detail on production, development yardage, accident statistics and manning levels. I hadn't had the time to complete the report and I wasn't convinced he ever read it. I decided to put my understanding to the test. So, without advising anyone I presented the same report for two months on the run. Guess what and no surprise to me it went unnoticed. *I wonder if………?*

The following morning further complications await. Tony Douglas has decided to take his own car. Usually they'd all travel together in the Manager's company car. Cuthbert and the Chief Engineer, Ken John have opted to travel with him. Leaving me to travel with the Manager. I guessed there would be a reason why. I was soon to find out.

"Mick would you mind driving please." *Would I mind driving? Not one bit. A top of the range Ford Granada – yes please. And it's automatic!*

"It would be my pleasure Mr Adder. Meant to ask. Are we meeting at Gadbrook Park."

"No, the Trentham Estate." *That's good easier to find.* "Have you ever driven an automatic before?"

"No actually I haven't but I'm sure I'll manage."

"Pretend you've only got one leg. The right. Put the left to one side and forget it."

"Sounds simply enough." I responded. I couldn't tell you how excited I was. So much so I never noticed him climb onto the back seat. The smell of the leather interior was intoxicating.

"Do me a favour Mick. Pass me the phone." I'd just sat down. The phone was on the passenger seat. It was another first for me. A car phone.

"There you go." He unravelled the attached cable.

"You'll need to plug it in to the cigarette lighter socket."

"Oh right." I did as instructed watching him in the rear view mirror for any further instruction. None came. I continued watching.

Opening his briefcase. He lifted a number of loose leaf papers and a folder spreading them either side of where he was sat. Reaching up he loosened his tie and undid the top button of his crisp white shirt. Sliding down into his seat he raised his left arm and placed it along the back rest. He picked up a fax from the pile and began to read. He returned my stare looking straight at me in the rear view mirror.

"Time we made a move, are you ready?" *Yeah I've been ready for the last five minutes.*

"Yeah Mr Adder lets be making tracks." And off we went towards the M56. I reach up to touch the peak of my imaginary cap. The car was a beauty to drive. Powerful too.

Fifteen minutes into the journey I notice he seems a little agitated and fidgety. A little on edge.

"I wonder what's happening at the pit."

"Why don't you give them a ring?"

"Yeah think I will." He picked up the handset and hit the required keys.

"Hello Control Room, it's me Mr Adder. Can you call me back on the car phone ASAP." He replaces the handset back onto its cradle. As way of an explanation he offered "Rather expensive these calls far better if they ring me," I say nothing continuing an occasional glance at him through the mirror.

The Manager had timed his actions to perfection as I brought the vehicle to rest at a set of traffic lights. We're surrounded by cars. Either side, front and back. The scene is set as the phone rings. Most of those passengers in the surrounding cars are staring at his brand new company car. He looks around to ensure he has the attention of his audience then towards the phone. His expression changes as he lifts the handset.

"Yes," he shouts into the phone. I try to imagine the conversation from the Control Room operator.

"Sorry to disturb you Mr Adder. I thought you wanted a call back?"

"Yes," louder this time his pained expression still in place. *He best be careful he may hang up if he continues to respond in this way.*

Having set the scene, he continues the conversation quieter now.

"Oh yes, right what's happening underground then?" for the audience he maintains his look of anger. The Control operator updates him on everything happening underground. Before long, the traffic lights turn to green. The cars in front begin to move off. His audience move on.

"Okay yeah I've got that. Yeah no that's fine nothing else…" He replaced the receiver. "Can't understand why some people feel the need to go on and on." I smile and shake my head in response.

"Yeah, you're right. There's nowt as strange as folk."

"Mick there's a garage just round the next bend. Do me a favour can you get me the FT?"

"Will do."

"Oh, and a packet of mints if you don't mind. There's a fiver in the glove compartment." I park the car away from the petrol pumps and head over to the rack of newspapers alongside the entrance to the garage. FT selected I head into the shop. There's an array of mints on display alongside the special offer on Aztec bars. Trebor, Extra strong, Fisherman's Friends, Polo mints, mint humbugs Victory V's and more. What should I choose? I go for my mothers-in-law favourite Polo mints. The mint with the hole as she often liked to point out. Back in the car.

"There you go Mr Adder." I pass him the newspaper followed by the mints.

"Bloody hell Mick what are these?"

"Polo mints."

"I know that. I don't like them."

"Oh right."

"These are the poor man's mint. I prefer the Extra Strong mints ideally peppermint if they've got them." *Well why didn't you fuckin say? In my world a mints a fuckin mint.*

"Okay I'll swap them." I keep hold of the poor man's mint for myself and purchase a packet of his favourite. Back in the car he's reading the FT as I pass him his Extra Strong spearmint packet.

"No peppermint?" *Actually, yes but two of us can play at being the twat"*

"Sorry no. That's all they had." He seemed not to have heard as I begin to drive off.

"You'd find this interesting Mick. There's an article here *What's in a Title.* Seems we're being influenced by the Americans. The top man in an organisation is no longer just a Manager or Director. They're now referred to as CEO or President. No there's a thought don't you think?"

"Yeah very much so Mr Adder."

Sixty minutes later we arrive at the seven hundred acre Trentham Estate. Purchased by British Coal in 1984 to allow one of the local Staffordshire collieries to mine beneath without the hassle of paying subsidence costs. Although I had read somewhere they'd drained the lake to reinforce the banks. At one time the place had belonged to the Duke of Sutherland. Little was now left of the original Hall built sometime around 1833. The river Trent had at one time been diverted into the lake. Resultant waste from the local Potteries eventually polluting it causing the 4th Duke of Sutherland to abandon the place in 1907. The majority of the Hall was demolished in 1913 leaving only the outer walls of the Grand Entrance and Orangery. Nowadays the grounds were used for a variety of activities. They'd even built the Trentham Ballroom where a number of famous bands performed over the year. Back in 1984 I'd received my Mining Degree from North Staffordshire Polytechnic in there.

Around the corner from the hall was the famous Clock Tower and riding school built in the mid 1840's. We were meeting above the old stables in the conference room. I drove along the cobbled entrance parking below the long band windows separated by the Doric pillars. As I parked the car it would not have come as any surprise if the household footman had come running out to greet us. We climbed out from the car remembering to straighten our ties.

Our colleagues were already there standing in the foyer below the head of a stag with its huge antlers. They advise us we're already behind schedule. The Group team already assembled upstairs. Tony Douglas makes a point of siding up to me.
"Where the fuck have you been?"
"Mints."
"Fuckin what?"
"Extra strong not Polo." He looks at me as though I've lost my mind.

The Manager leads up three flights of stairs. We pass under portraits of Lords, Ladies, Dukes and Duchesses from a bygone area. There's four near identical portraits alongside one another. I assume those to be the Sutherlands 1st, 2nd, 3rd, and 4TH. One or two pictures of younger women standing alongside a dead red deer stag. I momentarily stop to take a closer look. Ken John the Chief Engineer whispers in my ear "They be the mistress's fella." The Manager turns towards us both.
"Come on we're late." I smile. *I wonder why?*

We eventually reach our destination. I glimpse my first maid of the day. She is dressed in black with a neat white pinafore adorning her front. She's serving the tea, coffee, and biscuits to the Group staff. As we enter the room adjoining the conference room another maid appears.
"Tea, coffee gentlemen?"
"Coffee please, just black." I'm first to reply. I begin to feel quite important although I know I'm not.

We join our Group colleagues and mingle with the regular niceties being exchanged. *"How nice to see you again." "It's been so long". "You look well are you working out?" "What an absolute pleasure."* I remain near the door, *one, two, three, four, five*..... I count fifteen Group staff. *Blimey their numbers have increased! Hold on where's the Group Director? That would make sixteen. So much for the cost cutting carried out at the individual pits Group are increasing their numbers.*

To be fair I do them an injustice. Without this important group of gentlemen who would produce the inordinate amounts of paperwork – Group memo's, Group instructions, Group directives, safety bulletins etc. etc. *We only produce coal..........*

"You're keeping yourself to yourself today Mick, how's it going?" My thoughts are interrupted by Tom Brian the Groups Assistant Director of Employee Relations. Immediately my guard is up conscious of whatever I say will certainly be fed back to the Assistant Group Director Operations.

"How nice to see you again Mr Brian....." I pause mid-sentence his lordship has arrived, the Group Director.

A gap appears through the assembled group as he heads towards the conference room. I can't help but stare the man oozes confidence. There's an air of sophistication surrounding the man an aristocratic quality which is not lost on us mere mortals.

As he passes by me our eyes meet and he winks, I wince. Could the Manager be right does this high ranking official really like me? Sadly, no he withdraws a handkerchief from his pocket and wipes the corner of his eye. He stops to examine the foreign body he's just removed. He continues to walk forward we fall into line and follow. The China cups and saucers we've been holding we place back on the side tables. Etiquette dictates they don't accompany us into the meeting.

The centre of the conference room is taken up by a large rectangular mahogany table. Chairs positioned either side. Identical sets of paperwork in front of each. The Group Director takes a seat in the middle of one side. His colleagues position themselves either side. We sit opposite. The Manager directly opposite the Group Director. He looks up; the room is deadly silent. He eyeballs each of the colliery team. Individually left to right and then right to left. He has our complete attention. His team look as though they've been rehearsing the move as they follow his actions. He addresses us collectively.

"Welcome to you all. For those that didn't know this is our first meeting of the newly formed Midlands and Wales Group." He waited as we absorbed this information. Something I think we were all aware of. "Now gentlemen have you had a good journey?"

"Yes, Group Director." We reply in unison the Manager adding.

"Traffic was a little heavier than normal."

"Oh, right that would explain you're late arrival." *Mints* I want to add. I don't. We wait for the moment to pass. I'm expecting the Manager to get a bollocking. No doubt that will be done later in private.

The headquarters staff stare at us from the opposite side of the table not saying a word.

"Right let's get down to business shall we."

The opening presentation is provided by the Manager. He presents whilst sitting at the table. It covers the results from the previous months tonnage from the coal face and coal headings. Yardage driven in the various developments, manning levels, and tonnage per man shift. We'd reduced the pit workforce from six hundred and fifty from when I'd first joined down now to just short of four hundred. I still hadn't gotten my head round the fact that the number of contractors had increased by more than the number of staff we'd lost but the tonnes per manshift had increased. I wasn't about to say anything though.

He continued to cover costs, initiatives we'd embarked upon, coal tonnage split by size and markets it was sold to. Cuthbert added his comments on the small profit we'd made. It seems to confirm everything the Manager has said. Obviously accepted by the Group Director as he begins to nod. That seems to be the signal for his team too. They nod in unison.

I consider if any of the figures presented are checked. I certainly didn't recognise the figures for the coal drivages on my side of the pit. I consider the risk he's taking as only last year an Area Director from another area had mysteriously disappeared after presenting inaccurate figures for the amount of coal stocks they held. He skilfully presents the information some good some bad. Sometimes a question is raised he has an answer for all.

I wonder if he presented to his wife and kids last night. My thoughts are interrupted the Group Director has a question. It concerns the coal preparation plant and its layout. Not an area I believe the Manager has ever ventured into. It was hard enough to get him underground. Without pausing for breath and before the question is completed he turns to our Chief Engineer. Some would suggest to involve his staff was the sign of a team player. Personally I think it was more to do with him not knowing the answer.

Ken John is another who can talk for England. He starts on his preamble before answering the question. I'm now losing interest and the will to live I casually glance at the agenda. Safety is next. I begin to feel quite nervous and a little sad too. After such a fine performance by the Manager I'm about to burst the bubble and bring us crashing back down to earth. Present a subject I know little about adding insult to injury presenting inaccurate information. *I don't think I can do it, not me, why me?*

"Thank you Mr John. Have you anything else to present Mr Adder?"
"No thank you that's me done."
"Any more questions from my team?" He turns left and right towards his staff.
"Okay then what's next?" He looks down to the neatly placed papers in front of him. "Oh, Mick it's you to present the safety report and the month's results."
I nod my mouth is dry everyone is looking towards me expectantly. I must remember to keep my arms down. To conceal the perspiration, I can already feel under my armpits. I collect my acetates my hands begin to shake. The overhead projector is in position at the head of the table I stand and feel my knees shaking. *For goodness sake pull yourself together. This is it boy make or break time you can do it.*

A little confidence has begun to return as I walk towards the head of the table. I place my first acetate on the overhead projector. My hands are shaking. All eyes are on me. *Oh, fuck how do I switch it on it's different to one we use back at the pit.*
"The on/off button is at the bottom to you left." Tom Brian adds smiling.
Total silence as I commence my talk presenting the first slide. I try to control my hand it begins to shake. The slides indicate the current figures in blue with the previous quarters in red. I highlight the fact how much better this quarter's figures are. Everyone is nodding in agreement they seem happy enough. Other than Cuthbert he's spotted my ruse. I watch with concern as he learns across to the Manager whispering in his ear.
"Mick just hold it one minute." It's the Group Director. He raised his arms and looks around to those gathered. I see the Manager shaking his head. He doesn't look happy. *That's me fucked then!* "Before you go any further I have to commend you and the team for such a remarkable turnaround. Absolutely remarkable." I'm not sure how to respond. Everyone's shaking their heads in agreement. Even the Manager has changed his opinion. "I've never seen the likes before. What a turn round." He turns to the Manager. "Mr Adder you'll need to fetch Mick to the accountability meeting more often."

I smile *not if I can fuckin help it.* And that's how the rest of the presentation continued everyone nodding and offering congratulations on the pits huge improvement in the safety stats. After half an hour of presenting I didn't want to sit down. The Group Director had other ideas.
"Right thanks Mick I think we get the picture. Now time is of the essence I've got an underground visit at the Complex in an hour. With Mr Adman your old boss. Wouldn't mind a word with you in private Mr Adder regarding the Boyd

205

visit next month." Once the Group Director and Manager left the room. The group began to disperse. I headed outside to get a breath of fresh air. I was soon joined by Cuthbert and his Marlborough.

"You jammy bastard Mick. Don't ever think I've seen anyone pull off a performance like that."

"Thanks Cuthbert. It's not what you say it's how you say it."

-

"Mick sorry to bother you on your day off but you've got a couple of important visitors tomorrow." It was a Monday. I'd taken a long weekend off. It was the start of the kids Autumn term. "There'll be two of them. They'll want to see T7's and then pop in and look at T4's maingate and return."

"What time?"

"Late morning, I can let you know first thing tomorrow."

"Okay, should still give me time to make a trip into 64's maingate and 28's. Where are they from?"

"The States, company called JT Boyd. Mining consultants."

"Dad, are you coming or what?"

"Sorry Mick kids on your case I see."

"Yeah promised to take them blackberry picking. Thanks for the heads up see you tomorrow." I replaced the receiver. *Where have I heard that name before? Sunday Times. The Government had brought them in to review our industry. In fact, the Group Director had mentioned it last month at the Accountability.*

"Dad?"

"Yeah coming."

The following day I'd gone underground early. D28's was in the process of being salvaged with the chocks heading for 64's. Both 64's developments were coaling. Control room called me just after eight.

"Mr Gibson, Mr Gibson."

"Hi Control, Mr Gibson here."

"Just to let you know your visitors are here. The Training Officer will escort them into Strata Top."

"Yep okay I'll pick 'em up at the manrider." *No Adder thought he'd have been with them?* I continued to the Access conveyors. The conveyors packed high with the black stuff. Good to see Zone A and Mr Blackhead contributing to the pits output. I decided to have snap early probably wouldn't get chance later.

I reached down and extracted a pink grapefruit from the front of my overalls. I looked behind to check there was no one following. Something I did ever since one of the Zone A beltmen followed me up the conveyor last year. Seems he had an allergic reaction to the smell of the fruit as I peeled it. He passed out unknown to me. He was found by his colleagues in a collapsed state inside the chute of Access 2. Fortunately, bar for some slight cuts and bruises he made a full recovery. Twenty minutes later I was at Strata Top. I hadn't seen a soul not even the haulage lads. I made my way through the air doors and sat down. Whilst waiting I made some further notes on my earlier visit.

Fifteen minutes later I saw three lights bobbing up and down on the conveyor. I moved forward and stood by the lockout box. The Training Officer gave me a wave as he approached.

"Yours I believe Mr Gibson."

"Thanks Glyn. Good morning gentlemen." I turned to face the two visitors as each clambered down the alighting station.

"Howdy Mr Gibson."

"Gents, let's not rest on ceremony please call me Mick."

"Mick it is then. I'm Chuck and this is JW." I shook hands with them both. Glyn turned to me.

"I'll be off then Mr. Gibson. Make sure you return these good gentlemen in one piece now."

"Rest assured our American cousins will be safe with me. See you later." I turned back to Chuck and JW. "Now JW, would that be for John Wayne." He began to laugh.

"Fraid not that kindly gentleman is way past his sell by date. It's John Wasikowska."

"See what you mean. I like JW. Right if you'll follow me.

We continued on into T7's. During the journey they stopped several times to examine the steel supports supporting the roadway.

"You know what Mick." Chuck was pointing to a piece of wire mesh that'd been pushed out between the arches. "That's the downside of using free standing supports. It allows the surrounding strata to move." I nodded in agreement. Ever since we'd replaced the square work with the bolts and straps we'd all seen the benefits. We turned and entered T7's maingate. I began to give a little background information on the workings.

"T7's coal face is the fifth retreat unit we've worked in the area. It'll be followed by T8's. A narrow panel between the access roads for these five. Thereafter followed by T4's. We've recently started the access roads which you'll have the pleasure of seeing later." The conveyor hadn't stopped moving since we'd entered the maingate.

"Yeah T4's your boss mentioned it earlier. He may have some different plans for that." JW responded. Instantly Chuck shot him a glance. It was as if he'd volunteered too much information. I pretended I hadn't noticed. *Different plans for T4 whatever could he mean by that?*

"Mick do you mind if we stop for a minute." Chuck asked. They were both sweating profusely. Stains of perspiration clearly showing through their overalls. "Do'y know I've done more walkin this morning than I would do in a week back in the States." I looked for further explanation. "We use battery powered vehicles to travel on."

"Sorry guys, I can't even offer you the diesel powered FSV's big no no!" I unstrapped a water bottle attached to my belt. "Here have a mouthful of this." Chuck nodded his thanks and took the bottle from me.

"What the hell are these?" JW had his hand resting against a seven-foot wooden leg. It was attached to the celstrap above with a "U" shaped bracket.

"Tell me about it. Waste of time if you ask me but part of the Manager's Support Rules." I leaned forward and kicked its base. It immediately dislodged.

"See what you mean. No weight on it whatsoever." JW had removed his cap lamp from safety helmet and was shining it up into the roof area. "Anything show on these?" Illuminated above our heads was a laminated sign it read:

T7s MAIN
TELL-TALE
VISUAL INDICATOR
No 19
HEIGHT 2.4 Mts

"Not a scorrick."

"A goddammed what?"

"Sorry fellas a Lancashire term. No movement at all."

"Just as Paul had advised." Chuck nodded at JW's response.

We continued. It was pleasing to see, particularly as we had visitors the belt was piled high with the black stuff. From my conversation earlier Control had informed me the shearer was on its third cut. The coal was giving itself up. I could see lights up ahead. The clanging of the stage loader chain becoming louder as we approached. JW who hadn't repositioned his lamp picked out a further laminated sign ahead. The letter **M** reflected in the distance.

"Manhole. It's a manhole part of the Manager's Transport Rules every twenty metres."

"Used for what?"

"To place yourself out of danger when an FSV approaches. You must have seen a number of them on the main loco tunnel on your way in."

"Sure, did son. That I can understand with a train heading towards you but a goddammed FSV. Wouldn't it be easier for it to stop and let the guy pass on foot?" JW had a point.

"What the hell?" By this time, we were stood adjacent to the manhole. JW was laughing "I don't goddam believe it." Chuck stretched forward to see what was amusing JW.

"Well I never shot holes! Mick you actually blast the sides to create this fuckin thing?"

"Well they don't make themselves!" I responded.

"Don't you consider the damage you're doin to the surrounding strata?"

"No, it's something we have to do. If we didn't, we'd get an arse wuppin off HMI."

"H fuckin M fuckin I? Who the fuck are they?"

"Are they fuckin stupid?"

"Do you mind if I don't answer that?"

"Good morning Mr Gibson." I hadn't noticed the face Overman approach.

"Oh, hi Alwyn, let me introduce you to our visitors. They're from JT Boyd an American mining consultancy." Alwyn being one of my older generation face Overmen. He wasn't one for holding back. He always said it as it was, regardless of the consequences.

"Fuckin mining consultants. I've met more consultants these last few months than I've had hot dinners now. There was a time whenever anyone mentioned consultant, I assumed they worked in a hospital. There's even such a person as a tree surgeon. I wouldn't want one of them operating on me. How do you do gentlemen? Welcome to our little coal factory" He offered his hand to both in turn.

"Good to meet you Alwyn. We were commenting on your manholes and the need for them?"

"My thoughts entirely. The Inspectorate need to wake up and see times are changing." With that Alwyn led us down towards the Stageloader. JW and Chuck were both smiling. They'd instantly taken to him.

As we followed Alwyn towards the face, I began to look around at the scene the guys from JT Boyd would report back on. On the ribside of the stage loader various discarded items lay where they'd been thrown. Sheets of six by two mesh, steel tins, celstraps, wooden legs and pieces of chockwood. Most arriving there as the shearer advanced into the maingate end. Others removed from the stageloader's chain conveyor by one of the maingate lads. Lengths of cable for powering the shearer, lay in brackets running along its side. In places entwined with the various lengths of hydraulic bagging. The hydraulic pump attached to the large white tank containing the hydraulic fluid.

I watched as one of the Americans pointed to a laminated sign in front of the two roadhead chocks that now came into view. The letter **M** reflected below which NO 4 could be clearly seen. They came to a stop alongside a narrow metal bridge sat above the side plates of the Stageloader. I couldn't hear what they were saying to Alwyn. The noise of the chain conveyor and methodical pumping of the hydraulics drowned out the sound of their voices. They waited for me to arrive.

"Mick we were just askin if we could pop over the bridge to go look yonder?" Chuck was pointing to the ribside of the first roadhead chock. "Good to see how the roof is holdin after the coal is extracted."

"Best if I lead." As I finished my comment the chain conveyor began to slow.

"What the fucks up now?" Alwyn's voice boomed out. In response the tannoy answered.

"We've got a steel bolt stuck in the chute."

"For fucks sake. Gents if you don't mind, I'll have to catch you up." Before any of us responded he'd gone. These older guys never ceased to amaze me. On the surface they seemed to shuffle about. Down here though they were like young pups.

"Right don't go beyond there." I gave the instruction as I pointed to the back-cantilever bar of the first roadhead chock. Chuck and JW were stood alongside.

"Goddammit I'd have to have seen it myself to believe it. What do you say JW?"

"Better than I could have imagined. It's crying out for it!" They were both looking along the length of intake road inbye of the coal face. It was standing perfect. Other than the waste which had entered from the face side. I noticed the chain of a damaged load binder hanging from one of the leg brackets. The roof celstraps and bolts in the same position as the day they'd been installed. Even the ribside coal pillar was devoid of any spalling.

"Mick your conditions are perfect."

"For what?" It was obvious these guys had been sent on a fact-finding mission.

"All in good time. I'm sure the Manager will update you and the management team soon." And with that the conversation was over.

We continued up the face to the return end. We didn't see Alwyn again. In addition to the steel bolt blockage, the chain had been damaged.

-

The update came the following week. Although from previous conversations with the Manager I was fully aware of what was coming. Already in use in the North East it had been agreed to operate the method at Point of Ayr. The system had been used in the past but never fully mechanised. This would be different.

"Well gentlemen that's it. Over the next few months, we'll cease any further developments for coal faces in Strata Top. T8's being the last retreat panel. T4's as you know was to follow will now convert to room and pillar. The new district will be known as CM1. No guessing what that'll stand for." I don't think the Manager had meant for that last comment to be a question.

"Continuous Miner 1." The Deputy Manager couldn't help himself. He followed up with a regurgitation of his phlegm.

"Yes, thankyou Mr Douglas the very same. As you can see we propose to use a five road, sorry room system taking the full height of the seam. Six metres wide rooms supported by thirty metre square panels of coal." The Manager replaced the acetate. "This will be followed by a further site to the North, CM2's. As you can see initially running parallel with T2's."

Kelvin raised a hand. "Mr Adder will CM1 and CM2 run concurrent?" One or two of the assembled group looked at one another. Paul Adder picked up on this immediately.

"If you mean Mr Blackhead will they run together the answer is yes." He turned towards the screen. "And as you can see extending off to the west behind T2 and T3." Kelvin had another question.

"All this is happening in Zone B. I'm guessing after S64's, sorry H81's no more coal faces. All production from the continuous miner districts?"

"Exactly."

Everything I'd seen and been part of over these last few years fell into place. For us to survive we had to take further cost out of the business. Introducing room and pillar took cost out in two areas, manpower and materials. Including the added benefit of avoiding any production gaps. Strata Top in the Two Yard gave us that opportunity. What we'd been unaware of was the work done by the Group's Technical Department. They'd been working with equivalent organisations in both the USA (United States Bureau of Mines, USBM) and Australia (Australian Coal Industries Research Laboratories, ACIRL). It was from this work they'd found underground conditions in the UK to be very similar to those in Australia. A number of senior people had been out there to see for themselves.

The next slide brought the system to life. "As you can see the five road system is achieved using this machine here." He tapped the screen with his pointer. "The Joy Continuous Miner or JCM as its commonly known excavates the coal. Followed by the bolter. We believe this will be the Fletcher bolter."

"What no more Wombats?" Denny asked.

"No more Wombats Denny everything from now on will be fully automated. I should have added we'll be seeking exemption from HMI to initially extend the cut from two point one metres out to three metres and thereafter six."

The following slide listed the possible equipment we'd be using:

- JCM (Joy Continuous Miner)

- 2 x Fletcher Roof Bolters
- 2 x Shuttle Cars / Uni-hauler
- Stamler

And the manning levels:

- 2 lads JCM (includes a cable man – driver was usually the chargehand)
- 2 operating the shuttle cars or Unihauler's
- 2 per bolter (4 total)
- one electrician and 1 mechanic.
- Deputy

Noah our roof bolting specialist was sat near to the Manager. He turned to face us all. "Can I just add monitoring and the use of tell tales will continue as we have done in T7 gate roads. Two point four metre holes with tell tales at twenty metre intervals. At sixty metres the five metres tell tales. And at one hundred and eighty metres the wire extensometers."

"Yeah thanks for that Noah. If I may continue."

"He's got his feet well and truly under the table." Evan whispered to me as the Manager continued.

"The coal is collected and transported using these." Again, he tapped the screen. "Shuttle cars. Although that's not finalised as yet. We may decide to use something called a Unihauler."

"Mr Adder."

"Yeah Gregor."

"These shuttle car things are they diesel powered?"

"No cable."

"Fuck it. I knew it more work." The Manager chose to ignore Gregor's comment. Denny however added.

"What's up with ye cock. Cleaner environment."

"If it's the shuttle car we go with there's a narrow chain conveyor that runs along its centre allowing the extracted coal to be evenly distributed along its length. Once full it moves out and is replaced by a second machine. Its load is then deposited onto what is described as a Stamler. The Unihauler is basically a huge bucket fitted with a plough.

The Stamler sits on the tailend of the thirty six inch conveyor. This will be installed along the middle room or R3 numbering from left to right. Again, a chain conveyor within the Stamler provides a regulated feed of the extracted coal."

This was great news for the pit. I was particularly happy as it was something new to get my "teeth onto." The downside however would see the loss of a lot of the men who'd been there when I'd joined. I'd learnt quite a bit from them. Some good some bad but I'd miss them regardless. This was now a young man's game. All those fifty and older were being offered good terms to retire it didn't make economic sense for them to stop on. Osian for one had inquired. I was sure Evan would be next. I must remain positive it was an exciting time. It was also time I asked my own question. Although I knew most of it already.

"Mr Adder timescale."

"Yeah right Mick just coming on to that." He placed the last of the acetates onto the projector.

"The equipment will start to arrive Feb/March next year. Build and training. We'll be looking to start operations sometime May/June. We'll continue to access the area via T4's maingate and return. The JCM taking over to complete and commence the five road system by August."

"What about CM2's?"

"The following year."

"Wow that sounds promising. Looks as though we'll be here for the long haul!" The Manager turned away from the screen to face us all. I'd never seen such a smile before.

"Now for the good news. Group have arranged for a number of you to see the system in action." *For fucks sake a trip to Australia!!!!!*

"Mick you'll need to appoint one of your Overman to be the CM Supremo – working closely with Noah. We're off to the USA!"

–

I never did get an answer to the question I asked at our first meeting. It concerned our up and coming visit to the USA. Why there and not Australia as this was the country whose technology we'd be using. I never pursued it as at least I'd been given the opportunity to go. There were five of us going from the pit including me and the Manager. These were Arfon my appointed continuous miner supremo, the pits roofbolting specialist Noah and the pits NUM delegate Bevin. Our mission was to discover the new world we'd be entering that of room and pillar mining. I had enquired of Bevin had he been around when it was first utilised at Point. His answer was not one to repeat although it did include the word "bastard."

The news hadn't gone down particularly well at home. Just over a week before Christmas. The Saturday we left was also the PTA dance at the kids' school. Although I made good my promise of helping to get the kids bikes from Chester before I left. My wife as always had given me sound advice. "Don't get up to any mischief and make sure you bring back something nice for me and the children." My role as Undermanager at the pit had been taken up by a young lad Karl Haddock. Karl had been appointed as the new Undermanager for Zone B. I had temporarily been appointed Assistant Manager. In title only. No extra pay, which I never mentioned to Mrs Gibson. I may have had a new title but in my eyes, I was still the Undermanager!

The week before we left, we'd had an audience with the newly appointed Assistant Group Director, Phil Fowler. He was very complementary towards the team at Point. How we'd readily accepted the need for adopting the new system of work. It was imperative we made it work as the very future of the pit depended on it. We were the pioneers and first to become part of an exclusive club, "the American Club." His comments actually made me feel quite important. Wanting to believe this was true. However, when he mentioned there would be no them and us, a term I heard someone use previously, it did put a little doubt in my mind. During his speech I looked across to the rest of the team. Everyone seemed spell bound. I was sure the Manager had tears in his eyes. All accept Bevin. He was smiling. A smile I seen so many times before. It suggested he'd heard it all before and in his words, "verbal diarrhoea."

It was at this point the Manager's newly appointed PA; Lizzy appeared. She was carrying a tray with two cups of tea. Bevin had been right. The tea was for the Assistant Director and the Manager. Paul recognised the impression this would give immediately.

"Lizzy, what about the rest of the lads?" Instead of keeping quiet her response confirmed Bevin's smile which had returned.

"I'm sorry Mr Adder you said it was only for you and the Director." She'd only been in position for a week. Already she'd earned the nickname Dizzy. To avoid any embarrassment myself and my three tealess colleagues declined the offer. Probably just as well as the Director was coming to the end of his sermon.

"Above all else gentlemen make sure you enjoy yourself. We'll meet again on your return."

The Manager passed out a sheet of paper with the itinerary.

"So, a week from now we'll be leaving. One o' clock the bus will leave promptly. We'll be joined by one of Mr Fowler's colleagues from Group Tom Brian. There's also a gentleman some of you may know. The BACM President, Sidney Cider. Staying overnight at a hotel close to Gatwick airport. Our flight leaves on Saturday. The Sales Director from JCM Graham Michaels will meet us on arrival. He'll try to join us for dinner on our first night. As you can see, we have five underground visits planned."

"Mr Adder."

"Yes Arfon?"

"There seems to be a lot of gaps between each visit. In fact, nothing on our first day there?"

"Well spotted Arfon. Still to complete including one or two surprises. Right if there's nothing else?" That was our cue to leave.

The following week passed quickly. Things remained quiet at the pit at home too. I didn't want to admit it, but I was excited. And then it happened we were on our way. Setting off exactly as planned at one o'clock. Prior to boarding the bus Mr Adder had passed to each one of us an envelope. We'd each been given five hundred dollars spending money. Tom Brian accompanied us on the coach. We arrived at the hotel later than planned eight thirty. Friday was not the best day to be travelling down the M6 let alone the M25 and M23. It was already dark.

I say hotel, parking up in the courtyard it was more akin to a stately home. To add to our surprise several young men were waiting outside the entrance. They were dressed in what could only be described as butler outfits. As we climbed off the bus each ran forward to remove our luggage. The lads and I were speechless. Except for Tom Brian.

"Nothin like travelling in style."

Inside the entrance was even more lavish. Gold decoration covered the whole of the interior. The long reception desk's mahogany surface gleamed under the chandeliers. There was no queuing up to register. A single envelope on individual silver trays with each of our names had large brass chunky keys ready to take. I looked towards all my colleagues all were smiling. Bevin too. I could just make out a comment as he took his key. "For fucks sake!" I even caught my reflection on the desk.

The bedrooms too were exquisite. Four poster beds that I bet Royalty would be more than happy to use. The walls were separated into panels divided by strips of dark grained oak. Between which the red velvet patterned wallpaper added to the luxury. I headed quickly to the en-suite. We'd been told not to change we'd go straight to dinner when we arrived. The en-suite was in fact a room just a little smaller than the bedroom. Standalone gleaming white porcelain bath on gold feet. Taps of gold designed as a swan's head. The basin itself would have suited as a small bath.

After the sumptuous four course meal we retired to the lounge. Never in my life before had I seen such an array of malt whiskey. The whole room was surrounded by glass fronted cabinets stacked out with the stuff. The butlers having moved our luggage to our rooms and served at dinner were now in attendance once more. Each time we pointed to a decanter they would advise of its contents and deliver to our fine crystal cut glasses. Cigars were to follow. British Coal had done us proud.

Tom Brian took the opportunity to pass each of us a small parcel. It contained a variety of goodies as gifts for the people we were to meet. He requested we didn't open until we arrived in the USA and to place the parcel in our hold luggage. I wondered how we would answer the airline's check in staff when we would be asked the standard security question. "Have you packed this bag yourself? Have you been asked to carry anything on board by another person?" We could to all intents and purposes been passengers off the Mayflower heading to Cape Cod. I asked if the parcel contained beads and maybe a mirror. The response had been muted. Either it completely went over everyone's head or they were too pissed to even try.

When I finally got to bed in the early hours, I checked the package regardless. British Coal pens, couple baseball caps, some miniature oil lamp key rings, a decorative plate illustrating the Western Area coalfield and a set of place mats with pictures of coal mines long gone. The biggest prize was a small figure carved out from coal. I put that to one side that would be coming home with me. Fortunately for us all the flight out the next day wasn't until five pm. We arrived in St Louis at two thirty the following morning our time. Eight thirty pm theirs. We were staying at the Marriot Hotel. Noah our roofbolting specialist had been lucky to gain entry to the country. After warnings from the flight deck before we landed and the instruction on the entry visas not to bring foodstuffs into the country. He'd arrived at the Immigration desk eating an apple, part of his British Airways breakfast.

As Arfon had said prior to leaving there'd been some gaps in the itinerary. Our first full day was one of those. Again, as the Manager had commented we wouldn't be disappointed. I woke from my room looking down on the old Court House. We spent most of the day in and around the Gateway Arch. The view had been inspiring, the Gateway to the West as it had been described. What struck me more than anything was how young America was in terms of time. The museum at the base of the arch was split into time zones. Standing there it only seemed like yesterday General George Armstrong Custer had been getting his arse wupped at the Battle of the Little Bighorn. Thereafter we had a look around the town and our host Graham Michael's arrived earlier than expected. He suggested we go for a spot of lunch to Lynn Dickey's Sports bar.

The bar was owned by Clifford Lynn Dickie, hence the name. He'd been a quarter back in the country's National Football League. We only knew this because our guide for the tour Graham seemed to be a follower of the NFL. The evening meal was on a boat seafood restaurant on the Mississippi. It was called the J Lee Jackson.

The following day was to see the start of our underground visits. We set off from the hotel in two Lincoln Town cars. Designated drivers being Paul Adder, Tom Brian and occasionally Graham Michaels. Before arriving at the mine, we booked into our second hotel, the Drury Inn.

The mine, Monterey Coal Company No 2 was situated near to the village of Albers, Clinton County, Southwestern Illinois. Graham pointed out the mine in the distance. If he hadn't mentioned it we wouldn't have been aware. In the distance across a large expanse of ploughed field five circular towers stood proud. They reminded me of grain storage towers. However, Graham advised they were the ventilation shafts. Access to the mine would be via a drift. The day itself was very cold but the sun was shining brightly, just as I liked it.

We were met by the Mine Superintendent and lead into a large conference room. Here we were joined by several engineers and given an overview of the mine and its workings. Noah who seemed to have an ongoing problem with his water works requested the toilet. It hadn't helped the fact the previous night we'd stayed up till the early hours consuming copious amounts of bottled beer. Coors and Budweiser if I remember rightly.

The Mine Superintendent was explaining how the workforce of two hundred and fifty men produced nearly three million tons of coal each year. They were the second highest producer of coal in Illinois. The mine had been operating for fifteen years and was owned by Exxon Coal USA. In that time, it had produced more than seventeen million tons. Production remained consistent. The week before they'd achieved another record week's output tonnage.

The mine's biggest problem was the high sulphur content of the coal. Since the Clean Air Act had come into being tougher pollution controls had been put in place. He used the term "acid rain." Now where had I heard that before? Other issues they faced included competition from other fuel sources and some very bitter labour disputes.

Noah returned, "Problem with vandalism I see?"
"Sorry son, you'll have to explain."
"All the toilet doors are missing."
"They never had any son!"
"You mean if someone is taking a dump. It's in full view of everyone?"
"We don't pay the men to come here and take a shit." Wow I thought he'd given a perfectly good answer. Bevin who was sat alongside me, leaned across.
"Don't you be getting any ideas now Mr Gibson!"

Kitted up with overalls, safety helmets and safety gear we headed across to the drift entrance. Although the term used by the mine's management team was adit. The entrance to the adit was constructed with arches below which steel square work supported the main coal conveyor. Boarding the rope haulage manrider was not very different to what occurred back home. Low lung flat trolley with numerous wooden benches to sit on. The big difference however there was no roof to the trolley.

"Where can I put this?" Paul held up his camera. He'd been taking numerous pictures since we'd arrived.

"Take it with you. You'll get some good shots down below." We looked at one another with surprise. Taking a camera underground in the UK unless intrinsically safe was a no, no. I made a mental note to fetch my camera.

We descended at a rate of knots for about ten minutes until we levelled out. The smell of being underground once more very apparent. With our cap lamps switched off the darkness inside the mine was total. I bet it was the same the world over. I found it to be quite comforting in a way. From what I could make out from our guide most of the mines in the area followed the coal. Hence from the surface outcrop the access tunnels were constructed. Shafts although used were in the main for ventilation purposes and not for accessing seam as we did in the UK. A further twenty minutes saw us alighting at the inbye manriding station. He advised us we were some three hundred and eighty five feet underground at this point. I hadn't noticed until I'd climbed out of the vehicle that the steel supports had been replaced by bolts along the roof and along the sides. Just bolts and patch plates. I looked towards my colleagues. Arfon hadn't realized it, Noah seemed quite excited looking around and taking in the scene around. Bevin however did not look happy at all.

Waiting for our arrival was a battery-operated manriding bogey. It seemed the Yanks never walked anywhere. Once onboard we set off. This time on the flat and at speed along the eighteen by seven foot roadway Everywhere coated in what must have been their equivalent to stone dust. There wasn't a soul about. We must have entered the working as we crossed numerous identical tunnels. Then without warning a yellow vehicle passed one of the pillars to our right. Low slung with a single operator positioned to the side. Below him the figure twelve could be clearly seen. At the front, a huge bucket.

"Unihauler!" Graham shouted. We turned towards him, "Battery operated." That seemed to be our que. At the next x-cut on the right we turned in and came to an abrupt stop. He continued the conversation. "You'll be using shuttle cars. They do the same job but don't use batteries."

We followed on foot the direction the Unihauler had taken. It wasn't long before we could hear coal being cut. Ahead the Unihauler was stationary. The machine cutting the coal was in action. Above the din Graham shouted.

"Continuous Miner." Paul responded.

"Joy?"

"Why would you use anything else?"

This was our first sight of a JCM in action. It was formidable. The huge orange body of the machine standing out proudly against the black of the coal. The coal had no response to the cutting mat, and its array of tungsten carbon picks ripping the coal from its natural position. For millions of years it had laid dormant now within seconds it was being smashed to the floor.

As the machine edged forward two gathering arms clawed the smashed coal towards the chain conveyor centrally placed below the cutting mat. The mineral passing along the centre of the machine and out onto a further conveyor at the rear. The coal spewed back into the Unihauler's bucket. It was full within minutes. Out the corner of my eye a second Unihauler arrived taking its position as soon as the loaded one moved out. So, this is what they meant by continuous mining.

I walked forward because as, yet I could not see the operator. Straining to see where he was sat a person appeared from the far side of the machine. He was holding what looked like a control box, pressing various buttons as he walked forward. "I don't believe it; he's operating it remotely!" I said to no one in particular. Graham was looking towards me and smiling. He nodded to confirm my comment. The operator walked towards me.

"Howdy, where you boys from?"

"North Wales." He moved his head to one side. A lack of understanding written across his face. "Sorry, the UK." This time he nodded as if agreeing with me. He followed it by spitting out a gob full of chewing tobacco. I smiled it was like a scene from the old westerns.

"Want some?" He reached into his trouser pocket and pulled out a pouch. "Red Man, best there is." It seemed bad mannered not to accept. I took it from him. Emblazoned on the side the figure of a Red Indian below which the name of the chewing tobacco. I took a small amount and placed it into my mouth. It was beautiful, sweet too. I passed it back. "Thanks buddy." He nodded and continued to follow the machine. I looked across to the Superintendent to see what if any interaction there was between the management and men. My question was answered when he passed the JCM operator an unopened packet of Red Man.

We followed the Unihauler out to its delivery point. The Stamler positioned at the tail end of the main coal conveyor accepted its delivery. The bucket positioned itself above the unit. The operator using his controls to operate a plough to push the coal out. From here the chain conveyor ensure a steady load was delivered onto the conveyor.

Our guide then took us into road that had previously been cut. In place of the JCM was another machine we hadn't seen before. It had a central position for the operator when it was driven. Either side an extendable gibs where the drilling rods were mounted. This was the roof bolter. Each side had a cab for the protection of the operatives. The exposed ground in front of the machine was supported by an extendable gib supported by a huge central ram.

On the journey back out I reflected on what I'd seen. If at Point, we could get to half of what they did I'd be pleased. I felt very excited that we would be using this method of mining. The lads at the pit were ready to take anything on and certainly one of the few pits where I'd worked were there were never any issues regards industrial relations.

Back on the surfaced showered and changed we sat down once more in the conference room. The Superintendent needn't had asked us if we were impressed. Our constant questioning of what we'd seen confirmed it. For lunch they distributed a menu from a local sandwich bar. A place called Subway, which none of us had heard of before. They suggested we wouldn't be disappointed, we weren't. After we left, we did a little shopping in the world-famous Dillard's and then onto a pasta bar where I had swordfish for the first time.

The next morning was an early start. We were heading to a mine operated by Peabody Coal, Marissa Mine. We were met by the Mine Superintendent who as he explained had been called to an important meeting at Group. Our guide for the day would be his number two "Big Ron." No further description was required. One of those guys you'd pretty much agree to anything he asked you to do. However, his size and physique masked the kind, empathic personality of the man. An individual you could take to immediately. He explained later the meeting his boss was attending concerned the Clean Air Act. Something we were aware of from our visit to Monterey No 2. The coal they mined here also contained high quantities of sulphur. Peabody Coal were in negotiation with the mine's main customer Illinois Power. The company planned to mix Marissa's coal with that mined from Peabody's mines in Wyoming.

Once more we accessed the underground workings via an adit. This time we travelled on a trolley loco. Electrically operated, the power being supplied to the train via the front trolley and its pantograph. Big Ron explained once the pan was in contact with the double wire above current was passed to the trolley. The return current ran through the rails.

Initially descending through square work supports before levelling out under the roofbolted area of the room and pillar workings. Ron advised us to avoid any contact with the bare wires above our heads. He need not say anymore, we guessed what the consequences would be. That certainly kept us in our place during the decent into the workings. As we travelled along the pitch-black tunnel an occasional spark from the wires above illuminated the area around. Cables and pipes hanging from the supports above.

After travelling for thirty minutes the area ahead was full of activity. Cap lamps clearly seen from several moving bodies.

"Snap time." Graham sensed the question we wanted to ask. The loco came to a halt. "Right guys, coffee straight ahead." I assumed Graham had organised a flask for our use. How wrong was I. On a long wooden bench several coffee percolators were in use. Packs of Styrofoam cups lay alongside.

"Help yourself guys." Ron went ahead to talk with the group of miners.

"I don't believe it." Noah exclaimed as I began to pour us all a coffee. We each turned to see what had caused his comment.

"For fucks sake." Bevin was next to comment. "A fuckin women?" Well that was a first for us. Back in the UK the Mines and Quarries Act 1954 specifically decreed the prohibition of females being employed below ground.

Ron returned with a smaller guy following. Anyone next to Ron would seem smaller. He immediately saw our astonishment at seeing the two female miners.

"And why not? They need to make a livin just as we do." He had a point. Something I'd never considered before. The smaller guy stood alongside Ron.

"This is Billy, he's our engineer for the team." Billy looked relatively young with one of those faces that seem to be in a permanent smile. He had tobacco stains on his chin.

"Howdy yawl."

"Hi Billy."

"I've no doubt you will be asking if he's electrical or mechanical." Graham had joined the conversation. "In the States they don't differentiate. He what you might call an electromechanics."

"Right come on you guys let's make a move." We followed Ron on foot to the next x-cut. Once more we were met by a battery operated manrider bogey enough space for us all. Billy headed towards it. Ron had other ideas. Alongside it was a two-seater vehicle it resembled a beach buggy. At the back of it a huge white board proclaimed:

The Best Safety Device is a Careful Man

"Who's comin with me?" Before any of us could respond Paul picked up his pace.
"I think that should be me." He said smiling. I overheard Sidney muttering.
"Why would it be anyone else?"

As we travelled in towards the working area I could see the potential of what we could do in the Two Yard back at Point. It was ideal. From what we'd experienced so far on each of the coal faces conditions would be ideal. Although we had yet to receive the new equipment

Later that afternoon we boarded a flight for Pittsburgh. As we boarded two female cabin crew greeted us. The taller of the two was the image of an actress. I couldn't remember her name; she'd played a part in A Fish Called Wanda. We sat to the left of the isle. The first row was taken up by Paul, Tom, and Sidney. The row behind them was already occupied by a young couple. I, Noah, and Bevin took the next row leaving Arfon to take the aisle seat next to the young couple. Graham Michaels had made alternative arrangements to get to Pittsburgh.

Before we'd even taken off, I'd dozed off dreaming of Jamie Lee Curtis. She was gorgeous for no apparent reason she began to shake me. What did she want? "Mick, Mick." The elbow in my ribs brought me back to reality. It was Noah he was laughing. Alongside I could hear Bevin too.
"Listen to that cunt." He was pointing to the row in front. By now I was fully awake. Arfon was talking to the young couple. Sounded as though they were discussing the Royal Family.
"But I thought his name was Edward."
"Yeah." Her partner added. "Charles, Ann, Andrew and Edward?"
"No, Edmond. Charles, Ann, Andrew and Edmond." Arfon responded with conviction.
"Well strike me down with a feather. After all these years I thought his name was Edward. Edmond who'd have thought." I joined in the laughter. Poor old Arfon and he hadn't had a drink.

At the airport we picked up two black Lincoln Town cars. Graham Michaels having arranged them. He was on hand to meet us. This time we booked into the Howard Johnson Motel. Having unloaded our gear we headed straight to Station

Square for dinner at The Grand Concourse. It was to be another first for me. Lobster. I hadn't a clue how to eat it. Fortunately, a kindly waitress spotted my predicament and provided with what I could only describe as a nutcracker.

Next day we visited Penn Allegheny Mine. Owned by a mother and son. The first mine we'd visited and not part of a corporation. We entered on the flat through a yellow concrete portal into the side of what could only be described as a mountain. Scribed on the portal were the following words:

THROUGH THESE PORTALS PASS THE *Finest* **MEN IN THE WORLD**
Our **PENN ALLEGH COAL MINERS**

I assumed from this we wouldn't be seeing any females underground this time.

Leaving the mine, I got the chance to drive the Lincoln. I was fascinated it was first car I'd ever seen where the doors automatically closed themselves. And it had speed control. We headed to a place nearby called Jacks Bar. Set in the countryside. A huge log cabin. Outside several bison were roaming freely. It was the first time any of us had seen such a live animal other than on the telly watching John Wayne. I hoped the steak I ordered wasn't related to those we'd seen. They were magnificent looking animals. Ordering a beer wasn't as easy as imagined. The waitress was keen we chose from the variety available, Coors, Budweiser, Michelob, Miller, Milwaukee, Keystone. The list was endless. By the time we got back to the hotel we were all ready for a kip.

That evening we were in for a big surprise. The Manager had advised us to wear something decent as we were to be entertained at the local exclusive Pittsburgh Golf Club. Special guests of John T Boyd. The same company whose consultants been on an underground visit to Point two months previous. Bang on eight two white limousines arrived.
"Your carriage awaits." Paul exclaimed. He seemed excited. We all were.
"I've seen it all now." Perhaps not for Tom Brian. Something he was well used to working for Group headquarters.

Each of the cars was occupied by JT Boyd employees giving us a commentary of the surrounding area after we left the hotel. I was surprised to find after a short distance the deterioration in the housing. It seemed we were passing through Lower St Clair, a village built in the early fifties. It had been a public housing project nearly six hundred units in total. All similar in design with an outside veranda. At first glance full of character however on closer examination even with the regulation rocking chair outside the porch they looked run down. Something I'd witnessed previously living in Liverpool.

223

And then in the blink of an eye we were approaching the outlying expanse of land surrounding Pittsburgh Golf Club.

"Originally built in 1896 as a family club. It had several celebrity patrons including our very own JT Boyd. The area itself is known as Squirrel Hill." As we turned in through the entrance. The golf club was directly ahead. Constructed of white marble. Four tall pillars adorned the entrance. Either side huge windows covered in what looked like the finest lace curtains. Above which a veranda. It resembled a miniature Whitehouse I thought. It looked Georgian.

Coming to a halt. In the darkness outside doormen approached each vehicle. Their faces lit by the tall gas lamp posts set either side. We climbed out and headed towards the huge oak panelled doors. As if by magic they opened before us. The splendour continued unabated inside. The entrance hall was laid out with oak flooring littered with numerous coloured rugs. The walls covered in an orange wallpaper divided between oak panels. As we entered the main dining area a few guests had already arrived. I was still taking in the scenery. Each wall seemed to have its own ornamental fireplace. The patrons had a taste in chairs. A variety of Chippendale and Adam Lyre backs stood proud around numerous worktables. I thought I spotted a Sheraton Parlour chair in an adjoining room.

"Welcome gentlemen good to see you all. I hope your stay has been pleasant thus far?" What followed was beyond all our expectations. An evening with the great and good of Pittsburgh. A meal worthy of Royalty steaks the likes of which none of us had seen before. The red wine was on continuous tap, the quality I'd never tasted before. Each time we'd empty our crystal cut glass a maid would be on hand to replenish. I had enquired off one of them where the wine was produced. I could see it was a Cabernet Sauvignon from its label from somewhere called the Tusk Estate. This meant little to me.

"Why sir it's from Napa specially shipped in for Mr Jim himself." Her reply meant even less. More importantly it was exceptional. Bevin's continuous supply of Michelob I guessed was from somewhere other than Napa.

The night finished in what I believed to be the drawing room. The wine now replace by brandy. Poured from huge glass decanters in addition to huge Montecristo Churchill cigars. We were all fully engaged with the offerings. Other than Bevin who insisted on smoking his dwindling pack of Woodbines. A night to remember would be an understatement. The surprising thing however was we never once discussed coal mining.

The following day we had our final underground visit. Dianne Mine owned by the Canterbury Coal Company. As with the previous visits the underground operation was a delight to see. I began to feel at home in this new working environment. I felt privileged to see first-hand how the American miners and management produced coal. We'd been allowed to see inside "their world." I know back home some would see this as a "jolly." In some ways it was but for me it was proof BC were serious about the new technology. I believe we all felt the same way. Paul Adder had confided that he would be pushing to get more visits in before the new equipment was to arrive. He impressed me with his view that this should include the lads themselves, those operating the machines. I was surprised by his comment but pleased.

Arriving back up the drift we headed across to the management offices. It was another very cold dry sunny day. Something I loved but rarely got at home.
"What are they? And what are they doin there?"
"You don't have em back home son." The Mine Superintendent replied to Noah as we reached the door to his office." We all looked to see huge stack of wrapped birds piled high against the entrance. I walked closer to touch them. Still frozen.
"Yeah, sorry chickens…"
"You must be feedin them on something special son. They're goddam turkeys. Christmas turkeys for the workers."
"Wow"
"They taste good too."

We continued into the office and sat round a large table in the middle of the room. The Mine Superintendent sat at his desk directly opposite. It was positioned below a large window. The sun shining directly through. In places the glass offered some discolouration reflections of purples, yellows and blues.
"Coffee boys?" The assistant Superintendent asked as he entered the room.
"Please." We answered in unison. After he left we continued with our barrage of question. I could see Paul Adder smiling. I guessed he was pleased to see his team had lost none of its enthusiasm for what we'd seen.
"That must be a real treat for the men. Those turkeys we saw."
"Do it every Christmas. The women get one too."
"Sorry forgot you have female miners too."
"What you don't have em back home."
"No, we.." The door to the office opened suddenly.
"Coffee gents." The assistant Superintendent offered. He was carrying a large tray with mugs of steaming hot black coffee. He was followed by another guy again with a huge tray of bread rolls. "Turkey rolls too."
"Blimey that's one way of keeping the workforce happy."

225

"You might think so." The Superintendent threw his hand back pointing with his thumb to the glass window. "We had a strike couple of months ago. Some of the more hardened union men didn't take too kindly to our offer."

His comment caused us all to stare towards the discoloured glass.

"Bullet holes?" Arfon commented.

"The very same boy." I looked around at my colleagues. They looked as I felt. Other than Bevin he was smiling.

An hour later we set off for the last hotel of our stay the Sheraton in downtown Pittsburgh. It would be the last time we travelled in the Lincoln Town Cars that we had become so accustomed to. I was travelling with the Manager, Tom Brian, Bevin and Arfon. Graham Michaels was taking the other vehicle accompanied by Sidney and Noah. Tom raised our expectation of the view we would see as we crossed. He explained, not that any of us had the knowledge to question his comment. Pittsburgh was known as the City of Bridges with the world's only recognisable trio of identical suspension bridges. He named each one as the Roberto Clemente, Andy Warhol, and Rachel Carson. We'd be taking the Andy Warhol to cross the Allegheny River.

As we approached he suggested we sit back and take in the scene. He wasn't wrong. As we turned to enter the bridge the whole city was lit up in an array of illumination bringing to life building and structures of various shapes and sizes.

"Different view from the Menai now." Bevin added. "I suppose that would be the same for you Mr Gibson?"

"What would that be Bevin?"

"Runcorn bridge." I began to laugh as I continued to take in the view.

"Right lads I know you must all be feeling exhausted by now but it's a quick turnround." Paul Adder interrupted our thoughts. "Special night tonight so you'll need to be wearing your best bib and tucker. We're repaying Jim Boyd for his hospitality last night."

"And what a way to repay it." Tom added. "Christopher's restaurant." The name meant little to any of us.

"That's right Tom one of the finest restaurants in this part of the States."

"Have you been there before then Mr Adder?" Bevin asked as he nudged me in the side.

"No not exactly."

"Well how do you know then now?" Arfon added.

"I've been and can vouch for it." Tom had come to the Manager's rescue again.

"That's settled then. We'll meet in the foyer at six thirty."

We took two yellow cabs to the restaurant some twenty minutes away. We arrived to find Jim already there. He was in the bar. We all grabbed a beer and were then escorted to our table. By now I was beginning to accept the luxury we were being exposed too. Nothing was a surprise anymore or so I thought. We were taken to a table in the centre of the restaurant. The largest there was set out for nine. It was the view that hit us as we entered the room. The exterior of the restaurant was enclosed completely by huge glass panels. If we thought the view from the bridge was exceptional this was at another level, literally. Other than Jim Boyd and Tom we stopped in amazement. I took the opportunity to make a move towards the table and sit next to the main man. Paul Adder when he joined us didn't look so happy. I'd obviously taken his seat. Tom sat on the opposite side. I was determined to get a view from Jim on his findings to date on our industry and particularly on the future for Point of Ayr.

"Well Jim before we start I'd like to say thank you for last night and for the assistance given to arranging our underground visits." Paul opened the conversation. Well that was my first surprise of the night. I'd thought Joy and Graham Michaels had organised the same. We all nodded in agreement to show our thanks.

"Well thank you Paul. It's been good to meet your team I'm sure you and everyone at Point of Ayr will make this exercise a huge success.."

"More drinks gentlemen?" The waiter had arrived at the table. Ordering drinks before dinner each evening was a drama in itself. Both Paul and Tom were determined on ordering the wine. I'd made a note that to date they'd shared the honours. I watched as Paul placed his hand on the table searching for the wine list. The look on Tom's face suggested it had already been decided. Smiling he lifted the list from below the table.

"Two bottles of the Argentinian Merlot, Matias Riccitelli."

"An excellent choice sir Rio Negro. One of the restaurants favourites." I had to give it to Tom he certainly had a way with words. I wasn't sure Paul could have carried that off.

It was another memorable night and not all for the right reasons. As much as I tried I couldn't get any inside information from Jim. Not that I thought he was hiding anything. I guessed he just didn't know the detail on Point. I decided to stop asking questions and listen to the conversations around the table. More so as I began to slur my words. Looking around the table I counted nine empty bottles of wine. The last full bottle was directly opposite Arfon. That didn't include Bevin's empty Michelob bottles.

"John have you visited any of the Welsh mines yourself." Bless we all knew when we'd had enough.

"Who the fucks John, Prince Edmond?" Sidney's comment caused some laughter around the table. Undeterred Arfon continued. This time he began to gesture. It wasn't hard to see what was coming next.

We watched as if in slow motion as the bottle toppled over. Arfon was sat directly opposite Jim Boyd. The red wine flowed slowly over the crisp white tablecloth. Leaving in its wake a narrow red stain initially before its path widened. I don't think Arfon had appreciated the drama unfolding as he continued to talk.

"Or maybe any mine in the England." The wine continued to move forward. We watched. My proximity to Jim suggested it would land directly in his crotch area. Once more it was Sidney that broke the spell.

"For fucks sake Edmond!" The comment caused Jim who up till this point was mesmerised by the red wine pushed his chair back. Just in time as it reached the end of the table. Our waiter who'd been hovering in the distance soon arrived.

"Soon have this sorted gentlemen." He began to dab the stain with a white cloth he'd had up till this point draped over his arm.

We left soon after. Jim seemed glad his exposure to British miners was over. The best was I got the blame. Paul suggested I needed to get to grips with the team and ensure something like this never happened again. As it was our last night giving him that assurance was guaranteed a positive outcome.

Arriving back at the hotel there was quite a bit of activity in the bar area. I wasn't sure if the Americans referred to it as a disco. It was in full flow. Tom ordered us all a beer. I say all Graham Michaels had said his farewell outside the restaurant and Arfon had gone to bed. I was stood next to Tom watching the dancing. Bevin and Noah were on the far side of the room. I couldn't see Paul or Sidney.

"Hey you pretty boy." I turned having been tapped on the shoulder. *Bloody hell Whitney Houston.* What I can only describe as beauty in its rawest form was smiling at me. She was absolutely gorgeous.

"Like what you see?" For some reason Bevin had suddenly appeared stood directly behind her. He was shaking his head from side to side.

"Hundred bucks and I'm yours for the night." I was still unable to speak. Obviously, my lack of response caused her to turn towards Tom Brian.

"How about you mister silver fox?"

"No thanks darlin. I'm happy with my Budweiser." He responded raising his bottle as if to confirm his comment.

"Your loss baby." She walked off.

"Never paid for it and ain't goin to start now." Tom responded to no one in particular.

"Lucky escape there Mr Gibson." Bevin was now stood alongside the two of us.

"Maybe not for Noah." Tom nodded towards the other side of the room. Whitney was now in full conversation with him.

"He might be discussing the length of his resin and the hole diameter for insertion." Bevin added.

We stayed watching the dancing for a little longer. Tom and Bevin decided to call it a day. We'd lost sight of Noah. I went outside to take one last look at the nightlife around Pittsburgh. To my astonishment there were a number of open topped horse and carriage's outside the entrance. Beautiful looking animals. I'd always wanted to own a horse. People leaving the hotel were climbing on board and heading on to their next destination. *Wow seems the yellow cabs were replaced by a horse and carriage. Is that Sidney?*
In the distance I could see Sidney. I wasn't exactly sure what he was doing. I guessed the amount of alcohol was blurring my vision. I walked towards him. He was talking to one of the horses.

"You're the most beautiful thing I've seen all night." I wondered if I'd heard correctly. I guessed I had when Sid gently took the horses head in his hands and began to kiss it. It was time for bed.

The next morning at breakfast Sidney wasn't feeling too good.

"Hangover mate?" I'd just come into the restaurant for breakfast.

"Oh, hi Mick yeah I'm not one hundred per cent this morning. I kept dreaming about horses for some reason?"

"How strange, must be that Kentucky bourbon. I'm sure some ham and eggs will sort that plus a few coffees."

"I'm not sure I'll ever be the same. Not with the news to come."

"Whatever do you mean?"

"Well I'm not supposed to say but at the BACM conference next May we've got the new Minister for Energy presenting."

"And?"

"Well according to my good mate Dr Ken he's going to confirm the industry is about to be privatised."

"I think we're all expecting that at some time."

"We all know they've appointed JT Boyd to advise on the privatisation."

"Yeah."

"They're talking about bringing the number of pits down to seventeen possibly lower."

"What? No fuckin chance. We're at fifty now."

"Mick you may not know this, but all this hype of increased productivity isn't helping either. In the 91/92 financial year we produced only one million tonnes less coal but with fourteen thousand fewer employees. In the last year we produced three million tonnes more than we could sell. Do you know what stock levels we're at now?"

"Morning you two." Arfon had joined us.

"Good morning Prince Edmond."

"Oh, you are so funny."

"Morning Arfon. Go on Sid surprise me."

"Over forty two million tonnes!"

"For fucks sake!"

"Exactly my point... Here he is Mr Transmit." I looked across to see Paul Adder enter the restaurant. It was my que to leave.

"Sorry Sid I need to make a move. I need to get the missus a present before we set off for the airport."

"I thought I saw you with a load of shopping yesterday?"

"You did. Stuff for the kids and I got a pair of Ralph Lauren jeans and a denim jacket." I walked straight across to Paul.

"Morning."

"Morning Mick where the hell did you get to last night?"

"Bar all night. And you?"

"Some late night shopping. Get the missus a present."

"That's where I'm off to now.

As much as I tried I could not find anything I thought suitable for the wife. Perhaps I was still under the influence and time was pressing. Finally, I'd run short of time. I consoled myself I get her something from Duty Free at the airport. Failing that there was also the onboard sales. We arrived late in Boston. No time for Duty Free. To my relief I was able to purchase perfume on the aircraft. The icing on the cake, or so I thought, was a pearl necklace. Majorcan pearls to be exact. Something to go with a set of earrings I'd bought her the year before whilst we were on holiday with the kids.

We left Boston at seven thirty in the evening. I was sat next to Sid.

"Going back to our conversation earlier. The Chairman continually harps on about the dash for gas, why so?"

"The Government has got itself into a right mess. By creating a generating duopoly each generator only has to mimic its rival to remain competitive. There's an incentive to avoid the risk of acting differently. If one generator decides to burn horse shit the other will follow to ensure its rival doesn't gain any advantage."

"Fascinating." I responded. Sid let out a huge yawn.

230

"Listen Mick if you don't mind I'm fucked. I need some shut eye. We'll speak later.

The remainder of the flight was uneventful. I finally nodded off. We arrived back at Heathrow ten past seven in the morning.

Later that afternoon I arrived home. Outside the front door my wife and kids had put a huge sign up wishing me a happy birthday. I'd almost forgotten I was now thirty three. It was great to be home. Between them they'd made a huge chocolate sponge birthday cake with candles. The kids couldn't wait to see what I'd bought them. For my daughter I'd got her a black barbie doll, T shirts and trainers. My son too was happy with his baseball cap and gloves. T shirts too and a pair of trainers. Between them the latest Michael Jackson CD Thriller. I'd been told it was yet to be released in the UK. They both seemed pleased.

My wife however seemed less enamoured with her Majorcan pearl necklace. The turning point came when I showed them my denim jacket and jeans.

"You go all the way to America and get yourself and the kids something from there. And what do I get? A Majorcan pearl necklace!" I ducked as she threw it towards my head. Soon followed by the birthday cake. It was a mistake I would never make again!

7. 1992 The Announcement

The management team had been asked to attend a Manager's update on the Thursday afternoon. I'd assumed it was to do with our recent visit to the USA. I wasn't wrong. Although there was to be an additional announcement I wasn't expecting.

I was sat next to Kelvin. "I hope this isn't going to take too long. What's with the projector and screen." Chairs had been grouped together at one end of the conference room opposite the screen. I'd assumed they'd been left there from a previous presentation.

"You on a promise?" I responded.

"No, me and Dafydd are playing golf later."

"You seem to spend more time with him than your missus. Something I need to know?"

"Cheeky bastard. In fact, we're meeting up with Evan and Osian at Rhuddlan golf club. You should come."

"Mate I wish I had the time. Not sure my missus would take too kindly to it…"

The coughing from the corridor brought an end to the conversation. The door opened and in walked the Manager followed by Tony Douglas and Bill Hooper. Tony was still coughing as the three took up their positions at the front of the room. Tony and Bill sat down. The Manager remained standing. He turned to look at Tony who by this time had given up trying to regurgitate the phlegm.

"Right gentlemen let's make a start. I've an update from our USA visit. Bill will announce who will be in the next group to go and when. Most important of all is the follow up to all the work that was done on TQM."

"Not more fuckin consultants." I heard Gregor mutter from behind me.

"Due to the success of the first visit to America, Peabody Coal have agreed to send some of the team from Marissa Mine once CM1 is up and running." I nodded this was good news. They were a good bunch of lads and very knowledgeable. The Manager continued for another five minutes on progress of the equipment. Each time placing a picture of the item on the projector.

"He's got an album you know of the pics he took when we went over."

"Who?"

"The Manager."

"Bet most of them are of you."

"Fuck off."

Finished he sat down. Bill Hooper stood just as Tony Douglas began to cough. The Manager reached across and poured him a glass of water from the small table alongside the screen. He took a mouthful. At which point he began to choke. This drama had become a regular feature with the Deputy Manager. I was beginning to wonder if it was his attempt to gain attention. It certainly did with the Manager. He began to pat his back at the same time ushering him towards the door.

Everyone was watching the spectacle. Most of us well used to it by now.

"Laryngopharyngeal reflux." Kelvin whispered. "LPR."

"Fuckin LPR?"

"The very same. Caused by poor diet and fizzy drinks." I began to laugh. The Manager having seen Tony out returned to his seat.

"Sorry about that. Right Bill."

"As I was saying the next group to go will be led by Mr Douglas and Mr Blackhead."

"For fucks sake." Kelvin whispered again.

"Looks as though you'll be taking your own album with you."

"What'd mean?"

"LPR. Long playing record."

"Wow you're so fuckin funny."

"Thanks Bill. Right gentlemen final update. You'll remember.." He paused for effect. "Must be over twelve months ago now." Bill Hooper began nodding in agreement. "Mr Adman and Mr Button had introduced you to TQM. Total Quality Mining. They'd engaged PA Management Consultants to carry out some investigative work." The whole room nodded in agreement. "Well we've now received a programme on introducing the concept here. Ideally timed I would suggest with the new system of working." I don't think any of us in the room fully understood it had been so long ago. The Manager too lost his train of thought. He reached across to Bill who passed him a sheet of paper.

He began to read form it.

"Things never happen overnight, particularly when a culture change of this size is undertaken. If we do not progress with Total Quality Mining then we shall not become the supplier of choice of our customers. It is this forward looking attitude that will ensure our future and make us part of the nation's energy supply industry for a long time to come."

"It's coming."

"What?"

"His favourite phrase." I turned from Kelvin and continued to listen.

"I believe that Total Quality Mining is the future and we have now taken the initiative to develop the skills that we need to progress forward. I know that some of what you are about to see and hear may be difficult to take on board.."

"Told ye."

"Straight away, but with some hard work and commitment the training you are about to receive.."

"May we be truly grateful."

"For fucks sake Kelvin I'm trying to listen to the man." The Manager continued.

"Can be most enjoyable and rewarding."

He reached down and placed a further acetate on the projector.

"To help us achieve this I've listed a number of you to assist in introducing the concept and for you to train as Facilitators." I scanned the list. My name was at the top. *A fuckin Facilitator, don't you think I've got enough to do with the day job.*

"Bloody ell Mick something else to add to your CV."

"It's not just you, he's got six names in the hat. You, Len Saddle, Ioan Sword, Iolo Pyke, Osian, Ithel, Dafydd and Billy Blunt."

The Manager replaced the acetate and began to refer to a number of source booklets.

"There's a total of eight Source Books
   1. What is Total Quality Management
   2. Customer First/Quality First
   3. Managing for Total Quality

4. Teamwork for TQM
5. Putting TQM into practice
6. People Make Quality
7. Overcoming Barriers to Implementation
8. Making TQM Stick

I'll be advising the rest of the colliery when each person will be required to attend the training sessions."

"Mr Adder you mean everyone?"

"I certainly do Dafydd. This is only going to work if we include everyone."

Bless poor old Dafydd he did tend to ask the most obvious questions. I guessed the training wouldn't make much difference to him and his bosses daily routine. They spent ninety nine per cent of it on the surface anyway.

I sat and thought through the implications of the Manager's announcement. Upper most in my mind was how all this could be included on what we were already involved in. Where and when would we as Facilitators be trained? The Manager must have read my mind.

"I'll be holding a separate session with the Facilitators to agree time away from the pit for training. I'm guessing at the moment Kinsale Hall."

"Where's that?" Iolo asked.

"Just down the road. Near Mostyn. A week and probably residential." *Fuck how do I explain that to Mrs Gibson. Down the road and staying in a hotel. Not long back from the States. It was only last year I'd spent two weeks in Chalfont St Giles at the Vache.*

"Where will the training be carried out for the men?"

"At the moment Denny we're planning to book the Springfield." Bill Hooper responded."

I guessed the cost for the amount of printed books and the consultant fees had been hidden under the Capex for the continuous mining equipment.

"Mick you're very quiet today. Any questions?" *Why the fuck does he always pick on me.*

"No all good Mr Adder." I really wanted to ask was it his intention to increase the working week and did he really believe the shite about being part of the nation's supply industry for a long time. What exactly is a long time?

"Right if there's no more questions. Thank you all for attending."

The residential took place two weeks later and was actually quite enjoyable. We were wined and dined each night. Company was good and the consultant who lectured us on the principles of TQM made it interesting. I was learning quite a bit of new stuff. I particularly enjoyed hearing and understanding how other companies had used the concept to improve their performance and become a quality company. British Airways for one with Lord King and Sir Colin Marshall were one example. I began to dream what it must be like to work for one of those organisation.

After a day's session which became quite exhausting we'd retire to our rooms for a shower and to get changed for the evening meal. The restaurant was quite small and accessed up a short flight of stairs. Positioned to one side was a large tank. It contained a lobster. Being rather naive I assumed it to be for decoration a pet even. Each night we arrived it seemed to wave to us. Its large front claw tapping on the side of the tank. To all intents and purposes, it looked as though it was waving and welcoming us to dinner. Then one night I arrived later than normal. Everybody had finished eating. The tank was empty.

It wasn't till we started back at the pit that I found out the truth about Larry the Lobster. Billy Blunt had been carrying around in his wallet a piece of its claw. The night I'd arrived late for dinner he'd ordered it as his main. Consuming it before I'd arrived. I wasn't happy.

The presentations to the staff began the following month. As suggested the event was held at the Springfield over six weeks. It wasn't everyday so I was able to monitor the preparation for the arrival of the new equipment for the continuous miner operation.

Visits from various sources continued unabated including one from Sidney Cider. A member of the American Club.

"Now lad how's it goin?"

"Sid how nice to see you. What do we owe the pleasure?" I was sat at my desk.

"Just popped in to see his Lordship. I'm visiting a number of UK collieries to update those Manager's that didn't attend the last BACM conference. We received a presentation from the Governments new Energy Secretary." He passed me a single sheet of paper. "It don't read good lad."

I took it from him and quickly scanned the content. It contained the usual about the industry under threat and the tough challenges that lay ahead. How we all needed to focus on reducing cost, improving productivity and bringing in new technologies.

"Doing our bit there Sid."

"What?"

"New technologies, the continuous miners." He nodded as he lit up a fag. I continued to read. It talked about the Government's commitment to the industry. We all had a view on that statement! Privatisation was now openly talked about. We all knew it was coming. New coal contracts currently under negotiation between British Coal and the generators. The new contracts would establish BC's future coal market. It emphasised the need for long term contracts and firm prices. Allowing the coal industry to be the supplier of choice.

"What do they mean by giving the management and workforce the opportunity to bid for business?"

"Fuck knows."

"At least they're confirming their intention to protect pensions."

"Jury's still out on that lad."

The next piece was a little concerning.

"The electricity generators will seek the most cost-effective fuel. What's a CCGT?"

"Combined Cycle Gas Turbines. Chairman's always on bout it. Dash for fuckin gas."

"The comment on CCGT was mentioned as an answer to the old and inefficient coal fired power stations."

"I must say Mick you seem to have a grasp for the likely threat. Daft cunt down corridor seems to have a different view. What's that all bout?"

"What?"

"The book The Power of Positive Thinking."

"Oh, the one by Norman Vincent Peale. Not a bad read actually. Gary Player reckoned it helped him to be a success in life."

"Who the fuck's he?"

"A golfer."

"Adder doesn't play golf does he?"

"No but…" I stopped and continued to read. Sid was never going to see eye to eye with the Manager. I guessed it was after our visit to the USA.

Removing the coal fired stations would reduce gas emissions producing acid rain. They will also help to reduce the emission of greenhouse gases. Although economic the most cost-efficient power stations can produce electricity significantly cheaper than alternative fuels. In large due to the high capital cost of constructing these new stations. He confirmed collieries that were not competitive would close.

"He mentions Boyds. They're advising the Government on the technical aspects of privatisation. We met the main guy Jim when we were over there didn't we?" Sid had just started on his second fag.

"Yeah that's right. Remember the night in Christopher's when young Arfon spilt that bottle of red wind on the man himself."

"Oh, I remember it well. Manager wasn't very happy. Mentions the use of roof bolting to help reduce unit cost. To compete with imports and gas that's got to be about us. Did I mention they came over here last October. Went to have a look around T7's."

"All good stuff lad but I don't trust the Yanks…" Before he could say anymore the office door opened. It was Evan soon followed by Arfon.

"Hi lads." They both had an unlit fag hanging from the corner of their mouths. "Evan let me introduce you to Sid Cider the BACM President. Sid: Evan is my Colliery Overman."

"How do you do Evan." Sid held out his cigarette lighter.

"Good to meet you Sid and thanks." Evan responded as he inhaled on the cigarette.

"And this guy needs no introduction."

"Prince Edmund how good to see you again." Sid began to laugh.

"Fuck off." Arfon responded as he accepted the lit up lighter from Sid.

"Right gents I'll leave you to catch up I'm going for a bath. Overtime meeting is a three. See you later Sid." I continued out the office. I'd have liked to spend a little longer with Sid however from experience if I had I'd still be there the following day. Sid once he had you engaged in conversation never stopped.

"Come in Mr Gibson. Mr Gibson."

"Hi Control."

"Just taken a call from Asyn. They're on stand…"

"Why, what's up?"

"They've been struggling all morning bringing the chocks in near to the maingate. They've got a couple they can't move at the moment. Reckon he's goin to be at least an hour."

"Let him know I'm on the way. Just at the top of the manrider now. Does Mr Adder and Douglas know?"

"Can't get in touch with them at the moment. I believe they've gone over to the Coal Prep Plant with Billy Blunt and Ken John."

"Okay." *Those fuckin chocks must be at least twenty years old by now. Same ones that we were using on 42's when I first arrived.* It wasn't just the age of the chocks that were giving us problems. Fact was the coal face T8's was only 37m in length. A narrow panel of coal running through the middle of previously worked out faces in the Two Yard, T2 and T3 to the north and T5, 6 and 7 to the south. The pillars of coal either side of the maingate and return allowing bed separation above the coal face itself. Not that we'd had little choice. We needed the coal until the continuous miners were ready to operate.

Within twenty minutes I was walking down the maingate. I'd already passed two lots of the face men working on moving the stone dust barriers out. Arfon had made use of the men during the stoppage. Manning levels were becoming more of a problem as we attempted to reduce cost. The stageloader operator was on his knees cleaning out the tailend of the conveyor.

"Morning Bryn." I stifled a yawn. I wasn't feeling my usual self. Having worked the last three weekends on the trot I was feeling a little exhausted.

"Morning Mr Gibson."

I continued forward onto the coal face. I could hear the shearer taking the strain on the haulage chain. Asyn and three of the lads were perched between the chocks. I couldn't make out the individuals just the cap lamps.

"Hold it, hold it." Asyn shouted. "Fuckin hold it I said." His voice rising each time.

"Okay keep your fuckin knickers on. I heard you the first time now."

"Morning boys." I interrupted.

"Bora da Mr Gibson. Won't budge a fuckin inch!" Asyn responded. The shearer operator slackened off the chain. I could see the red light on the lock out box and climbed onto the AFC. The twenty two millimetre haulage chain crashed onto the pans.

"Have you tried more of a direct pull?"

"You name it we've tried it. Hasn't moved a gnats cock!"

"What about putting the chain around the front legs of the third chock and feed it back?" I asked.

"I'll try anything. Go on lads do as the Undermanager has suggested." Asyn replied. Two of the lads climbed out from between the chocks. They removed the bolt from between the links of the chain and walked towards chock three.

"Throw them some slack Gareth." The machine operator edged the shearer closer to the maingate end. I reached down and assisted in pulling the chain.

Having secured it both men moved back into the chock line.

"Get yourself out of harms reach Mr Gibson." One of the lads shouted.

"I'm fine. Go on take the strain."

"You watch yourself Mr Gibson."

"I will. Go on start pulling." The haulage chain straightened. Very slowly the troublesome chock began to move.

"Go on, go on she's moving."

"Come on you little bastard keep fuckin coming."

The crack and loud bang of the haulage chain breaking came without warning. Where it had been attached to a bracket on the shearer had snapped on the weld. Everything happened in slow motion. I could hear voices but not what was being said. As I was the only obstruction between the shearer and chock the chain hit my legs and then began to wrap itself around my shins. The impact sent me flying backwards. I'd been warned but had chosen to ignore it. I wasn't sure if I'd lost consciousness. It had happened so fast. I didn't remember falling. One minute I'd been standing now laid out flat.

"Mick, Mick. For fuck's sake you okay?" The shouting from Asyn brought me back to the present. I realized my helmet was missing. I climbed back to my feet and repositioned my helmet.
"Yeah I'm good." I wasn't I was in agony.
"Stretcher, stretcher someone get a stretcher."
"I don't need a fuckin stretcher."
"Pethidine?"
"No, I don't need any fuckin thing. Now I've sorted the chock out get me some coal."

I made my way back into the maingate and sat down. The alarm on the stageloader started up. We were coaling again; I was in agony. To add to my discomfort the phone on the stage loader rang.
"Mr Gibson it's for you. The Manager." That's all I needed I could hardly stand.
"Thanks Bryn. Mr Adder, Mick."
"Are you okay?"
"Yeah. Why wouldn't I be?"
"I've just heard you were involved in an incident on the face."
"Oh that. Was nothing."
"Good to hear it. Wouldn't want my favourite Undermanager getting injured."
"How kind of you. And yes, we're coaling again."
I spent the following day in the office I could hardly walk.

–

Over the coming weeks the new equipment began to arrive. We'd agreed to build the Joy Continuous Miner in a roadway supported by steelwork. This would help with the lifting and assembling of the various parts. Joy had provided three reps to help the pits fitters and electricians assembly the machine. Gethin and Ifor were on hand every day to offer support to their men. To ensure we met the agreed timescales the build took place over three shifts including the weekends.

Gregor had arranged for a series of electrical panels to be placed at various positions in the district. Once the JCM was built it was tracked into one of two blind ends for access to the room and pillar district CM1. Here the operators could practice cutting with the reps in attendance. The roof supported by roof bolts, initially installed using Wombats.

239

The Fletcher bolter build had a separate location. All agreed we'd concentrate on building one machine at a time, again over three shifts. The thinking was to get one available for the training the operators sooner rather than later.

The Joy shuttle car build had been fairly straight forward. Taking place in one of the cross cuts. The two machines were completely built within a week. From what I'd seen in the States these had the potential to be the most dangerous piece of kit. The cable providing power to the machine was wound on a spring loaded drum. Each time the machine started from a stationary position it would whip up into the air. Far from ideal if a person was crossing over it and caught them between the legs.

The final piece of kit, the Stamler we left for the time being. There was little point in building it outbye from where it would be operating. Once we had a series of roads constructed we'd build it then.

Whilst the build was taking place the drivage towards the new workings continued. The area of coal was accessed via two drivages. The intake seventy five metres in length using the JCM. By the end of July1992 it had established the five road system. The Dosco Roadheader was used in the return. A distance of one hundred metres. This included a fifty metre length at 1:4. This broke through at the end of August.

A connecting road was driven between the two. Up to this point the JCM was tracking a distance far in excess of what it was supposed to do. Until we'd established the five road system we had little choice. The design layout for the room and pillar had been agreed with the Group's Technical department. The criteria for the size of the rooms and pillars was to support the roof and economic coal extraction. This had been agreed at thirty metre square pillars with rooms extracted to a width of six metres.

During the latter part of summer, only eight months since we'd returned from the States we were ready to go. Ahead of schedule. We'd got the surveyors to produce a plan for my office. Using it to agree the pattern of work with the lads before they went underground. It hadn't taken long before they just got on with the job. There were no set rules. Productivity measured by tonnage and efficiency measured by both bolters in action. This allowed the JCM to have available three places in which to cut.

The essential job was making sure we kept the bolters supplied with the relevant materials. Boxes of fast and slow set resin. Celstraps for the roof and sides, patch plates, mesh, and bolts.

Arfon arranged with stores to get packs of supports produced. The larger FSV fetching them in and parking up in the cross cuts. Bolts and resin were stored on the bolter. The system of work relied on the JCM to extract the coal with its gib cutting from floor to roof. Left to right. The cutting mat just over three metres wide required two swipes to open the six metre wide road.

All the machines powered from cables. Shuttle cars ran with a cable reel attached to the rear allowing them to travel from the JCM to Stamler. The shuttle car would position itself at the rear of the JCM to allow loading of coal and then travel and unload at the Stamler. The bolters were just left to do what they do best and that was bolt. From experience we learnt to position the Stamler two clear cross cuts back. This allowed for separate routes for the shuttle unloading and that travelling back empty to the JCM.

The district was a pleasure to be in. The working areas in Zone B were now reduced to the coal face T8's and CM1's. Unless I had other inspections to carry out most days I'd visit the face first and then make my way along R5 to watch the lads in action. Roof and sides suitably dusted with stonedust from Rick's duster. Regular supplies of calcium sulphate crystals kept the floor solid. Entering the district was eerily silent. In the background the hum of the thirty inch ventilation ducting providing ventilation to the forward heading. We had advanced a sufficient distance now to start erecting brattice sheeting in the cross cuts to create a circuit. As I got closer to the working area the sound of the shuttle car became apparent. It produced a gentle hum hardly discernible as it travelled with its load to the Stamler. The clicking of the cable reel as the vehicle stopped and restarted. For some time now we'd ensured everyone underground wore reflective jackets more so with these vehicles trundling around at speed.

Although I never admitted it to anyone it was exhilarating watching the JCM extract the coal – crunching, chopping allowing the coal to fall to the floor. There two continually moving paddles on the base of the machine scooping up the extracted mineral onto the centrally positioned chain conveyor. Travelling along the centre of the machine passing alongside the operator and then spewing into the waiting shuttle car. Without being told the lads would reduce the depth of cut if the roof became friable and adding additional bolts to assist.

CM1 became the place where visitors and dignitaries visited including Government Ministers, the Military, overseas – France, Canada, and the States. British Coal Directors and management teams from Selby, Thoresby, Harworth, Asfordby even Ellington colliery in the North East. And of course, Coal News. Nothing better than getting our mug shots in the news.

Elsewhere in the country mines were still being closed. We were told there was little to worry about the future looked promising.

–

"Morning Terry."

"Bora da Mick."

"How long do you reckon you'll be?"

"Say another hour. Just got to complete the stitchin and put the structure in. We'd be complete by now but the fuckin FSV ran out of diesel."

"What!"

"Fuckin nightshift. Second time this week."

"I'll have a word. How far have you moved the Stamler?"

"Another sixty metres right up to the tash."

"How are the lads today?"

"One or two are a bit down. I've told them to get their sorry heads outta their arses. What will be will be."

"Very diplomatic Terry."

"Anyway, Bevin was in the canteen when we arrived first thing. Tells me he and the Area Secretary are off to a briefing tomorrow with the Group Director. Says that we're not on the hit list of thirty pits earmarked for closure. What's your view Mick? Ever been in this position before?"

"Yeah actually I have. First pit I ever worked at Cronton. Back in eighty-four just before the strike. The closure was announced back end of February from memory and production ceased the following month."

"Same month as the strike started?"

"Yeah the very same. I was a Deputy back then NACODS the union I was in attended several meetings in London at Hobart House. The appeal meeting, I believe they were called. All the main players were there Northard, Evans even Scargill but it came to nothing. Took the closure of Cortonwood before everything kicked off."

"What happened did the men come out?"

"No, would you believe they allowed us to continue working. Flying pickets arrived once. Stayed for half a day and disappeared never saw them again. We continued salvaging the place."

From the crosscut ahead a light appeared. "Terry, bolting complete ready to start coaling."

"Okay start filling the shuttle cars. Belt won't be long." He turned back towards me. "So, what do you think?"

"If I were a betting man, I'd say we'd be okay. Last week could turn out to be a production record, although not confirmed yet. The recent investment in all this new kit and how you and the lads have adapted to the new system of working is a credit."

242

"Mr Gibson, Mr Gibson." Once more we were interrupted. This time control room from the tannoy.

"Sorry Terry I'll have to make a move. Probably the Deputy Manager after me. He wants me back up the pit early today."

"Go on then what do you think?"

"All the signs are good. However, I have this naggin feelin."

"Mr Gibson, Mr Gibson."

"Sorry Terry I'll have to go. See you later."

Back on land -

"What's all the commotion?" I was sat at my desk having just returned from underground. Osian and Reece were sat either side.

"No idea." Osian walked across to the window. "There's a group of lads gathered outside in the car park. Must be the announcement it was due this week."

"I don't think so. It wasn't due till Wednesday or Thursday."

"Could be, looks like the press. There's one guy taking pictures of the headgear.

"Mick." Tony Douglas appeared. He was holding a board. "Do me a favour and get some lads together. Need to get a shot of this." He held the board up.

POINT OF AYR
CONGRATULATIONS
20,137 TONNES
RECORD OUTPUT
10th OCTOBER 1992

"Wow, excellent news it's true then?"

"Yep sure is. Only got confirmed early today. Manager thought it would be good for some PR and morale. Particularly as this is the week." I suppose it was inevitable we'd be breaking a record. What with the two coal faces, S64's and T8's and CM1's finally producing coal. I turned to Osian.

"Could you do me the honours, us three plus a mix of fitters and electricians ideally in their black."

"I certainly will."

"Hold on though Mr Douglas, shouldn't we get Mr Blackhead and his team on the shot too?" I turned to Reece. "Where are the Zone A team anyway? They're normally first up."

"Missed the manrider. I reckon another twenty minutes."

"Can't we wait? I mean 64's contributed too."

"No time. Manager's being interviewed now. Once they're done with him, they'll be on their way."

243

"Okay such a shame. Osian make sure we get a fitter and a lecky from Zone A."

I grabbed the board and we headed out to the Coal Prep Plant. The guy from the Daily Post had wanted a shot with coal in the background. A few minutes later Osian appeared. Followed by another six lads, two from Zone B and the others from Zone A. The photographer from the Daily Post wasted no time in organising us, Myself and Osian held either side of the board with a couple of lads kneeling in front.

"Now lads. Big smile, thumbs up." We all duly obliged.

"Hold it." Behind the photographer Tony Douglas was waving. He wasn't going to waste an opportunity to get in the papers. I couldn't believe it Bill Hooper the Personal Manager was following. Both in their clean bib and tucker and wearing helmets. Not that I had anything against Bill, but I don't think he'd been underground in his life. And what would Mr Blackhead say when he got up?

"Right think that's us done."

"Don't forget to pick up your commemorative mugs."

"What?"

"Yeah, the Manager ordered them Friday ready for today. So, he already knew?"

"He wanted it to be a surprise. They're in the canteen, Storm's handing them out now." With that we all headed back across to the main building. Just inside the canteen a table was piled high with cardboard boxes with several mugs standing loose. Inscribed on each in red were the words:

Record Output
20,137 Tonnes
10th October,
1992

Alongside there was a picture of a Welsh Red Dragon and a sketch of the pit's number three headgear. Very impressive.

"Come on Cariad are you goin to give me one?"

"Osian your dirty old bugger now. If I were to give you one, I'm not sure you'd last the session."

"Worth a try though darlin." I reached forward to Storm.

"There you go now Mr Gibson. Osian you see that's how a proper gentleman behaves."

"Thanks Storm." I winked at Osian as I turned and headed back to the office. The Manager was outside the main entrance as I passed. He was being interviewed by a reporter. I made a slight detour to hear what he had to say.

"Yeah a workforce of four hundred and twenty-nine. August last year was our previous best seventeen thousand seven hundred and twenty-nine tonnes. Puts our tonnes per manshift up from seven point eight to just over nine. The men have worked tremendously hard to turn out excellent performance levels in a very difficult climate. The colliery has recently invested over a million pounds on the latest high-tech equipment for a brand-new system of mining."

I had to give it to him he was good and so positive. I wished I could have some of what he was on. I needed to read the book he had given me. He continued. "The men have worked hard to install the new system and have adapted to the change very well. The pit is now starting to reap the rewards for all their efforts as our current crop of records confirms." *Not quite true Mr Adder we did have two coal faces assisting production.*

"What about the comment from British Coal Corporations Midland and Wales Group suggesting the future of the pit and all those in the Group would depend on negotiations with the electricity generators?" The reporter asked.

"The mine is producing coal at thirty pound a tonne cheaper than imported coal."

I continued back to my office.

—

The next day everyone seemed content. Several lads had picked up the early morning addition of the Daily Post. Which I had yet to see. There was a general sense of calmness about the place I was sat in my office with Osian.

"How the fuck does Bill Hooper get on the photo?" The spell was soon broken by the appearance of Kelvin Blackhead. He was holding a copy of the Daily Post.

"Sorry mate I knew it wouldn't be fair without you and your team in the photo." Osian reached out for the paper.

"Bora da Mr Blackhead. Now let me see what all the fuss is about." Beneath the heading **Miners smash records at colliery** there was a picture of me and a few others holding up the placard Tony Douglas had provided.

"Not a bad picture of me. If you don't mind me saying Mr Gibson, you look as though you've got your thumb up your nose." He passed the paper to me. I nodded in agreement not the best shot.

"He might have had his thumb up his nose but at least he got his mug shot on."

"Talking of mugs did you pick yours up?" Osian asked laughing.

"Fuck off." With that Kelvin left us. Later in the baths we were together getting changed to go underground, he was still sulking. As were his two deputy engineers, Dafydd and Owain.

"Bit of an atmosphere in here this morning cock?"

"Morning Denny. Yeah Zone A not the happiest of bunnies today." I received no reaction from Kelvin or his colleagues."

"Anyway, just to let you all know Ken John has just come out of the Manager's office. Seems the Manager and NUM officials have been called to a meeting at Staffordshire House. Tony wants us all to stay on land. Thinks there's going to be an announcement."

"Bout, what?" Dafydd asked.

"Bout pay rise ye daft fucker what do you think!"

Back in the office I was soon joined by Kelvin.

"Listen mate I never wanted them to take that photo without you there."

"Oh, don't worry about that now. I'm over it. More to the point what do you think goin to happen?"

"I'm guessing they're about to announce we're stayin."

"Do you really think so?"

"Come on we've done everything asked of us and broken the weekly output record. There's nothing more certain."

"I hope you're right. Took a call from a mate of mine last night. Reckon Trentham and Silverdale are on the list plus your last pit Parkside."

"The big hitters, I just can't see it."

"Well we're sure to find out soon enough."

Later that morning Tony Douglas called us both into his office.

"Gentlemen could you arrange for as many men into the pit canteen at the end of the dayshift. Get some of the noon lads in there too." Tony didn't look good he was as white as a sheet.

"You spoke to the Manager then?"

"Just come off the blower." We both looked at him for further explanation.

"And?"

"Sorry, Managers asked me to address you altogether." For the first time I had a bad feeling. It didn't look good. Neither of us said anymore and headed back to the office.

"The pit will cease production in March 1993", as the Deputy Manager finished the sentence the whole room fell silent. This was it then seventeen years to the day I'd joined the mining industry. For the first time in my life I was to be out of work. Michael Heseltine, the President of the Board of Trade, had announced up to thirty one out of the fifty remaining deep mines face closure. The silence in the canteen seemed endless. One or two of the lads began whispering between themselves.

"How the fuck does that work Mister? It was only last week we broke our best weekly performance two hundred and one thousand three hundred and seventy tonnes."

"Was it fuck!"

"That's what it says here in today's Daily Post." Terry the chargehand grabbed the paper from his colleague.

"Twenty thousand one hundred and thirty seven tonnes knob head!"

"Now lads let's stay calm. This has been as much a shock to me as it was to you. And yes, as you quite rightly say Dai in the light of our recent successes which culminated in the record output last week. However, Mr Adder has given a commitment to the Group Director."

"Fuckin commitment. You've got to be fuckin joking!"

"Fat lot of good fuckin TQM did then?" Someone else added.

"Without it we may have closed sooner."

"Fuck off as usual you're talking utter fuckin shite!" I turned to see a very angry chargeman from CM1 shaking his head *he's certainly got a point.* Mr Douglas ignored the comment

At the back of the room the sound of something being smashed. I turned to see several lads who'd been drinking from their recently acquired Edwardian Gift Ware mugs no longer holding them. White porcelain was littered against the back wall. In places the distinct picture of the Welsh Red Dragon lying amongst the fragments. I decided to go for a bath. Denny was already in there.

"Looks as though that's it cock! What will you do?"

"Not sure mate I'm sure something will come up. Can you do my back." Just before I left that night I took a call from Ron Groves. Which was typical of the man. He had his own problems. Bickershaw was closing too.

I arrived home earlier than usual that day. My wife greeted me as I walked through the door.

"Job hunting this weekend dear?"

The following day when I arrived copies of a Special Edition Coal News lay scattered outside the lamproom. Dayshift obviously not happy about its contents. There were numerous copies lying around on my desk too. A picture of the Chairman Neil Clarke alongside his comment *"Scant reward for effort."* Under the headline **NO MARKET FOR 31 PITS** further detail was provided

"Production at 31 of Britain's 50 operating collieries is to cease because there is no market for the coal, they mine. Twenty-seven are to close and four to be retained on a care and maintenance."

I think what really hit home as I scanned the front page were the nine bullet points at the bottom of the page:

- Markets for only 19 pits
- 31 collieries to cease production
- Four mines to go on Care and Maintenance
- 30,000 jobs to be lost
- Redundancy terms renewed
- £10,000 lump sum restored
- Compulsory redundancy
- Appeal procedure withdrawn
- Industrial action will jeopardise redundancy payment

"Bora da boss." I looked up.

"Bevin you're in nice and early this morning."

"I, thought might be wise to see the lads before they went under."

"Sorry I never got chance to see you again after the sad news."

"We're organising a campaign to save the pit now."

"Good luck with that. I'm not sure how far you'll get."

"Oh, now Mr Gibson it's not all bad news. The Area Secretary thinks we'll get the decision reversed. Reckons when he and Mr Adder met the Group Director yesterday, he seemed extremely embarrassed by the decision. It was as much of a surprise to him as anybody. Reckon we'll get a reprieve."

"Bloody hell Bevin that's positive. I reckon you're spending too much time with the Manager!"

Later that day the Manager issued a communique:

Dear Colleague,

By now you will all be aware that the Pit is to close at the end of March 1993. This was as much of a shock to me as it was to you and is particularly upsetting in the light of our recent successes which culminated in the record output last week.

However, in the five months remaining, I intend that the installation of H.81's will go ahead as planned. The Continuous Miner Project will be maintained, and we shall continue with our plans to reduce bolt density, bolt length etc. to prove beyond doubt that the system will work.

None of this is possible without your co-operation, and it is important that we produce as much coal as possible during the next few months.
This will ensure that the level of your wages is maintained, and that the Pit remains cash positive.

If we fail and the Pit loses money, then the closure will be brought forward, and this will benefit nobody.
Redundancy is now compulsory and applies to everyone who works at the Pit – Mineworkers, Supervisors and Management alike.

None of us now have a job beyond March, but up to that time all I can ask is that we conduct ourselves in the same professional manner that permitted us to achieve last week's record results.

Today I have spoken to all the Unions at the Pit and am assured of their support in trying to achieve the highest output we can.
Let us all do our best to see the Pit out in good style with safe and efficient working right up to the end.

And that was me attaining the position thirteen years later and four years into the job the dream was coming to an end. The pit was to close in March the following year, the industry in terminal decline. For the first time I began to question the authority around me. The superiors I reported to, each day and their effectiveness. Knowing all the effort I and others had put in would make no difference it was over. That's when I began to have my next dream one I had dropped into over the last year. As the pressure intensified on us to reduce cost, increase productivity with fewer and fewer men. Instruction from above became less and less logical I had begun to dream of another life. A life I knew existed but never entered.

I'd seen it at first hand many years before whilst taking the staff bus from Anderton House to North Staffordshire Polytechnic. During the time we were completing the HNC course we sometimes waited for the bus inside the Coal Board offices. Waiting in reception I'd watch the various office workers going about their daily business looking extremely important travelling from one office to another. Each carrying various amounts of paperwork. I'd assumed those with most documentation were the important ones. First time outside the pit canteen I saw female staff.

Over time it became apparent that most of them carried the same pieces of paper throughout the day. The really important guys were those sat in the offices and attending meetings, including their assistants and their assistant assistants.

–

Later that day I was sat in the office alone. My thoughts wandered to those men that I worked alongside. What would become of them. The senior officials would survive I had no doubt. Retirement beckoned. The fitters and electricians had the skill set for further employment. But what of those who had none. Other than their pit skills. What of the beltmen? The lads at two o'clock in the morning walking in alongside you to repair the broken Access 1. There were no better men to have round you at that moment. What would they do? Manual work? Less pay. They'd get their redundancy. The original ten k appetiser had been reinstated. How long would it last for though?

The current contract with PowerGen and National Power was for sixty five million tonnes, this was expected to reduce further possibly down to forty million tonnes. British Coal would be competing with heavily subsidised nuclear power which is given a guaranteed market. Planned for new gas fired power stations. Electricity was being imported from France. Plus, a small but growing contribution from what was known as renewables. Then there was oil, Orimulsion, and imported coal.

Coal stocks were a problem too. Generators had thirty three million tonnes, BC fourteen million at the pithead with production adding two hundred and fifty thousand tonnes per week. Add to all of this the depressed energy market. World coal prices as low now as they've ever been. Imported coal delivered to coastal power stations at prices BC cannot compete with. National Power and PowerGen had announced the closure of eleven coal fired plant. The new Killingholme gas-fired station had come on stream – the "dash for gas" had begun.

–

"Will you be joining us then?"
"For what?"
"There's a march through Prestatyn on Saturday in support of the pit. The NUM are attempting to raise support for its continued operation amongst the locals. All our friends are going, kids too."
"Yeah I'd heard. I'm working though."

"I thought that was next week. Anyway, you'll be back in time don't forget it's Halloween too. The kids are looking forward to dressing up and doing some trick or treating."

My wife had a point how was I going to tell her I wasn't actually working I was away with the senior team on a team building weekend in Derbyshire. Just over two weeks since they'd announced the closure of the pit and we were still going. I had raised my concern with a number of colleagues and at the Manager's daily meeting the week before. Paul Adder had however been adamant.

"Mick as I've said in my message, I want us all to work right up to the end."

"Yeah I know and understand the point you've made but don't you think this is a little insensitive?"

"It's still work." I looked at the man to see if there was any indication of humour in his comment. None. Was I surprised? No not really the man seemed to lack any moral compass. The same man that was continually telling me "there's no them and us, we're in this together."

"Listen something I've been meaning to tell you." My wife looked at me with the same expression she'd used over the years. The one when I was about to let her down.

"And?"

"I'm actually away from Friday on a management conference. The Manager's taking his senior team to Derbyshire. We're discussing the best way forward after the recent announcement."

"Why Derbyshire?"

"Manager thinks it best if we're offsite. So, we can't be distracted."

"Piss up more like!"

"Yeah I've no doubt we'll have one or two drinks."

"One or two? Who are you kiddin? You best tell the kids. I guess they won't be surprised. Dad putting work before them again.

In the way of an apology I did something I'd never done before. I'd taken the kids to school before setting off for work on the Friday. I'd picked them up on a few occasions but never taken them.

Once back at the pit I had some time to kill. There were seven of us attending. This included Tony Douglas, Billy Blunt, Ken John, Bill Hooper, and Cuthbert. We weren't setting off till two thirty that afternoon. I went underground to CM1's. Being late underground I travelled alone reflecting on the previous weeks and how everyone had reacted to the news.

For me there was still a possibility of a move to one of the pits staying open. However, that seemed unlikely. It was time for a change. The industry was coming to an end. The chairman at the time Neil Clark had been warning us all through his regular column in Coal News of the "dash for gas." I'd never really believed it would affect us. We'd done everything asked of us. We'd introduced a new method of work, reduced manpower with the inherent increase in productivity. We'd even broken the pit's weekly output record at the beginning of the month.

I had been contemplating becoming a milkman. To get away from the daily grind of management shite. Working for myself and getting a franchise with Dale Farm. I was sure my redundancy would give me the chance to buy in. Or like one of my uncle's join the police he'd done quite well on it. Retiring at an early age on a good pension. I may even have to leave Wales something I didn't want to do.

Before I knew it, I was at Strata Top and finally CM1's heading along R5 only excavated in June. The place looked immaculate. The roof and sides looked solid. Shining my cap lamp on the tell tales as I passed them. No discernible movement exhibited by any. Arriving at XC2 I turned left heading towards R3 the main coaling route. As expected, the conveyor was stacked high with the black stuff. Continuing forward it wasn't long before I could see activity ahead. One of the shuttle cars was offloading its load onto the Stamler.

"Hi Mick, didn't expect to see you today. Thought you and Adder were off on a jolly?" The dayshift chargehand had appeared behind me. I'd been so engrossed in the activity ahead I hadn't seen him approach.

"Thought I'd pop in and see how things we're going before I left."

"Yeah, all good. The lads are crackin on with it. Did we get any feedback from the Group Director's visit earlier this week?"

"He was as always impressed with the set up. To see how we were reacting to the recent news. I think he was taken aback with the fact you and the lads were just gettin on with it."

"No choice have we really? Adder already said we'd close earlier if we didn't perform."

"I that's true. Tell me though how are the men feeling?"

"Very worried. It's the not knowing what we'll do next. If there's anything out there for us. The contract lads from South Wales have obviously been through this already. It's a bit scary to hear how whole communities have been destroyed. One of the lads now they're workin away from home are tellin us how the kids have been alienated from their Tads. Because they're not around during the week tryin to earn a crust livin away. Kids think they can do what they want. Mam's tellin them wait till you Tad's back he'll sort you. When he gets back all he spends his time doin is tellin em off."

"Hello Mr Gibson, come in Mr Gibson." The tannoy burst into life.
"Hi Control."
"Mr Gibson could you give the Manager a ring."
"Will do."
"He must be missing you already Mick?"
"I don't think so. Anyway, Terry good talking with you. I'll probably see you next week. What shift you on?"
"Afters but I'll be comin in a couple of hours earlier. We're having a teach in on the new shorter bolts and increased cutting depth."
"Oh yeah, I'll be at that too. See you then."

I headed back out this time along R4. Once more I shone my cap lamp on the surrounding roadway. Rick's duster had been a godsend. Everywhere coated in a thin layer of stonedust. The roof celstraps with bolts protruding holding the six-foot rectangular mesh securely against the roof. Along the sides of the road there was no mesh. Contorted celstraps holding securely the shape of the coal excavated. Little if any spalling apparent. The laminated signs indicating the position of tell tales clearly showing. This time the thirty inch ventilation bagging hanging adjacent to a number of cable hangers with the black cables powering the JCM, roof bolters and Stamler. I spotted a phone in the next cross. Walking across I stood on a smaller cable lying on the ground. One of two powering the shuttle cars. I stumbled slightly as I entered the next roadway. A layer of dust rose from the floor, unusual in the newer roadways since we'd started a programme of floor consolidation using calcium chloride crystals. I made a note to speak with the Dust Suppression Officer.
"Hello, Mr Adder. I've been asked to give you a call."
"Mick, where the hell are you? We've decided to leave a little earlier. Everybody else is ready."
"I'm on my way. See you shortly." I replaced the phone. I smiled and there's me holding up the senior team.

The teambuilding weekend was being held at a place called Callow Park Country Retreat in Wirksworth, Derbyshire. It was sited near to the shore of Carsington Water. I had assumed that being as close as we were to the lake, we may have had the opportunity to try our hand at sailing. This was not to be.
On arrival the Manager introduced us to the team organising the events. We were told that to get the most out of the next three days we shouldn't take things too seriously and should enjoy the occasion. We had five months left at the pit and should make the most of the hospitality provided.

On the whole it had been an enjoyable few days. We'd experienced more abseiling. This time off the side of a bridge passing over the river Derwent. The height we dropped from not as high as that I'd done at Hope from a viaduct. Clay pigeon shooting something I'd never done and mountain biking. This event hadn't been solo. Billy Blunt and I had ridden a tandem together. How we never managed to gain a serious injury was pure luck. Particularly after a steep downward ride when we'd been travelling at fair old speed. I was in the front and applied the brakes. Unfortunately, only the front set were working. It was purely by chance Billy never ended up over the handlebars.

The orienteering went without incident even though we managed to get lost a number of times. Canoeing was also another activity I'd never taken part in before. I'd been partnered with Bill Hooper. We were using Canadian canoes not the most stable at the best of times. Try as we might the canoe never stayed upright for more than a couple of minutes. The highlight of the exercise, however had to be the river crossing. The majority of us positioned ourselves on one side of the river Derwent equipped with a bow and arrow and two separate long lengths of rope. The plan was to attached the thinner length of rope to the arrow and shoot it across to the other bank. Tony Douglas had volunteered to remain on the opposite side and accept the delivery. I claimed although not true to have some experience of archery.

Try as I might I was unable to hit Tony. I don't think anyone noticed my intention although the Manager eyed me suspiciously and was heard to comment. "I'm glad I'm not on the other side opposite Mick." I think he had a very good point. Finally, having achieved the delivery the thicker rope Tony hauled across and secured it to a large willow tree close to the bank. We did likewise on our side. We all crossed without incident with the Manager being last to go. Try as we might swinging on the rope, we couldn't get him to fall in. It was only when I spotted a number of large stones the fun really started. By the time he'd reached us he was wetter than if he'd fallen in. All credit to him though he took it in the spirit it was meant.

Our last night we were all in high spirits and rather than go out to the local as we'd done the night before we decided to stay put. The fact there was to be a Halloween disco had in no way affected our decision.
Straight after the meal I went to call my wife to see how the march to save the pit had gone. She seemed pleased and guessed there were nearly eight hundred people attending. The colliery band had led the procession. Even the shopkeepers had shut up shop and came out to applaud those marching. The kids had enjoyed it too. The Point of Ayr Colliery band lead the procession

followed by the campaign to Save Point of Ayr Colliery. As Mrs Gibson had said it had been a real family affair. Mums, Dads, and Grand-parents. All wearing stickers proclaiming Coal Not Dole. Children too, some in pushchairs all carrying placards which read "Please don't sack our dads." Some even brought their dogs. Others included local fireman and postman it had brought Prestatyn High Street to a standstill.

The protest received huge coverage from the media and was attended by the local Mayor, Labour MP David Hanson, Shadow Welsh Secretary Ann Clwyd and Plaid Cymru's Elfyn Llwyd. Notable by their absence but of no surprise was Michael Heseltine, David Hunt, Secretary of State for Wales, and the local MP Rod Richards.

"Mick, phone quick before the kids wake." I never seemed to hear the phone it was always my wife. I jumped out of bed and headed towards the stairs. Glancing at the clock as I did so. *For fucks sake two thirty.*

"Hello."

"Mick sorry to get you out of bed. Just taken a call from Terry in CM1's they've got a break running along in the roof running parallel with the coal pillar. Terry's asked us to call you and patch you through." Terry the chargehand was running the CM1 operation on nights.

"Guttering! Where's Delwyn?"

"On his way in from Pit Bottom."

"Okay let's speak with Terry." I waited a couple of seconds before I heard a click. I could hear the muffled sound of a shuttle car underground. "Terry you there?"

"Yeah, hi Mick sorry to call you at this hour but I think we've got a problem." I remained silent. "One of the lads noticed some fine dust falling from the roof as he was offloading. On further examination he spotted a fissure open up between the side of the Stamler and coal pillar. He notified me immediately. By the time I got here. The fissure had spread, it's now about four yards long and still moving." His comments pushed my tiredness to one side. I was now fully awake. If the break spread too far the strata between the two pillars would cantilever bringing the roof down. Something similar had happened at one of the Nottinghamshire pits some months earlier. Three men had been killed.

"Terry you need to support it and quick."

"Yeah on it now. I've got the shuttle car fetching chockwood in. We'll build as many stacks as we can alongside the pillar without affecting the access for the cars."

"What about some additional bolts?"

"Yeah got that covered too. I've sent Billy out with the FSV to pick a Wombat up."

"Good man. I'm on my way."

An hour later I was on site with Terry. Two stacks built and a third being constructed. Another team were peppering the area with bolts.

"Excellent job Terry."

"Yeah the lads have done well. Should be coaling again in about an hour I reckon."

"I wouldn't worry about coaling again. Make sure you complete the job."

"What about our fuckin bonus now." He responded laughing. "Don't worry Mick we'll sort before we start up again."

I didn't hang around much longer Terry had everything under control.

I arrived back at work the next day later than normal. I headed straight to the Manager's office. Mr Douglas was already underground.

"Sorry to bother you Mr Adder." The Manager was sat at his desk. He was reading the Financial Times.

"Morning Mick come in. See we've been mentioned in the paper."

"Oh right. Thought I'd give you a quick update on last night."

"Seems the Government are very close to making a decision."

"First time I've seen guttering as bad as that."

"I've no doubt in my mind we'll get through this review. The pit has become a shining example of what can be done. Fancy a brew?"

"No, I'm fine."

"What were you after anyway?"

"Thought I'd give you an update on last night." I repeated.

"Oh that. Mr Douglas went straight in this morning. Tells me it's all sorted now." He turned the page. "I wonder how my British Gas shares are doing?"

"Right I'll be off." I left the office without him uttering another word.

–

To reduce costs further we'd already reduced the length of the roof bolts from two point four to one point eight metres. The next stage was to reduce still further. This time down to one point six. This would reduce the material cost by up to a third. Under the supervision of Noah, a number of blind ends were created off the main coal run and trials established. Monitoring stations using a device called a Sonic Probe Readout would allow us to understand how successful this would be.

We took the opportunity to trial roof bolts without the use of Celstraps. These being replaced by patch plates. Using patch plates as against Celstraps was certainly another cost saving but encountered an ancillary problem. Maintaining the pattern of bolting. Something the regular visits we received from the Group Technical Department was emphasised on more than one occasion.

The exercise in the remote part of the workings allowed experimenting with the depth of cut. Not that we had any plans. We'd already extended from three to six metres. What we wanted to observe was the length of time unsupported roof would stand. These trials were never signed off from Group Technical Department. It was something we wanted to understand better. Safety was paramount. Any such areas were fenced off and the appropriate noticed displayed to avoid any persons accidently walking in. We already understood the dangers of "guttering." What I hadn't appreciated at the time was the potential for complacency. With all the trials taking place and the relative success achieved it could be perceived that anything was possible.

-

To our surprise and delight the Manager had arranged for Big Ron and Billy to visit us. The guys we'd first met at Marissa Mine It was an ideal opportunity to see what the experts thought of our performance. We'd only been operated the room and pillar system for a matter of months. It was pleasing to hear from Ron how impressed he was. Particularly as only two months previously it had been announced we were closing. As a reward he'd brought over a box of Red Man which we evenly distributed between the teams.

As a thankyou myself and Mrs Gibson took our guests to Liverpool to see the Albert Dock. Ron who was interested in ancestry told us his relatives had sailed from Liverpool towards the end of the nineteenth century. The highlight however was the tour of the Beatles museum. Ron was a big fan. Afterwards we met with the Manager for dinner before they flew back home the following day.

-

"Don't be such a ponce now. There must only be a metre and a half before we prove that fault. Keep going."
"For fucks sake Arfon we've extended the cut to six metres not eight."
"Hold it look the roof!"

Terry the chargehand had on this occasion decided to drive the shuttle car. The first he knew there was a problem was the sound of a loud crack above his head. Before he had chance to look up. A weight hit the back of his helmet forcing his head forward. Darkness enveloped the cab. For what seemed an eternity he sat there semi-conscious. It was the tannoy alongside the car that brought him back to the present.

"Arfon, control here mate. We're getting a build-up of methane along the return road. A few outbye monitors are hitting one and a quarter per cent and rising. Is there a problem down there?" Terry reaching behind him shoved a stone slab back from his body. He grabbed the side of his cap lamp and switched it back on. It made little difference a fine airborne dust hung in the air obscuring the light. Scrambling down to the side of the car he located the tannoy. His head hurt like hell.

"Control it's me Terry. There's been a fall in CM1."

"Terry, sut ydych chi? Anybody hurt?"

"Yeah I'll be okay but Arfon and Paul are up by the machine. Not sure how they are."

"Where exactly? Can you get out?"

"Yeah, I'm goin to check on the others. R1, XC9."

"Okay mate. I'm going to get help to you now."

Lewis next put a call through to Delwyn. His instruction had been short and precise. "Put the Emergency Procedures into action." He would make his way there with all due haste. Procedure dictated the Mines Rescue Brigade be called first. The local volunteers and then the permanent brigade. However, as he did on most occasions, he called the Undermanager.

"Mick, we've got an emergency at the pit. Roof fall in CM1's at least three men trapped." Fortunately for me I'd finally invested in a new phone. The handset was alongside the bed. "I'm on the way. Give Evan a call too, I'll see him there. Make sure the cage and loco are waiting. Who's involved?"

"Arfon, Terry and Paul."

"Where abouts?"

"R1, XC9 and there's a build-up of gas on the return side.

"Thanks."

My wife hadn't moved. Best I leave it that way. Within five minutes I was driving to the pit.

Driving through Rhuddlan my mind was racing. *Just over a week to Christmas, what a time for this to happen but whenever would it be a good time?* I knew once the rescue lads landed there'd be restrictions on those going down. This would include me. However, I'd be there before then. I need to get in and see for myself the situation. Evan could take the rescue lads through the plans. Arfon shouldn't have been on the nightshift. He was covering for one of the Deputies on leave. We didn't have any spare capacity within the Deputy numbers. More had taken redundancy since the announcement.

Before I knew it, I was parking the car up outside my office. Within twenty minutes I was walking along the main drag into the district. I travelled to the incident site via the maingate. Control having briefed me the methane content had now risen to over two per cent. Approaching the fall area, the tannoy came to life.

"Hello control, hello control." It was Terry. I ran across to the nearest tannoy.

"Terry, Undermanager here what's the latest."

"Hi Mick. I've managed to reach the lads. Arfon seems okay he was semi-conscious when I reached him. He can't move though there's a huge fuckin boulder on his leg. Paul's still out though. Bad news his right hand has been severed. Arfon had a first aid tin on him so I've managed to stem the flow of blood. Could do with some morphine or pethidine whatever we're using these days. Before he regains consciousness. Oh, and Arfon's methanometer is reading off the scale. It's getting pretty fuckin hot in here. We need some air and fast."

"Stay by the tannoy I'll give you a shout as soon as I'm on site."

"Mick, it's me Delwyn. I'm at the entrance to the fall. I've got an idea. If we turn the compressed air off and Terry breaks the six-inch range where the lads are, I can attach the air bagging to it."

"Did you get that Terry?"

"Yeah Del give me a shout as soon as its off." I continued forward. Within five minutes I could hear Delwyn and the lads ahead.

"Terry, compressed air is off." Delwyn and the team began dragging a 12" ribbed ducting to the main thirty-inch ventilation bagging. He saw me approaching.

"Hi Mick, this will have to do." Again, the tannoy burst into life.

"Mr Gibson, Mr Gibson it's me Evan."

"Hi Evan, rescue lads there yet?"

"Just arrived they've put the pit on lockdown. They're asking can we send all the men not involved out of the pit."

"Yep already sorted. I take it you've got enough info to brief them on location and casualties?"

"Yeah I was listening in."

"Let them know there's a loco waiting for them."

"Will do."

"Evan, how we fixed outbye with the gas? Booster's okay."

"Yeah at the mo all good. Listen Manager's here wants a word."

"Hello Mr Adder?"

"Mick you near a phone?"

"Not at the mo."

"Give me a shout when you do. Is there anything you need?" I looked towards Delwyn.

"No not at the moment we just need to get the lads out."

"Hi Del we've got air flowing in gas has dropped." Terry had interrupted our conversation.

"Nice one. How's the other two?"

"They're both fully conscious. Paul's in fuckin agony though. He's desperate for morphine."

I turned back towards Delwyn. "Have you got a key to the Morphine Safe?"

"Yeah why what you thinkin?"

"I noticed on the way in a flat with a number of methane drill rods. What if we could extend them and shove them down the six-inch range with the morphine attached?"

"Worth a try." He turned to Billy the FSV driver. "Bill take the machine with the haulage lads and load me as many drill rods as you can."

"Will do Del."

"Plus, a couple of stretchers from the meeting station." He turned back towards me. "I'll go and fetch the morphine." Delwyn followed the FSV out.

It was the first time I was able to take in the enormity of the situation. I walked back to the entrance of XC9. The fall from where I imagined the JMC to be had extended itself to where I now stood. The cavity above what had been the roof must have been ten to fifteen feet tall. Bits of stone were still falling. Various lengths of roofbolt lay scattered around the fall area. Some still attached to the distorted celstraps. Solidified length of resin still clinging to the bolts. A number of surplus tell tales barely visible under the stone. We may have had the three lads safe for now but how would we get them out? The last thing we wanted was anymore casualties. I spotted a phone on the far side of the road and walked across.

"Mr Adder."

"What the fuck has Arfon been up to? You know this could jeopardise our future trials." The Manager was referring to the reduced length of bolts and density.

"To be honest with you it's the last thing on my mind. We'll be closed in three months anyway. What fuckin difference does it make?" He sensed I wasn't in the best of moods and changed his tact.

"We'll leave that for now. We need to get them out. Arfon will have some explaining to do."

"He certainly will."

"Hold on a mo Evan wants a word."

"Hi mate."

"Do you remember those three-foot arches Bleddyn showed you down by the old stables?

"Yeah quite a few sets if I remember with two-foot struts."

"That's them. Would they be any use to build a false tunnel alongside the road?"

"And fetch the lads out through that?"

"Yeah, the only other alternative is to fetch the other JCM out of CM2's and that's goin to take some time before we can drive a relief road."

"Evan, I like it. Can you arrange it?"

"Yeah already on it. I redirected some of the lads on their way out. Should have them in about an hour. Thirty metres I reckon."

By the time I got back to the fall area Delwyn was well on his way to delivering the morphine. As each rod was attached to its neighbour one of the lads pushed the rods forward.

"The eagle has landed," It was Terry again. In the background I could hear the squeals of pain. I assumed it to be Paul. Terry managed to drag the tannoy up to the JCM after the electricians extended the green line. Two minutes later he was back on. "Sorted." He was referring to the morphine injection which I'd guessed as the squealing had stopped. "Managed to free Arfon's leg too."

"Hello Mr Gibson."

"Hi Arfon, how are you now?"

"Certainly, better than Paul, I feel so bad over the situation."

"Enough of that for now, we'll deal with that later. Job now is to get you lads out and you'll be pleased to know we have a plan. Just sit tight."

I heard a number of men approaching and turned to see some of the pit's part time rescue lads. Reece was leading the group. Four in total.

"Hi Mr Gibson, all under control I see."

"Yep we certainly are Reece. This may be a waste of your lads time."

"Never a waste always good for the practice. I think you'll find the permanent lads feel the same." He turned to indicate the permanent brigade had arrived. After the introductions, the Brigade Commander agreed too. He would use his men to assist in building the false tunnel. Unlikely they would need to use their breathing apparatus each man removed it and stacked to one side.

Twenty minutes later we started. A further FSV had arrived carrying tins and two-foot mesh. We completed the first ten metres without too much trouble. Where they could the men left the larger pieces of stone in situ, the smaller pieces man handled through. A jigger pick was passed to the front for those pieces too big to move. Reece who'd been leading from the front moved back out into the main tunnel. He was wet through with perspiration.

"Getting a little warm in there." I passed him a water bottle.

"We thought it would. Delwyn's managed to source a small auxiliary fan with about thirty metres of ribbed ducting. Just setting it up now."

"We're through." A shout came from the tunnel.

"Looks as though it won't be needed now."

My involvement for the last hour had been little more than an observer. The professionals had taken over. I had nothing but admiration for the way in which they worked. Tirelessly without stopping in such a confined space. Each of the stretchers was passed down the line. Re-emerging with a body on each. The medic from the group place an oxygen mask on Paul. Whilst checking his pulse. He was unconscious.

"He's good to go." He then directed his attention to Arfon who was now sat up. "Him too."

"I'm fine I can walk."

"You'll be doin no walking mister stay as you are." Terry was last out carrying a bag.

"Anyone need a hand?" The laughter was muted.

"I'll take it off you." The medic had retrieved a plastic container from amongst their gear. Once opened a couple of packs of frozen peas could be seen. He took the bag off Terry and placed it in.

"Do you think you can save it?"

"Probably not but it's worth a try."

And that was that. Paul returned to work four months later with his artificial hand. Now deployed to work in the lamproom. Arfon however, resigned the following week. We never saw him again.

-

8. 1993 The Reprieve

I'd just returned home from work. A number of the management team had been exploring the idea of taking the wives underground. Our way of saying thanks in a way for all the shite they'd put up with over the years. Long shifts, continually falling asleep when arriving home, phone calls at all hours of the day, residential courses, cancelled holidays the list was endless.

"Who'll look after the kids?"

"I've told you already. I've arranged with your Mum and Uncle John to stay the weekend. We'll only be there a few hours. Come on it's a marvellous opportunity to see what I do."

"Where will we get changed? I'm certainly not getting showered with the other wives."

"You don't have to. You can do that when you get back home."

"I appreciate the opportunity but let me think about it."

"Don't think about it for too long. We may not stay open."

"I thought you said it was looking hopeful."

"I said hopeful not definite."

"Well you just make sure you keep applying for other jobs. I don't know what we'd do if you lost your job. You're not getting any younger."

"Thanks."

The following Sunday we arrived at the pit. My wife Annie had made use of some old jeans, T shirt and jumper. The relevant size safety boots, helmet and gloves were provided by the Training Officer. There were a total of six ladies, me and Dafydd had agreed to accompany them. Once suited and booted Dai the lampman took them through the standard safety talk. This included use of the self-rescuer. Next stop the lamproom. It was at that point I realized we hadn't arranged for a searcher.

"Dafydd who's goin to search the girls?"

"Good point Mick, hadn't thought of that one." Dai overheard our conversation.

"I'll do it. It would be my pleasure." Dai hadn't stopped smiling since we'd arrived in the lamproom.

"I bet it would." Dafydd responded. "I think Storm's in work. She's doin a stock check now I think. I'll give her a call."

Storm agreed.

"Thanks Storm."

"Croeso Mr Gibson. You know I'll do anything for you." Fortunately, my wife was out of earshot. Having picked up our tallies we made our way to the shaft top. It was always interesting for me when taking visitors underground. Particularly for those first timers. Today was no exception. The excitement and anticipation was quite evident.

The cage was waiting as we arrived at the shaft side. Gate lifted and in position the Banksman stood by.

"Bora da ladies. Silver tally if you don't mind. Keep the brass on you until you return to the surface."

Dafydd entered the cage first. I stood back and watched as each of them moved forward. Stepping gingerly over the gap as they entered the cage. The look of excitement had been replaced by concern as each looked around at the holes and gaps in the cage construction. Arriving at Pit Bottom we made our made towards the manrider. The loco attached was puffing out clouds of diesel. The ladies were looking around exclaiming how tall the tunnel was expecting it to be a lot smaller. The ride in went without incident.

Arriving at the Durbog manrider we agreed I should lead. The belt was standing. I walked on ahead followed by each of the wives. I positioned them kneeling down with at least three yards between each. Once in position Dafydd contacted the Control Room.

"Hi Control can you start the Durbog manrider." Without waiting for a response, he climbed on to the belt. We waited for the pre-start alarm as the belt started up. Nothing happened. "Who's in Control this morning?"

"Elis I believe." I responded as Dafydd climbed back off the conveyor.

"Probably reading Hare and Hounds."

"Why the sudden interest?"

"Him and his missus have just bought a horse. He's getting as bad as Idris and his Gamekeeper's Weekly. Hello Control, hello Elis can you start the Durbog manrider." Dafydd waited alongside the tannoy this time. He needn't have bothered as the pre-alarm kicked in.

We arrived at the top. As with anyone's first visit the Durbog manrider provided plenty of excitement. The women proved to be no exception laughing as they alighted. We continued into the district passing the GMT where Dai Fingers had been inserting a new hydrant.

"Bora da ladies. Enjoy your visit now." One or two of the wives must have noticed his hands. If they hadn't his next move ensured they did. He placed the stub of a finger into the pool of water surrounding his feet. Placing it in his mouth. "Salt. I guess you didn't know you were under the sea now did you?"

"Thanks Dai I'm sure the ladies will appreciate your comment." I continued walking wanting to avoid any mention of his missing fingers. We'd be there all day."

"Once you get to XC15 you're not very far from the lighthouse at Talacre now. Found a crab once I did now."

"Behave Dai." Dafydd responded.

We continued forward conversations amongst the group referencing Dai's comments. "I didn't know they worked under the sea." I heard Lucy Blunt ask my wife Annie.

"Yes, I did. Mick mentioned it to me once. I used to take the kids and the dog there whenever he was working a weekend. Which was most weeks. It was the closest we could get to him."

As we made our way into CM1'district my wife exclaimed. "I can't believe how white the place is."

"Stone dust. We spray it on a regular basis. Especially when we have important visitors."

"What's it for? Surely not just to keep the place white."

"No, it's used for its incombustible properties. If there's a methane gas explosion tests have proved it mixes with the coal dust and reduces the effects of the explosion."

"Nice one Dafydd I'm sure the girls needed to know that."

Once we got to the working area the lads had just completed a move up. We'd arranged with them to cut out one of the rooms so the ladies could see the operation in action. It went without incident. It wasn't until we'd arrived back on the surface that one of them shouted.

"Wait till you see your face. It's black."

"You too." My wife turned to me. I nodded. I'd never really given it a thought but for someone on their first underground visit it must have been a surprise.

It had been well worth the effort. My wife was full of adulation. She had been so impressed with what we did and the conditions we worked in. I became her hero and could do no wrong. It lasted a week.

"A fuckin diesel operated bus! It's more like a fuckin museum piece. Where the hell has it come from." I was stood in one of the crosscuts in CM1. Gethin was observing the first of three loads of new equipment being delivered. The Manager had never gotten over how he'd been driven around underground when we'd visited the USA. He was continually going on about it. The vehicles we'd seen in the States had been battery operated. As we had no charging station in place underground there was little if any chance of this happening. However, when the opportunity for a second-hand diesel vehicle became available the Manager jumped at the opportunity.

"I believe it's come from Thoresby. Before that, although not confirmed, Wistow. Before that Ellington and before that Bilston Glen."

"I rest my case."

"Gethin mate I don't disagree what you're saying but the Manager is adamant. If you just get it built we both know it'll never be used but it will keep the man happy." As we were discussing the subject E3 arrived.

"For fucks sake Billy go easy." I shouted towards the FSV driver as he made no attempt to handball the second load off the flat bed. By providing short jerky movements the load slid off.

"Sorry Mr Gibson I thought it was scrap."

"I me too Billy lad." Gethin shouted back laughing. "Did you see any narrow pipework at GMT?"

"Yeah but it looks damaged. Attached to what looks like some kind of filter." I turned towards Gethin. He was shaking his head.

"It'll cost you know."

"Whatever it takes."

"I can't guarantee it'll do the job though." Now that comment from Gethin was a worry. If he couldn't get it to work no one could. "I'll speak to Denny when I get up."

"Thanks mate."

And that was it no more was said on the matter until the following month.

"Go on then Gethin tell him." Denny offered. I was sat with my team in the office first thing. I was just about to go down and see the Deputy Manager.

"What would that be then gents?"

"Well Mick I've got some good news and some bad news. Which do you wants first."

"I'm feeling positive. Go with the good first."

"I've got your diesel bus built."

"And it doesn't work?"

"Oh, it works alright."

"What's the bad news then?"

"For about five yards and then it stops. Needs to be primed it does now. Every time it stops."

"Well it's good enough for me."

"Fuckin ell cock. What if Manager wants a ride on it?"

"Is that likely to happen? Think he's got rid of his pit gear."

Some weeks later, however. "Dewi sorry mate I'll have to go need a shit I'll catch you up in the lamproom." Dewi was currently covering for Evan who was off sick. Osian reckoned he had a problem with his liver.

"Not a problem I'll have a fag first and see you there. Where you off to today?"

"The face."

It was quite unusual for me to take a shit before going underground it was something I used to save for later in the day. Must have been something I ate the night before, come to think of it our daughter had made a cake at school. I left the office and headed to the toilets situated off the corridor just as you entered the executive area.

The toilets consisted of a single urinal, two cubicles and a wash basin. Above which was sited a soap dispenser and paper towel container. Entering the first cubicle I was about to drop my trousers my stomach had already begun to rumble.

"For fucks sake," I exclaimed. Fortunately, I'd spotted the loo role holder. I quickly moved to the adjacent cubicle. *Thank fuck for that.* In place a full role of tissue. I sat to contemplate the day ahead.

I hadn't been sat for more than a minute when I heard the door to the toilets swing open with a bang. *Someone's in a rush!* They entered the cubicle next to me. I could clearly hear the guy's belt being undone and his zipper unfastening. The guy sat down, and I waited for what was coming then a long drawn out fart.

"I don't believe it fuckin hell." Gregor's voice was clearly heard I waited. Then a tapping on the adjoining wall, "Hey mate do us a favour can you pass me some paper." I didn't move nor make a sound. "Hey I know you're in there." I ignored him again. On finishing I removed a single piece of toilet tissue and passed it under the dividing wall.

"Gibson you cunt." Containing my laughter, I jumped up washed my hands and left through the adjoin door to the Undermanager's baths. In the background Gregor continued to hurl obscenities at me.

"You look happy." Kelvin greeted me as I pitched up at the adjacent locker. "What's up with Gregor? I smiled as I removed my tie placing it in the locker. "Wait till you get around to the other side. All the lockers have got Lynx shower gel plus brand new towels. Must be another visit?" Before I could answer the door to our changing room opened.

"Mick Manager wants to see you" Billy Blunt entered the Undermanager's baths.

"What the fucks up now we're just about to go underground?" Ignoring my response, he turned his head towards the toilets.

"What's up with Gregor?"

"Haven't a clue."

"Anyway he wants to speak with you immediately."

"Mick don't worry I'll hold the cage." Kelvin added.

"Thanks mate I'll be as quick as I can."

I knocked on the Manager's door and walked in. At the same time, he was walking out the bathroom comb still in hand.

"Mr. Adder you asked to see me?"

"Yes, Mick I certainly did and apologies on the short notice, but we have a high profile visit today."

"Another?" Ever since we'd started room and pillar mining there wasn't a day went by without someone coming to see the operation.

"It's the Group Director…"

"He was only here last week."

"If you'd let me finish." The Manager paused for effect. "He's got some high profile visitors from the military. They'd planned to meet up at Staffordshire House and head off to the Trentham Complex, but it seems one of the coal faces has a heating, so he needs an alternative venue. And as you're the new shining star he suggested here."

I'd been called some names in my career but never a shining star. I smiled.

"All three groups will be represented, Army, Navy, Air Force and fairly high ranking too." He reached down to a fax on his desk. "Group Captain, his name Alan Croft, a Squadron Leader, Lionel Jet, an Admiral Horatio something or other, Colonel Bartholomew and a Major Tom, both these two where at the Falklands plus the Director himself."

"That explains the Lynx and towels."

"Yeah I got Bill Hooper to pick some up on his way in."

"What time you expecting to come down?"

"I'm guessing about eleven, eleven thirty. By the time they travel across, give them a drink; I'll do a short presentation and then off to change. Should be with you at lunch time ish?"

"Don't be too late wouldn't want to be in there at shift changeover."

"Get the lads to stop over then. I'm sure a spot of overtime would be welcome."

"I'm not so sure they will but I'll try." The recent announcement and cut back on costs including overtime hadn't gone down well with the men and who could blame them. "Anyway, I need to get moving or I'll miss my ride, see you later."

"One other thing don't forget the diesel bus, have it waiting at the bottom of CM1."

"What? Oh, right yeah will do." *Fuck that's all we need.* I made my way back to the baths.

Finally changed I made my way out to the lamproom. I stopped.
I thought Kelvin had mentioned something about Lynx shower gel and towels? I looked around to check. I could only see the new towels. I never gave it another thought and headed out.

"Change of plan Dewi. Need to check on CM1 Manager's coming in with the Military. Who's the Dep?"

"Caerwyn."

"You're fuckin kiddin me?"

"Oes is that a problem Mr Gibson now."

"One fuckin big problem. He doesn't like going where's there's no steel. To be fair though Dewi you wouldn't have known that. The lads reckon he suffers with IDLR. Come on lets go."

"IDLR?"

"It's a piss take. I Don't Like Roofbolts, IDLR." I don't think my explanation registered with Dewi.

"I'm ever so sorry now Roger Tree is off today."

"When we get to the Two Way you need to give him a call. Let him know we've got some important visitors."

Kelvin true to his word had held the cage. I walked in followed by Dewi. Gate closed we began our descent. "You alright cock. You look a bit preoccupied."

"Fine thanks Denny. Just been told we've got a visit. Could do with Gethin being around."

"What for cock?"

"The diesel bus Manager will be wanting a ride in it."

"No chance cock. It's fucked. Smoking like the Crem at St Asaph. You'd be better giving them a piggyback cock."

"For fucks sake Denny can you just get him anyway."

"Now there's no need to be like that. Keep yon knickers on. I think he's up there anyway. Gone in early with Ifor one of shuttle cars broken down." I began to realize the day wasn't going to pan out as I'd like. However, I'd have to deal with each problem as it arose.

Once at the Two Way Denny put a call through to Gethin. He arranged we meet in R1 between XC2 and XC3. The Diesel manrider had been parked up there since its assembly. Dewi was having trouble contacting Caerwyn.

"Mr Gibson I can't get hold of Dewi I'll go on ahead. Control will continue calling him on the tannoy now."

"Thanks, Dewi. See you in there later."

"Want me come with you cock?"

"Up to you Denny. What did he say about the shuttle car?"

"Electrical problem. It's in R5."

"Does Gregor know?"

"Not sure cock. He's in a meeting with Billy and Dafydd."

"Fuckin electricians. They spend more time on the surface than the Manager. Come on let's go see Gethin."

I could smell the machine before I heard it. As we turned into R1 we saw it. It looked almost new. The lads had given it a good lick of paint. Gethin looked up as we approached.

"Fucked Mick. It'll run for about five yards. Starts smoking then stops. I reckon the bore of the pipes supplying the fuel is too narrow. Not getting it enough fuel causes it to overheat. Before you ask we've been on to the manufacturer they don't want to know. Ain't that right Denny?"

"Sure, is cock. Well Mick do you have a plan?" I was thinking.

"What's its maximum speed?"

"Supposed to be 15 mph. Best we've had is 10."

"What if we keep it to a steady 5?"

"Fuckin hell cock. It'll take you a month of Sundays to get in."

"I'm not planning it'll take us all the way just give 'em a chance to experience the ride. I'll tell them we've received a bad batch of diesel causing the problem."

"Why not tell them the truth."

"Don't you think I've tried…" I turned as I heard someone approaching. It was Dewi he didn't look happy.

"Mr Gibson I've found Caerwyn he's in a right state now. Sweating like a pig he is now. Up by the Stamler he won't move now…" Dewi stopped to catch his breath as the tannoy burst into life.

"Hello Mr Gibson, hello Mr Gibson."

"Dewi can't we replace him with someone else?"

"Fraid not now. I've got three officials off at the moment. There's a bug goin around. Managed to get hold of Reece though he's coming in early."

"Hello Mr Gibson. Come in Mr Gibson." The Control Room operator shouted again. I turned and headed towards the tannoy.

"Hi Lewis Mr Gibson here."

"Just to let you know your visitors are on their way in." I turned to Dewi.

"Manager said lunch time." Dewi shrugged his shoulders. Lewis as by way of offering an explanation continued.

"They arrived early they did now."

"Thanks Lewis." I turned once more to Dewi. "Sorry Dewi you're goin to have to hold the fort."

"What me? Me as the official in CM1?"

"You'll be fine. Who's the chargehand?"

"Terry T."

"Go and have a word let him know the situation. We'll worry about Caerwyn later and how we get him out." Denny and Gethin had said nothing up to this point. Gethin had continued investigating the engine problem.

"Gethin would you have a problem being my driver?"

"What? Fuckin hell cock Ken John won't be happy."

"Denny I'm not particularly bothered whether he's happy or not needs must. You okay with it Gethin?"

"You're the boss."

"And you my favourite Assistant Mechanical Engineer. Right I need to be movin. Need to get to the Durbog manrider."

"How many will need a ride?"

"There's six plus Adder."

"It'll only take six."

"Put Adder next to you. I'll walk. We'll meet up in R5 near XC1. At least if it starts smoking there it'll blow away from us. Catch you guys later."

I continued out towards the Top of the Durbog planning my excuse when the manrider broke down. Just as I arrived the control shouted over the tannoy system.

"Mr Gibson, hello Mr Gibson."

"Hi Lewis."

"The Manager has asked me to let you know he's at the Two Way with the MOD. *MOD you'd think we were going to war. Why doesn't he just say he's with his visitors?*

"Thanks Lewis. I'm in position. Ready and waiting." By the time I'd finished the conversation I could see a number of lights bobbing up and down at the bottom of the brew. The belt was already running. I guessed the Manager was allowing the Group to get on first with the Director. Knowing I was in position he would take up the rear. We'd carried out this procedure many times before between us. I walked across to the lockout.

The Group Director was leading. He spotted me and greeted me with a nervous smile and that bloody wink. I don't think he was comfortably leading. I moved forward onto the wooden ramp that led down from the conveyor. Luckily, I did the Group Director stumbled as he alighted. Stepping forward I went to grab him then thought better of it. He took my hand instead. I was surprised how soft it was. I guessed he did the washing up at home. He gave me another wink. Instead of moving straight off he momentarily stood to take in his surroundings. Not the done thing. I spotted immediately the next problem as a huge figure of a man ran straight into us both. I quickly pulled the Director forward. The Colonel following before the others landed. Once order had been restored the Group Director took control and introduced me to the Group.

"Mick this is Group Captain Alan Croft. His colleague Squadron Leader Lionel Jet. Colonel Bartholomew Brittain." The man was huge. "And Major Tom Watson. And last but not least Admiral Horatio Hamilton." I shook hands with each in turn.

"Right if you don't mind gents follow me." I walked off. The Manager was soon alongside.

"You okay Mick? You seem a little preoccupied."

"Mr Adder might be worthwhile if we give the diesel bus a miss."

"Why?"

"We're having a few problems with it."

"Never mind problems you'd best get it sorted. The Group Director went to a lot of trouble getting us that."

"But...."

"No buts Mick." I said no more.

We continued into CM1's towards the diesel bus. Gethin was already in place. He smiled as we approached. "Sut ydych chi."

"Da iawn." The Group Captain responded to everyone's surprise. As way of an explanation he continued. "My mother's family are from Haverfordwest, Pembrokeshire." Impressive I thought.

"Right if you could all take a seat. Mr Adder if you don't mind could you sit here now." I pointed to the seat alongside Gethin. He walked forward and took his place. It was at this point he realised who the driver was.

"Gethin?"

"Bora da Mr Adder. I'm just helping out." The Manager turned towards me for an explanation.

"Short staffed. Right if you're all ready. Hold on to your hats." Gethin started the machine up. It started immediately thankfully soon followed by a cloud of smoke.

The Manager gave me a quizzical look. "you not riding with us?"

"No room. I'll be fine. I'll walk alongside." We began to move forward. The smoke was far worse than I thought. To watch the thing proceed was painful. I reduced my pace as I began to get too far ahead. Nobody seemed concerned at the speed they were travelling. I was just happy they were moving. The smoke and smell of diesel was a concern, however. Then the tannoy burst into life.

"Who the fucks running the bus?"

"What's up?"

"The lads are about to walk out. The smoke's filling the headings."

I needn't have worried seconds later the thing juddered and spluttered then stopped. No matter what Gethin tried it was having none of it. We'd travelled no more than thirty yards.

"Sorry gents looks as though we're walking from here on in."

"Whatever's the problem Mick?" The Director asked.

"We received a bad batch of diesel. Looks as though some of it is still in the system." The look on the Manager's face suggested I was talking a load of shite. I was. As I walked on ahead the Group Captain caught me up.

"I've often wondered what it must be like working down a coal mine. Used to go for long walks on the beach with my grandparents in Pembrokeshire. You can see numerous outcrops of coal in the cliff faces."

"Yeah know what you mean. We did a week there on a geology course." I answered. He knew I wasn't happy we'd only managed to get thirty yards on the bus.

"For what it's worth old bean I've had similar issues in my career even at my level." I was surprised by his comment and appreciated his sympathy.

"Thanks."

"Remember the Falklands War."

"I certainly do. You guys gave those Argies a run for their money."

"We did and we got the result we wanted. However, it wasn't plain sailing."

"What do you mean?"

"The runway at Port Stanley."

"The one you guys bombed using the Vulcans. What an achievement."

"Off the record. We never hit the runway."

"You did. There were pictures on the news. What was his name? Brian Hanrahan you know the guy famous for *I counted them all out and I counted them all back*. He showed pictures of the bombs that hit the runway. I remember seeing one crater. 1,000lb bombs were used if my memory is correct."

"Fake. Pictures were taken at RAF Finningley. Made to look like we'd hit the runway."

"Why would you do that?"

"After all the trouble we'd gone to get the Vulcan Bombers ready and the expense of prepping the Victor's to refuel. Then flying eight thousand miles from London to Stanley with a stopover on the Ascension Isles no one dared tell Thatcher we'd missed. She'd have had us all in front of a firing squad." I couldn't help but laugh. There's me worrying about a bloody diesel bus. It put the whole thing into perspective.

The walk in was a good chance to get to know the group individually Alan Croft was close to retirement. Based at RAF Finningley which was about to close as a base. Once home to the Vulcan bomber. The end of the Cold War had seen a reduced presence on the Eastern seaboard. There was talk it may be developed as a commercial airport.

Lionel Jet known to his friends as LJ in addition to being a Squadron Leader was also Navigator. He sat behind the pilot in the Tornado Jets they flew. Something I couldn't get my head round if he was the Leader.

The Colonel, Bartholomew Brittain had done well for himself. Originally from Barbados his family had come over here after the war. On the Windrush. His father had set up a successful business as a barber in the East End. Bartholomew however had other ideas. His grandmother in her younger days had fallen in love with a young British Army officer. It had never worked out after his move back to England. During his time with her she'd often reminisce on how things might have been. Each time however she'd confirm to the young Bartholomew that she wouldn't have changed a thing. Just to have him in her world. So, from a very early age he knew what he wanted to become. It was a wonderful story.

His colleague Tom Watson was nearing retirement. A veteran from the Falklands war where he'd seen enough action to last a lifetime. He'd been attached to a Gurkha Regiment. He'd been amazed at the fear these guys had put into the Argies during the conflict. He and many of his colleagues believed it was like having an additional battalion on the British side.

The Admiral another interesting character had been in the Navy all his life. Man, and boy. A long family tradition. His father had been an Admiral of the Fleet. I couldn't but ask the obvious question.

"Were you named after our famous Sea Lord?"

"Good god man of course I was. Another family tradition. My father's name Collingwood Hamilton."

"You can guess my next question then?"

"Well young man my answer will surprise you. Yes, my family are related to the lady in question. Sad how it all ended really…" Our conversation was interrupted when a bolter appeared up ahead. Instinctively I knew something was wrong when the lads never acknowledged our presence. Something they always did particularly when we had visitors.

Dewi appeared. He seemed not to notice my visitors. He was sweating too. An unusual sight. "Down to one bolter, cable damage we think. It's in R4."

"Where's that one heading?"

"R1."

"Where's the JCM?"

"On stand in R2."

"Can't you keep it cutting with one shuttle?"

"Nowhere left to cut."

"What….

One of the lessons learnt from the recent trials in extending the cut was the number of rooms we could leave open at any one time. We tried to keep it to three, four at a push with the both bolters in operation. But five! My concern was justified when the tannoy once more burst into life.

"Terry roof fall in R3."

"For fucks sake Idris I leave you for five minutes and you brought the place in. I'm on the way back."

I turned to Dewi. "Where is Terry?"

"He took the FSV out to pick up the spare cable reel." No fuckin wonder we were in trouble. The one person I could rely upon wasn't even in the district.

The visitors hadn't taken much notice of the conversations taking place. Neither had the Manager. He was in deep conversation with the Director.

"Dewi, as soon as Terry appears ask him to see me. I'm taking this lot into R4 to see the lads bolting. We need to see something working."

"Right will do now. Wela I chi."

"Yeah see you later too. Right gents we're heading this way." I pointed across in the direction of R4. "Just remember when you see a cable on the floor make sure you…" Before I could finish the sentence the Manager came alongside and whispered.

"Mick what the fuck is goin on I haven't seen a shuttle movin yet?" The Manager's comment had distracted me. I watched as the Major continued towards R4. He'd just placed the tip of his foot on a narrow cable. A shuttle car cable. I tried to finish my sentence and shouted "…stand on it…" Too late. Without warning the cable flew into the air taking the Major with it. What happened next was quite remarkable. If I hadn't seen it myself I would have found it hard to believe. The Major did a complete somersault and landed back on both feet. As if by way of an explanation the Colonel who was now stood alongside me said.

"Parachute Regiment." For what seemed like an eternity I stood without uttering a word. The silence broken once more by the tannoy.

"Bolter 2 now running. False alarm cable hadn't been damaged." To add to our change in fortune the JCM appeared out of R2 heading towards R3. To my relief Terry was driving it. He shouted across to me.

"Mr G shuttle car should only be another hour. I'm just heading into R3 to do a clean-up. Then we'll move the bolter from R1 into R3. Once you've seen the bolter in action head over to R1 we'll be cutting by then." What a guy order had been restored. Terry had saved the day.

"Thanks Terry." I shouted. "I owe you one."

"Pack of Red Man would be appreciated."

"Consider it done."

As they watched its operation I continued to provide a running commentary on how we'd increased the density of bolts when we encountered bad ground. It seemed to satisfy the audience all accept the Manager who eyed me suspiciously.

In R1 the JCM was churning out the coal. Terry having taken control of the machine. Just doing enough to keep the one shuttle in action. I looked around at the group. They seemed satisfied with what they saw. The two fellas from the army looked particularly excited. I think a large part of that was the noise and the shear power the JCM demonstrated.

Next stop was the Stamler. To my surprise Caerwyn was still there still sweating and now shaking.

"PTSD?" The Major asked me.

"PTSD?"

"Looks as though he has it. Ex-military?" The penny finally dropped.

"No nothing like that. Our Caerwyn here suffers with IDLR."

"Guessed as much." His answer was a surprise.

The Manager went over to Caerwyn to enquire to his wellbeing. He got no response.

"Bout of Welsh flu. Pretty bad this time of the year. Seems to be affecting my officials more than most." The explanation seemed to satisfy the Manager as it explained Dewi being there and Gethin operated the rider. Everyone at this point distanced themselves from Caerwyn. We began to head out. I was hoping they'd not ask about a ride out. How wrong was I when Gethin appeared.

"This way if you don't mind gents." He shouted as he approached us from R5. "Manrider this way." I quickly made my way towards him.

"Gethin what the fuck are you doin? I can't go through that again."

"Don't you worry now Mr Gibson." He responded smiling.

"Why? What have you done."

"Made some alterations to the pipework plus the return journey will all be down bank. You wait and see now. One thing though now. Don't expect it to be operational for another month. The engine will be completely fucked once we get out now." I said no more the man had never let me down from day one. I waited until the others caught me up. The Manager being first.

"Please don't tell me we're having to endure that painful exercise again."

"Oh, ye of little faith. Mr Adder when have I ever let you down." I walked off to the rider before he could answer.

Once everyone was onboard I climbed onto the back bumper. Strictly a no no but if Gethin was right I wasn't going to miss this for the world. It also helped that the Manager and Director were facing the opposite direction.

"Right Gethin all yours fella." The engine kicked in immediately and we shot forward continually gaining speed. Never mind a max speed of fifteen mph we must have been doin twenty at least. There was still plenty of diesel fumes passing over us but with the speed we were travelling and the assistance of the ventilation it was bearable. If anything, it added to the excitement. It was like being on Rhyl's Big Dipper. Each bump in the roadway lifted the group from their seats. The hallowing and laughter confirmed their enjoyment. I hung on for dear life. My concern was if the thing didn't stop. Within ten minutes my mind was put at ease as Gethin gently applied the brakes and brought the thing to a halt below XC1.

Wow it don't get much better than that. Each of the visitors to their credit shook hands with Gethin as they alighted. Once they'd repositioned their helmets. It was quite obvious from the comments the lads from the MOD had enjoyed their visit. I even overheard the Group Director comment to the Manager that we'd been the first pit to get the diesel bus working. No fuckin surprise there then. I gave Gethin the thumbs up as I followed the group back out.

Arriving back up the pit and considering the start we'd had it had actually been a huge success. The Group Director also having paid me a complement on the rider as we were coming out. "Well recovered." Were the very words used. I must admit I was feeling quite chuffed with myself.

I waited until the cage had cleared I was last out. To my astonishment Bill Hooper was waiting he didn't look happy. I overheard him say something about having to buy more Lynx shower gel.

Two hours later Dewi arrived back in the office. He'd stayed behind with some of the men to help get Caerwyn out of the District. They'd achieved it by placing a hessian sack over his head until they'd reached the outbye steel work. Dewi confirmed he'd be confined to Pit Bottom from now on.

The Manager had been pleased with the outcome too. Not that he'd said anything to me. He'd left soon after with the Group Director for a meeting at Gadbrook Park. It was Lizzy who'd popped in to advise us all sandwiches and cakes were available in the conference room. It was the leftovers from the visitors. After gorging myself on the tuna and salmon sandwiches followed by the two fairy cakes I headed towards the baths.

"Oright cock."
"Yeah all good thanks Denny thanks for your help today. Seems to have gone down well."
"Not me cock thanks Gethin. I'll just get a round of fucks of Ken John when he find what he's done to the rider."
"What exactly did he do?"
"Added an extra fuel pipe to engine. Played around with the intake manifold and carburettor. Strictly a no no but improves the engines rated output. Fucked up a number of bearing too." Denny's answer meant little to me.
"Oh.." I went to sit down to removed my boots. "What the fucks this doing here?" I picked up a bottle of Lynx shower gel.
"Dafydd left us all one. Seems he's got a locker full of the stuff." For the next month anyone using the Undermanager's bath didn't need soap!

-

"Mick can you grab Blackhead. Manager wants a word." I'd just got up the pit about to light up a cigar.
"About what?" I asked the Deputy Manager.

277

"An update. See you in the conference room." He left. The update he was referring to we'd guessed was coming. The local and national new had picked up on the Government's plans for the industry going forward.

Since the announcement we'd all just got on with the job. It was the uncertainty. If you thought about it would drive you nuts. I guessed as we should have closed this month we were staying open. The giveaway had been delivery of the new equipment for CM2's.

"Kelvin mate Manager wants to see us."

"What the fuck does he want now?" He responded smiling. I'd noticed the changes with Kelvin over the last few weeks. He seemed more relaxed and not on edge as much. "Come on then. Let's go and see the daft cunt."

"That's no way to refer to our leader."

"Don't make me laugh. I suppose Mr Positive has got an update."

"Probably."

By the time we arrived everyone else was in there. Mr Adder acknowledged the two of us when we entered.

"Right gentlemen if I could have your attention." Silence as the individual conversations ceased. "Some good news I guess we all could see coming. British Coal will be announcing an update later today. I've been advised by the Group Director Point of Ayr will be amongst twelve pits staying open. A further six will be put on care and maintenance. All this on the back of the Government's Coal Review." He stopped and waited for a response. Nobody said anything.

"I'm pleased that went down well." It took Gregor to break the silence.

"How long for?"

"Well hopefully till we go on to privatisation. That however depends on performance. We should hit the half million tonne mark this year with about…" He turned towards Bill Hooper.

"Three hundred and thirty staff thereabouts at the last count."

"Thanks Bill. That puts us in the right ballpark for productivity. However, I have to emphasis output must be consistent. CM2's must be ready and producing coal by November." He looked towards me. I nodded. Denny who was standing next to me whispered.

"No pressure then cock."

"Fuck off Denny."

"What if any information did we get back on the competition?" Billy Blunt asked.

"Billy if you're referring to the dash for gas. That continues. As does the operation of the Magnox nuclear stations. The future threat everyone is referring to are renewables."

"What about them fuckers across way drilling for oil?" Denny had such a way with words.

"If you're referring to Hamilton Oil that continues."

"Opencast?" Gregor added.

"As you might expect. Continues unabated. Gents it's not all bad news they've promised a subsidy to cover the difference between coal we produce and that which is imported. This obviously helps us with Fiddlers Ferry.

"What about those fuckers down road at Connah's Quay." The question caused most of us to turn towards Gregor. As we didn't have a clue as to what he was talking about. He looked towards us all. "Bloody sour gas."

"What the fucks sour gas."

"Same as natural. Just contains more hydrogen sulphide."

"Why didn't you say. Just rotten fuckin eggs." Gregor and Denny when they got going were fun to listen to. However, the Manager was losing control of the meeting.

"Right gents can we have a little order." Silence once more descended on the room. "If there's nothing else." He waited. "Thanks everyone let's get back to it."

Before I turned to follow the rest out the Manager walked across. "Mick, Tony could you two give me five." The Deputy Manager and I remained where we were. As soon as everyone had gone he came across to us.

"We've got the new Deputy Chairman here in three weeks. He'll have with him a number of Directors to look at our progress in CM1's." The news came as no surprise. I'd contemplated asking the Manager if we could sell tickets to add another revenue stream but thought better of it. Just in case he agreed.

"Yeah no problem. I suppose he'll want to see the new kit being built for CM2's?"

"Yep I think that would be a good move. Okay? Right thanks gents catch you later."

As planned the visit took place with the Deputy Chairman. Both the Manager and Tony Douglas attended too. I was surprised how open he was in his conversation with the Directors. I was able to learn some detail on the agreement in principle with National Power and PowerGen for new contracts. Sales of one hundred and sixty million tonnes of coal over next five years. Forty million tonnes this year and thirty million tonnes in each of the next four years. However, this included a substantial price reduction. This year alone price per tonne would reduce from forty pounds to thirty two. This equated to over five billion pounds. The visit went without a hitch. Everyone seemed well pleased, particularly the Deputy Chairman. I enjoyed these sorts of visits.

-

"Well I didn't see that coming. Where you off to?" Kelvin and I were sat in our clean office something Mr Adder had been promising for some time now a reality. Kelvin had just returned from a meeting with the Manager where he'd handed in his notice.

"British Airways."

"British fuckin Airways! How did you manage that then? All that time with Mr Douglas at weekends taking flying lessons."

"Fuck off pilot? Now wouldn't that be something. No, the wife's uncle works for their cargo side of the business in Singapore. They're looking for someone to run the Gatwick operation over here."

"You don't know anything about cargo."

"Doesn't seem to be a problem. They're looking for someone with experience on the health and safety side plus dealing with unions. Seems they have a lot of internal issues. Regardless of what we've heard during the TQM sessions about BA being a quality company."

"When you goin?"

"End of month. The Manager's arranging a farewell doo!"

"Not convinced by the reprieve then?"

"Mick, both you and I know whatever happens the industry is on its knees. Have you seen the figures? They may be talking about saving twelve pits but for how long? There were twenty-eight thousand of us employed in the industry end of last year. A total of sixty pits. The writings on the wall. We're fucked all of us. Even Mr Positive."

"Yeah I know. You're probably right."

"There's not probably it's a fact. Between you and me Tony's asked me to see if there's anything for him."

"Not sure they'll let him fly. Not even those big fuck off 747 cargo flights in and out of Hongkong!"

-

"Mick will show you round. What's it been now Mick six years?"

"Tell me about it. Yeah must be about that now." *Yeah and the sooner I can get out of here the better!* I was sat in the Manager's office with Paul Adder and the new Undermanager Robin Martin. He seemed a nice lad. "Let's hope you stay longer than the last fella."

"Who was that then?"

"A guy called Karl Haddock. How long was he here for Mick?

"Bout nine months."

"What happened?"

"Mr Douglas our Deputy Manager sent him round the twist." Paul Adder began to laugh.

"He's having you on. He got a job in Zambia. Copper mine I believe."

"Yeah true but it was our illustrious Deputy Manager who convinced him. "By the way where is he today?"

"Interview with British Airways I believe."

"Mick you're unbelievable, all you seem to do of late is take the piss." *I wonder why?* "Anyway, Robin I've got to make a move. Meeting at Group. They're providing an update on the plans for privatisation. I'll leave you in Mick's capable hands."

Robin and I left and headed towards our clean office.

"Right fella that's your desk there." Robin walked over and sat down. He began to open each drawer. From the corridor I heard the distinct sound of Bevin talking. As much as I liked the man. He was a member of the American team. Something he continually reminded me of. Of late he was continually asking my view of the future. Something I had about as much knowledge as the he did. I quickly and very quietly pushed my chair back and headed to the large window. Having opened it to its full extent I lifted myself out and jumped to the floor. Quickly reaching up and pushing it back to its original position.

"Prynhawn da. Aw sorry to disturb you. Have you seen Mr Gibson?"

"Yeah he's there........" From outside I pictured Robin pointing to my empty seat. "Well he was.... Must have nipped out."

"I'm guessing you're the new Undermanager Mr Martin?"

"Yeah that's me."

"Hi, I'm Bevin. NUM Branch Delegate and a member of the American team. Good to meet you. Tell him I called, Wela I chi." Bevin left.

Crouched on the ground below the window the mid-afternoon sun on my back. It felt good. The conversation from inside had stopped. I popped my head back up.

"He's gone then?" Robin turned his head and began laughing.

"Yeah, what's all that about then?"

"He's a lovely guy and best NUM fella I've worked with but talk. If you think Adder's bad spend a day with Bevin. Did he tell you he was in the club?" I was now sat back at my desk.

"He did."

"I'll tell you about it later. Come on we need to get moving. I promised Adder I show you S64's and the developments for H81's. If we've time we can pop into CM1's and the new place that'll be starting up soon CM2's.

-

As agreed with the Manager the equipment continued to arrive for the new development in CM2's. In addition, the Three Yard drivages began to access additional reserves for CM3's that however was not planned to start up until 1995. By November 1993 we started up as planned. It had been timed to perfection as the following month we had a further visit from the boys from JT Boyd.

-

"Gentlemen what an absolute pleasure to see you both again."

"Mick the pleasure's all ours boy. I brought you a little present from the US of A." JW handed me a package. I guessed what it would be.

"You're so kind." I opened it to find two dozen packs of Red Man. I removed one. "If you don't mind I'll pass these to the lads when we get inside."

"Mick you do what you damned well like with em." Chuck added.

"Where to first boys? CM2's." The Manager who'd been stood back whilst the banter took place answered.

"I think that would be good Mick. I'd like to see how things are progressing." Probably just as well as it would be his first visit also.

The visit went without a hitch. The following week it was announced the pit would be going through to privatisation. Rumours were rife we'd be taken over by RJB.

-

9. 1994 Privatisation

"Mick we've hit a fault in R3 and R5 upthrow."

"Thanks Terry. Can we access further to the west?"

"Yep on that now." We'd only established CM2 five months ago and out of nowhere we'd hit faults just beyond XC8.

"And nothing showing in R4?"

"No, very odd if you ask me. Hold on a mo." Terry had been interrupted by one of his team. "R6 now as well."

"Okay push on to the west see if we open up at least three further headings. I'll have a word with the Manager. Be with you shortly." I replaced the receiver.

"Trouble?" Dewi who was now my new Colliery Overman. Evan had gone missing literally no one had seen him for weeks now. Dewi however only had a few weeks to go he was retiring too. He was stood facing the far wall. An underground plan showing the workings pinned to the wall. He had a cigarette in one hand and was tracing out the current active headings.

"Give us a minute I'd best go see the Manager."

This predicament was a major concern. About the time Dewi was to retire there was an announcement due. British Coal would list the pits going through to privatisation. All indications suggested Point would be on that list. Particularly after the excellent visit and feedback we'd had from Chuck and JW late last year. It was vitality important we kept production at the current level. Any drop could send out the wrong signals to the bean counters.

"Mr. Adder sorry to disturb you." Paul was leaning back in his chair. Now in his customary position both feet on the desk. He was reading a copy of the Financial Times.

"Oh, hi Mick, come in and take a seat. How do you fancy owning a mine?"

"What?" His question had taken me completely by surprise.

"There's an article here about Hatfield Colliery just outside Doncaster. Seems the Manager there has completed an MBO with British Coal."

"Eh MBO?"

"Management Buy Out."

"Oh right. Yeah as long as we had plenty of coal to go at."

"I've heard. Received a call from Control. We've hit a fault in CM2's. I've arranged to go under with David Jonathan." David Jonathan or DJ as he was fondly referred to. And he didn't operate a disco. He was a geologist who'd been assigned to the colliery. Originally from Group HQ. In the drive to prepare for privatisation a number of individuals had been assigned to those collieries remaining.

"We plan to open up towards the west. Keep the coal coming."

"Good I'm sure it'll be fine. Have you told Mr Douglas?"

"No not yet. He's already down pit with Robin problems on 81's?"

"Now wouldn't that be something owning a mine." He'd gone back to reading the paper. I'd never seen such a change in a man. Ever since he'd read some book *The Power of Positive Thinking* by an American *Norman Vincent Peale*. He'd been so taken by the book he'd gone out and bought us all a copy. I'd yet to start on mine. Billy Blunts had gone directly into the bin. Something to do with it being "religious crap."

"Okay I'll see you in there," I received no response.

Arriving in the district the air resembled a fine white mist. I'd been prewarned and quickly positioned my dust mask. Visibility had been reduced to no more than ten yards decreasing as I got to the working area. I arrived in R4 and removed my mask we were cutting coal. Terry T appeared alongside.

"Bora da Mick did we expect this?"

"Not sure. Manager doesn't seem too bothered. He'll be in later with the geologist. Remind me, how many places have we hit the dirt?"

"Just the three R3, R5 and R6. R4 is still in coal. So too R7, R8 and R9 seem okay at the moment. I'm a little concerned continuing to cut where we've hit the dirt. We're knocking shit out of the machines. We're going through picks like there's no tomorrow."

"Let's hold fire till DJ's had a looksee."

"Oh yeah you said."

"Let me put a call through to the stores see if we've got any dirt picks left over from CM1's."

"Right I'll get back to the lads Wela I chi."

"Thanks T. Meant to ask what are you doin in here anyway?"

"Asyn asked me to pop in. Short on drivers."

I made my way back out to check on CM1's. All seemed okay. Two hours later I got the call.

"Hello Mr Gibson, hello Mr Gibson."

"Hi Lewis."

"Manager's at the Two Way he asked I let you know. He's with David Jonathan."

"Thanks Lewis. I'm on my way."

"Oh, by the way. Iolo asked me to pass on a message regards the JCM picks. There's half a dozen boxes he'll send in with the afternoon shift. He's put another order in for a further twenty boxes."

"Thanks Lewis."

I continued out. Half an hour later I caught up with the Manager and David in R3.

"Morning both." They were examining the white stone wall now fully exposed.

"Morning Mick."

"What have we got left in the way of dirt picks?" The Manager asked.

"Sorted. A load coming in with the afternoon shift and more on order."

"David reckons we'll face the same problem in R7, R8 and R9 in about forty metres. Should be able to get another crosscut in before then."

"See here Mick." David held out an A3 plan of the workings. "I'll arrange with the surveyors, but I reckon if we concentrate in R3 and R5 at 1:4 for about eighteen metres we'll be back in coal. Then we can open up again to the five road system hopefully."

"It'll also give us the chance to access the Five Yard." The Manager added.

"Sounds like a plan. Keeps the coal coming while we get through the fault."

And that's exactly what we did. Without losing any production we accessed the coal through the fault in both roads. Two weeks later we had five rooms available.

At Christmas, my wife and I would carry out the Christmas shopping in the beautiful City of Chester surrounded by the magnificent sandstone Roman wall and the interior black and white Tudor buildings. It was something we both looked forward to every year.

I loved to "people watch" and in particular the office workers going out into the city for lunch. I watched with interest their furrowed brows contemplating where they would spend the next hour taking refreshment. What a problem they had! Where to go for lunch the big decision for the day. And there was me pink grapefruit stuffed down my overalls. Excited at eating it on the conveyor belt travelling out from the mine covered in coal dust.

I'd never contemplated working anywhere else; however, the recent threat of closure had got me thinking. What would it be like working outside the pit?

For the first time in my career it was becoming more and more a chore turning up for work. I needed afresh challenge I was ready for a promotion. It had been suggested some time ago that Tony Douglas was moving on. A promotion to Deputy Manager would suit me fine but was that ever likely to happen? Paul Adder had been far better as a Manager than I thought he'd be. Generally leaving me alone to manage my section of the mine. I'd been at the colliery now for six and half years.

The industry was about to be privatised. British Coal had increased the offer of redundancy. Each day more and more of the older generation were taking their money and moving on. We'd even had an influx of Officials from the Lancashire collieries that had already closed.

I was still thinking about a Dale Farm a franchise. I could do that. Up early without any hassle that could be the future. The thing is though I did like meeting people. It would probably be a nice change but was it really me. What had I done now? Nineteen years in the industry was it really all coming to an end? Then one day totally out of the blue......

"Mick?"

"Yeah," I recognised the voice.

"How do you fancy coming to work for me at Coal Investments? You'd be my Deputy Manager."

It had recently been announced that the preferred bidder to take on the last remaining operating pits was RJB. Coal Investments unable to secure any operating pits had a different strategy. To take over those currently on care and maintenance. One of those mines Hem Heath was managed by Wayne Hickox. Wayne I'd first met on joining the industry.

"You still there." I'd had so many disappointments to date I could hardly believe my ears.

"Yeah sorry Wayne caught me by surprise. Deputy Manager you said?"

"I did. Plus, we'd be introducing the room and pillar system of mining and we think you're the man to do it.

A promotion a fresh challenge. My expertise required for the room and pillar operations Maurice Adman was there as too was Ken John. Building a pit from fresh a completely new start and approach. The ex-commercial Director from British Coal had pulled a team together to open up a number of mines Hem Heath/Coventry/Silverdale/Annesley Bentinck/Markham Main)

"Can I have a think about it?"

"You certainly can."

"How long to make a decision."

"Tomorrow would be good."

Having discussed the situation with my wife my mind was made up. Although she thought the idea was crazy. "Can't you see the industry is coming to an end. You need to find something new. A different industry something that's expanding coal mining in the UK is dead."

"Yeah you're probably right. I'm not sure though it's going to happen where we live now. If we move to Staffordshire I'll be central for all the motorways. I may even get a job working at an airport like Kelvin Blackhead did."

"The kids love it here though."

"I know. I love Wales too, but I need to work. We could always move back when I retire."

"Well I'll tell you this. If and at the moment it's an if we do move we ain't moving again. I can promise you that for sure."

I went to see Paul Adder. I guessed that like Kelvin when he left the Manager would arrange a farewell doo. There'd even be flowers for Mrs Gibson.

"You want to what?" He looked at me in disbelief. He began pacing up and down the office. He didn't look happy.

"Yeah fraid so I think it's time." He continued pacing up and down as his face reddened. I wasn't sure why he was so agitated.

"Where will you go? Have you had a job offer?"

"I'd rather not say at the moment."

"You have to I need to know."

"Why?" He seemed unable to answer the question he began to stutter. I actually felt sorry for the man. There was a knock at the door. The coughing and regurgitating of phlegm needed no introduction. The door opened.

"Sorry to bother you Mr. Adder."

"Not now Mr. Douglas can't you see I'm busy." The door closed without response.

I thought to myself well it can't do any harm.

"I've had a job offer from Coal Investments." How wrong was I. Without warning he slammed a clenched fist onto his desk. And there was me thinking how pleased he'd be for me.

"The competition, how could you? I can't let you go to them!"

"It's a promotion. I'd be going as the Deputy Manager."

"I want you here as my Deputy Manager."

"Mr. Adder with all due respect you've been dangling that carrot in front of me for the last two years."

"Well you can't go. I won't let you. So that's that." He sat down back at his desk and started signing reports. I left his office somewhat bemused and headed back to my clean office.

No more was said on the matter although the calls from Coal Investments were coming thick and fast. They were after my passport details. I was to lead a team across to the USA to see once again room and pillar in action. I'd made a mental note as soon as I arrived to get the missus a gift.

I said nothing to anyone at work. However, a month after offering my resignation. I was travelling along the main Tunnel. Contemplating my next move when the tannoy burst into life.

"Hello Mr Gibson. Mr Gibson."

"Hi Lewis this is he."

"Mr Gibson can you give the Manager a call. Says it's urgent."

"Will do, thanks."

"Mr Adder Mick here."

"You're to make your way out of the pit immediately. Speak to no one. I've had clearance to let you go. Clear your desk." The phone line went dead. I didn't get chance to ask about a farewell doo and flowers for my wife.

Walking out along the Main Tunnel I reflected on the last six and half years. Some good some bad but most of it good. Evan and Osian were gone. Dewi had recently finished. It was now left to the new lads. The likes of Hywel, Reece, and Asyn. All good lads. I guessed Robin would now become their Undermanager I was sure they'd fare well. It wasn't that I was just leaving Point of Ayr. After nineteen years with the nationalised coal industry I was to join and work in the private sector. Coal mining with a new private company Coal Investments. What would the future hold?

-

The End

10.APPENDICES

The Characters

Manager:
Ron Grove
Maurice Adman
Paul Adder
Wayne Hickox

Deputy Manager:
Paul Adder
Tony Douglas

Assistant Manager
Tommy Oldham
Mick Gibson

Secretary
Bronwen
Lizzy

Personal Manager
Bill Hooper

Undermanager
Paul Taylor
Mick Gibson
Kelvin Blackhead
Robin Martins
Karl Haddock

The Wives and Relatives
Annie Gibson
James Gibson
Elizabeth Gibson (Lizzie)
Uncle John
Mrs Blunt

Colliery Overman
Zone B - Bleddyn
Night Shift - Delwyn
Afternoon Shift - Gruffyd

Zone B - Evan
Zone A - Dewi

Overman
Osian
Lewis
Evan
Arfon

Face Overman
Alwyn
Hywel
Asyn (Huw)

Deputy
Caerwyn
Owen
Reece
Edwin (VG)

Control Room
Idris
Lewis
Elis

Canteen
Storm

The Men
Dai - Lampman
Rhys Llan (from Llangollen)
Aled Flint
Dylan Denbigh
Arfon Shit
Llewellyn Ffyn (from Ffynnongroyw)
Llew and Gordon - Trackmen
Terry T – FSV Driver / Chargehand
Billy B – FSV Driver
Dai Fingers
Keith – Haulage
Bryn - Stageloader
Billy Nelder

Tommy Twat (TT)
Ged – face chargeman

Loco Drivers
Ivor
George
Tomos
Gordon

43's Maingate
Baeddan the Boar
Dai Dyserth
Dai Denbigh

North Headings
Tom, Rick, and Larry

42's Coal Face
Ithel the Little - Chargeman

The Beltmen
Gareth
Owen
Tecwyn

Mechanical Engineer
Gerry Tuffman
Ken John
Clark Michaels

Deputy Mechanical Engineer
Denny Richards – Zone B
Owain Jones – Zone A

Assistant Mechanical
Gethin

Workshop Fitter
Little Rick

Shaftsman
James Runner

Electrical Engineer
Billy Blunt

Deputy Electrical Engineer
Gregor George – Zone B
Dafydd Jones – Zone A

Assistant Electrical
Ifor

Accountant
Cuthbert Sum

Store Manager
Iolo Pyke

Surveyor
Len Saddle

Geologist
David Jonathan

Rockbolting Specialist
Noah

Safety Engineer
Llewelyn Larry

Ventilations officer
Joe Tree

Coal Prep Manager
Llyn Garvey

NUM Delegate
Bevin

Payroll
Ioan Sword

The USA Team

Tom Brian – NW Group Assistant Group Director Employee Relations
Sidney Cider – National President BACM
Bevin – NUM Delegate
Noah – Colliery Roof Bolting Specialist
Arfon – Overman Zone B Continuous Miner Ops
Graham Michaels – Sales Director JCM
Phil Fowler – NW Group Assistant Group Director Operations

TQM Facilitators

Osian and Billy Blunt
Ioan Sword and Iolo Pyke
Mick Gibson and Len Saddle
Dafydd Jones and Ithel the Little

The Military Visit

Group Captain Alan Croft
Squadron Leader Lionel Jet
Admiral Horatio Hamilton
Colonel Bartholomew Brittain
Major Tom Watson

Area / Group Staff

Deputy Chairman
Area Director
Assistant Director
Group General Manager / Director
Assistant Group General Manager
Assistant Group Director – Larry Button
Operations Director – Larry Button
Operations Director – Phil Fowler

Mining Terminology

Advance Coal Face – The long face of the seam extracting all of the coal, accessed through an intake and return. The roads servicing the face are maintained.

Airlock – Area between a set of airdoors separating intake from return air.

Alighting Station – Platform to allow riders to disembark from a manriding conveyor or locomotive carriage.

Armoured Face Conveyor (AFC) – Means of transporting coal off the coal face.

Anderson Shearer Loader (ASL) – Coal cutting machine used on the coal face.

Auxiliary Fan – Ventilation fan.

Arch – Free standing steel support (arched or square work).

BACM – British Association of Colliery Management.

Banksman- Competent person for the purpose of receiving and transmitting signals at the top of the shaft.

Baths – Showers.

BC – British Coal.

Beethoven 100 Shot – Type of exploder.

Belt Structure – top rollers / bottom rollers / stand / side irons.

Bi Di – Bidirectional – reference to shearer cutting in both directions

Boarding Station – Area used to access a manrider (loco, conveyor etc.)

Bretby – Cable handler running in spill plate on the coal face.

Caisson Method – Method of shaft sinking through unstable ground using compressed air in a pressurised chamber.

Caunch / Kench – Extracted strata above a coal seam to create a roadway.

Cage – Lift / Means of travelling the shaft. Covered in completely at the top, closed in at the two sides to prevent persons or things projecting beyond the sides. Suitable gates at each end with a rigid steel bar easily reached by all persons in it.

Calcium Sulphate crystals – used for consolidating floor dust.

Capex – Capital Expenditure.

Celstrap – Steel strap used to support roof via roof bolts.

Cap lamp – Battery operated lamp attached to helmet.

Carlton – Make of pipe, typically 6" used for supplying compressed air and/or 3" for pumping out mine water.

Chew – tobacco.

Chock Fitter – Fitter on coal face providing maintenance on powered supports.

Chock Stack – means of support using chock wood.

Chock Wood – Timber – generally 6" x 6" x 2 or 3 feet long.

Cock/Cocker – person (typical Lancashire expression).

Collier – Faceworker.

Contraband – Smoking material e.g. cigar, cigarette, pipe, match, mechanical lighter or other contrivance for smoking.

Cowl – Semi-circular metal guard surrounding the cutting disc of a shearer.

Crosscut – Connecting road between an intake and return road.

Cross Measure Drift – any drift driven otherwise than in coal or for the purpose of getting coal.

Crust -Wage.

Cunt – Term of endearment.

DAC – Tannoy / means of underground communication.

DC – Deputy Chairman.

DERDS – Double Ended Ranger Drum Shearer.

Detaching Gear – Attached to the shaft cage. Allows the cage to be detached during an overwind.

Development – Tunnel / Roadway.

Deputy Official of the mine, appointed by the Manager to be in charge of a district. To have charge of all workmen in that district and all operations carried out by them therein. To secure the safety and health of those said workmen.

District – underground area of the mine delineated on a plan.

Donkey jacket – Workwear warm jacket.

Dowty Prop – single hydraulic support.

EBG – Elsewhere Below Ground.

EVRS – Early Voluntary Retirement Scheme.

Firedamp – Methane.

Flame Safety Lamp (Oil Lamp) – Originally designed to provide a safe means of underground illumination. Thereafter replaced by electric cap lamps. Primarily used for testing the general body of the mine air. Officials and Workmen's Inspectors lamps have a self-contained relighter device. This allows the injection, for gas testing purposes, of samples of mine air collected by means of a bulb.

Free Standing Support – Steel support arch / square work.

Face conveyor – AFC.

Gaffer – Manager / Boss.

Gate End – End of the coal face.

Gate Conveyor – conveyor leading to/from the coal face

Gnat's cock – short distance.

Goaf (Waste / Gob) – Area behind coal face after coal extracted.

Gobbin – Spit.

Half a Bone – Overtime between shifts.

HMI – Her Majesty's Inspector – Mine's inspector appointed by HSE.

Hessian Bag – Sandbag – generally used for packing/support of roof at gate ends.

Horseheads – RSJ used to support roof beams.

Inbye – Tunnels / roads leading away from pit bottom.

Job and Knock – Used to describe a set task. Once complete team return to surface.

JCM – Joy Continuous Miner.

Jolly – Holiday.

Kench – Strata above the coal seam being extracted. Typically, at the gate end.

Keps – Means of supporting cage when at rest.

Kibble – Small manriding cage attached to a steel rope.

Lashing chain – metal chain with hook. Used for pulling vehicles underground by attaching to a steel rope.

Lifting Station – Area identified for use of lifting gear.

Loadbinder – Means of securing a load to a vehicle.

Locomotive – Train (usually diesel operated).

Longwall Mining – Using the advance or retreat method as against Room and Pillar (Pillar and Stall).

Maingate – Intake road to the coal face.

Manhole (Refuge Hole) – Provided along lengths of haulage road to protect individuals from moving vehicles.

Manriding Station- point at which men would board manriding carriages for transport.

Meeting Station – Area identified at the entrance to a Deputy's District.

Mesh – Welded wire mesh panel.

Methane – Explosive Gas see also known as Firedamp.

ME12 -Type of exploder (up to 12 shots).

Mine – A place for the purpose of extracting mineral carried out by the employment of persons below ground. Includes surface land, buildings, structures and works surrounding or adjacent to the shaft or outlet in connection with the working of the mine.

MINOS -Mine Operating System.

Moggie – Mice.

Mon – Man (typically Lancashire).

NACODS - National Association of Colliery Overmen and Deputies.

NCB – National Coal Board.

NUM – National Union of Mineworkers.

Onsetter – Competent person in attendance at the entrance of a shaft to receive and transmit signals when any person is raised.

Outbye – Area away from the coal face towards pit bottom.

Overman – Person superior to a Deputy but inferior to an Undermanager.

P1 – Type of explosive typically used in stone / cross measure drifts.

P4/5 – Type of explosive typically used in coal.

Pack – Used to support the area adjacent to the main gate of a coal face. Typically using paper or hessian sacks filled with waste material. In more recent times man made bag filled with concrete type material.

Pantechnican – A series of rail mounted vehicles typically carrying electrical panels, cables, hydraulic tank, and pump for powering face supports.

Pantograph – Means by which current is collected from contact wires.

Panel Train – Electrical panels on rails as above.

Panels – Used to provide electrical power for underground equipment.

Pikrose hauler – Winch equipped with a steel rope for transporting equipment/material underground.

Pinch – An amount taken as in snuff.

Pit Bottom – Area at the bottom of the shaft.

Pit Top – Area at the top of the shaft.

PLA – Power Loader Agreement.

Powered Support – Hydraulic prop mechanism to support the coal face.

Pull Lifts – Lifting Device.

Pushover – Term used to describe the movement of the AFC on a coal face, generally after the shearer has extracted coal.

Ramming stick – Wooden rod used to position sticks of explosive and ramming material into a drilled shot hole.

Red Man – American chewing tobacco.

Retreat Coal Face - Driving parallel roadways to the proposed extent of working, thereafter the coal face was driven between them. Coal was then worked coming outbye, as opposed to going inbye which was normal (advance coal face). While this system involved major expenditure in driving the gates before any coal was removed, it had the advantage of identifying unexpected faults, seam thinning etc. It also removed the need for ripping, and left the goaf behind, reducing the risk of heatings.

Return gate - A tunnel typically leading from the coal face towards the outbye district.

Ribside – opposite to faceside.

Rick's Duster – Metal container (usually an empty five gallon oil drum) containing a small venturi coupled to compressed air. The operator uses an external three inch hose to blast stonedust onto the surrounding roof and sides of a road.

Rip – Extracted strata above a roadway. Usually where the free standing support has been distorted.

Roof Bolt – Steel or wood of various lengths. Used to provide additional support to unstable ground.

Room and Pillar (Pillar and Stall) – Consists of driving headings in the seam for coal extraction and leaving pillars of coal to support the roof.

Ropeman – Person employed to splice steel rope on haulage system.

RSJ – Rolled Steel Joist.

Scorrick – Small portion.

SERD – Single Ended Ranger Drum Shearer.

Shaft – Link between pit top and pit bottom.

Shear – Length of coal cut on a longwall face.

Shearing – Cutting on a coal face.

Shunt – Length of rail used for storing vehicles for storing supplies.

Side Ranters – RSJ used to support legs whilst being secured to cross beam.

Seam – Band of coal.

Self-Rescuer – Respirator to protect against carbon monoxide.

Schaeffler – Type of Exploder.

Shuttle car – Vehicle used for carrying extracted coal. Operated by electrical cable.

Skippy – Kangaroo (native to Australia).

Snap – Lunch, Bait. Grapefruit.

Snicket – Small tunnel at the return end of a retreat coal face.

Spalling – Falling mineral (typically coal).

Spill Plate – Attached to a pan (typically AFC) main use for carrying cables.

Spontaneous Combustion – spon com / oxidation of coal leading to underground fires / heating.

Stable – Accommodation for horses / An area at maingate end of a coal face. Created by drill and fire technique in place of a Bi Di.

Stamler – Loading device used in conjunction with a shuttle car/ Unihauler.

Stemming rod – Wooden pole used to place explosive to the back of a drilled hole. Followed by packing material.

Shearer – Type of cutting machine used on coal face to extract coal.

Square work – Free standing steel support.

Stageloader – Chain conveyor positioned perpendicular to AFC. Used to transport coal onto maingate conveyor.

Stint – work area on a hand filled coal face. An amount of work carried out.

Stitching machine – device used for applying fasteners to lengths of conveyor belt

Stonedust – Limestone dust.

Stonedust Barrier – classed as either heavy or light. In the event of a methane explosion the discharged dust mixes with coal dust to avoid its ignition. Coal dust explosion is more violent than methane explosion.

Strut – metal bar (flat or tubular) to attach adjacent free standing steel supports to one another.

Silvester – prohibited lifting/pulling device similar to a Tirfor.

Tailgate – Return end of the coal face.

The Searcher – Person appointed to search for contraband.

Tie Bar – See strut.

Tins – corrugated steel sheets used for cover between the free standing support.

Tirfor – lifting / pulling device.

Top Shunt – Manager's office (typically Lancashire term).

TQM – Total Quality Management / Mining.

Transfer Point – point at which one belt conveyor loads on to another.

Traveller – person accompanying a Deputy usually on overtime.

Trunk Conveyor – Coal carrying conveyors outbye of the coal face.

Tunnel – Extracted area of ground used to access coal seams.

Twat – Term of endearment.

Undermanager – Person appointed by the Owner of the Mine and providing daily supervision of persons working in the mine. Every part of the mine worked must be under the jurisdiction of an Undermanager and supervise all operations.

Unihauler – Battery operated machine used to transport extracted coal from JCM to Stamler Loader.

Victaulic – make of pipe, typically 3" used for supplying water (fire fighting range)

Vulcanise – means of joining lengths of conveyor belt. As against using mechanical stitching. Two ends fused together.

Waste (Goaf / Gob) – Area behind the coal face after coal has been extracted.

Wanker – Term of Endearment.

Winder - Person operating the engine transporting the men up and down the shaft in the cage.

Wint Hole – Short tunnel driven in coal to access retreat face to improve ventilation over top motor.

Wombat – Handheld drilling machine used for roof bolting.

Workwear – underground clothing provided by the NCB. Generally consisting of overalls and underwear, vest, and T shirt.

Welsh Phrases

Bora da – good morning
Cariad – love, darling
Croeso – you're welcome
Da iawn – very well
Diolch – thankyou
Diolch yn fawr – thank you very much
Hwyl fawr – goodbye
Nac oes – no
Noswaith dda - good evening
Nos da – good night
Oes – yes
Pemblwydd Hapus – Happy Birthday
Prynhawn da – Good afternoon
Sori - sorry
Sut ydych chi – how are you / how are you doin
Sut Mae – hello
Tad – Dad
Ti - You
Wela i chi – see you later

Access Roads to Underground Workings via Shafts and Drift

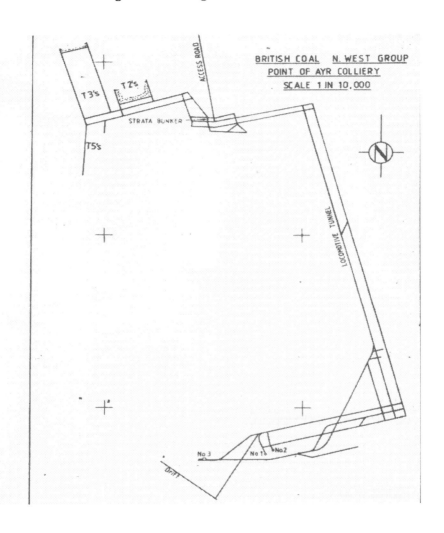

Strata Top - Two Yard Seam - Zone B - Progress Plans
Coal Faces T2 & T3

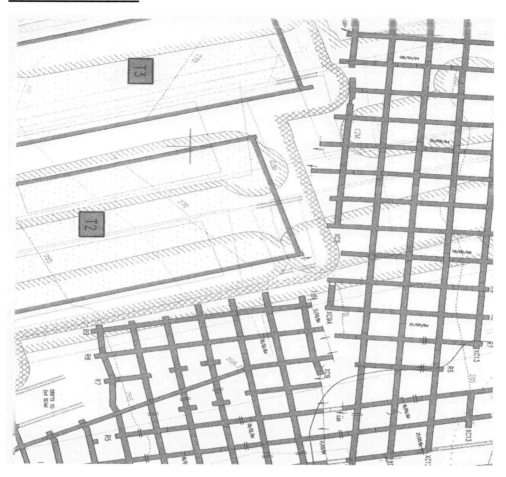

Coal Faces T5, T6, T7 & T8

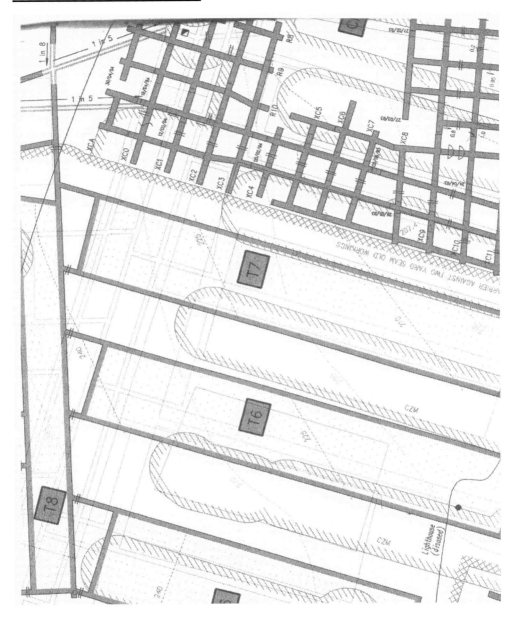

Continuous Miner 1 District

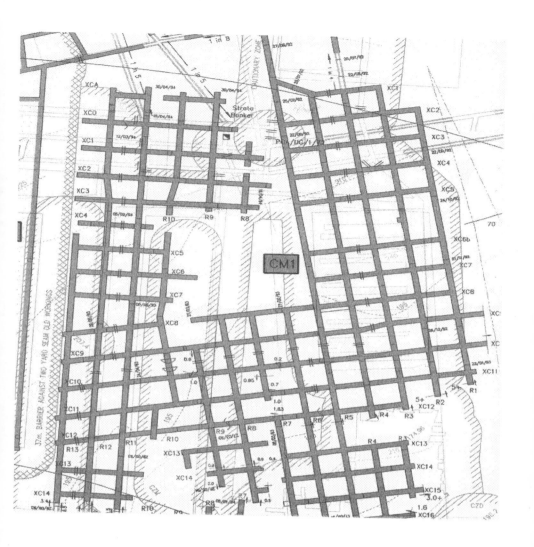

Continuous Miner 2 District

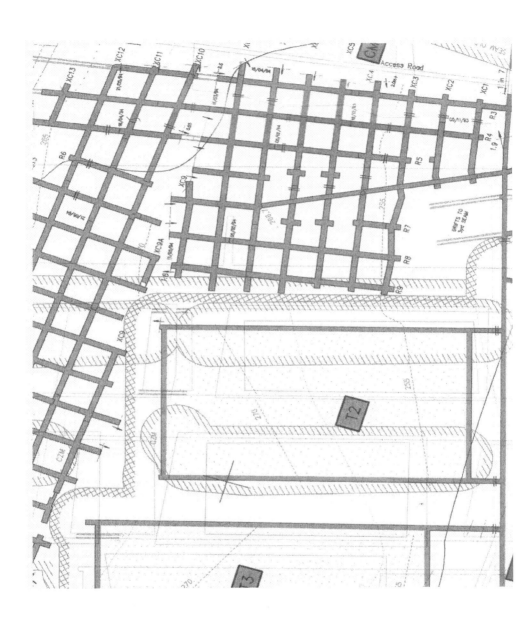

Coal Seams

GENERALISED VERTICAL SECTION

FIVE YARD 304cms.

40—45m.

THREE YARD 243cms.

30—38m.

TWO YARD 213cms.

32—45m.

DURBOG 398cms.

20—35m.

STONE COAL 450cms.

30—35m.

HARD FIVE QUARTERS 243cms.

70—80m.

BYCHTON 213cms.

Point of Ayr Underground Workings

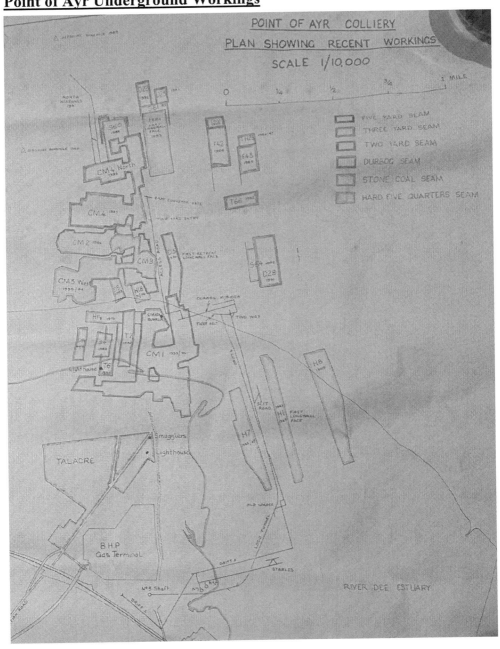

Coal Production 1975 to 1994*

Year	Number of Deep Mines	Deepmined output (Million tonnes)	Employment (Thousands)
1975	241	117	252
1976	239	110	250
1977	231	107	248
1978	223	108	240
1979	219	108	242
1980	213	112	237
1981	200	110	172
1982	191	106	164
1983	170	102	148
1984	169	35	139
1985	133	75	114
1986	110	90	91
1987	94	86	75
1988	86	84	69
1989	73	80	56
1990	65	73	49
1991	50	73	38
1992	50	66	28
1993	17	50	10
1994	16	32	7

*Department for Business, Energy & Industrial Strategy – Historical Coal Data: Coal Production – 1853 to 2018

Room and Pillar – Continuous Miner Operations (showing 2 Fletcher Roof Bolters in action)

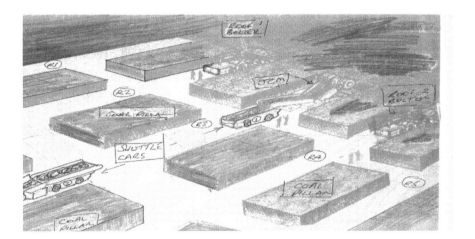

Room and Pillar – Continuous Miner Operations (showing Stamler and Conveyor)

Printed in Great Britain
by Amazon